PEREGRINATION SERIES

BOOK 5

THE FINAL BATTLE;
BATTLE OF THE BEASTS

S.G. Boudreaux

THE FINAL BATTLE;
BATTLE OF THE BEASTS

Peregrination Series Book 5
S.G. Boudreaux

Peregrination Series Book 5

SG Boudreaux

ISBN   9781733963688 (paperback)
ISBN   9781733963695 (digital)

Copyright 2019 by S.G. Boudreaux

Zanchier Publications
PO Box 12936
Lake Charles, La. 70612

Printed in the United States of America

Sgboodro2@yahoo.com
www.SGBoudreaux.com
www.Zanchierpublications.com

Peregrinate: To leave one's homeland and wander
for the love of God; to travel, especially on foot.
(v.) to travel over or through something.

Glossary

Cruciform Church   a tetraconch plan or design, meaning a cross structure with equal length of sides. Later designed as a cross within a square.

Siq   The narrow passageway and entryway between two cliffs into the ancient city of Petra, Jordan.

Kabihanxu (ka bi HAN j<u>u</u>) The firebird's scientific name. A colorful, four-legged bird type creature that breaths fire

Pagorinx (PA gor inx) A large wild cat-like creature residing in the Xantifal Mountain range in Zanchier.

Tanmoyaro Draconomai (*Tan mo Yar o)(Dra CO no mI*) Mountain of the Dragons.

Yarequu (Yar **a** Koo)   A horse like creature residing in Zanchier, that stands twenty to twenty-five hands high and has a width of up to eight hands. It is larger than a Clydesdale, has three-toed split hooves, braided, twisted mane and tail, has spikes that slant upward at each leg at the knee joint. It is charcoal in color with streaks of white and teal around its eyes, ears, and mouth, and running down its neck, fanning out and blending into its coat. These streaks are also evident around its hooves and the spikes on its legs.

Monshokto- (Mon SHOK toe)   A large Zanchier creature, that is mainly a land dweller and lives by Everly Lake. They eat plants and fish and are defensive creatures. They have a near flat face, one horn in the center of its head and can makes a deep reverberating sound. It is very hairy and is the color of sand and grayish-brown rock, allowing them to appear as boulders on shore. It has a long thick tail, walks upright on two legs, and runs on all four. They can hold their breath for fifteen minutes at a time underwater.

Some of the storms that are listed in the book series are factual storms that took place throughout history. Some places in the books are actual places and researchable. Some places are fictional and are made up for the benefit of the storyline.

This book series is a work of fiction. Although it is based upon some biblical truths, all characters are fictional and in no way represent any living or deceased persons. Any similarity is purely coincidental.

Author's Note

First, welcome to any new readers who may be beginning with this fifth and last book in the series. I encourage you to go back and read books 1-4 to fully understand who the characters are and what the books are all about. Also, a big shout out to all my loyal fans who have returned to read the ongoing story entitled the *Peregrination Series*. I hope you've enjoyed the last four books E*arth, Wind, Fire,* and *Water,* and that you will find even more fun and intrigue, and that the ending of this series is all that you expected and more.

Book 5 will pull together all the twists and turns that have taken place in the last four books, and, even has a few more surprises for you.

The next series that I will be writing is a spin-off of this one. It is titled *Zanchier,* and each book will have its own subtitles. It takes place in the strange and interesting world that I created for the *Peregrination Series* in *Book 2: Wind.* The world of Zanchier kept occurring and turning up in unexpected ways as I wrote the last three books, and so it encouraged me to write a spin-off. You may recognize a few of the characters that are represented in the *Peregrination Series,* but the books *Zanchier* predate the *Peregrination Series.* I am expecting this new series, *Zanchier,* to be a total of three books.

Thank you for your support and if you enjoyed the *Peregrination Series,* I hope you will follow me over to Zanchier and enjoy a deeper glimpse into that spectacular world.

Prologue

The Peregrines have located most of the Armor of God. They must find the last two pieces, the Shields of Faith —which must still be located, and the Swords of the Spirit —which were dismantled long ago and melted down. The new blacksmith, Dekker Smit Vandenberg, must refashion the swords for them and make them strong enough to do battle against something powerful in the Final Battle. The Dragoman are hoping to find more information about the Final Battle against dragons between the pages of the *Book of the Keepers*. Which until now, was unable to be read due to the strange language in which it was written. They recently discovered this language to be a unique blend of Akrotiri's ancient language and another form of Greek.

Marnor Draiwood, the Scaither leader from Zanchier, was somehow able to peregrinate to Reader's Island after the massive demon battle the Peregrines, Dragoman, desert people, and Zanchier creatures all just fought. Many of their friends, both human and animal, perished in that battle. Because of their past connections, Caroline and Sofia are having issues with Marnor's presence, which is causing tensions on Reader's Island. Seth and Oz also have issues with Marnor due to the treatment of the two women and many others by the Scaithers, a rogue band of evil people whom Marnor was the leader of until very recently.

Uriah has disappeared, Petra is still being held prisoner, Safra is now a younger version of herself, and new relationships form as others grow stronger. Annabelle, the newest and youngest Keeper has unexpectedly bonded with Nicholas who is as surprised by this as everyone else, his past hurts still vivid memories.

Now, on with the next and last story in the Peregrination Series of novels.

For we do not have a high priest who is unable to
empathize with our weaknesses, but we have one
who has been tempted in every way, just as we are-
yet he did not sin. Let us then approach God's throne
of grace with confidence, so that we may receive
mercy and find grace to help us in our time of need.

Hebrews 4: 15-16 NIV

Chapter 1

Reader's Island, Present Day

Simon stood at the coffee pot waiting for the dark liquid to finish
brewing. Although the events of the previous day had everyone
exhausted, including himself, he still could not seem to be able to
get much sleep. Thoughts of yesterday's losses and the
brutality of it all plagued his mind. He knew from experience that it would pass, he just wondered if they were to
face another such battle in the future. He wasn't sure they
could all handle another fight like that. In all of Simon's
thirty years of being a Dragoman, they had never fought in
a war as large as what they had faced yesterday. They had,
for the most part, come out unscathed. Except for the loss
of many friends The Twelve still remained intact, meaning
the future of mankind was still secure, hopefully.

These new Peregrines fought like no other he had ever
seen before. The gifts they were given were quite different
from some of those of the past. Perhaps God was preparing
them. Knowing The Twelve were now selected and assem-
bled meant that the end and the final battle was close at
hand. They had only one more piece of armor to locate, and
the swords to refashion before they were ready to face what
they recently discovered as four beasts or dragons.

Everything Simon knew about dragons from all the folklore given about them meant they may well face giant beasts that could breathe fire. He wasn't sure the armored pieces could handle that sort of heat. If they didn't melt from the contact, they may likely heat up to the point of cooking the Peregrines in the very thing that was meant to protect and aid them in the fight. What also concerned him was the fact that perhaps whatever beast they fought may do more than just breathe fire. The four beasts may well have very different capabilities. He only wished there were some way to find out what those capabilities were, and what sort of beasts they were to fight. Perhaps they could take the *Book of the Keepers* to Heba today for translation, and the material to make the capes as well. However, if the Peregrines were to face fire-breathing dragons, then perhaps cloth capes may not be such a good idea after-all. He would have to research that in the ancient archival books they found. Surely, the answers to all their questions were in them somewhere. The books had certainly answered some of the previous mysteries already, such as Seth and Jason appearing together in the same portal from different places. And what they were to do with this new breed of warrior known as the Keepers, whom all four were very young people. Annabelle, the recently found ten-year-old girl being the youngest ever to be called to this lifestyle.

The coffee finished brewing, and Simon grabbed one of the largest mugs he could find and filled it to the top. He added a spoonful of sugar and a dash of cream to his cup, took it and walked outside to the patio area. It had to be near four in the morning. He would sit outside, drink his coffee, and enjoy the constant island breeze created by the rolling seas that surrounded the forty-nine square mile island. The sunrise should be coming up in a couple of hours, so Simon sat in the quiet, fragrant, soul-soothing, peace of the island. The early morning birds chirped occasionally, and he sat with his eyes closed, relishing the feel of the breeze upon his skin and the scent of the tropical flowers that filled the island paradise. Simon inhaled deeply of the smell of jasmine wafting past on the soothing brush of air that caressed his upturned face. He took a few more deep breaths before opening his eyes and taking a few sips from his coffee mug. The taste of the coffee soothed his insides as much as the feel of the breeze and scent of flowers soothed his outside.

Simon loved the island, but he did miss his own home on Barrier's Edge at Garganthera. However now, with the demons attacking and destroying most of the Dragoman safehouses, the island was truly the only safe place for everyone. He missed the solitude his place offered him, but there were many places on the island here where someone could find solitude should they need it.

Nuncio suddenly came to his mind, and Simon's demeanor turned to one of remorse once again.

"What am I going to do without you, old friend." Simon exhaled heavily and peered up at the still star-filled sky. He would miss Nuncio dearly. They had fought this war together for more than thirty years. Nuncio had been at it for forty years, but now he was at peace. Resting in the saving knowledge of Jesus. He no longer suffered the constant pain of the wretched injury he sustained thirteen years before. He had wanted to go out in a blaze of glory, and by god, he certainly did that.

Simon smiled at the image of his dear old friend standing firm, seated upon his steed on the battlefield, his sword raised and ready, a smile as big as life written across his face. Nuncio had lived a long and useful life, working for the good of mankind until the day he died. He had served honorably, and Simon would make certain that everyone who had perished serving God would be remembered and honored when the final battle was over. He had lost many friends over the years living this way. But it wasn't something they could just quit doing. It wasn't a life you just chose to ignore.

However, some Peregrines and Dragoman from earlier on apparently did choose not to follow God's leading. Toren Pascal Degare' was such a person. What a shock it had been to find that Seth Jager and Jason Marshal were half-brothers from different time eras. Simon sometimes wondered how many more half siblings Toren had fathered out there in the first dimension, or perhaps in other dimensions as well. Could the man have actually fathered children all over time and space? It was something to which he was certain they would never really know the answer. At least Jason and Seth had found one another.

That miracle in itself was another mystery. The Dragoman had always believed that the Chosen were randomly selected by God. However, recent events might prove otherwise.

Hiram Burke who was a Dragoman thirteen years back had a daughter who was now called as a Keeper. And Seth and Jason, both half-brothers from the same Peregrine father who served a thousand years ago, were both also called to peregrination. Then, there was the strange incident of Caroline Jager, Seth's wife, being called to peregrination as well. They are the only family members that Simon knew of that had ever been called to serve. Everyone else was called singularly. However, now that Simon thought about it, no one else was married before they peregrinated. Sure, they may have been involved or engaged, but not yet in a truly committed relationship. If Simon was correct, none of them had children to leave behind either. Except for Toren Degare', but he did so after he was called to peregrinate. As did Hiram Burke, Bridget's father. Then there was Safra. Her father Sage Driscoll had been none of the above. Just a man called and committed to serve God's chosen. Safra was the same as her father, she served the Lord's cause and his people. Maybe there was much more to being called than Simon knew.

"Lord," Simon exhaled, exasperatedly, "if I am to figure this out, you're going to have to help me with it."

He sat pondering his thoughts and drinking his coffee until the sun peeked above the edge of the horizon, sending a splash of instant light and color across the sky which was reflected in the smooth surface of the water.

Just after sunrise, others began making their way outside to enjoy the sights and sounds the island had to offer. Safra headed toward Simon with coffee cups in hand, not only for herself but for Simon as well. She sat the cup in front of him with a grin and took a seat beside him.

Simon smiled at her. "Thank you, Safra." He took the second cup gratefully, sipping from the fresh, hot liquid. Safra knew him well, even this younger version of herself. He remembered her looking this way so long ago. It made him wonder why he chose to bring Safra here from the 1950s era of Morocco instead of this younger version. She had obviously known something he did not. He would miss his older, wiser, gentler, stubborn friend. But he knew she had been growing tired and was feeling useless as of late. She knew she wouldn't have been of any use to them on the battlefield yesterday, and so had gone back in time to get her younger self to help in the war. And help she did. Safra was a great warrior, even at an older age, but the woman who now sat beside him had amazed all who managed to catch a glimpse of her in action yesterday. She had proven to be a force to be reckoned with, even without any special powers like those of the Peregrines and Dragoman.

Simon thought about something that captured his attention. How did Safra peregrinate without the aid of someone else? Did someone go back in time with her? No one said as much. Perhaps Nuncio or one of the others who died in battle yesterday had taken her back while they were making camp in Timna Valley. He decided to ask her instead of continuing to speculate.

"Safra, can you tell me who peregrinated with your older self when she went back to get you?"

"No one. She came alone."

"How is that possible? She was never able to peregrinate alone before."

"I think it has something to do with the Portgen. Neither of us had problems walking through, and she left the island through Barrier's Edge, alone."

"Strangely curious," Simon answered, drifting off into deep thought.

As he sat there drinking his coffee and his mind tried to figure out why neither of them perished while attempting to travel, Marnor Draiwood appeared outside on the patio. When he spotted Safra, he came straight for their table.

Simon watched him approach and looked at Safra.

"What on earth is he doing here?"

She looked at him. "I thought he was with all of you."

"No. He isn't. I'm uncertain as to who the man is all together. All though, I do think he is somehow intertwined with Bridget and Caroline."

Marnor stopped at the table looking at Safra, about to speak. Simon stood and interrupted him.

"Excuse me but, who are you and how did you get here on this island?"

Marnor looked nervously at Simon. "Marnor Draiwood. I came with all of you from the demon fight."

"How is that possible? Only Peregrines and Dragoman can walk through time."

Marnor shrugged his shoulders. "I don't know. All I know is I didn't have any trouble with it."

"Well, Marnor Draiwood. Where exactly is it that you come from?"

"Bakrashan," Marnor stated.

"Where exactly is Bakrashan?"

"In Zanchier."

"The world Oz and Sofia were trapped in for thirteen years?" Simon asked, surprised.

"Yeah," Marnor said a bit sheepishly.

"Didn't you say your last name was Draiwood? Is that any relation to Mary Draiwood?"

Marnor shifted his stance nervously. "She was my mother."

"How were you able to leave that place?"

"I made a pact with a demon that possessed me. I guess that's how I was able to leave."

Simon's brows shot up in surprise. "I'd say you're very lucky to be alive *and* in your right mind."

Marnor shook his head in agreement.

"So, you're Bridget's brother?"

"Half-brother. Hiram was *not* my father," he said with disdain.

"Yes. I've heard about you as well." Simon looked disapprovingly at him over the rim of his glasses.

Marnor swallowed hard and shifted feet. "I'm sure there is a lot more that you haven't heard. But I've changed. Only recently, but I *have* changed."

"Regardless, I don't believe that you staying here on the island is where you need to be. This place is for Peregrines, Dragoman, and Keepers only. No one else has ever been allowed here. We'll have to decide what to do with you I'm afraid."

Marnor didn't say anything. He clenched his teeth, and his jaw tensed in agitation, but he silently hung his head. He wasn't used to being told what to do. But if he was going to have any chance of staying with these people and his half-sister Bridget, he needed to learn to bite his tongue. He was determined to do what he needed to, too have the chance to get to know Bridget. She had saved his miserable excuse for an existence all because he was her brother. He needed to know what made these people different. He had never met people like them. Well, he had, but he was so busy torturing them and thinking them to be liars that he never took them seriously.

"I know that my being here isn't what you expected, but I just want the opportunity to get to know my sister. I figure I'm here for a reason. Can you just give me the chance to prove myself?" Marnor stated.

Simon looked at the man. He had heard some of the stories that Sofia and Oz told about their time in Zanchier and their dealings with the Scaithers.

"I'll discuss your fate with the other Dragoman. But for now, we have more important things with which to deal. You have a day or two of reprieve. Make the most of your time here. It will likely be short lived."

Simon looked at Safra. "Would you mind keeping an eye on this man?"

"Not at all, Simon. I'll make certain he behaves while he's here. He can help with taking care of the manor and such."

Simon looked at Marnor, then walked away toward the house. He had much to think over. He decided to make a list of things that needed to be done so they didn't miss anything. With Nuncio gone, he would have more on his own plate. He would confer with Malachai, Vashti, Prisca, and perhaps even Ryan. They were the only Dragoman left now. Everything rested on their shoulders. As Simon entered the large Caribbean style, mansion-sized home, Seth and Caroline were walking out. They bid each other good morning in passing.

Seth and Caroline walked out on the large patio with their breakfast and found a place to sit. Seth noticed Caroline tense up slightly at the sheer sight of Marnor Draiwood. Seth figured it was time for her to fill him in on why the man made her so obviously uncomfortable. She did threaten to, and almost did, kill the man after yesterday's battle.

"All right, Caroline, what's the deal with this Marnor character? What did he do to you to make you so angry?"

Caroline slid the capped sleeve of her T-shirt up slightly to reveal the branded mark she was given when she was held as a prisoner, and future conquest, of one Riglan Mortruff's while back on Zanchier.

"This, amongst other things," she said morosely.

"He's the one who had you branded?" Anger began to build in his chest as he turned to glare at the man.

"Not exactly. He's one of the men who captured me, hauled me out of the Xantifal Mountains, threatened me, tied me up, kept me prisoner and, actually put the red-hot iron to my skin. All at the orders of a man called Riglan."

Seth stared at the man, and with every explanative she spoke Seth's knuckles grew tighter over the arm of the chair, to the point that he began crushing the steel beneath him.

Caroline noticed the damage he was inflicting on the lawn furniture and reached out to calm his nerves.

"Seth," she said soothingly as she touched his hand to get his attention. "I think the poor chair is calling uncle." She gave him a small smile.

Seth released his hold on the chair arm, not realizing what he had done until she brought his attention to it.

"Sorry, but I'd really like to get my hands on that guy. When I think about what they did to you, and what else they might have done, it infuriates me."

"I know. But, apparently it was all a part of God's plan. That *is* how I received my tribal mark. Although, I have to say, I would have been happier if he had chosen a more pleasant way to mark me." Caroline sarcastically grinned.

Caroline thought about the ceremony they were ready to perform on her that night in the Scaither camp. She didn't tell Seth that part and she wasn't ever going to. She new he would make good on his threats to kill the man, and she didn't want to burden his soul with unnecessary information. She had also made Bridget and Oz promise never to say anything to him about it either. It was in the past. Or, at least it had been until Marnor somehow managed to show up, not only in the first dimension, but, here on the island as well. Her one place of solace and refuge from the ungliness of the world. Until now.

Caroline glanced around the patio looking for Sofia. If anyone had a reason to hate Marnor Draiwood, it was Sofia. She had been held prisoner by the Scaithers for ten years. Not only that, she was a beautiful woman, and had been used and treated cruelly by Riglan, and she suspected, by Marnor as well.

She saw Sofia coming out of the house. She watched her eyes scan the group and land on Marnor. Sofia squared her shoulders, breathed deeply and stepped outside. Caroline waved her over to sit with her and Seth. Sofia's expression seemed to be one of relief. The two of them hadn't spoken much since returning to the island and hitting the ground running, literally. But they both shared a special bond and understanding that few others here could grasp. Caroline couldn't imagine the horrors she had faced in bondage with those abusive people for ten years. Caroline only had one whole day, and it had been enough to give her nightmares.

Seth began to stand as she approached the table. Sofia smiled at his gentlemanly manners and waved him to sit down. She placed her plate on the table and pulled out her chair to sit.

"Seth, I haven't had a man stand in my presence since I was married to Caislan. You don't have to make any special effort for me." She grinned.

Seth smiled. "Sorry, just habit."

"I know."

Sofia sat, prayed quickly over her food, and then smiled at them. "So, what do you two have planned for the day?"

Caroline knew she didn't want to discuss Marnor and was happy to oblige her direction of conversation. "Not really sure yet. After yesterday, I figure everyone will be taking it as easy as possible."

"True. I could certainly use a day to while away my time." Sofia sighed and grinned.

They all grinned at each other.

Seth sighed. "Well, with everything going on, I doubt we'll get a full day. But I for one don't think we need any sparring practice today. I think I might go fishing in one of the boats. Surely Clancy and Henry could use some fresh fish for tonight's dinner."

Caroline smiled. "Sounds good to me. Sofia, would you like to tag along with us?"

"Thanks, but I think I'll pass. Besides, I figure you two could use some time alone. It's kind of hard to get that when you live with forty or so other people." She chuckled slightly, and they joined her.

"True," Seth said, looking at Caroline. "So, what do you say. You ready to go fishing? It'll take us maybe twenty minutes to gather everything we need and walk down to the boat docks."

"I'm very ready. I think the last time I went fishing was a couple of years ago on one of our dates." She smiled.

"Yes, and if I recall correctly, you out-fished me three to one." Seth laughed. Caroline and Sofia laughed with him.

Sofia smiled at them. "You two have fun. If anyone asks, I'll let them know where you went and that you will be back in a few hours."

"Thanks, Sofia. You're sure you don't want to tag along?" Caroline asked, glancing at Marnor questioningly.

Sofia smiled at her attempt to keep her away from Marnor. "No, thanks. I'm sure I'll find something to do today." Sofia watched as Seth and Caroline picked up their dishes and walked inside the house.

It wasn't long after they left that Marnor walked up to the table.

"Shraiva, can I talk to you a minute?"

Sofia tensed at the sound of the name she was given as a prisoner of the Scaithers; never turning to address the man.

"My name isn't Shraiva. It's Sofia. If you call me that one more time, I'm not going to be responsible for what I do to you."

"Sorry…Sofia. It's just, that's all I've ever known you by. Riglan never told us his girls real names."

Sofia tensed again at him mentioning her being one of Riglan's girls. Like she had had any choice in the matter.

"Look, Sofia," Marnor stumbled over his words. He stood there looking at her stiff back, trying to find the right thing to say. "I'm sorry, for everything that you ever went through. I know I don't deserve your forgiveness, I just want you to know that I really am sorry for what I did and what I allowed to be done to you. To everyone who was ever like you. I just…wanted you to know that.

Marnor waited for a response for a few seconds. When she didn't turn or respond he walked away, headed inside for kitchen duties.

Sofia watched him go inside the house. She didn't know what to say or how to react. She had suffered so brutally at the hands of the Scaithers for so long, she didn't trust herself around him. She even still felt a bit intimidated by the man. It was all she could do to threaten him without fear of pain being inflicted on herself. She knew she would eventually have to forgive him. It was what God expected of her. She just didn't know how much forgiveness she had in her.

She felt someone's hand upon her shoulder and she jumped.

"Sofia, are you all right?" Rourke, her long time friend was standing beside her chair, watching Marnor enter the house.

"Yes, Rourke, I'm fine. Thanks."

"I didn't mean to startle you." Rourke sat beside her in one of the chairs and leaned toward her. "You just looked like you needed a little help. Do I need to have a chat with that fella'?"

Sofia grinned tightly at him. "No. It's fine, Rourke. Thanks all the same. Marnor and I just have a… long history. And it isn't a pleasant one."

"Well, if you ever want to chat, I'm still here. I always have been," he said with such emotion that her insides shook like jello.

"I may take you up on that one day. You might regret it though." She nervously laughed, glancing back toward the door Marnor had disappeared through moments earlier.

"Never. There isn't anything you could tell me that would change the way I feel about you. I never lost hope that you'd return you know."

Sofia smiled warmly at him. "I know. But right now, Rourke, I just can't handle a relationship."

"I understand." Rourke grinned softly at her. "I'm not planning on going anywhere. So, whatever you decide, just know I'm here for you. In whatever capacity that might be."

She smiled at him and took his hand in hers in a friendly gesture. Pleased to know she still had the support from old friends who knew her before her Zanchier experience. She wasn't so sure that he would still be interested in the *after Zanchier* Sofia though. She was forever a changed woman. With more baggage than any one person deserved to carry. Including herself.

Marnor walked into the kitchen where the chatter around the large kitchen table ceased at his appearance. He stood looking at them for a second and then walked toward Clancey and Henry for instruction. The chatter soon resumed amongst the group of people gathered there. He glanced back over his shoulder at Bridget, who occasionally glanced his way as well. He wanted to talk to her but wasn't sure how to start. He turned to the sink full of dishes and began to clean up, glancing back and forth between Bridget and the chore before him.

He walked over to the table to pick up the dirty plates and cups that had been scooted to the table's center. When he passed by Bridget, he stopped briefly. Marnor's nerves were as tight as they could get with all the confrontations today already, and it was still early.

"Uh...Bridget," he stammered, "can we...talk later?" He stared at the dishes in his hands, not daring to look at her.

"Yes," she said, looking up at him, "whenever you're free."

He grinned nervously at her, bowed his head in thanks and walked away.

Bridget watched him go, then looked at her friend Dominic who watched Marnor with caution as well. Dominic gave her a questioning look that asked if she were crazy. She smiled at him, then curiously and demurely watched her brother go about his duties.

Dominic watched Bridget, worried what this new relationship with Marnor may do to her. Or more importantly, where it might lead her. He didn't like Marnor, at all.

For it is God's will that by doing good you should
silence the ignorant talk of foolish people.

1 Peter 2:15

Chapter 2

Breakfast had come to an end and everyone scattered across the island, some just taking time to refuel, and some still to mourn the loss of dear friends.

Simon, after making his list, met with the other Dragoman, Safra, and Oz in the archival library to discuss what still needed doing, and how to best go about accomplishing the tasks at hand. They all gathered around one of the smaller tables in the room, their already small group dwindling with each new demon war.

Even though Safra was technically not a Dragoman she was always involved in the meetings, her skills and wisdom being particularly useful in such areas. Oz was Prisca's husband, and a long-time Peregrine and faithful member of the cause. And after he and Prisca spent thirteen years involuntarily separated, none of them balked at Oz being present at meetings. The two of them were now inseparable for the most part.

Simon got to the point. "We have several things that we need to address here. First, we need to decide what to do about Petra. We can't keep our efforts focused on tending to her needs while she stays locked in her room. We simply no longer have the time or man-power for it."

Malachai said, "Well, what about exiling her like we discussed in the last meeting?"

Prisca added, "She would likely just find her way back to the island."

"Perhaps," Vashti said, "but not if we sent her to Zanchier."

Oz spoke up, "True. That place is hard ta' get out of. But, after bein' stuck there fer thirteen years, an' seeing the things done ta our kind, I don't recommend it. Killin' 'er would be more humane than sendin' 'er there."

Simon sighed. "Well then, we'll just have to keep her locked up for a bit longer until we can come up with a logical solution. Now, onto number two. Can any of you think of a way to protect the island from Uriah returning?"

"Do ya' think he'd dare show 'is face here again?"

"Seeing who Uriah has become makes me think that he is capable of anything. Especially since he still possesses a Portgen."

Ryan spoke up. "There is s...still tracking c...capability inside the Portgen."

Simon sat up at that. "Ryan, have you tried tracking his Portgen?"

"No. That o...option was for each Dr..Dragoman to be able to tr...track their Peregrines from their o...own d...device."

Malachai stated, "My Portgen is upstairs in my room. I'll go get it." He stood and dashed out of the room and up the stairs to retrieve the device. When he returned a few minutes later, he had turned the device on and quickly handed it over to Ryan.

"Here, Ryan, I'm not sure how to do what you suggested. I haven't had to use that feature yet."

Ryan took the device, pushed a few buttons on the Portgen, and a blip appeared on the screen. He then turned a few knobs this way and that, pushed a few more buttons, and the location of the blip was revealed.

"It s...says he is in D..Dover, England, in the y...year 15...7..5."

Simon grew curious. "What on earth would he be doing there?"

"When did Bridget say her pa' died?" Oz questioned.

Simon grew thoughtful. "I believe she was an orphan for two years before she came to us. Meaning that Uriah went back before Hiram's death."

Vashti asked, "Why would he do that?"

Simon looked at her. "Probably to try and convince Hiram to join him in the NKRO, and to try to overthrow our plans."

"The what?" Oz asked confused.

"The New Kingdom Rulers Order. Something that Hiram Burke put into plan fourteen or fifteen years back. Apparently Uriah is a follower, along with many others."

"Surely his foll'wers aren' 'round anymore. I don' think anyone else here on th' island is a b'trayer," Oz stated.

"I don't think any left here is a follower either, save Petra of course."

Prisca said, "She said she had given that up after Uriah betrayed her."

"Let's hope she is being forthcoming about that," Simon answered.

Malachai said, "There were a lot of other Peregrine and Dragoman who were unaccounted for after all the disappearances thirteen years back."

"Well," Oz said, "I can vouch fer some a' the ones who were pushed inta' the port'l with me an' Sofie."

"I don't think we'll get an accurate count regardless," Simon said. "Besides, unless you're certain they all died back on Zanchier, then we have no way of knowing if Hiram went back to Zanchier to take those out of there that were loyal to him. Remember, he did have an easier way into and out of Zanchier."

The blip on the screen stopped transmitting at that moment and the Portgen went quiet. Ryan looked at Simon.

"I think he t…turned his off."

"Why would he do that?" Simon asked.

"Well," Ryan fidgeted in his seat, "when we track a p…person, it shows a b…blinking dot on their screen, but no sound, for safety reasons."

Simon asked, "So Uriah knows that we are tracking him?"

"Probably," Ryan stated.

Simon sighed. "Well, at least we have an idea of what he's up to anyway. Ryan, is there any way for you to monitor Uriah's Portgen from the mainframe in the computer room in case he turns it back on? Which I am certain he will likely do."

"Sure, Simon. It w…won't be h..hard to add." Ryan stammered.

"Good. Now, onto number three. We now know that the language used in the writing of the *Book of the Keepers* to be a blend of Greek and an ancient form of Akrotiri. Dekker said that his friend Heba can translate, but we must take the book there. We also need to take her the cloth to be sown for the capes for The Twelve. We need to do this as soon as possible."

"Why not go today?" Malachai asked. "I for one would like to see this underwater city."

"Yes, we can do that. As long as we can round up everyone we need. Dekker, and Gabriele for certain will have to go," Simon replied. "And a few of the other Peregrines, just for safety reasons."

Prisca questioned, "Is there anything else we need to discuss?"

"Just one. I am curious as to how that man Marnor came to be on the island?" Simon replied.

"I wondered that myself," Malachai stated. "How is it possible that he's here? Has a non-chosen person ever been on the island before?"

Simon glanced at him. "Not to my knowledge. But Safra did say that she also had no trouble peregrinating alone. Also, there is the possibility that he is one of the chosen. A new Peregrine could still appear."

Malachai's brows knit together. "Hmm..I guess your right about that last statement."

"Could the Portgens make traveling easy for anyone?" Vashti asked.

"It is possible, since we no longer rely on storms, the Portgens could make it possible for anyone to travel. But how would we know for sure?" Simon stated.

"Don't we already?" Prisca said. "Is not Safra, and possibly Marnor evidence of this?"

"Perhaps, but we won't know for certain until we try it. The only problem is, I don't know anyone who's life I'm willing to risk just to find out," Simon answered her.

Everyone shook their heads in agreement and confusion.

"That Marnor fella' was possessed by demons. That's how he left Zanchier," Oz said.

"Yes, but not how he came to the island," Simon stated. "We'll have to work on that mystery later, after we get the book translated, the capes made, and the search for the next piece of armor underway."

"Agreed," Malachai stated.

"All right, everyone. Let's go see if we can round up an expedition party to return to Akrotiri." Simon grinned at them.

They all left the library, and Simon went to retrieve the ancient archive book they called the *Book of the Keepers*. Dubbed so for the intricately ornate carvings of strange beasts and dragons that adorned the cover. He grabbed the key and book and resealed the vault.

Simon walked out of the front door and turned toward the stables. He could usually find several people out that way, either getting in a workout, or tending to the horses. Although he seriously doubted anyone would be in the mood or shape to work out today after yesterday's battle. As he strolled across the front yard he crossed paths with Odessa who was heading toward the house.

"Simon," she called to him and waved. She jogged a bit to catch up with him. "I had a dream last night concerning the next piece of armor."

"Well, that is good news."

"Perhaps, but, the dream was a little vague about where to find it. It showed shields, I assume the Shields of Faith, but where they were located is sort of confusing."

"Oh? How so?"

"Well, I keep seeing different places and landscapes. There isn't one particular place that I can pin down and say that it's right. There are some that appear above ground and some below. I haven't gotten a really clear image of anything. I just seem to be having a very hard time concentrating lately. I seemed to get distracted easily. "

"I'm sure your visions will clear. Just give it some time and maybe go somewhere quiet when you feel one coming on."

"That's just it. I haven't been able to figure that out yet. They just sort of appear."

"Oh well. Perhaps you will be able to in time. Now, onto another subject. We have to make another trip to Akrotiri. Care to join us?" Simon asked with amusement. Knowing full well she would likely decline given the interest in her by King Pyrrus on their last visit.

"No thanks!" she said adamantly. "I've had enough of that place *and* it's king." She grinned and giggled slightly at the memory.

They smiled at each other and parted ways, Simon continuing his original direction. Upon entering the stables he was pleased to find Gabriele, Timothy, Jason, Seth, Caroline, Nick, Nadia, Annabelle, Bridget, and Dominic. Also present were three of the groundskeepers and one Marnor Draiwood. They all were grooming or tending to the needs of the animals. Simon wasn't sure he liked talking business in front of Marnor. He didn't know or trust the man.

"Hello everyone, I need to speak with you all for just a moment. Especially you, Gabby."

They all stopped what they were doing and came to stand by Simon. All except for Marnor Simon noticed, who continued on with what he had been tasked with. He knew he was not included in the request and apparently chose to mind his own business unless called upon. *Smart man,* Simon thought. He then turned his attention to the group that had gathered around him.

He decided to keep Odessa's dream to himself for now until they had more to go on.

"We need to make another trip to Akrotiri today for several reasons, and we need you, Gabby, to help us with the journey. Your gift, combined with the Staff of Moses, made travel possible."

Tim asked, "Couldn't you just put in the coordinates and go by Portgen?"

Jason answered, "Not to Akrotiri. The city is located deep within the center of a mountain, and apparently the tracking and navigational systems can't penetrate that deeply."

"I'd like to see the place. Do you mind if I go along this time?" Timothy asked.

"Not at all. We need a few of you to come with us just in case there happens to be any trouble again," Simon stated.

Timothy smiled, ready to go on the adventure that he missed out on last time due to his no longer being one of the twelve, and the fact that he had a massive chip on his shoulder at the time. Besides, he had another reason. He wanted to get to know Gabriele better. He had grown to like her quite a bit over the last few days and wanted to spend as much time as possible in her company.

"No thanks," Nick spoke up. "I'm mainly over my fear of big water, but that doesn't mean I want to walk the ocean floor again anytime soon." He grinned a bit painfully.

Everyone chuckled at his revelation. "I'll go Simon," Nadia spoke in her thick Russian dialect. "Like Timothy, I would love to see Akrotiri as well."

"Great. It seems we are getting a party together." Simon smiled.

"How many people do you need or want to go, Simon?" Seth asked.

"I'm certain this journey will be a simple one. I doubt we will face any problems like last time. We are just taking the Keeper's book for translation, and the material for the capes to the city for Dekker's friend Heba to work on. So, a small party will be fine. Dekker will also be accompanying us, along with the other Dragoman. We are all attending for the purpose of translating the *Book of the Keepers*."

Gabby asked, "So when do you want to head out?"

"As soon as we can get everyone together. The journey shouldn't take too long. But, with the book needing translated, we may need to stay overnight. It's a fairly decent sized book and may take us quite a while to get through. That is, if Dekker's friend Heba can actually translate it."

"Okay," she replied, 'I'll go pack and get ready."

With that, she, Nadia, and Timothy all went to the main house to do exactly that.

Nadia decided to see if Sofia wanted to tag along since she also missed the last trip to the ancient underwater city. She saw her sitting outside under the veranda speaking with Rourke, Clancy, and Shannon, and diverted her direction toward them.

She approached the table as everyone waved at her.

"Hello," Nadia smiled at them. "I came to see if Sofia, or any of the rest of you want to go on the Akrotiri expedition? We are packing to leave very soon."

Sofia shook her head in agreement. "Sure, I'll go. That would be an interesting trip."

"I'll go as well," Rourke said, "as long as we retired people are still considered useful to the cause after the last battle."

Sofia smiled at him. "I'm sure Simon won't mind any of you coming out of retirement permanently."

They all smiled back at her.

Clancy looked at Shannon, then at Nadia. "I don't think I'll tag along for this one. I'm perfectly resigned to retirement until absolutely needed again." He chuckled.

"I as well," Shannon agreed, smiling at him.

"Well, I guess we should go pack then," Sofia said standing, followed by Rourke.

They said farewell to Clancy and Shannon, and the three of them headed to their rooms to prepare for the trip.

Back at the stables, Simon was still conversing with Jason and Seth about what to watch for and tend to while all the Dragoman were gone.

"Jason, you, Seth, and some of the other leaders will have to keep an eye on things here at the island. Ryan, of course, will be staying. And you will all have to watch Petra. Tend to her needs, food, that sort of thing, until we can decide what to do with her."

Marnor couldn't help over-hearing their conversation and spoke up. "I don't mean to interrupt but, I can take care of the woman. Take her meals and things to her. I've already helped Clancy and Henry do it this morning anyway."

Simon looked at him, unsure whether to trust the man with such an important task. "I'm not sure that's a good idea. Petra is a traitor, and a trained Peregrine at that."

"I understand that. But I am used to being in charge and handling large groups of people. Most of who I'm sure were stronger and more obstinate than this woman Petra. Anyway, just a suggestion. I'm just trying to help out here. Earn my keep somehow."

Simon looked at the others questioningly and sighed. "Well, if one of the leaders wouldn't mind accompanying you while you take care of that, then I suppose it would be all right. But let me warn you now. Petra says she has changed allegiances, just as you say you have. If I find out that either of you schemed against us, or helped Uriah Mose, I will kill you both myself. Do I make myself clear on that?"

"Perfectly," Marnor answered without flinching.

Simon breathed deeply and exhaled, then turned to Jason. "Make a schedule amongst yourselves to accompany Mr. Draiwood when tending to Petra."

"Sure thing, Simon. And don't worry, we won't let him out of our sight." Jason looked at Marnor who stood coolly and unflinching, his feet spread apart slightly and his hands grasping the handle of the resting shovel in front of him that he had been using to muck out the stalls.

Marnor bowed his head slightly at them, an agitated smile on his lips. It was apparently going to take a lot to get into good graces with these people, but he couldn't expect anything different after his past actions and dealings with them. He turned and went back to shoveling.

Simon left the stables to pack while Jason went in search of the other leaders to give them a schedule as Simon had asked. Seth and Caroline left the stables as well to take a walk just to be alone for a while. Nick and Annabelle took a horse ride to get her used to riding the animals, leaving Dominic and Bridget in the barn with Marnor, who saw this as a chance to speak to Bridget.

He stood up from his work, and cleared his throat, looking at her as he sat the shovel down. He walked over to where she and Dominic were standing, laughing and playing with two of the stalled horses.

"Bridget," he said, clearing his throat again. "Can we have that talk now?" He looked back and forth between her and the young man who was giving him the evil eye.

Bridget looked at Dominic, gave him a reassuring smile at the look on his face, then turned to Marnor.

"Certainly."

"I just wanted to say, thank you again. You had no reason to go out of your way to save a man like me. No matter who I am. I don't deserve the kindness that I've been shown. Everyone here, even though they are unsure about me, has been accepting of me."

"That's how we are, Marnor. Even though you've done things to people, it is required of us to forgive."

"I don't understand what you're talking about. What do you mean it's required?"

"It is our faith and beliefs in God. He has forgiven us all our sins. So, therefore, we are to forgive others."

"I've never heard of anything like what you all believe, but I would like to learn. I really did have a change of heart back on that battlefield yesterday. And it wasn't necessarily the fact that I almost died, but more the fact that you and your friends went out of the way to help me when I least deserved it."

"Well, Marnor, even though I wasn't exactly happy to find out my only living relative in the world was a Scaither leader, you are my brother. You are the only blood family I have left. Most of these people here are like family to me, and I would do anything for them. You will have to earn that sort of trust from me, but I am willing to try, if you are?"

"I would like that a lot, Bridget. Maybe we can talk more after dinner tonight. Maybe get to know a bit about each other."

"Perhaps." She grinned.

"Not alone," Dominic answered protectively, looking at Bridget with concern.

"You, and anyone else is welcome to join us," Marnor said, looking at him.

"Good." Dominic stood straighter and puffed his chest out a little.

Bridget turned her head to hide the spreading grin that was threatening to take over her face at the actions of her friend. Dominic had grown quite protective of her ever since Tintagel and her run in with Uriah when he was being hard on her about her father's sins. She didn't want him to think she was laughing at his display of manhood. He certainly wasn't afraid to speak his mind or take on the man who stood almost a head taller than he did. She began to walk from the barn, followed by Dominic, who threw warning glances over his shoulder toward Marnor.

Dominic knew better than to warn Bridget about the man. She had every right to talk with him, but he would make darn sure that Marnor didn't have a chance to hurt her. He didn't know why he felt so protective of her, but he did. And she didn't seem to mind him butting into her life. So, until she said something about it, he would do just that.

Almost everyone gathered at the beach to see the peregrination group off on their latest mission.

Marnor followed along, curious about what all the interest was concerning. He wanted to learn all that he could about these people and their so-called peregrinations. So, he took every opportunity to witness all he could for as long as they allowed him to do so.

Gabriele held the Staff of Moses while Oz stood near the rear of the group, ready to connect his Portgen to Gabriele's powers. The traveling party also consisted of Simon, Safra, Malachai, Vashti, Prisca, Timothy, Nadia, Sofia, Rourke, and Dekker.

"Everyone ready?" Simon announced.

They all chimed in with a "Yes," and Gabriele gripped the staff with both hands as she had done before, creating a protective bubble around them. Oz's Portgen latched onto the power shield creating a complete connection, encompassing all twelve of the traveling group.

Simon glanced at Jason and Seth one last time and nodded, letting them know that he was depending on them to keep things running smoothly on the island until the traveling party returned. Jason and Seth nodded their understanding in return, and the party began their walk into the ocean, soon disappearing beneath the crashing waves of the island's surf.

Marnor stood there, stunned at the capabilities of these people. Not only could they travel through time, but they could walk underwater as well. He turned to find Bridget and decided to follow her to wherever it was that she went. Wanting the chance to talk with her some more.

Jason watched the group go, then turned and announced, "All right everyone, back to your daily chores, or whatever it was you had planned for today. If anyone needs anything, then come find me or Seth. I plan on heading to the sparring field. I have a few knew moves I'd like to try out if anyone else cares to join me."

Most everyone followed him to the sparring field, including the Keepers, who decided amongst themselves they needed some more battle training. Especially sweet little Annabelle who was in tears after her first battle yesterday.

Alec looked at the young girl. "Annabelle, if you want to come with me and Odessa, we will teach you to shoot a gun and a bow."

"Thank you, Mr. Alec, sir."

Alec grinned at her politeness. "You can just call me Alec. None of this mister stuff," he said, making an unpleasant face, then smiled at her.

She smiled broadly back at him, then turned to look at Nick. "Will you come too, Mr. Nicholas?"

Nick looked at the girl to whom he had unwillingly started getting attached. "Sure, but the same goes for me as well. No mister, just Nicholas or Nick." He smiled at her as they all walked to the shooting range, realizing that his heart was beginning to go into dangerous waters, a place he hadn't been in a long time. This little girl could be the undoing of years of hard work to guard his heart from forming attachments. He glanced at the heavens, wondering what God was up to just as Annabelle grasped his hand with hers and he felt his heart melt a bit more.

Forsake your folly and live and proceed
in the way of understanding.

Proverbs 9:6

Chapter 3

Akrotiri, Ancient Underwater Grecian City
Present day

As the peregrination group exited the water onto the shores of the marina in the city of Akrotiri, they were greeted with less fear than last time. Dekker also knew many of the people present at their appearance and was able to settle the fears of those taken by surprise by people rising up from the depths of the water.

Many Akrotirians remembered them from their last peregrination to the city, and although surprised to see them again, knew them to be of no threat to anyone.

Many conversed a few moments with them, curious about them and the new things that Dekker had experienced upon his leaving with these strange people. They were also surprised by his new glasses that now enabled the once nearly blind man to be able to see. He gave them a brief explanation as to how they worked, then excused them all, claiming the need to see Heba as soon as possible. They waved goodbye to the friendly people, then headed inward toward the city and Heba's home.

It took them a brief fifteen-minute walk to reach Heba's place. Dekker knocked on the door which soon swung open to reveal a very shocked Heba. She smiled from ear to ear at the appearance of her old friend.

"Dekker!" she breathed in excitement. "I thought I would never see you again." Her Grecian dialect was understood only by Dekker.

"Hello Heba." Dekker smiled back, leaning in to give her a hug.

"What strange thing are you wearing on your face? Can you now see?" she asked surprised.

"They're called glasses, Heba; like Simon has. And yes, they enable me to see. Very exciting indeed." He smiled.

"Please, come in, everyone," she said as Dekker translated, stepping back to swing the door open wide. Heba continued, "I'm not certain if we can all fit inside my small place, but we can try. Please, you're welcome to find a place to sit."

Everyone said hello, introducing themselves as they passed through the door, finding a place inside to stand or sit, per Dekker's translated orders.

Heba closed the door behind the last person and turned to face Dekker.

"So, to what do I owe this pleasure?" she asked.

"We are in need of your special talents," he answered.

"What can I do for you?"

Dekker explained the need for the capes to be made from the cloth they laid out on the table for her, explaining she would be paid well for her services. Then he took the book that Simon handed him and asked her if she could help them translate it.

"Of course I can. Although, we may need to travel to some ruins on the outer part of the city where the ancient writing is carved into some of the stone there, where many of the ancients still live. Some of the symbols in this book are very old. I do not know some of these, and I'm not sure there is anyone left who can help us."

"We can only do what we can," Dekker replied.

Heba placed the material, thread, and measurements provided to her on a corner shelf, and then packed a small bag with a water bladder and some snacks.

The large group left the small house and walked through the city to the edge where the ancients lived. Most of the Peregrines marveled at the scenes before them. An ancient civilization preserved for hundreds of years beneath the water, inside the bottom of a mountain, was a sight to see. It was unlike anything any of them had ever seen on their past peregrinations.

Malachai spoke to Vashti as they walked.

"This place is amazing. To think we are in present times, and yet this place looks like it existed before the BC era."

"Yes, I know," Vashti agreed. "I feel like we have missed out on so many things as Dragoman. There are so many undiscovered places to see. Why did we as Dragoman, stop taking peregrinations with our mentored people? It isn't like there is some rule that we can't go along as well."

"No, there isn't. But until recently, we all traveled during separate times and to separate places. Our Peregrines traveled by twos before this. This way of traveling, in one large group, is just a recent necessity."

"True. I suppose that is one answer. Well, I for one plan on taking more adventures in the future. God has given us wonderous places to see and explore."

"I agree." Malachai smiled at his wife, their secret relationship coming to light only recently along with several other couples.

They continued following Heba as she led them to the outskirts of the city where the walls crumbled from years of neglect due to the lack of habitation. Only a very few people lived this far from the city's center and the king's palace. They walked past small waterfalls that cascaded down from someplace high within the mountain, providing fresh water to the city. The flowing water pooled in depressions that were staggered all over the ground, overflowing in spots and running into the ocean at the water's edge. Near the waterfalls, vegetation sprouted and vined in all directions, climbing over the old dwellings and through the crumbled stones and partially standing windows. There was no wildlife here, except for some burrowing creatures. The people here depended solely on the sea for their lively hood, and whatever they could grow in the city gardens.

They soon reached a small area where about fifteen, small, stone, houses stood still intact. There were a few children or younger people there, mainly just very old people sitting around a fire pit in the village center.

Gabriele, ever the observant one, noticed a cauldron with something bubbling inside and a steaming pot of what appeared to be a dark liquid, perhaps their version of coffee.

Heba turned to Dekker and spoke, then he turned to the group.

"Heba says for everyone to find a place to sit or look around if you like. She and I are going to find her grandfather and return shortly."

While Heba and Dekker disappeared behind some more of the small huts, everyone else did whatever they wanted. Gabriele watched as Simon cautiously took a cup of the dark liquid offered to him from the pot. He thanked the giver with a slight bow and smile, then sipped from the cup.

Gabriele had to stifle a laugh that tried to escape her lips at the look on Simon's face. She wasn't sure if it was a look of disgust or if the man simply couldn't breathe. Simon sputtered a bit, then cleared his throat, took a deep breath, and handed the cup back to the giver. The old ones around the fire erupted in laughter and chattered amongst themselves, looking at Simon in amusement.

Simon looked down and spoke, knowing they likely couldn't understand him.

"I'm afraid your drink is a bit too strong for me, but thank you all the same." He coughed and sputtered again and the old ones giggled some more, shaking their heads in acknowledgement.

It wasn't long before Dekker returned, beckoning Simon over to him. They spoke for a few seconds before Simon turned to address the group.

"I and the other Dragoman are going with Heba and Dekker to see about translating the book. You are all free to roam and explore. I'm certain we will be busy all day. Gabriele, you were here with us last time. If you could show everyone where Dekker's home is, you can all settle in and put your packs and bedrolls away. See you all later tonight."

With that, Simon, Malachai, Vashti, Prisca, and Oz, followed Dekker behind the huts and disappeared. The others turned to Gabriele.

"All right, you all follow me as we go back to Dekker's place. I'll fill you in on what happened last time if you haven't heard yet. Then you can explore the city of Akrotiri for yourselves. Just try to stay away from the palace or any guards."

They all then waved goodbye to the people in the small village and went back the way they had come just thirty minutes earlier. As they walked, they all gazed at the strange beauty that lay within the mountain's core.

Gabriele was always fascinated by each new, unique world they discovered on their peregrinations. And this modern age city, stuck in the ancient past, locked deep below the ocean's surface was no exception. Although it was crumbling in many places, the city still had a mystical, magical charm about it. The strange light that gave a sense of daylight reached most everywhere, except for dark little niches here and there. The waterfalls cascading from deep within the dormant volcano split and ran in all directions into the water of the sea which, strangely enough, created a cove of sorts, several hundred feet below the ocean's surface just on the inside walls of the mountain.

How a city could sustain itself like this was a miracle. One that Gabby knew to be of God. She smiled to herself as she thought about the work she did for that very same God. She was specifically called by Him to this life. And although it could be very hard and treacherous at times, she felt honored to be a part of it.

"Penny for your thoughts." She heard someone say, then turned to see Timothy walking up beside her.

"You were watching me?" she asked him with raised eyebrows.

"It's kind of hard not to notice the look of awe on your face." He grinned lopsidedly.

"What can I say. I enjoy my life, and I am grateful for what I get to see and do. All while serving my God and living out my faith."

"I never really thought of it that way," he said thoughtfully.

"Perhaps you are not a believer?" she questioned him with a quizzical look.

"I am. I have been since the day I peregrinated. But I didn't try to get closer to God. I guess I figured that, since I was doing what I was called to do, that I was good. I realized my mistake just recently. After the whole Kristen thing, and then Uriah, I decided I had better start paying more attention to Him. Plus, Simon had a good talk with me, and it opened my eyes to my thoughtlessness."

Gabriele grinned at his confession. "Good. It's kind of redundant to be a warrior for God and not believe in who you serve."

He smiled at her reply. "I agree."

The two of them chatted as they walked, soon coming to Dekker's home where everyone placed their unnecessary items, listened to Gabby about their last visit, then split up into groups to explore the area, Timothy sticking close to Gabriele's side.

Reader's Island

Jason was the first scheduled to help Marnor deliver lunch to Petra. As the two men walked the stairs to the second level of the house, Marnor spoke.

"Jason, I just wanted to thank you for healing me and saving me from death on the battlefield the other day."

"No problem."

"I know you don't know me, but you've likely heard of some of the things that I've done."

"Yes, I have."

"Look," Marnor said, stopping on the middle landing where the large staircase split. "I know I have to prove myself to everyone here. Especially those that I hurt. But that day on the battlefield, something changed in me. I'm not sure what, but I saw something in you people; in my sister; that I've only ever seen once before. And that was almost fourteen years ago when we first encountered your kind. The only difference now, is that kindness was extended to me this time. Me. The one person who *did not* deserve it. And *that* is what made me change."

"That is what grace is, Marnor," Jason said, turning to take the next flight of stairs to the upper level, followed closely by an attentive Marnor. "Jesus Christ first offered tremendous grace to us. God sent Him to die for our sins, so that we could have a personal relationship with Him. Now, as believers, we must offer the same to everyone else, no matter how much they've done to us. But only if forgiveness has been asked for. Now, since you've been given such grace, you must make amends to those who you've hurt."

Marnor shook his head in understanding but was unsure who this Jesus person was. He had heard God mentioned many times in his encounters with these Peregrines and remembered what many of those they captured and tortured years ago had said as they slowly died from that same torture.

They stopped outside Petra's bedroom door and he looked at Jason who continued.

"Marnor, if you need to talk or ask questions, you can ask anyone here and they will *all* likely tell you the same thing. But if you want to ask me, your welcome to anytime."

"Thanks. I appreciate the offer."

"Now, about Petra. We aren't for certain where her allegiance lies, so keep the talking to a minimum, and don't take your eyes off of her for a second."

Marnor shook his head in understanding and held the food tray in his hands, as Jason took the key and unlocked the door. Petra was sitting in a chair staring out of the spell-protected, sealed, windows. She turned to them as they entered the room. She looked at Marnor with curiosity. She glanced between him and Jason.

Jason recognized her questioning look. "Petra, this is Marnor Draiwood. He'll be a regular visitor with you."

She shook her head in curious acceptance, then asked morosely. "Am I to be kept in my room forever? Locked away, never to see the outside again?"

"That's not my decision to make, Petra. Besides, you did this to yourself."

"I know." She sighed heavily. "But I've changed. Really I have. I'm going stir crazy in here, all alone. I miss being with people."

"You'll have to discuss that with the Dragoman when they return."

"When will that be?"

"Not really sure. Tomorrow maybe."

Petra sighed again.

Marnor watched the exchange between them, realizing that he himself had free reign of the island —under supervision of course— and he was a complete stranger to most of these people. And those that did know of him, knew him to be the cruelest of men. What had this woman done to be locked up here in her room?

"I'll walk you down to the restroom. Some of the women will be up later to allow you to shower," Jason said, then turned to Marnor. "We'll be right back, Marnor."

Marnor watched how Jason handled the woman as they left the room. He walked behind them, stopping at the door, and watching what needed to be done as she was led to the bathroom. Even though she was a prisoner, she was still treated and spoken to with kindness and decency. *He* had certainly never treated the enemy this way. He hoped that they would soon allow him to handle this one task on his own. He felt a need to earn the trust of these people. To prove that he was a different person now. But he doubted that they would ever trust the likes of him with anything real, especially to tending to this woman who was held prisoner. He was curious to know what she had done that was so terrible?

They soon returned to the room and Petra plopped down on the chair in front of the desk to eat. She seemed completely defeated, sniffling a little as a stray tear or two streaked her cheeks. They left her alone once again, locking the door and returning the keys and the previous day's used tray to the kitchen. Jason left, going about the day's business. Marnor went about washing yesterday's dinner dishes from Petra's room, deciding that he would sneak back up later to talk to the woman through the door. She had to be lonely, and he had little else to do. Surely just talking to her wouldn't be a bad thing. Maybe the two of them could find their way together? She would likely be more open to talk with him than any of the others, no matter what Jason said.

Stables

Jason walked down to the stables to find Seth, Caroline, and many others there tending to the animals. After yesterday's battle, a few of the horses had perished and several received minor injuries. As a trained veterinarian, he took it upon himself to see to their care. He was glad to see many others there already, tending to the animals' needs. Their bandages had already been removed and the wounds cleaned. Jason approached Seth.

"Seth, are there anymore clean bandages and topical medicine in the tack room?"

"I believe so. I was going to rebandage the wounds, but I wasn't sure about a few of the injuries. Some are pretty deep."

"Don't worry about those. I may need to stitch a few of them. Especially since the horses keep moving around."

"How are you going to manage that? It isn't like you have a lot of equipment to keep them still."

"No. But, they are pretty tough animals. I doubt they will even feel it much. If need be, I'll run through the barrier to find some tranquilizers for them to calm them down so that I can do what needs doing."

They all continued tending to the animals. Cleaning wounds, brushing them down, shoeing, or grooming them. A few hours later, the work was complete and the group returned to the main house for some lunch, grateful that Clancy and Henry had taken up the cooking again. They all thanked the men for the delicious meal of fresh fish, caught earlier that morning by Seth and

Caroline. They retired to the patio once again to eat, the constant cooling breeze of the island the main draw to dining outside.

Bridget watched Marnor choose a seat off to the side, alone. She looked at Dominic, who always seemed to be close by lately and excused herself.

"Dominic, I'm going to sit with my brother and eat. This is the perfect opportunity for us to have a chat."

"Bridget, I don't know about h…"

"Dominic," she said quietly, yet forcefully, "I am having a chat with my brother. Either you deal with it, or not. It doesn't matter. I will be fine. I can take care of myself you know."

She almost grinned at the look on his face but decided not to. It might have hurt his ego all the more. She picked up her food and walked over to Marnor's table, several pairs of eyes watching her, including Caroline.

Caroline didn't like that man, and she surely didn't like Bridget cozying up to him, half-brother or not. She would certainly be keeping her eyes on the situation.

Bridget approached the table and sat across from him.

Marnor watched as she sat down, a bit taken by surprise at her willingness to sit with him.

"Hello, Marnor." She grinned at him and waited for a reply.

"Bridget," he said, clearing his suddenly tightening throat. He wasn't good with relationships or talking. But he would certainly give it a try.

"Well," she said, taking a bite of food and chewing, watching his face.

His eyebrows shot up in question.

"You said you wanted to talk to me. So, here I am."

Marnor cleared his throat, a bit uncomfortable at her straight forwardness. "I'm not sure what you want me to say."

"Well, you did ask to talk to me, so I assumed you *knew* what you wanted to say." She watched the confusion flit across his features. "Oh, all right. I'll start the conversation. What do you want to know? Surely you have all sorts of questions. Whether they pertain to mother, my father, or what you're doing here. I know *I* certainly have some."

"Yeah, you're right. I do want to know a few things. First, I guess, is why you saved me yesterday. You risked your own life to save me. I've never done anything good for anyone. You know what kind of person I am and the things I've done."

"You're right, Marnor. You have done horrid things. I've only heard about what the Scaither's are capable of from Oz. And I know what you did to Caroline, and likely Sofia as well. But, God says that we are to forgive what others do to us."

"Why?" Marnor asked anxiously. "I don't understand that. Why are you supposed to forgive the people who torture you, hurt you, even kill your friends and try to do the same to you?"

"Because Marnor, Jesus did the same for us. He is God's son, who was sent to pay the price for all of our sins by dying on the cross. He took all of our sins away so that we could have life everlasting."

"I don't think He would want me or be able to make atonement for the things I've done."

"There is nothing He can't make right, Marnor. Even your sins. It's all a bit confusing until you accept Jesus as your savior and start reading the Bible."

"You're right. None of it makes any sense to me. But if there is a way to make restitution for the things I've done, and to be like you and the other people I see here, then I'll give it a try. I want to stay here, Bridget. I'll do whatever I need to do to make that happen."

"Well, Marnor, it's more a matter of the heart. If you accept Jesus just because you want to stay here, that isn't the correct reason. You must *really* want to change; your way of thinking, your actions, your words, everything. You have to turn your life over to Him. Let Him lead and guide you from now on."

Marnor looked at her. He wasn't so sure about giving control of his life over to someone or something else entirely.

"How do I do that?" he questioned her, looking a bit uneasy and taking a deep breath.

"It's simple really. Just pray and ask Jesus into your life and be willing to change."

Marnor took another deep breath and said, "Okay, how do I do that."

Bridget grinned softly at him, instructed him to bow his head, close his eyes and just talk to God. She started by giving him an example, then waited for him to take up where she stopped.

Marnor felt a strange sense of peace come over him. He couldn't quiet explain what it was, but for the first time in his entire life, he felt different; at ease. He finished his prayer and opened his eyes to see Bridget smiling at him.

"Now, you are a child of God, Marnor. You have his protection and will always be welcomed into the kingdom of heaven."

"Just like that? Does that mean I can't die or something?"

"No, nothing like that. We can all die at any time. But now, our souls are saved from hell. When we die, we can be certain that our souls will live in heaven with God and Jesus, instead of hell with the demons."

Marnor understood that aspect. He had already been tormented horribly by possession. In fact, it was that possession that made him realize how much he had hurt others. The constant pain and torment he had suffered for a time made him realize what an evil man he had been. Even with the things that he did to others, it in no way compared to what he had seen and witnessed while possessed. He never wanted to experience or feel that way ever again. And if Bridget was right, now he wouldn't have to. If that reassurance was all he ever got out of being what Bridget called a Believer, then that was all he needed to convince him.

Marnor grinned for the first time. A true grin of relief and happiness.

Bridget smiled broadly at the change in him already.

Marnor knew he needed to change more, but he was willing to learn and do whatever was needed of him to become more like the people that he was beginning to admire more with each moment spent in their company. Especially his little sister Bridget. She was an amazing young woman. He had only had a few encounters with her before leaving Zanchier, and even then she had made an impression upon him. He had known then that she was different, like some of the Peregrines he had met before. Her beliefs and lack of fear had impressed him so much that at the time, it had angered him. Now he understood where her strength came from. He only hoped that he too would find the kind of strength and reassurance that she exuded. He knew one thing, now that he had a sister; the only family he had left; he would protect her at all costs.

He and Bridget sat chatting about the past. Answering questions for one another about their own childhoods, their parents, and what made them the people they had become. They talked well into the afternoon, with Bridget's friends glancing their way as they passed them, curious what they could be talking about for so long. Caroline and Dominic being the two that were concerned the most.

They each prayed silently for their young friend, that this man Marnor wouldn't turn her heart away from them, or God.

My help comes from the Lord, the
Maker of heaven and earth.

Psalm 121:2

Chapter 4

Akrotiri, Underwater City

Simon and the others listened intently, each making notes and writing the translations that Heba and her grandfather spoke as Dekker diligently translated. They had been working at the translations for the majority of the morning and her grandfather was growing tired.

Simon said, "Dekker, let's take a break for a bit to give him a chance to rest. Besides, we need to scrounge up some lunch. I'm famished, and I'm certain that everyone else is as well."

Malachai grinned. "I could certainly eat."

Dekker replied, "I agree." He turned to explain to Heba and her grandfather, and they all left to head to the market for some fresh seafood, fruits, and vegetables. After retrieving the necessary food items, they headed back to Dekker's home for lunch. None of the other Peregrines were there, most likely they were all out exploring.

Malachai pulled out a chair and sat down at the table with his food. "I wonder if we are going to be able to get the whole book deciphered by tomorrow."

Simon turned to answer. "Most likely not. And I don't think we can afford to stay here for more than a few days. If the translations take more than two days, we'll leave the book here. Perhaps a few of us could stay behind as well to transcribe the translations. After we figure out how long it will take to get through the first chapter of the book, we'll decide on the next plan of action."

Dekker spoke up. "I can stay behind, Simon. I'm used to it here."

"I'm afraid, Dekker, you'd have no choice in the matter either way. You're the only one who can communicate with Heba and her people. Of course, King Pyrrus and his men speak English and Akrotirian, however, I don't wish to involve any of them if at all possible. We don't need a replay of the last visit." Simon's raised eyebrows and a stiff grin relaying his take on the memory.

"Too right," Dekker replied.

Vashti looked at the men. "Why don't we just see how the rest of the day goes, then we can figure this out. We already have the first ten pages transcribed. Perhaps it won't take as long as you think."

Simon looked at her. "Yes, but I don't wish to wear Heba's grandfather out in the process."

"He seemed like he was enjoying reading it. I think the book fascinated him."

"I'm sure it did. It fascinates us too. If we could leave the book here for them to translate and we could return to the island, then it would be ideal. However, I don't want to have to make another trip back here if there is no need. Besides, the Peregrines will need to leave soon on the mission to find the last piece of armor. Meaning, Gabriele will have to leave with them. She's the only way we've found so far to travel down here. Without her, we may not be able to return."

"Yes. I see your point. We may not be able to make it back to retrieve the book," Vashti replied.

Prisca looked up from her plate. "Then that means we have the same problem with the capes. What if we can't get back to retrieve them either?"

"Goodness. I hadn't thought of that," Simon said. "We have a few things to think through don't we?"

Dekker said, "What if we take Heba back to the island with us? She can sew the capes there. Probably much faster as well once she learns to use the modern machinery."

Simon looked nervous. "I'm not sure she would be able to walk through the portal."

Malachai stated, "Marnor did. He is not one of us. Safra did as well, and she was never able to do so before Ryan made the Portgens."

"Yes, I understand all of that. But are you willing to risk the woman's life just to find out?" Simon warned.

Malachai stated in frustration. "There has to be a way to test this theory."

"I'm afraid the only way to do so is to jeopardize another human life," Simon explained.

They all sat quietly for the next few minutes. Each pondering the unanswered questions and trying to think of a solution to the seemingly unending problems they always seemed to face.

Safra, Nadia, Sofia, and Rourke walked the city streets of Akrotiri, marveling at the ancient architecture that seemed to withstand the test of time.

Safra was amazed. Of course, she realized that there were no elements to wear at the stone here beneath the volcanic mountain. The city, although crumbling with age in some spots, still stood in all its glory. The statues of the gods that these people worshipped, standing tall and erect throughout; a few of them visible high above the buildings in some areas. From her vantage point at the top of a crumbled mass of stone, she could see almost the entire city below. She marveled at the arched entryways and the marble columns that graced nearly every doorway and open courtyard. The end supports for the strange type of grapes they grew here were even tiny Grecian columns. She was surprised at how the city seemed to exist, even though she knew they did without some very important staples. God had provided a way for these people to survive —even here beneath the earth's surface— for hundreds of years.

"Safra, are you coming?" she heard Sofia call her.

"Yes. Be right down."

As she began her descent from the tops of the stone, a loose rock gave way and she slid with it to the ground below. The motion and noise caught the attention of the others.

Rourke ran over to where she landed. "Safra are you all right?"

"Yes, I'm fine," she said, standing and brushing at the dust and dirt on her clothing. "No injuries to report."

"Good." He grinned.

Unaware they were being followed, and watched, they left the area to explore some more.

The seven curious children that sought after the strangers to their world quietly followed after them. They had never seen people like these before. They also remembered the way they fought in the battle with the King's men the last time they were here. Children weren't allowed to watch the gladiator fights, but they always managed to find a spot from secret hideaways along the top of the coliseum walls. They had also watched the strangers disappear into the ocean when they last left Akrotiri.

Kobal, the oldest of the children who followed and watched the strangers from their hiding place amongst the forgotten city dwelling, noticed the woman slip on the crumbling rock. When she seemed all right, the group left again headed inward toward the palace walls. He crept up slowly, following as closely as he could without being seen, trying to keep the other younger ones quiet. They liked this new game of watching these people. He wanted to find out as much as he could about them. They talked funny and dressed very oddly.

As he and the other children walked past the spot where Safra had tumbled down from the top of the stone pile, one of the smaller children noticed something lying on the ground. She reached out and picked up the strange looking rectangular box with all the buttons.

"Kobal, look what I found!" she excitedly said, showing the older adventurous boy her treasure.

Kobal and the other children gathered around her.

"Give it to me, Kida. It might be dangerous."

Kida pouted at the thought of giving up her treasure, but if she didn't give it to Kobal, then he might not let her come on anymore of his adventures. So, she reluctantly handed it to him.

Kobal looked at the strange device. It had some green lights glowing on a strange little square in the center of it. And the lights flashed on and off, like the light bugs that flew near the freshwater streams on the city's outer borders. He looked at the buttons on the front curiously.

He looked at the other children gathered around him and asked, "Do you think we should push the buttons to see what happens?"

They all glanced at each other, some shrugging their shoulders, others shaking their heads no, and still others anxious to see what would happen.

"I say we try it. What could happen?" Kobal bravely stated.

With that, he randomly began pushing buttons on the front of the device.

"Oh no," Safra said worriedly. "I've lost my Portgen somewhere."

Sofia's eyes grew wide. "We need to go back and find it, quickly."

Rourke knew the reason for her concerned demeanor. "I'm sure it's fine, Sofia. Besides, since Ryan installed the fingerprint scanner upgrade, no one can open the device except the person to whom it belongs."

Safra looked at him curiously. "I don't think my Portgen had that feature."

Nadia asked, "What do you mean? They all should have had it installed."

"Maybe my older-self forgot to get that upgrade," Safra stated.

Sofia nervously said, "We need to find that device."

They all turned around and ran back the way they had come, searching every inch of ground as they went.

Gabriele and Timothy walked the streets of the city chatting congenially with one another.

Tim was shocked at how relaxed he was with her. He felt he could talk to her about anything. He had never felt this comfortable around a woman before. In the past, he was always too busy impressing them with his long list of accomplishments, his cars, his money, or his good looks. That's all they had ever been interested in anyway. Except for Kristen, she never bought into the whole charmer routine, and he was now glad of it. Uriah had been right about his feelings for her. It was more of a competition with Sean Doran to see who she would choose. Thankfully, she chose Sean. Tim felt like he would have grown tired of her after a while. He had liked her, but it was more physical attraction than anything else.

Gabriele was a different matter all-together. She was as straight-forward a person as he had ever encountered. She told you how it was, regardless of your feelings. But at the same time, she was cautious with her words. She didn't offer her opinion very often unless she felt she had something useful or important to say. And when she did speak, people tended to listen.

Tim looked at her, studying her features. Her hair was so black it shimmered with hints of purple. The straight silken strands and page boy style cut, swished about her head with each slight movement. She was very pretty, in an exotic way. She was taller than most oriental women he encountered in the past. Probably due to her British genetics from her father's side.

Gabriele turned to notice him looking at her.

"Is there something on my face or in my hair?" she questioned, reaching up to feel for any foreign matter.

Tim grinned at her unassuming nature.

"No. Just noticing how attractive you are."

Gabriele looked at him with a raised eyebrow.

"What. Now that Kristen is taken, you're on to your next conquest?"

Tim sighed audibly. "No, it's not like that. Besides, she made the right choice with Doran. I don't think we would have lasted long. I think it was more of the thrill of the chase with her."

"And I'm *not* thrilling to chase?" she teasingly asked.

He smiled broadly at her words and tone.

"I don't plan on chasing you. I plan on getting to know you for real and seeing where it goes," he answered her honestly.

Gabriele stopped at his words and looked at him. Just as she was about to reply, she stopped. She felt something in the air. Tim must have noticed her demeanor change because he asked, "Gabby, is something wrong?"

"Sorry. I think I felt a portal open."

"What do you mean? How can you feel when a portal opens?"

"Ever since the last demon battle, where my power connected with all the Portgens to make a protective barrier around our army, I've been able to sense or feel when a portal opens."

"You're sure that's what it is?"

"Not really, but I think so."

"Who would be opening a portal down here?"

"I don't know, but I think we better find out. I think it's coming from that direction," she said pointing. " Let's go." The two of them took off at a steady trot.

Kobal and the other children watched in amazement and fear as a bright light appeared directly in front of them. He dropped the Portgen, almost frightened now to touch it.

"Kobal, what's that?" Kida sheepishly whispered, tugging at the older boys' shirt.

"I don't know, Kida." He stepped a little closer, the other children following his example. All trying to peer at the strange sights visible on the other side of the bright light.

Kobal's foot nudged the Portgen when he stepped closer to the light and he bent down and picked it up. He held it in his hand while he cautiously held his other hand out toward the portal.

"No, don't, Kobal," one of the older girls warned. "You might get hurt."

"How? It just looks sort of like a doorway, but to another place." He ignored the girl's warning, and as the other children watched in apprehension, Kobal slowly stepped through the portal.

Safra, Sofia, Rourke, and Nadia ran as quickly as possible. When they turned the corner of an old building they saw some children standing in the road, an open portal directly in front of them.

"Stop!" Rourke barked, startling the already frightened children. Fearing for their very lives, he yelled, "It's dangerous! Don't go near it."

The four Peregrines stopped in their tracks. Suddenly joined by Gabriele and Timothy from another direction.

Just then, Kobal stuck his head back through the portal and stepped back out of the opening, dropping the Portgen. All the children ran off, afraid they might be in some sort of trouble.

They all stood looking after the quickly disappearing boy, shocked that he was able to pass through the portal. Rourke walked over and picked up the discarded Portgen, shutting down the portal and returning the device to Safra.

Rourke turned to his group of friends. "You all saw that, right?"

"Yes," Safra answered. "I for one am very grateful. That boy could have died."

"Yes, but he didn't. And unless he's a new Peregrine, Dragoman, or Keeper that we have yet to discover, I'd say it was safe to assume that anyone can travel by way of the Portgens."

Nadia said, "All the more reason to make certain that all of them have the fingerprint scanner installed."

They all agreed with a shake of their heads.

Sofia looked at Gabriele. "Where did you two come from so quickly?"

Gabby looked at her, unsure whether she wanted everyone to know she had yet again received another gift of sorts. She decided it would be best to tell them, and explained to them what she said to Tim.

"I'm not sure I envy you that one." Sofia smiled at her.

Safra added, "Yes, I would take that to mean you might attract energy or electricity. Best be cautious during an electrical storm."

Gabriele's face scrunched up in realization. "Thanks for that," she said apprehensively. She certainly didn't take to possibly attracting lightning. That was Uriah's gift.

Rourke spoke after, saying, "I think we need to find Simon and the others and let them know about this little hiccup. If those kids come back with adults or armed guards who believe their story, we could have a serious problem on our hands."

They all left quickly, headed back to Dekker's to grab their packs, and then to find the others.

Simon and the other five in his group finished their dinner, left their packs and bedrolls at Dekker's -planning to return for the night- and went back to Heba's grandfather's village for further translation. They had only been there about an hour when Gabriele and the others showed up, Rourke suddenly appearing inside the house.

"Simon, can we talk to you and the others for a minute," he said urgently.

"Certainly."

Simon and the others followed him outside as he explained about what had happened and that maybe they should leave Akrotiri.

"Well, we at least have one question answered for us," Simon said, looking at Malachai and the other Dragoman. "Do you really think that it's necessary for us to leave here?" Simon asked Rourke.

"It depends on whether or not those kids talk about what they saw, and whether anyone believes them."

"I'll admit it could have an adverse effect on our purpose here. But then again, perhaps not. Besides, we really need to finish deciphering this book. I do have one question though. Do you know where it was that the young man went? The last time we were here we couldn't get a signal on the Portgens. It seems strange that he actually got a portal to open."

"No, I don't. Do the Portgens have a storage for memory of such things?"

"I have no idea. That's a good question for Ryan when we get back. I say we all just stick close by. Perhaps Heba and her grandfather could come with us to Dekker's home. That way, if we have to leave in a hurry, we will be close to the water's edge"

"Simon," Dekker interjected, "perhaps it's best if we stay here. It is less likely for us to be found out here than at my place. They found you all there last time, remember?"

"True. All right, Rourke can you and the others bring our packs and bedrolls back here?"

Timothy spoke up, "Already done, Simon. We grabbed them when we picked up our own."

"Good thinking." Simon grinned at him. "Well, you all hang close by and the rest of us will return inside to see about translating more of the book."

After they went back into the house, Rourke formed a plan.

"I think the rest of us need to spread out and pick some higher places to keep watch until the others are ready to go. Yell if you see anything that looks suspect. We won't have much time to leave unless we can get the Portgens to work again."

They all agreed and split up in all directions to keep watch, Safra staying near the house to quickly alert all inside should the need arise. She prayed that they could accomplish what they needed to do before leaving Akrotiri. She felt responsible for this forced rush. She should have been more careful with her tools. Especially one like the Portgen.

Fortunately, as the day passed by and the hour grew late, no one came looking for them. Or, if they did, they didn't search this far out.

Dekker asked Heba to send a scout to his place to see if anyone was waiting around at his place for them to return.

Heba sent a few of the village's older boys to the waterfront to watch Dekker's home for thirty minutes. They were to return and report before Dekker and the others could leave. Heba was curious about the extra security and asked Dekker why.

He explained to her what had happened with the device that allowed them to travel between worlds.

"Does that mean that I could go with you?" Heba questioned him.

"I'm not sure, Heba. I suppose it means that it's at least safe. But why would you want to go with me? Your home, your family, is here. What about your grandfather?"

"All my life I have lived for everyone else. I wish to live for me. I wish to follow you, Dekker. Wherever that may be."

Dekker finally realized what she was saying. Why he had never noticed her feelings for him before, he didn't know. He truly liked Heba. He just never thought of her in a romantic way before. Of course, he never really had thoughts about a relationship with anyone recently.

"Are you certain, Heba? You may never be able to return here."

"Yes, I am certain."

"Then I will ask Simon. It may be best to take you with us anyway to finish the translations and to work on the capes."

"Thank you, Dekker."

"Don't thank me yet. You may wish you never left. There are many dangers that await us in the places we must go. These people fight against great evil almost weekly."

"I understand. I will not be a hindrance to you or the others in any way."

The young men soon returned with good news. They had seen no one interested in Dekker's home. The Dragoman felt it was safe to return to Dekker's for the night.

Dekker walked with Simon on the way, explaining to him Heba's wish.

"I don't know, Dekker. Do you think it's a good idea to bring her along? You know the lifestyle we lead."

"I explained all of that to her, and she understood. Besides, it would be more beneficial for the translating and the capes."

"I thought she didn't know some of the ancient language?"

"She didn't. But spending time with her grandfather and helping to translate today, she's learned a lot of the symbols, and made notes on most of the others. It couldn't hurt to take her. If anything should go wrong, I'll bring her back myself."

"Well, I'll need to discuss this with the others before agreeing. I'll let you know tomorrow morning."

"That will be fine, Simon."

They reached Dekker's during the darkest part of the dimming light, which was still nearly as bright as sunset. They decided that everyone would stay in Dekker's blacksmith shop instead of splitting into two groups of six as they did last time, with half staying in his home. Dekker would stay upstairs alone just in case anyone came by looking for them.

They all quietly settled in for the night, with several taking turns with the night watch. They would change out every two hours until daybreak.

Safra and Simon took the first two hours. They talked only when necessary as they scanned the city streets through the small hammer and anvil cutouts in the door of the shop.

Safra decided to offer her apologies for their situation.

"I am sorry, Simon. This is all my fault. I should have been more careful with that device."

"It isn't your fault, Safra. You aren't used to such things. Traveling by storm did have its advantages."

"Perhaps. But that boy could have died today."

"But he didn't, now did he? Besides, we learned a very valuable lesson today. And received the answer to an important question. God has a purpose for everything, Safra. And this is no exception."

"I suppose you're right."

"You know, you used to be the one to give me these pep talks." Simon smiled at her.

Safra smiled back at him. Her *older-self* had been that person. She had a lot to learn about the woman she would become. Of course, that could all change now that her life was completely different. At least *old Safra* had left her a book explaining the strange things, people, and places she needed to know about. If they ever got any down time, she would spend it reading and learning all she could about these people she now fought with, lived with, and could potentially die alongside. She shut off her thoughts and got back to the task at hand.

54

Have I not commanded you? Be strong and courageous.
Do not be afraid; do not be discouraged, for the Lord
your God will be with you wherever you go.

Joshua 1:9

Chapter 5

Reader's Island

By the time Bridget and Marnor finished talking it was close to dinner. Bridget walked with him to the kitchen. Helping out there had become one of his jobs since he had come to the island. Plus, he needed to take Petra's food to her.

Marnor felt a sense of peace and calm like never before. He wasn't sure if it was just the beautiful island he was on, the way the people here behaved, his growing relationship with Bridget, or his acceptance of the God they all served. Whatever it was, he liked it. He planned on making the most of this new life he had been given.

Bridget said goodbye, promising to find him at dinner and disappeared. Marnor went to the kitchen to find Seth waiting on him with the tray of food they would deliver to Petra.

Marnor took a deep breath to steady his nerves. The man didn't like him, and with good reason. He was massively large and tall, and intimidated Marnor very much.

Seth looked at the man on whom he had been waiting. He could tell he rattled Marnor's nerves. *Good,* he thought. He didn't mind meal-time delivery to Petra, but he didn't relish having this man along with him. He knew he had to come to terms with what he did to Caroline. He just wasn't sure how long that would take.

Seth picked up the key from the tray without so much as a word to him, and Marnor picked up the tray to follow behind.

They silently left the kitchen, climbed the staircase, and stopped in front of Petra's bedroom door. Seth turned to look at Marnor.

"No speaking to her, understand," Seth warned.

"Why?" Marnor braved the question.

"Does it matter? The Dragoman said no talking, and that's how it's going to be. If you have a problem with that, then find another job to do."

Marnor looked at him and shook his head in understanding.

They opened the door to find a freshly showered Petra sitting and reading a book. Marnor wondered when she had been taken to clean up. He looked at the woman, and for some reason, actually felt sorry for her. This revelation stunned him. It had been ages since he had felt compassion for anyone. He had apologized to Sofia and Caroline because he knew he had to do so too survive here. It was expected, but not truly heartfelt. Even though he said it was at the time. It was more out of instinct to survive. But what he felt for this woman, Petra, was a completely knew sensation. He wasn't at all sure that he liked it. It made him feel weak, like back when he first joined the Scaithers. Riglan had punished him anytime he showed any sort of remorse or kindness. Or, when he whined about being abandoned by his mother when she left with Hiram Burke. He had learned very quickly to be brutal and unforgiving to survive the world of the Scaithers. He had climbed the ranks quickly, the youngest ever to do so. Except for Riglan of course. The man was born evil, just like his father had been.

Seth noticed an emotion flit across Marnor's face and a sort of discomfort in his body language. He wondered what was going through the man's head. He would have to keep a very close eye on this one. He didn't trust him at all.

Marnor switched out the trays as Petra asked Seth a question.

"Have Simon and the others returned yet?"

"No, they haven't. We don't expect them back until tomorrow or later. Is there something you need?"

"Yes. Out of this room. I'm going crazy in here!"

"Well, you shouldn't have betrayed your friends, Petra. You're locked *in here* because of your own actions. People can't trust you."

"I know. You don't have to keep *lecturing* me about it."

"It's just that you seem confused as to why you're being punished."

Petra exhaled sharply. "Can you, or someone else, *please* take me outside for a while? I promise to behave. I don't *have* anywhere to go anyway. The island has been my home for the last fifteen years."

"I'll see what we can do. I'll speak to the other leaders about it."

"When," she anxiously asked.

"At dinner, tonight."

"Thank you, Seth."

"Don't thank me yet. You may not like the answer. Now, do you need the restroom?"

"No, maybe before bed. Thanks."

Seth and Marnor left the room and returned to the kitchen in time for dinner to be served. Seth went out to sit with his friends, calling all the leaders together at one table.

Marnor sat alone in the kitchen, pondering the feelings he had experienced upstairs, when Bridget walked in looking for him. She walked over to where he sat and placed a book on the table in front of him.

"What's this?" he asked, looking at the book.

"It's a Bible. I thought you might like to have it since our last talk this afternoon."

He looked at it and said, "You assume that I can read?"

Bridget looked startled at that. "I'm..I'm sorry, Marnor. I didn't realize that you couldn't."

"I can a bit, just not well. Never had a need for it. I was never one to go to the Academy when I was younger. I never found *my talent*. People like me were sent to work in the mines or harvest fields." He finished with an underlying tone of resentment.

"Well, perhaps I can teach you a little."

"You would do that for me?" he asked, surprise in his voice.

"Certainly, Marnor. I would do it for anyone. Especially so for my brother." She smiled gently at him.

"Thanks, Bridget."

"When would you like to get started?"

"Maybe later, after dinner?"

"All right. I'll see you then." Bridget smiled at him then waved goodbye and left the kitchen.

Marnor could feel his throat begin to tighten and tears stung the backs of his eyes. He shook off the feelings, unwilling to shed those tears. He just didn't understand where all the grace and forgiveness kept coming from. Bridget was truly remarkable, and he was fortunate to find her. He had been fortunate to find this island. If this God they all talked about was real, then perhaps he should learn to read better so that he could learn more about Him. He looked at the book lying beside him on the table. He reached out and stroked the leather covering, tracing the letters with his fingers. He could read the word Bible, since that was what Bridget had called it. He had never been given a book before and he wasn't sure how to feel about it.

Seth discussed Petra's request with the others at dinner. Everyone chiming in on their opinion.

Jason said, "I don't know if that's such a good idea."

Nick replied, "It's not like she could get very far."

"True," Zaccai said, "we would just have to watch her closely. I know I would feel the same if I were in her shoes.

Zeke stated, "Yeah, but it is her own fault that she is in her predicament. She purposefully deceived everyone *and* tried to steal the books to help Uriah take over the entire world."

Zaccai countered, "Yes. But she was deceived by the man she thought loved her. Most people have done far greater foolish things for love. I don't agree with what she did, but I don't see the harm in her request."

Seth said, "What if she makes a run for the barrier, and succeeds?"

"Then she is no longer our problem," Zaccai stated. "She can't really hurt anyone anymore. And if she is stupid enough to return to Uriah, then that's her problem."

Caroline said, "I think we could at least let her walk around outside for a bit. They do that much for true criminals in the prison systems."

"Caroline, this doesn't concern you, you don't need to worry about this. The leaders have to decide and agree," Seth said.

Caroline sat up straighter and looked at Seth. "Well, then. Excuse me everyone. I'm not qualified to listen *or* give my opinion here." She stood, picking up her plate and glass and walked away.

"Caroline...stop!" Seth stammered. "I didn't mean it like that!" he called to her retreating back.

Zaccai looked at him as if he were crazy. "You're either a very brave man, or a really stupid one, Seth Jager."

"Apparently, it's the latter. Just an idiot with words mostly. Excuse me while I go find my wife and explain myself and grovel *heavily* for forgiveness. I'm sure you can all come to a decision on your own." Seth got up and followed after Caroline.

Jason took what was said and stated, "Caroline is right. Prisoners do get to walk around in a fenced area. If two of us take to watching her at a time, then I don't see why she can't take her meals with us. Then at dinner get a reprieve from her room until we go to bed."

"I think that is very fair," Zaccai stated.

Nick and Zeke both agreed. Zaccai would let her know of their decision when she and Caroline went to take her to the restroom later. She would be allowed to have breakfast, lunch, and dinner with the group, with a slight reprieve, then returned to her room for the rest of the time.

Zeke watched Seth trot across the patio, trying to catch up with the quickly moving Caroline.

"Poor guy's in for a fight," Zeke stated with a grin.

"He'll be lucky she doesn't take his head off." Zaccai smiled.

"Yeah, relationship problems," Nick stated plainly.

"I'd give anything to have that kind of problem," Jason stated flatly. "Fighting with Memnah is fun. If only we got to see each other enough to actually fight."

Jason suddenly stood and walked away as everyone quietly sat and watched, feeling sorry for the man. Zaccai and Zeke looked at one another, linking their fingers under the table in appreciation of having their significant other right there.

Jason decided he would take the rest of the evening to make a trip to see Memnah tonight. He was missing her terribly, especially now. He would let Clancy or Shannon know where he was going, Seth as well if he happened to run into him, which he doubted. He happened to pass Shannon in the hallway upstairs tending to the bathrooms and told her his plans, asking her to let Seth or one of the other leaders know. He grabbed his pack, weapons, and Portgen, opened a portal right there in his room, and disappeared into the desert and the setting sun as it sank below the Negev Desert, just on the outskirts of Memnah's village.

Sean sat with Kristen, Bridget, Wade, and Dominic around one of the lit firepits on the patio playing charades with Annabelle. He realized how fun the young girl was to be around and how she brought an element of play that they all seldom had the opportunity in which to participate.

Sean had always wanted a sibling, but never had any. Kristin was an only child as well. Bridget too. However, Dominic came from an extremely large family, and Wade, well, Sean had never really asked him. Wade was a quiet, soft-spoken guy. He never said much at all to anyone. He was friendly enough, just quiet. Sean decided to rectify that.

"Wade, do you have any siblings?"

Wade looked surprised. "Yeah, an older brother, and two younger sisters. Why do you ask?"

"No reason. I just realized that I really don't know much about you or your life before you came here. And we've been working together in Prisca's group."

Wade shrugged his broad shoulders. "Well, umm…there isn't much to tell. My oldest brother plays football for a major league team, and my parents wanted the same for me. I wonder how everyone is doing. It's been about six months since I first peregrinated. I was closest to my youngest sister. We got along pretty well."

"How old is she?"

"Eight. She was born with some birth defects that caused her some health issues. She's fine and all, just a little on the shy side, and unsure of herself sometimes. I always felt like I had to protect her. I worry about her a lot. You know, wonderin' if she is doing okay and all."

Sean realized that he hadn't thought about these younger people having to worry about such things. He certainly never had. He was beginning to understand Wade a little more.

Annabelle sat beside Wade. "I'm sure she is all right, Wade. She probably misses you a lot. But God knows what he's doing. He isn't just using you here, but back home as well."

Kristen looked at the young girl. "That's a very grown-up way to look at things, Annabelle."

"Back in the orphanage, the teachers tried to tell us to look on the bright side of things. Most of them were really nice. We used to play the thankful game a lot. All the kids would list something that they were thankful for while living at the orphanage."

Kristen and Sean exchanged looks. Kristen thought, *it's sad that this bright, cheerful little girl didn't have parents to love her.* Kristen felt fortunate to have had the love and caring that her parents so often displayed to her. She had been one of the lucky ones. She knew that. And now to have a man like Sean Doran love her as well…she almost felt guilty. Some people would never experience real love of any kind, and she had found it twice.

"That is a very good game to play, Annabelle. Why don't we all play that game now. There are lots of things that I am thankful for right now. For one, I am thankful for Sean." Kristen looked at Sean, noticing the comical, playful look of pretend cockiness in his demeanor. Everyone giggled at his silly antics.

"Your turn, Sean." She smiled.

"I am grateful that God brought me here to this lifestyle so that I could meet Kristen. We would have never met otherwise."

"I'll go next," Dominic said. "I'm grateful that I found another family almost as big as the one I left at home."

Wade said, "I'm thankful that I can speak with animals. I've always liked animals."

Bridget said, "I've been having a hard time lately finding anything for which to be thankful. I have so many dark things in my family's past. I was alone for so very long, with no one at all. Then, Caroline showed up and has become like a sister to me. Then we met Oz, who is like a great big bear of a grandfather. And, of course, all of you have become like family. But I am truly thankful to have my brother, Marnor, here with me. It's nice to have a living relation. I didn't even have *that* before I peregrinated."

Annabelle smiled broadly. "You're all very good at this game. Now, it's my turn." She sat for a minute and thought. "I am grateful to have a new family as well. Even though the demon war was very scary. Ms. Nadia is helping me with that though, and Mr. Nicholas. I'm very grateful for both of them. It's almost like having a real family."

Sean looked at Kristen with concern in his eyes. He wasn't sure Nick was up to that just yet. Sure, his family problems had been a very long time ago. But Sean didn't think Nick's heart had yet healed. He looked at Annabelle talking animatedly with the younger people, and grinned. He wasn't sure that Nick would have much of a choice in the matter. This little girl was a force to be reckoned with. And she had her heart set on Nadia and Nick.

Seth's night had not gone as well as he would have liked. He had tried his hardest to explain to Caroline that he was sorry and that it had come out all wrong, but she was still angry and wouldn't even let him in their bedroom last night, so he had spent the night on one of the couches in the upstairs library.

He sat up and stretched his long frame, feeling a small crick in his neck and shoulder from the stiff couches. They were large settees, but he was an extra-large man, and didn't quite fit.

He walked to the door of his room and knocked.

"Caroline, are you up?"

He stood there for a minute, softly knocking and calling to her.

He heard a dull click, but the door stayed closed. She had unlocked it but hadn't opened it. She was still mad.

Seth opened the door and watched his wife take her clothing behind the dressing screen to change.

"Caroline, honey, you need to talk to me eventually. How many more times do you want me to say that I'm sorry? I know that what I said sounded bad. But I just didn't' want you to have to worry about all of that. That's all that I meant. I'm sorry it came out the way it did. Please forgive me." He walked to the dressing screen and waited for her to come out.

Caroline stepped from behind the screen and looked at him.

"You hurt my feelings, Seth. And you disrespected *and* humiliated me in front of everyone else. I felt like a child being scolded."

"I know, and I am *so* sorry for that. It's just that I'm feeling a bit more overprotective of you right now with that Marnor character being on the island. I just don't want you to have to worry about anything else."

Caroline softened toward him just a little. She hadn't realized that Seth was taking her past encounter with Marnor to heart so strongly.

"Seth. I am over what he did to me. I was just initially shocked at seeing the man in Timna, then here on the island. I'm not afraid of him. I'm much stronger than him now anyway and trained to be a fighter. I don't think about him much anymore. Besides, all of that was a means to an end. A way God used to mark me. He never allowed my vows to you to be broken."

Caroline wished that she could take back those words as soon as they left her lips.

"What do you mean? Did that man or someone else try to take advantage of you?" he seethed with anger at the question, knowing full well that *something* had happened.

Caroline held up her hands to calm him down. "No, not Marnor. Although he knew what was planned." Caroline sighed, "Seth, come sit on the bed with me. I might as well tell you the whole story."

Caroline and Seth sat and discussed her bondage for that one day. The things that she experienced and what God had saved her from.

"Why did you never tell me all of this before?" Seth's muscles tensed in every part of his body, his mind a whirlwind of images and awful possibilities.

"Because I didn't want to upset you with unnecessary details. Seth, please don't let this make you angry. I am fine. I truly suffered very little compared to how much Sofia has. If anyone has a right to hate Marnor Draiwood, and any other number of Scaithers, it's her. She endured *ten years* at their hands. She's never told me about her bondage with them. But from the way they treated the imprisoned women, I could put two and two together for myself."

She touched Seth's arm, their fight from earlier a mere memory. He was truly in anguish over what she had revealed. She had so wanted to spare him the details.

Seth looked at her. "Is there anything else? Don't leave anything out, Caroline. I want to know the truth about all of it."

"No, there is nothing else. I promise. Not even a conversation. Now, promise me you won't retaliate toward Marnor. Seth, I'm serious. It won't do any good, and it'll likely just upset Bridget. Besides, forgiving is what is expected of us."

Seth looked at her, noticing the concern that was evident in her expression.

"Fine. I'll behave, as long as he does. But I can't say that I'll be forgiving the man any time soon."

She leaned forward, placing her hands on each side of his rough, beard-shadowed face and planted a kiss on his lips.

When they separated, Seth said, "And, you need to keep an eye on Bridget. The two of them are getting awfully close."

"I know. I'm watching. Now, what do you say we go get some breakfast," she said standing.

Seth followed suit, sighing heavily.

"Can I at least shower and change first?"

Caroline apologetically smiled at his request. She had briefly forgotten that she had made him sleep elsewhere last night without so much as a change of clothing. "Sorry, Seth. Yes, of course you can. I'll wait right here."

"Great. Thank you." Seth grabbed a change of clothing, rubbed the knot in his shoulder, and left the room for one of the bathrooms.

Caroline smiled after him, giggling to herself at how miserable he had looked when he asked her permission to shower. She sure did love the big lug. He may not be the best with words at times, but his heart was true, and she was grateful for such a man with whom to share her life.

After he returned, they met with almost everyone else down in the kitchen. They decided to sit at the large table in the big room as they discussed the day with Clancy, Shannon, and Henry over breakfast.

"Oh, Seth," Shannon interjected in their conversation, "Jason told me last night to let you know that he went to see Memnah. Surely he's back already, but I didn't see you last night to let you know."

"Thank you, Shannon."

Zaccai and Zeke entered the kitchen with Petra between the two of them and sat her at the end of the long table. Everyone watched her sit, smiling as she did. Obviously happy to be let out of her room. Shannon was the first to approach her and hand her a plate of food. The exchange between the old friends was friendly but sad. Petra thanked her for the plate.

As they ate and chatted amiably, Marnor entered the kitchen for a plate of food and to begin the day's chores. He grabbed a plate and sat at the counter on the opposite side of the kitchen. He looked up to see Petra sitting there and the two called Zaccai and Zeke on either side of her.

Seth watched Marnor as he entered the kitchen. He also watched the odd reaction he had to Petra. His mannerisms didn't depict him to be as dangerous as what Caroline and Oz had told him. Of course, being out of certain environments tends to change a person. Maybe the man had changed? Seth would still watch him every opportunity he got. Marnor must have sensed Seth watching him because he turned at that moment, looked at Seth, nodded, then went back to eating breakfast.

Seth's blood started to boil again, but he took a few deep breaths to calm his nerves. He promised Caroline he would behave. He certainly didn't want to get into another fight with her. Besides, the man hadn't done anything but nod at him. However, Seth couldn't help imagining the horrible things that Marnor did and said to his wife, and the horrid things he likely did or allowed to happen to Sofia. He preferred it if Marnor acted like he didn't exist at this point. He certainly didn't need him acting all friendly-like. Seth decided to avert his eyes from the man's profile to try and steady his quickly unraveling nerves. His mind would take a bit more to clear. He had always had an active imagination. And right now, it was wreaking havoc on his soul.

Seth stood and bolted from the kitchen toward the sparring fields to work off his pent-up frustration and anger. Caroline watched him leave in a hurry, worried about his state of mind at the moment. She glanced at Marnor who also noticed Seth's hasty retreat. The two of them locked eyes for a brief moment, Caroline refusing to look away. She would not let him intimidate her. Marnor nodded at her as well, looked back at the doorway that Seth had just left through, stood up, and turned to the sink to start on breakfast dishes.

Caroline went after her husband, just to keep an eye on him. She knew he needed to work through this by himself. But she would try to stay near to him today to make certain he didn't do anything stupid.

Not long after she found him at the sparring field, others came out to join them.

Alec and Odessa were still working with the Keepers on their shooting abilities, while the rest of the Peregrines decided to join Seth in the sparring arena. They spent the remainder of the morning working on fighting techniques.

Lunchtime came quickly and found Sean and Kristen taking their turn to watch Petra. Marnor watched Petra from afar as he sat at the table with Bridget, learning to read from the Bible she had given him.

No one had seen Jason yet this morning and Seth was beginning to worry when he suddenly made an appearance on the patio with a plate of food in hand.

"Where have you been all morning?" Seth asked.

"With Memnah."

"You stayed in Timna last night?" Seth asked with raised eyebrows.

"Yes. But, not with Memnah. I stayed in a tent with some of the other bachelors in the tribe. I was very tempted to stay with her, but I wouldn't jeopardize her reputation like that."

"And this morning?"

"We went riding out over the desert, hung out, and just talked about all sorts of things. We haven't yet spent that much time together. It was nice. Something I hope we get to do more often in the future."

"So do I, brother." Seth gave him a reassuring pat on the shoulder.

Akrotiri

Morning came uneventfully much to everyone's relief. Simon and the other Dragoman decided that it would be safer and less nerve wracking if they just took Heba and her grandfather to the island with them, instead of being in a constant state of panic over possibly attracting attention after the fiasco with the Akrotirian children yesterday. It had at least proved to them that anyone could travel with the Portgen. Which made Simon realize the benefits, and the problems, that such information could bring to light.

After breakfast, Simon filled everyone in on the plans for the day. Dekker went to tell Heba, then the two of them went back to Dekker's to get Simon. They all took a trip to her grandfather's village to ask him to come with them. After much reservation on his part and much convincing on theirs, he hesitantly agreed to go with them, with Simon promising to return him home as soon as possible.

By the time everything that Heba and her grandfather would need was gathered up, and the group got ready to leave, it was nearing noon. They gathered on a more remote spot by the water and began their journey home to the island. Heba and her grandfather were both fearful and excited at this strange journey they were beginning.

Not only so, but we ourselves, who have the first fruits of the
Spirit, groan inwardly as we wait eagerly for our adoption to
sonship, the redemption of our bodies. For in this hope we were
saved. But hope that is seen is no hope at all.

Romans 8: 23-24

Chapter 6

Reader's Island

The peregrination group to Akrotiri arrived back on the island
just after lunchtime. Heba and her grandfather were in awe of the
sights, sounds, and smells around them. Not to mention the
unbelievable walk across the bottom of the ocean floor. They
stood on the beach at the edge of the water watching the expanse
of ocean and the waves rolling in and crashing at their feet.
Having never before seen the sun or sky, they were giddy as
children looking at the expanse of blue, the white puffy clouds,
the bright yellow sun, and the constant cooling breeze supplied
by the ocean's waves brushing their skin.

Dekker was thrilled for his friends and the things that they
were experiencing. He hoped they would enjoy their stay on the
island.

"Heba, you two come along and we'll get you both some
lunch," Dekker explained.

As the group walked to the house, and others began noticing
their arrival, they began to enquire after Simon of the two
strangers traveling with them. After explaining, they continued
inside, got the travelers fed, then found Heba and her grandfather
a place to sleep. They would use one of the staffers cottages that
once belonged to a couple who worked on the island before the
demon war that had taken their lives just days ago. Simon and
Dekker decided they would give Heba and her grandfather a tour
of the island after they had a chance to unpack and rest a bit.

Nick ate lunch quickly and left the house a bit earlier, deciding to work in the barn with the horses, cleaning stalls, and brushing down some of the animals. Everyone was supposed to tend to the needs of their own animals, but with twelve people gone on a mission, he decided to take it upon himself to help out. Besides, he wasn't one to just sit around. He had just finished mucking out a few stalls and picked up the comb to brush one of the horses when Annabelle and Nadia appeared inside the barn. He glanced in their direction but kept to the task at hand.

"Nicholas!" Annabelle squealed in excitement.

Nick couldn't help but smile. For some reason she had taken a shine to him, and he was beginning to take to her as well. Annabelle ran over to him and threw her arms around his waist. He looked up to see Nadia enter behind her, the two of them locking eyes for a few seconds. Nadia smiled at him and Nick grinned back.

"I didn't know you all were back yet," he stated.

"Only just. Annabelle and I ran into each other and got to talking and decided to make some plans for the rest of the day."

He pulled Annabelle away, then stepped back a bit himself. "Is that right? Well, what are you two up to this afternoon?"

"Nadia and I are going fishing, and we wanted you to come along as well." Annabelle smiled broadly up at him.

"Well, I have a few horses to comb down first. Maybe you two could help me finish them, then we can all go."

"Sure!" Annabelle smiled.

He looked over at Nadia who grinned broadly as well, shaking her head yes.

"All right then, you two grab a comb and pick one of the horses tied outside their stall."

"Okay!" Annabelle happily giggled.

Nick looked at Nadia as Annabelle skipped off to the tack room to grab each of them a comb.

"It looks like the two of you are growing close," he said to her.

"Yes," she said as her features turned more serious. "She has been sleeping with me in my bedroom since the battle. The first night, she had a nightmare and came running to my room. I'm not sure why she chose me, except for the fact that her and Bridget's room is right next to mine."

Nick looked at her. "Maybe she recognizes a kind heart when she sees one."

Nadia grinned at his words. "I think most everyone here has a kind heart. The nature of our calling, you know."

"Maybe, but she must see something special in you."

"Perhaps the same thing she sees in you?" she questioned, as sadness briefly overshadowed her features.

This made Nick very curious. It reminded him that he wasn't the only person with a past. *What was Nadia's story?* He wondered.

Annabelle soon returned, smiling happily, and thrust a comb into Nadia's hands. They all smiled at one another and commenced to tending to the horses as speedily as possible. They finished the task within the hour, then returned to the main house storage, packed the fishing gear and some snacks and beverages, and headed to the end of one of the covered docks to spend the rest of the afternoon.

Nick breathed deeply of the salty air, feeling more relaxed then he had in years. Annabelle was good for him, and spending time in Nadia's company wasn't bad either. She was easy going, easy to talk to, honest, and he had to admit, not bad in the looks department. Although, he was definitely not looking to start any kind of relationship. He could handle being friends with her, for Annabelle's sake.

Whoa, Nick! He admonished himself. *You're getting too close to this girl Annabelle for your own good,* his head rationalized, trying to overrule his heart again, for his own sake. He glanced over at the young girl who sat on the edge of the dock, her bare feet swinging in the wind, pole in hand, and a smile as big as any he'd ever seen. His hardened heart softened just a tad more; no matter what his head warned him against.

At that moment he glanced up at Nadia, her slim profile looked relaxed and content as her shoulder length, ash-brown hair whipped lightly about her face. Nick felt his heart skip a beat before he abruptly turned away, taking a deep steading breath.

Get it together, Nick ole boy, before you mess up their lives like you did Jenny and Cassie's! He cleared his throat, squared his broad shoulders, and put the screws back in the door around his already tattered heart. He would be civil and kind, but he couldn't handle getting involved again. No matter how much he seemed to be drawn to both of the women, young and older, beside him.

Annabelle chattered on and off all afternoon, and Nick did his best to answer her politely but to not engage too much. She started looking at him with questions on her face as to his sudden change in demeanor. Nadia must have noticed too, because she would glance at him sideways each time he gave Annabelle a clipped or nonchalant answer to one of her questions. Apparently Annabelle had had enough. She sat down her pole on the deck, stood up, and walked over to Nick.

"What's wrong, Mr. Nicholas? Did I do something to upset you?" she asked him. Her little face pointed downward as her eyes occasionally glanced up at his face.

"No." Nick sighed, aggravation starting to show in his stance. "I just…I can't do this with you."

"What? Fishing? If you didn't want to come, you could have just said. I would have understood." She pouted a little.

Nick began to feel like a heel, which only added to his frustration. "No, it isn't that."

"What then?" Annabelle turned her face up to his. She reached out to take his hand and he flinched, pulling away from her.

"I can't do this relationship thing with you. Look, you're a sweet kid. But, I just don't have time for all this family type stuff you want to do all the time. I'm not your father, Annabelle."

Annabelle's eyes began to fill with tears. "I'm sorry, Mr. Nicholas. I..I didn't mean to make you angry." She turned and ran from the dock toward the main house in the distance. Sobbing as she went and swiping at her eyes.

Nick suddenly felt like the biggest jerk that ever was.

Nadia came over to stand in front of him. The hurt and anger in her eyes pierced him to his very soul.

"I understand that you may have been hurt in the past. But not likely more so than anyone else. You don't hold the title for biggest heartache, Nicholas." Her anger fueled her words.

He seethed. "You have no idea what I've been through!"

"No. I don't. But *neither* does Annabelle. And she doesn't deserve that sort of treatment! That little girl has lived her entire childhood inside an orphanage, with little to no love to be found. Kindness perhaps, but not love. She's drawn to you for some reason. Out of everyone here on the island, she chose you. Why? I don't know and likely never will."

"I didn't ask for that!"

"No! You didn't! But maybe God knew that you needed her as much as she needed you. Perhaps if you tried trusting in the One who called you, you'd be more willing to let go of the misery in which you so relish to live."

They stood there for a few more seconds looking at each other before Nadia turned to leave. She stopped only briefly to say, "Whatever happened to you, Nick, is no reason to shut your heart up. Especially when that little girl is offering you all of her own."

He watched as she turned her back to him and trotted across the pier in search of Annabelle.

Nick sighed heavily again. What was wrong with him? He knew better than to treat Annabelle that way. And the way that Nadia had looked at him made him feel less of a man. He had lost the respect she had for him in a few short seconds. Suddenly a Bible verse came to his mind. He couldn't recall exactly, but he remembered it mentioning the tongue being sharper than a two-edged sword. Boy was that ever true! And he had just used his to cut that sweet innocent child to pieces. All because he couldn't handle her loving him.

"Good job, you moron!" he chided himself. He turned and started gathering all the fishing equipment and baskets.

Sean and Kristen were walking along the beach when they noticed Annabelle run past them, sobbing.

"Annabelle?" Kristen called to her. She started to go after her when Sean grabbed her arm.

"Wait a minute, Kristen," he said, noticing Nadia not far behind her. The look on her face was one of concern and anger. Sean looked out over the water along the dock where they had just been. He saw his friend, Nick, out on the end picking up equipment.

Sean sighed heavily, his heart aching for his friend who, just recently, had told him about his past. Nick had a lot of healing to do, and Annabelle was apparently making it a bit harder on him.

"Kristen, can I meet you back up at the house in a bit. I want to have a talk with Nick."

"Sure, Sean. I'll see you later."

Kristen turned in the direction of the house, deciding to see if she could find Annabelle or Nadia and see what was going on.

Sean turned onto the dock and ventured to the end where he found Nick, slowly picking up the discarded items.

"Hey, Nick, you want some help?"

Nick stood and looked at the young man who had been like a brother to him for the last six years.

"I screwed up bad, Sean."

"You want to talk about it?"

"Let's just say a made a huge mistake. I really showed my rear-end this time."

Sean just listened as Nick stopped picking up the equipment on the deck and stood to look at him.

"You know my past. Annabelle was getting too close, making me feel things that I haven't felt in years. Not to mention Nadia. I started to feel like I could have something real again, and my stupid head had to jump in and run my mouth. I'm afraid I made a real mess of things with her."

"Who? Annabelle, or Nadia?"

"Both," Nick said, defeated.

"Ah," Sean said as realization began to sink in. Nick was falling for both of them and it scared him to death.

"Nick, you've spent the better part of your adult life feeling responsible for your marriage ending and your daughter's death. Perhaps Annabelle and Nadia are God's way of telling you that you've tortured yourself for long enough."

"Maybe. But I'm not good at relationships. See, I just ruined two more."

"Yeah, because you wanted to. Just go find them and apologize. I'm sure they'll both understand if you explain fully. It's time you stopped carrying that burden around, Nick. Give it to God. He really is trying to give you another chance here."

"I know." Nick sighed.

"Besides, like it or not, Annabelle sees you and Nadia like her parents. She is so ready to have a real family."

"How am I supposed to give that to her right now with the way we live?"

"I don't know, Nick. But God has opened the door for it, so it can't be impossible. It won't always be this way either. Soon, we'll all have regular lives. The whole *saving the world* gig is going to end. Now let's get this stuff picked up, and you can go find both of them." Sean slapped his friend on the shoulder to reassure him, and they picked everything up and went to put it away.

After everything was where it belonged, and with some more urging from Sean, Nick went in search of Annabelle. Hopefully, he would find Nadia as well. He had a lot of explaining to do, and he would rather do it at the same time then repeat himself. He only hoped they would forgive him for being so callous and foolish.

The day was growing late, evening on the island was approaching quickly as Jason searched for Simon and the other Dragoman to inform them of their decision as leaders, to allow Petra to dine with them and to have some free time after dinner. He wanted to tell them before they saw her outside of her room. He stumbled across Simon in the computer room with Ryan, talking about one of the Portgens.

"Simon, can I speak with you a moment?"

"Certainly, Jason. I'll be right with you."

Jason waited in the hallway while Simon finished his conversation with Ryan. It didn't take long before Simon headed his way.

"Now, what's this about?"

"Well, while you and the others were gone, we had to make a decision concerning Petra. She requested some time out of her room. We decided she was of no danger to anyone here and granted her meals and an hour or so after dinner, while under constant surveillance. I hope this is all right with you and the others?"

"Well, it seems that you all could make a decision where we could not. I believe that will be fine with the others. I'll try to let them all know before she's brought downstairs. Besides, it's not like she's killed anyone. At least not that we are aware. Unless of course she was involved with the whole betrayer situation thirteen years back?"

"Unless she willingly admits to that, we'll likely never know the answer to that question," Jason stated. "Oh, by the way, how is it possible that so many strange people are coming to the island? I thought that only Dragoman and Peregrines could travel through time. Are the two you brought today new Peregrines or Dragoman?"

"Well, not exactly. They are the people who are translating the *Book of the Keepers* and Heba is making the capes for The Twelve."

"So, anyone can travel through time with the Portgens?" he asked anxiously.

"I believe so, Jason."

"You know what this means for me, Simon!" Jason said excitedly.

"Yes, I do, my boy. Just don't forget your missions. You have one more piece of armor to find, and Memnah would not be able to go with you."

"Why not?" He asked incredulously.

"She's not a Peregrine or Dragoman. She has no special skills or abilities. It would be extremely dangerous for her."

"Simon, she's already fought with us in two demon wars, and survived. As a matter of fact, if it weren't for Memnah and her people, we might have failed at both of those wars. None of us might be alive today."

"You have a point, my boy. And I do understand how you feel. I will speak to the others at dinner, and if they see no problem with Memnah coming here, then I have no problem either. But don't get too excited yet. We don't know what the others will say."

Jason's huge smile spread from ear to ear, and he was nearly unable to control his excitement. Simon had never seen Jason this happy about anything before. He had always been militaristic in his actions and emotions. Now, he was as giddy as a schoolboy.

"I understand, Simon, thank you," Jason said as he nearly skipped down the hallway and out the front door.

Simon couldn't help but smile and be happy for Jason, even though he feared that all these new people coming to their very private island could become a real problem. How were they going to explain to all these new people what they did and make them understand that they could not take part in most of it?

Simon sighed heavily, tired from the last several days activities, and all the new problems that were arising. Sometimes he wished that Ryan had never invented the Portgens, but then again, the devices had certainly made life simpler for everyone.

Simon went into the archival library where the Dragoman and their guests were hold up, still working on deciphering the *Book of the Keepers*. He explained to the others about Jason and Memnah, and they all agreed that she should be allowed to join him here on the island. Simon would give him the good news at dinner, and he would likely go after her immediately.

"I believe it's time for dinner everyone. And by the way, Petra will be joining us for meals and a brief refrain from her confinement after dinner. The leaders made that decision while we were gone. I for one, will honor their decision."

"I agree with that," Prisca stated. "We've confined her long enough. She'll never be able to prove herself if not given the chance."

"True," Vashti chimed. "The meal thing is a good start to trusting her again."

Everyone gathered outside on the patio for dinner. The Peregrines and Dragoman, sitting together at the massive wood and iron table where they would occasionally hold dinner meetings. They had much to discuss this evening with the group, so it made it much easier to do so all at once.

Sean and Kristen again took the task of tending to Petra this evening. It was Nick and Nadia's turn to watch her, but with the afternoon's events, they took over for them. Nick had yet to find Nadia or Annabelle to talk with them, and Sean figured it would be terribly awkward for them both. They put Petra at the table with Clancy and Shannon, surrounded by most of the other island staffers. Clancy assured Sean they would watch her. Marnor took a seat across from her to maybe get to talk with her.

Sean and Kristen found a place at the table beside Nick. As they sat waiting for the others to have a seat, Nadia and Annabelle arrived, sitting together at the other end of the table. Nadia looked in Nick's direction, and then quickly turned away. Nick fidgeted in his seat, feeling uncomfortable. He would get up to go sit beside them, but it would be best to wait until after dinner for their discussion. He certainly didn't want to cause a scene during dinner and the meeting.

Everyone was seated and served, and friendly chatter floated around the table. Nick noticed how quiet Annabelle was being tonight. His heartstrings grew ever tighter knowing he was the cause of her unhappiness. As dinner was beginning to finish up, Simon stood at the head of the table, his spoon and glass in hand. He clanged the side of the glass with the spoon, sending a ringing into the air, catching the attention of everyone. The chattering soon grew quiet as they all waited on what Simon had to say.

"Good evening everyone. Most of you have already met our two guests this afternoon. Heba and her grandfather, Renquin. They are of course from Akrotiri. Most of you have wondered how Marnor and these two have come to be here on the island. Well, it seems that since the invention of the Portgen, anyone who stumbles across the devices can time-travel. So, you all need to make absolutely certain that your fingerprint scanners are installed on your Portgens and that they work as they should. I don't need to explain the dangers of someone coming across an open Portgen. Now because of this we have some good news. Jason has asked permission to retrieve Memnah and we have agreed that she should be allowed to come here." Simon smiled at Jason when he spoke the last sentence.

The entire table erupted with cheers for Jason. They all knew how hard the long-distance relationship was for both of them.

"I assume you'll be off to retrieve her this very night?" Simon asked him.

"You would be correct, Sir." Jason's smile was never ending.

"Now, onto the next business at hand. Petra," Simon addressed the woman, "I'm glad to see you've gotten a reprieve from your confinement." He turned to the rest of the table. "She will now be having meals with the rest of us. Our next bit of news is that our next mission will be approaching soon. Odessa did have a dream about the last piece of armor, only the details were a bit fuzzy. As soon as we are given clarity on that we will schedule a time to leave. We have discovered that the Swords of the Spirit will have to be refashioned. Meaning the forge in the barn will have to be restructured and a form made for the swords. Dekker is a master blacksmith and will be remaking the swords per the instructions that were found in the *Book of the Keepers* during translation."

Zeke interrupted with a question. "Simon, why aren't the instructions for that found in the *Book of Armor*?"

"We believe the *Book of the Keepers* was written at a later date than the *Book of Armor* and that the swords were dismantled after that book was written. So, the *Book of the Keepers* tells the story why and what happened to the swords. The message that was found with the jewels and the key for that book states that the jewels are in fact pieces of the swords. Each jewel will be placed inside the hilt of the sword that represents that particular tribe. We are also concerned about the beasts The Twelve will face at the end. They are dragons of sorts. We don't know what these beasts will be capable of, but we are going with folklore and legend and taking all things into consideration."

"What does that mean exactly, Simon," Seth asked.

"Oz told us of minerals native to the mines of Zanchier called Rhenium and Ruthenium. These minerals are prized for their properties in Zanchier where some of the native creatures breathe fire. Such as the Kabihanxu, Han, and other firebirds that you all had the privilege of seeing in battle a few days ago. We have now discovered Hiram's secret way into and out of Zanchier by way of Storm Valley alone. We Dragoman will launch an exploration party to Zanchier to locate and purchase enough of these minerals to coat the Armor of God so that you won't all cook within your metal, protective, suits."

"Isn't that place really dangerous," Nadia asked.

"Yes. Which is why we will take the Keepers with us. They can control the animals to help us."

Marnor grew nervous at the mention of Zanchier. He'd spent his whole life trying to get out of that place. Now he feared they may make him return.

"Any more questions before we wrap this meeting up?"

"Just this," Rourke yelled, "I say we celebrate tonight with a party!"

Everyone cheered their acceptance of the impromptu party, clapping and whistling.

"So be it then!" Simon smiled.

"Well Mrs.," Clancy leaned over to Shannon, "I think that's our cue to whip up some party desserts and beverages."

Shannon giggled at her husband's wriggling eyebrows and statement. "All right then, let's get to it."

Clancy looked at Rourke. "See to it that Petra is put back in her room."

Petra laid a hand on Shannon's arm. "Wait, please. Can't I help in the kitchen? I promise not to try anything."

Clancy looked at the others there. "Who's willing to come sit in the kitchen while we bake and keep a trained eye on Petra?"

Several of the housekeepers agreed to the task.

"All right. I'll clear it with the Dragoman." Clancy left and walked over to speak to them.

Simon returned with Clancy to chat with Petra.

"Petra, we're going to allow this. But please do *not* disappoint us, or we will have to take stronger measures next time," he warned her.

"I promise, Simon. You won't find fault with me again."

Everyone split, going in different directions, planning, and gathering things for the party.

Marnor followed them into the kitchen to help. This would give him the perfect opportunity to talk with Petra.

The groundskeepers and other housekeepers set about moving furniture out of the way for a dance floor and setting up a table for the cakes and beverages to be placed.

Jason took off for Timna as quickly as he could, to deliver the news to Memnah and bring her back tonight to see the island and partake in the night of revelry.

Most of the Peregrines and Dragoman pitched in wherever they were needed, and all went to find a nice outfit to dress up for the evening.

Nick managed to catch up to Nadia and Annabelle before they disappeared for the night.

"Annabelle, may I speak to you and Nadia privately?"

Annabelle held onto Nadia's hand, partially hidden behind her tall frame. She looked up at Nadia, who gave her a nod of acceptance.

"Yes, Mr. Nicholas," Annabelle replied formerly.

Nick's heart raced and ached at the same time. He knew he hurt her, and it showed in her reply. They were back to Mr. Nicholas.

"Can the three of us go somewhere quieter to talk? There's too much activity and excitement around here."

Annabelle shook her head yes.

Nadia asked, "Where would you like to go?"

"How about we walk down to the water. I know it's a way's off, but it shouldn't take us long. We can even take one of the ATVs. I'll even have you both back in time for the party."

"All right, that would make a quicker trip of it."

"I'll be right back to pick you both up. I'll just get a key from Rourke." Nick left to find the man. He got the key, went to the shed and got the cart, then went to get Nadia and Annabelle who had walked out to the edge of the yard to meet him. They all loaded into the cart and headed to the beach to sit in the loungers and talk.

Nick's nerves made his stomach do flip-flops and his palms sweat profusely. He was about to take a complete one-hundred-and-eighty degree turn from where he was headed just a few days ago. But Sean was right. It was time he let go of the past and accept his future for what it was offering him.

Be anxious for nothing, but in everything
by prayer and supplication, with thanksgiving,
let your requests be made known to God;

Philippians 4:6

Chapter 7

Nick pulled the ATV to a stop just beside the beach loungers. He sat on one while Annabelle and Nadia sat on another directly beside him. Nick took a deep breath, unsure where to even start.

"First, let me say how sorry I am for upsetting you both earlier today. Especially you, Annabelle. There is no excuse for the way I behaved. There is a reason however, and I would like to explain to both of you why I acted the way I did."

Nick took another deep breath and exhaled.

"A very long time ago, I had a family; my wife Jenny, and our daughter Cassie. We were a very happy family until my daughter became very ill. She had a degenerative disease that made her body fight against itself. The doctors didn't know what it was, only that it was caused by the inability of my genes and Jenny's genes to come together in Cassie. The main problem with her disease was a deformity in my genes. Cassie didn't live very long after her disease started. She was only eight years old when she died. The whole ordeal drove me and Jenny apart. Mainly because I was afraid to have any more children. I didn't want to make them sick too and us go through it all again. Jenny left me, and we divorced. That was when I was twenty-nine. You see, Annabelle, I've spent so many years hardening my heart not to feel emotions for anyone. Until you came along. You have wormed your way into my heart, and it scared me to death."

Annabelle stood up and threw her arms around Nick's neck and just stood there, hugging him. Nick was shocked at first, then wrapped his arms around her small frame.

"It's all right Nicholas. I understand. And I'm so very sorry that you lost your daughter and your wife." She stepped back to look him in the eye. "I'll be your family. If you want me to?"

As tears filled his eyes, Nick chuckled at her innocent answer and her beautiful heart. He stroked her hair and looked at her. "You know, when I first saw you in Akrotiri, I couldn't stop staring at you. You remind me so much of Cassie. I looked at you and saw what she could have been if she had been a healthy child. I guess that sort of made me stay away some too. You reminded me too much of what I had lost."

"I'm sorry. I didn't mean too."

"No...no...Annabelle. That isn't your fault. It's also what drew me to you. That and your sweet spirit and heart. I'm so sorry for upsetting you and saying those mean things today. Will you forgive me?"

"Of course I will, silly. Because that is what family does." She smiled at him, wrapping her arms around his neck once again.

Nadia sat and watched the exchange, tears streaming down her cheeks. She had always known that Nick held a painful secret, she just didn't know how painful, or how close his story was to her own in some ways. Nick looked over at her as he hugged Annabelle, the tenderness in his eyes making her heart skip a beat. She was really beginning to have feelings for this man. She was already drawn to him for some reason. Ever since his partner Dinah had died in the demon war in Timna two months back, she had felt a strange pull toward him. She could only attribute it to God's design. Not to mention that he was very attractive both physically and mentally. He had a good heart, something she had trouble finding in the men she had encountered in her past.

They sat there for the next few minutes just chatting before Nick said, "Hey, do you two want to go to a party?"

"Yes!" Annabelle said excitedly. "I've never been to a *real* party before."

Nick and Nadia exchanged glances at her honest, sad answer. He said, "Well then, let's go. You need to get ready in a nice party dress."

Annabelle giggled with excitement.

Nick looked at Nadia. "So do you." He smiled at the questioning look on her face. "I overheard everyone talking about dressing to the nines. You will save me a dance, won't you?"

Nadia smiled at him. "Of course. You sir may fill my dance card."

They loaded up in the ATV and sped away toward the main house, ready to enjoy their evening of relaxation and fun. They put the ATV away, and Nick went to find Rourke to return the key while the girls went into the house to dress for the evening.

Annabelle looked at Nadia. "I don't think I have a party dress, Nadia."

"Don't worry Annabelle, with all the women around here, and the wardrobe room we have for missions, I'm sure we can find something that will work. It will be like playing dress up." She smiled at the young girl feeling a little giddy herself.

They ran into Bridget, Caroline, Gabriele, and Zaccai in the wardrobe room just off the second-floor library. All of them were sorting through clothing they might like to wear for the party, chattering and giggling as they searched.

It wasn't long before the men had the same idea. Their lifestyle didn't lend much in the way of needing nice clothing. The room began getting more and more crowded with people filing in to find something to wear. Soon nearly the entire household was in the room, as people came and went with their selections.

Jason nearly ran the entire way to Memnah. He was so excited he could hardly stand it. He couldn't wait to see her face when he told her she could go with him.

He ran to her tent first to search for her but did not find her there. He walked the village searching for where she might be when he heard music and singing. He followed in the direction from where the sound seemed to be coming. In the village center, around a large fire, some men sat on the outer edge of a large circle, while other men and women who were all dressed up, danced rhythmically to the sound of the instruments.

Jason had gotten to witness some of Memnah's culture, but nothing like this. Their time together had mostly just been the two of them off alone somewhere.

Jason watched from his place at the edge of the tents, wondering what the celebration was all about. He watched the dancers until one in particular caught his eye. Memnah was dressed in beautiful, sheer, and silken robes, of bright colors like the setting sun. Her face was veiled just below the eyes and she moved as gracefully as a swan gliding across the water. She turned in his direction and suddenly realized he was standing there. She stopped dancing and ran toward him, leaping into his arms.

"Jason, what are you doing here?" She smiled broadly.

"Watching you dance. What's all this about?"

"It is the wedding ceremony I told you about this morning, and this is the party to honor their future together. Weddings are always a large celebration. Why don't you come and join me in the dance? I'll show you how it is done."

"Well, we *could* do that. *Or* you could come with me to Reader's Island?"

Memnah stopped and looked at him. "You are serious?"

"Very. Apparently it is completely safe for anyone to travel with the Portgens. I only wish I had known sooner."

She squealed and bounced up and down in his arms. "This means I can go with you wherever you travel?"

"Yes, I think so. At least we can be together now, Memnah. No more separation."

They kissed each other in excitement and ran to tell Memnah's tribe leaders where she was going.

Jason and Memnah left the wedding party to go to her tent briefly.

"I just need to change," she said entering her tent.

"No, you look perfect. We are having a celebration on the island tonight and everyone is dressing up."

"This isn't too much?" she asked, looking down at the extravagant materials that encompassed her.

"I don't think I have ever seen anyone look more beautiful." He pulled her into his arms and kissed her.

After they separated, she smiled at him. "Sweet talker."

He grinned at her teasing. "Now, are you ready to go?"

"Absolutely. I have been waiting for this day for a long time."

They opened a portal in her tent and walked through to the island just outside the mansion. Memnah was flabbergasted at the beauty of her surroundings, and the size of the house. They saw several people beginning to gather on the front patio area. The hanging strings of lights twinkled in the twilight, waving gently in the cool ocean breeze. The sound of music playing and laughter, mingled in the air, carried on the wind.

Jason watched Memnah's face as the expressions of awe and joy graced her features, the wind gently blowing her veil and robes as they walked toward the house.

"Jason, I have no words. This place is unbelievable."

"Yeah, we like it," he said nonchalantly.

Memnah turned and gave him a look of teasing reprimand, knowing he was being facetious.

They arrived on the patio and Jason left her with Odessa while he went to change into something more formal. He did have a suit he had purchased long ago for a certain mission he had gone on to a more modern city. He just hoped he could still wear it.

He passed a very tidy, genteel fellow by the name of Alec, descending the staircase in a white, early 1900's-period suit, which fit him like a glove. His silk puff-tie, the color of his suit to offset his royal blue, silk shirt.

Jason whistled at him and winked as he passed by, taking two steps at a time.

"Thank you, dear!" Alec yelled to his long-time friend. He stepped through the doors, scanning the already large crowd for Dee. He spotted her standing next to Memnah. She wore a full dress that tied behind her neck, had no shoulders or sleeves, was v necked, tied at the waist with a thin, braided rope, and flowed outward with a high front just below the knee, and long to the floor in the back. The color and style was in an ombre' pattern, from soft blue at the top, to darker shades near the bottom. He couldn't take his eyes off of her. He took her hands holding them out from her body and spun her around, her full skirt twirling out around her.

"You look absolutely beautiful, Dee. The prettiest girl at the party!"

"Thank you, kind sir," she blinked at him flirtatiously.

A dapperly dressed Ezekiel, in a black tuxedo, welcomed a stunning Zaccai, dressed in a shimmering, slightly fitted floor length gown, befitting an African tribal princess.

"My goodness, Woman, you look ravishing," Zeke said, looking her over from head to toe.

"You look pretty amazing yourself." Zaccai smiled at him as she accepted his hand and they walked to the dance floor.

Everyone welcomed Memnah, several talking excitedly about getting the chance to show her around the island later. Simon and Safra led her over to the dessert table, as tray after tray of delectable treats began to line the tables.

Nick stood by the table in his suit and tie that he had found in the wardrobe room. It fit well enough, but it was just a tad uncomfortable, so he removed the tie, unbuttoned the top button of his shirt, and slid the tie in his jacket pocket. He turned to look at the doors of the house, waiting for Annabelle and Nadia to make an appearance. Just then Annabelle skipped through the door wearing a very colorful, Asian influenced smock and leggings with her hair tied up with strings and what appeared to be chopsticks. It looked similar to the one Gabriele wore back in Tintagel, England on a mission.

Just behind her was Nadia. Nick nearly choked on the drink he was sipping when she came through the doors. *Good Lord*, he thought. He knew she was attractive, but she cleaned up extremely well. She wore a shimmering gold top that was sleeveless and tucked into a sage green skirt that reached nearly to her ankles and was split to the knee on the left side, the split edged in a slight flowing ruffle. Her high-heels were strappy and open-toed, she wore long dangling gold earrings, and a slinky bracelet, and her hair was up in a tight bun with loose tendrils lying about her face.

Nick cleared his throat and sat his drink on the nearby table before his nerves made him spill more of it. Sean had appeared next to him out of nowhere.

Sean whistled. "Dude, you are *one* lucky man. She looks like a model."

"Cut it out, Sean. I'm nervous enough already," Nick chided him, walking over to meet the girls, and listening to Sean's sniggering as he went.

Sean took a drink of the wine in his glass as he scanned the room for Kristen. He nearly choked as well when Kristen appeared in a long, soft, flowing gown that fit her like a glove just passed the hips, and then loosened and fell to the floor behind her with a long slit to the knee right up the middle. The top was fitted, yet it had a thin sheer material that shifted softly as she moved. The sleeves were small and wispy, like the top, and sat just off the shoulder, billowing around her biceps. Her heels were black and open toed. Her long brown hair styled like that of a 1940s lady, softly laying on her shoulders and flowing smoothly down her back.

Nick watched her pass by, looked back at Sean who stood there with his mouth hanging open, and gave him two thumbs up. Now sniggering himself at the dumbfounded look on Sean's face.

"Sean, are you all right?" Kristen asked the still dumbstruck man.

He shook it off, cleared his throat and straightened his tie. Feeling rather underdressed next to her.

"You look…beautiful, Kristen." He cleared his throat once again and said, "Shall we dance." He led her to the dance floor, mesmerized by her grace and beauty.

Everyone looked incredible in their dresses and suits, most everyone dressed according to the period from which they came.

Whatever the height of fashion was for them at that time. It almost looked like a costume party with all the different types of attire present.

Petra was allowed to participate for the first hour, then she would be sent to her room for the rest of the night.

Even Marnor had been taken under wing by the kitchen staff and dolled up for the night in a nice shirt and a pair of dress slacks. He cleaned up surprisingly well, even garnering some appreciative second glances in his direction by many. Petra included.

Bridget ran up to her brother. "Marnor, you look rather dashing."

"You look very nice as well, Bridget" he said a little uncomfortable.

"Come dance with me." She pulled him out to the makeshift dance floor.

"I..I don't know how," he said nervously.

"I shall teach you then." She smiled at him and showed him where to place his hands and commenced to show him how to do a simple box step.

Jason reappeared wearing a classic black, slim-fit, suit and bow tie. Memnah looked at him with appreciation.

"My goodness but *you do* clean up very well, Mr. Marshal."

"Thank you, Ma'am." He smiled, pulling her into his arms and spinning her around the dance floor.

Caroline and Seth appeared wearing 1920's garb. Caroline in a flapper style dress and heels, and Seth in a suit with fedora hat, and wingtip shoes to match.

Sofia and Rourke showed up looking like they were going to a red-carpet event in Hollywood. She wore a fitted, red knee-length dress with capped sleeves, and classic black heels. Her long blond hair pulled back in a high ponytail and curled down her back. He wore a pale gray, fitted suit with a western bolo tie, and cowboy hat. Complimented by his gray and black, snake-skinned cowboy boots.

Rourke pulled her onto the dance floor.

She smiled at him and said, "This was a very good idea you had, Rourke. Everyone really seems to be enjoying themselves."

"I had to create *some* excuse to get you into my arms." He smiled mischievously at her.

Sofia threw back her head and laughed at him, truly enjoying the *kind attentions* of a man as a nice change.

Malachai and Vashti appeared. He wore the traditional robes of his Hebrew upbringing, and she in a beautiful, sequenced dress the color of emeralds.

A clean-shaven Oz and Prisca appeared looking quite royal. Prisca being of noblesse uterine blood herself, truly was a royal, dressed in a coral and white full-length dress, and slightly puffed sleeves just off the shoulder that tapered thinly to her wrists. The skirt was full but not to the point of puffing out around her. Oz was dressed in a mid-century suit with a long duster coat and a silk, floppy, bowtie finishing his look.

Simon watched the revelry, laughter, and jovial countenances of everyone; smiling and chuckling every so often at something silly someone did. He decided it was time for a photo before everyone managed to disappear later.

He stood on top of one of the sturdier chairs on the patio and said, "Listen everyone. I hate to interrupt, but I'd like for everyone to gather in the center here for a photograph. This evening calls for a picture to remember."

They all excitedly hustled to find a spot in the group, making sure everyone was visible for the picture. Even Marnor and Petra were included, standing next to each other accidentally. The photo took about five minutes to get everyone situated and to find a spot far enough away to get everyone into the photo. The camera was placed on a stand, put on a timer, and Simon ran into the photo and slid in beside Safra in the front. As soon as the camera flashed, everyone broke apart to continue with the revelry.

Simon stood back, grinning happily at the scene before him.

Safra watched her friend's smile and interrupted his thoughts with a request.

"Simon, come dance with an old friend." She pulled him onto the dance floor, and the two of them fell into perfect step with one another. Simon, of course, was an excellent dancer from way back.

Wade stood back and watched Gabriele and Timothy dancing together. He was hoping to get a chance to dance with her tonight. He really liked Gabriele, but with Timothy around he'd never get a chance with her.

Dominic noticed his friend's sour mood.

"Hey Wade, what's up, man? You look miserable, tonight is supposed to be fun." Dominic playfully jabbed him in the ribs.

"Yeah, I know," he grumbled.

Dominic followed the direction of his gaze.

"Uh-huh. So, you like Gabby and your jealous of Tim?"

"Shh…you don't have to tell everyone!" Wade whispered.

"Wade, Gabby is way out of your league man."

"We're the same age," Wade defended.

"Age has nothing to do with it. She is way too mature for you. Look, quit being a spoil-sport and come have some fun. It may be the last time we get a night like this." Dominic grabbed Wade by his jacket and pulled him over to the dance floor and started dancing around him like a fool.

Wade got so tickled at his friend's antics he couldn't help but loosen up. He was still agitated by the way Tim seemed to hover over Gabriele, but he supposed he should try to enjoy himself tonight.

As Jason danced with Memnah in his arms, he couldn't believe his prayers had finally been answered. Only, how would he let her go back to Timna tonight? She could stay here tonight, bunking in with some of the other women in the staff's quarters. But what about tomorrow, and the day after that? Jason decided he didn't want her to go back. Tomorrow, he would use the barrier to go to a modern city and purchase a ring. He would ask her to marry him. Then, they wouldn't have to worry about her reputation with her people. They would be man and wife. And the sooner, the better. He would ask her to stay tonight, after the festivities were over. But what if they had to leave tomorrow on a mission? They never knew when or where they would go, or for how long they would have to leave. He decided then that he would ask her tonight and worry about a ring later.

The hour was growing late, nearing midnight when they decided they should call it a night. Everyone agreed to help clean up in the morning, yelling their promises to the staff to leave everything until then as they all made their way to their rooms.

Jason and Memnah were two of the stragglers, still slowly swaying to the soft music beneath the pale moonlight.

Jason spoke, "I don't want to let you go. Tonight has been a dream come true that I don't want to end."

"I know. I feel the same way, Jason. But I do need to return to gather my things."

"What will your people say with you staying here with me?"

"Does it matter? I love my people, Jason. But I love you more. Your opinion is the only one that matters to me."

Jason stopped moving and looked into her green eyes.

"Memnah, marry me."

"Are you serious?" came her shocked reply.

He let go of her, placing his hands on his hips. "Of course I'm serious. Why else would I have asked?" Jason's brows knit together in confusion.

"Well, I don't know?" Memnah said, aggravated and placing her hands defiantly on her hips.

"Is that your answer?" Jason asked agitatedly.

"Of course it's not my answer," she replied, aggravated as well.

"So, is it a yes then?" Jason asked, his voice escalating in pitch.

"Of course it's a yes!"

"Then why couldn't you have just said that to begin with?"

They stood there looking at each other incredulously, and then suddenly burst out laughing, bent over with it. They threw their arms around each other and kissed happily between fits of laughter.

Those who were still outside with them first thought they were fighting, then they heard his question and her reply, and then saw them both laughing. They all burst into cheers and congratulations.

Memnah looked at Jason. "When?" she asked him. Anxious to be Mrs. Jason Marshal.

"As soon as possible. Tonight if you want."

"I would. But my people will be angry that we dismissed tradition. They will want to have a proper wedding."

"How long will that take?"

"Tomorrow." She shrugged and smiled brightly.

"Tomorrow it is then." They kissed each other again, and Jason decided it was time to let her rest. He walked her to the staff cabins at the rear of the house, kissed her goodnight again, then went to his room, feeling over the moon. He didn't know if he would be able to sleep tonight from all the excitement. In the morning, he would discuss the wedding with the Dragoman and ask them to give them this one day for the wedding. Then he would take Memnah to her village to prepare. They would be married before sundown, most likely in Memnah's village, amongst her people.

Jason must have finally dozed off last night, because by the time he awoke the sun was already shining brightly in the sky. He jumped out of bed, got dressed, and ran downstairs to locate Memnah. He wanted to make sure it hadn't all been a dream. Most everyone was up, and the clean up from last night's party had already been taken care of.

He saw Seth from the other end of the house walking toward him with a smile.

"Congratulations, Brother." Seth pumped his hand and slapped him on the shoulder.

"How did you find out already?" Jason asked quizzically.

"Everybody knows already. Alec woke up heralding it from the staircase." Seth laughed.

"Well, okay then. Have you seen Memnah yet?"

"Yeah. Everyone has her hold up in the kitchen talking wedding plans."

Jason smiled, feeling sorry for Memnah. Hoping she wasn't mad that he had overslept.

When he walked into the kitchen, the whole place erupted with applause and congratulations. Memnah looked over-whelmed already with all the attention. Happy, but none the less overwhelmed. Jason grabbed her away from everyone, trying to talk over all the questions being thrown their way.

"We'll be back later!" he yelled pushing her out the kitchen doorway and toward the house entryway and outside. "I need to get you home so we can get this thing started."

"Not home. To my village. This is my home now, with you." She wrapped her arms around his waist and kissed him.

"Right. And the sooner we get this thing started, the better." They left for her village to discuss the ceremony with her village elders. Once they met with them and the older women, the plans had been set for the ceremony to take place in Timna Valley in her village. Her people would make all the prepara-tions. Memnah would stay in the village until the ceremony, which was to take place at six pm., just before dusk. The after party would take place in the village as well, and everyone was invited.

Jason left Memnah there to go back to the island to inform everyone there of the ceremonial plans. He had asked Memnah what he should wear. Since he wasn't one of the men from her tribe, he needn't worry with their traditional robes. They decided that he would wear a silk white shirt, white pants, and a nice pair of shoes. She would of course wear the village's traditional gown and headdress.

As he sat in the living room discussing the plans with the rest of the island, he suddenly realized he had forgotten something.

"Oh no! What do I do about the rings? I don't think I'll have time to go buy any," Jason said, running his hands across his face in disbelief.

Simon answered with, "I think I have the perfect solution. I'll be right back." He left for his room, returning a few minutes later with a velvet box, handing it to Jason. "Will these do?"

Jason took the box and opened it. His eyebrows shot upward as he looked up at Simon, stunned. "Who's are these?"

"They were the rings I was going to use to propose to someone many years ago before God chose another path for me."

"The woman you told me about, right? Lilly." Jason remembered a previous conversation from a night not too long ago.

"Yes." A bit of sadness was heard in Simon's voice.

"I can't take these, Simon," Jason argued.

"Certainly you can, my boy. I will never use them. And I can't think of anyone else I would rather have them, then you and Memnah. I hope and pray they bring you good fortune."

"Thank you, Simon." Jason hugged the man who had been his mentor and friend for the last nine years.

"You're very welcome." Simon grinned at him over his glasses, wiping at a stray tear that escaped the corner of his eye. "I am *very happy* for you and Memnah, Jason."

Jason hugged him again and shook his hand. "Now, all I have to do is find something to wear."

All the women standing around started chattering. Caroline and Odessa each grabbed an arm and pulled him upstairs followed by the other women.

Seth and Alec looked at one another.

Seth said, "We better get up there and help the man out."

"I agree, my friend. There may be nothing left of him to marry off to Memnah by the time they have finish with him."

Zeke overheard the conversation, chuckling with knowing, as the three men climbed the stairs after the chattering women and the groom to be.

Go forth O daughters of Zion, and see King Solomon
with the crown with which his mother crowned him on the
day of his wedding, the day of the gladness of his heart.

Song of Solomon 3:11

Chapter 8

Jason stood in the wardrobe room as the women went on the hunt for appropriate *groom* material. He protested and argued against the outfits, shirts, and suits they held up to show him. All of them, in a frenzy to make Jason into a handsome groom. Finally, Caroline, listening to Jason's instructions from Memnah, found just the thing. She pulled a white, medieval, Viking-style shirt, in a loose-fitting, pull-over, linen material with a V-neck that was laced together with a long, small-tasseled string which hung loosely. The grommet and V-neck opening was bordered by a thin, navy-blue embroidery, ending at the neck opening. It had long sleeves, which were loose, straight, and thin, with an embroidered navy-blue cuff to match the neck opening.

Jason grinned at the shirt, finally grateful for a ruffle free option.

"That will work just fine, Caroline. Thank you." He smiled at his sister-in-law.

"Your welcome." She smiled back, then whispered. "I know better than to try to dress a modern man in ruffles." She winked and went about searching for a pair of white linen pants or slacks to match.

Seth, Alec, and Zeke stood by watching the chaos, laughing occasionally at the tormented look on Jason's face at some of the women's suggestions. They braved stepping in a few times to nix an idea or two themselves.

After about thirty minutes of dress-up torture, Jason finally had an appropriate outfit to wear. Caroline took the outfit to

Shannon to see about having it cleaned and pressed for the ceremony.

Jason went outside with Seth and Alec to spar and work off some of the pent-up anxiety over having to wait for another seven hours to see Memnah. The men were soon joined by most everyone else, and spent the afternoon practicing their skills and powers, and laughing at one another's jokes and the playful wedding gibes made at Jason's expense.

At two p.m. the party made their way to the kitchen for a late lunch, then everyone decided to start getting cleaned up for the big evening ahead. Some of the women walked up to their rooms to do just that.

Odessa said, "I can't believe we get to dress up again tonight and dance the evening away once more."

"Yes," Zaccai replied. "I could get used to more downtime like this." All the women smiled at each other.

"Last night was a lot of fun, seeing what everyone chose to wear. Some of the outfits were spectacular. We just need to be mindful with our choices today. Let's not try to outdo the bride," Caroline chuckled.

"True, but with her culture, I doubt that's even possible. Especially with what she was wearing last night. If that was traditional for being part of the wedding party, then I can't wait to see what a bride looks like," Odessa stated, recalling their conversation before Jason returned to whisk Memnah away onto the dance floor. They all agreed, remembering the beautiful fabrics and baubles Memnah had been draped in.

They soon separated at the second floor as people waited and took turns with the ten bathrooms shared by the second-floor bedrooms. Some people even went out to the staff cottages to use the showers there since the four downstairs bathrooms were also occupied.

The entire island was preparing for the wedding. That being thirty-nine people with the addition of Dekker, Annabelle, Heba and her grandfather, taking the place of the six that perished in the war, and the betrayal and disappearance of Uriah Mose.

Petra, however, was not allowed to attend. Everyone wanted to enjoy the wedding and not be concerned with the possibility of her disappearing.

Upon hearing this particular news, Marnor decided to stay behind, not really part of the group anyway. Besides, it would give him the opportunity to speak more with Petra.

Safra decided she would also stay behind, just to keep an eye on Marnor, and to make certain that Uriah didn't try to venture back while they were all gone. With that looming threat, Ryan had designed yet another piece of technology that would track any use of the barrier, setting off an alarm and leaving a tracking beacon behind and attached to the offender. It would also register anyone coming through a portal in the old lighthouse's Tesla coil system.

Ryan never went anywhere voluntarily and would stay behind as well. Monitoring all his computer systems constantly.

The hour was growing nigh, and Jason turned to Seth and asked, "Seth, would you do me the honor of being my best man? That is, if that's how they do things in her village?"

Seth smiled broadly. "Of course. It would be an honor on my part." They smiled and shook hands, as Jason handed him the rings, and nervously adjusted his shirt, nearly hopping in place.

Caroline, who was keeping an eye on the time, announced, "It's time to leave everyone!" They walked out onto the lawn, opened the portal to the edge of Memnah's village and the large party of time-travelers walked through to the other side.

Memnah was watching for the tell-tale sign of the light from the portal and instructed some of her people to go and fetch the groom and his party and show them where to go.

Many remembered the village from the demon war days earlier. But the transformation for the celebration of the wedding was unbelievable. When they had come to prepare the dead for burial, the village was drab and colorless and blended in with the desert around it. Except, of course, for the sparsely placed trees and plants around it.

Tonight, it looked more like a fantastical fairytale land. Lanterns were lit at every tent, and a large colorful piece of cloth was draped across the top of each. The people were dressed in colorful robes of linen, silk, or sheer cloth, all singing and humming in their native language.

They were led to an area where a beautiful arch had been set that was draped with colorful fine silks and sheers in shades of blue and white. Paper lanterns lined the sides of a thick, fabric-lined pathway leading to the arch. People began filing in to stand on either side of the lanterns as the sun began it's slow descent on the distant mountain top at the edge of the valley.

Jason and Seth were led to stand in front of the archway where the village Rabbi stood, Bible in hand. The man grinned and nodded at Jason, who nervously grinned back.

A translator stood beside Jason to tell him what the Rabbi said so he would understand.

Jason was grateful for that, knowing it was probably attributed to Memnah thinking ahead. He was suddenly shaken from his thoughts when he heard the rhythmic singing of the tribal people, as they chanted and rolled their tongues in sync with drums and tambourines. An occasional blast from a horn could be heard as well. He watched in anticipation as a group of women appeared at the end of the flickering, lantern-lit, walkway. Jason felt like he could crawl out of his own skin, the thrill of it overwhelming his body and spirit. The women split apart, and Memnah walked forward from behind.

Jason's breath caught in his throat, Memnah was a vision in whites and soft blues. Her gown was white silk and sleeveless, with a soft sheer blue fabric thrown over one shoulder and a teal color over the other. Her head piece was thick white over her head, and a sheer blue which lay across her nose and mouth. Small gold coins shimmered in the flickering light from around her headdress and the edges of the teal wrap over her left shoulder. Her visible green eyes shimmered in the flickering fire-light of the lanterns, relaying the emotion she felt at the moment.

Jason swallowed hard at the knot in his throat. She was stunning, and soon to be all his. She stopped in front of him taking his hands in hers. She smiled at him and they turned and faced the Rabbi.

The desert creatures called out as night began to fall. A slight chill overtook the desert night as a light breeze began to blow the gauzy material of Memnah's robes, adding an air of mystic to her.

The ceremony only lasted about ten minutes as they said their vows, then turned to face one another. The setting sun shone its last brilliant blast of light behind them as the two of them kissed, sealing their vows.

The village erupted in shouts of joy, laughter, and singing, as Jason and Memnah broke apart, smiling from ear to ear. They began their walk, arm in arm down the makeshift aisle as the villagers threw flower petals over them.

The celebration that would ensue was one of high energy, dancing, and merriment which would last the majority of the night and well into the morning hours.

Alec watched with interest as Odessa's expressions changed to all sorts of emotions as the ceremony played out before them. She went from happy crying, to stoic and rigid, then irritable, and then back to crying, but not the happy-looking sort.

He leaned over and whispered, "Dee, what in the world is going on with you right now?"

"Nothing." She shook her head.

"You can tell me anything. You know this. Just because we are in a relationship now doesn't change our communication. If anything, it should make it better."

As Jason and Memnah walked back down the aisle passing them by, they stepped from where they had been standing, and turned to follow them like everyone else. The large fire built in the village center roared, as music began to play and people instantly broke into singing and dancing.

Alec took Odessa by the hand and pulled her aside into a darker spot between two tents.

"Dee," he said, looking down at her trying to make her meet his eyes. She hesitantly looked up at him as he patiently waited for her to start talking.

She sighed audibly, letting loose a guttural moan of anguish, throwing her hands up over her face. "I'm sorry Alec. I just had so many different emotions watching the ceremony."

"I noticed. Would you care to elaborate?"

"Fine," she stated crisply. "When Jason and Memnah started their vows, I was so happy for them. I'm just amazed at how strong their love is. That started me thinking about how much time I've wasted. I mean, they just met a few months ago and already know they want to spend their lives together. It has taken me *forever* to let my feelings out. That thought made me really think about my life. Then, I got mad because I really feel like I have good reason to be cautious. But then…ugh…I got really angry because I felt like I was being stupid and overreacting over this wedding and how much I was letting it get to me, and that made me cranky. Then, I could see you watching me out of the corner of my eye, wondering what in the world I was thinking. I realized how wonderful and patient that you are and have always been with me. Why did it take me *so long* and you getting injured in battle for me to figure out that I actually love you? That made me sad because of all the *time* I've wasted because I don't know my own mind and I could have lost you because of my idiotic delaying!"

"Whew…good grief, Dee, you are being too hard on yourself. We have been *so* comfortable with one another for so long. And, you didn't know how I felt until I asked for more."

"I know, Alec! But I'm *so* sorry for dragging my feet for so long. I just get *so mad* at myself for thinking like this. I was abused for so long before peregrinating, that the thought of a relationship scared me. Then I get even madder for thinking that way because I know you would never do that to me. See! I'm an emotional roller coaster of crazy! Are you sure you want to do this relationship thing with me?" She threw her hands over her face again in frustration.

Alec took her hands in his and looked her in the eyes. "Dee, I would do *any* kind of crazy with you. You are all I have wanted for *nine years.* I love your craziness. It is part of who you are. I wouldn't change you for anything in the world."

Odessa started crying again, happy crying this time, and threw her arms around Alec's neck. He wrapped his arms protectively around her waist and they stayed that way for the next several minutes, just holding onto one another.

The music permeated the air and Alec began swaying with Odessa as the sounds and feel of the evening brought them closer than ever before.

Alec couldn't have been happier. He relished in the feel of her in his arms and knowing that he was in her heart made him look to the heavens and silently mouth a big thank you to God once again for answering his long-awaited prayer.

Seth and Caroline stood watching Jason and Memnah dance around the fire with the other villagers and several of their own revelers.

Seth couldn't be happier for Jason. He had agonized over his feelings for Memnah for so long, even to the point of almost giving up on their relationship. Only God had other plans in mind. He was grateful that Jason got his happy ending, just as Seth had gotten his. Yes, they still had hard days ahead. And any of them could lose their lives at any time. But they knew who controlled it all, and where they would go when they died. And that one day, they would all be together again.

Seth leaned forward from behind Caroline and wrapped his arms around her. They stood there watching the scene before them, smiling with joy and gladness.

Some of the village men led a white horse over to Jason and Memnah, which was also adorned in beautiful colorful silks and sheers over its haunches and around its neck and face. Its reigns also mirrored Memnah's headdress with shimmering gold coins that dangled from the fabric's edge.

Jason and Memnah climbed up on the raised box. Jason lifted Memnah into place onto the horses back, and then mounted the animal himself, sitting behind her and taking the reins offered to him by one of the men.

Simon opened a portal to the island, and Memnah and Jason rode through to the other side.

Seth sighed, teasingly saying, "There they go, riding off into the sunset."

"Seth, you know very well the sun *set* when they *kissed*. The wedding was so beautiful." Caroline sniffed, turning to face her husband, and sliding her arms around his waist.

"Yeah, well, it was an appropriate metaphor," he smiled.

She smiled at him, watching as he grew serious.

"Caroline, do you regret marrying the way we did?"

"What do you mean?" she asked, confused.

"You know. Rushing off to the justice of the peace. No formal ceremony."

"No. If we had waited, we wouldn't have been able to get married, and our whole future and present could be completely different now."

"True. We are the only married couple in history, that we know of, that ever peregrinated together."

"Yes. And what if God decided that to be the reason he made us both Peregrines? The sanctity of marriage being the reason we are both here now?"

"You make a very valid point." He smiled at her wisdom and leaned down to kiss her gently.

"I wouldn't want to change a thing, Seth."

The two of them swayed to the music still playing loudly throughout the village.

Seth looked around at all the activity still taking place. He smiled and looked down at her.

"Who knew Memnah's people were such party animals."

Caroline laughed loudly at his remark. "We'll have to keep an eye on her. She just might turn our straight-laced, militaristic, Jason Marshal into an uncontrollable, fun-loving guy."

"Wouldn't that be something." Seth smiled broadly. Sweeping her up into his arms and spinning her around several times as their joyful laughter mingled with that of the others, filling the night sky.

Reader's Island

Safra greeted Jason and Memnah, taking the horse as the two of them dismounted thanked her for her help, and ran into the house to celebrate the long-awaited honeymoon.

Safra smiled at their eagerness as they ran up the massive staircase to the second floor of the large mansion-style house. She walked the animal to the barn, removed all the dressings to make it comfortable, and placed it in one of the available stalls.

Marnor watched Safra from the sitting area, and saw Jason and Memnah run up the staircase, laughing and teasing each other joyfully in their haste. Safra would likely be at the barn for a little while, giving him the opportunity to speak to Petra. Jason and Memnah wouldn't be coming out of his room until morning. Now was the only chance he had. He would take the key with him just in case he might want to enter her room.

He ran into the kitchen, located the key, slipped it into his pocket and took a back staircase up to the second floor. He reached her door, and lightly tapped on it.

"Who's there?" he heard Petra ask from inside.

He cleared his suddenly tightening throat. "Marnor."

"Oh," he heard her say. "What do you want? You've already brought dinner up."

"I uh…just wanted to talk with you a bit."

"Oh…well, can you take me to the restroom?"

"Sure, I have the key." He pulled it from his pocket and unlocked the door.

Petra stepped back as he pushed the door open, the two of them nervously locking eyes.

"Thank you," Petra said, looking around for Safra. "You're alone?"

"Yeah." He looked down and fidgeted with the key in his hand as they walked the hallway.

"I'll make it quick then. I know this could get you into trouble." She entered the bathroom and locked the door behind her.

Marnor stood outside, glancing nervously down both sides of the long, ten-foot-wide hall. He heard the door lock click, and Petra made an appearance. They stood looking at each other once again, until Marnor stepped back and offered for her to go ahead of him. She stepped out beside him and they walked back to her room.

Petra asked in the awkward silence between them, "So, what did you wish to talk about?"

"Well, I was curious about why you are locked up like a criminal here. Although, I must say, you are still treated with kindness, strangely enough."

This caught Petra's attention. "Yes, considering what I was planning to do, they have been very kind. I'm not sure I deserve it, but it isn't like I've killed anyone. If that's what you're asking?"

Marnor half-smirked, half-laughed at her revelation. "I didn't think you did. They said you betrayed them somehow. Besides, I'm the last person to judge anyone about murdering people. I've done loads of that myself."

This made Petra a bit nervous. Marnor noticed the slight sway and reservation in her step.

"Don't worry, Petra. I'm a changed man now. I don't plan on hurting anyone, much less, you."

She grinned ever so slightly at his words. Stopping at her door and stepping inside.

"Well, I used to be in a relationship with a man named Uriah Mose."

"I've heard the others mention him before, and not in a good way."

"Yes, well, he has some very idealistic views of the way things should be run. And, he had me fooled into thinking that I was a part of those plans. But I was just a pawn in his game. A means to an end. He used me terribly and left me here to take all the blame." The pain and rejection of it all was still fresh in her voice.

"Well, I for one am glad he did, leave you here, I mean," he clarified quickly at the astonished, angry look on her face. Her gaze softened a bit, but she was obviously unsure of his intentions. He wasn't even sure of his intentions himself. He just felt drawn to her for some reason. "I better get this door locked back before Safra finds out I let you out. If she comes up later to take you to the restroom, just fake it."

She shook her head in acceptance of his offered plan and watched as he closed the door between them.

Marnor took a deep breath, his mind jumbled with all manner of things as he took the back staircase back down to the kitchen and placed the key back where he had found it. He was leaving the kitchen when Safra walked back into the house.

She stopped him and said, "Marnor, I'm going up to allow Petra to use the bathroom and to shower if she'd like. You'll have to come along I'm afraid."

"Can't that Ryan fella' go with you? I'm kind of tired tonight."

Safra looked at him with a questioning brow. She had noticed the way the two of them looked at each other and naturally assumed he would want to tag along.

"Sure," she answered. "I'll go let him know. I suppose you'll be heading off to bed early then?"

"Uh, yeah, I think I will."

Marnor turned and walked to the back of the house and out the door to the staff quarters. He showered, shut off the lights, and laid there staring up at the ceiling while his mind was a whirlwind of thoughts and emotions. Neither of which he was used to. He never had to think about things being right or wrong before. And he had never had these strange stirrings for a woman. Desires, yes. The Scaither life had been all about taking whatever you wanted with no explanation or apologies, except that which belonged to the Scaither leader. You didn't touch the boss's things. But here, his head and his emotions didn't line up very well. Here he had to watch everything he said and did. It was a constant struggle to watch his tongue and his temper. Now he had these other feelings for this woman Petra. It wasn't exactly desire, more like curiosity. He *really* wanted to know and understand her. Something he had never wanted with *anyone* before. He stopped caring about people when his mother had left him behind to fend for himself. He had become hardened at an early age. That is until Bridget and the demon war, and now this Petra woman. He sighed heavily, tossed his pillow a few times, punching it for comfort and to ease his frustrations. He closed his eyes, hoping his mind would shut down as well. It probably wouldn't be long before the others returned, and he didn't feel like chatting with the other single men on the island who he bunked with. If need be, he'd pretend he was asleep.

Reader's Island, Present Day

It was close to midnight when the partiers returned to the island, excusing themselves from the wedding celebration still going on in full swing back at Memnah's village.

Simon noticed that the house was quiet and dark, although Safra had left a few lights on so they could see upon returning.

He thought about his friend. He had missed her tonight. She was beginning to grow on him even more than she had before. Although now, these feelings were different. He recognized them to be sure. He was attracted to this younger Safra and her energy. He also knew that she felt the same about him. He recognized the look in her eyes at times. But he was too old for her. In truth, they were nearly the same age. But because of his creating storms three times in the past, he had aged fifteen years, putting him nearly twenty years her senior.

No, Simon had tried the whole relationship thing a few times already with no luck. First with his Lily back in Egypt thirty years ago. And then here, twenty years back with another Peregrine. She had perished as well during the betrayal and demon war nearly fourteen years back. He and she had an on and off again relationship over the course of several years. He smiled at the remembrance of his younger, cockier, self and the headstrong, defiant young woman named Hannah he had met once while here on the island. A year after her disappearance he finally gave up hope of ever seeing her again, until she reappeared one day out of nowhere, injured to the point of death.

Simon decided then that a relationship was not in the cards for him. He had decided that he would serve faithfully, looking only to what God had for him and nowhere else. Now, all of a sudden, these feelings were beginning to resurface. He sighed, knowing full well he would never act on them. His future was that of a warrior, fighting to save mankind. And hopefully God would see to giving him a warrior's death like his old friend Nuncio had experienced. Simon wasn't ready to die yet by any means, but neither was he interested in pursuing another relationship, only for it to fail. He walked to his room, entered, and closed the door, kneeling to pray to ask God to take away the feelings he was having for Safra. He didn't want or need them. They would only be a distraction for him in the days to come. Very dark days, he was afraid. Days that The Twelve would face fighting a very great and perilous evil. His focus for his prayer soon turned from himself to the lives and safety of the twelve people who would soon face, quite possibly, certain death.

You saw with your own eyes the great trials, the signs and wonders, the mighty hand and outstretched arm, with which the lord your God brought you out. The Lord God will do the same to all the peoples you now fear.

Deuteronomy 7:19

Chapter 9

The island was a buzz of activity the next morning as several of the men set about updating the forge to accommodate the making of the swords and for the melting of the Rhenium and Ruthenium to strengthen and coat all the armor pieces.

Simon and the other Dragoman made plans to visit Zanchier in the company of the Keepers within the next several days.

Marnor decided to stay out of sight as much as possible during such discussions, not wanting to remind Simon that he was still here and be made to return to Zanchier with them.

Jason and Memnah were inseparable, still honeymooning for as long as possible.

The rest of the Peregrines decided to have another sparring day. During which, they experimented with combining their gifts and abilities to see how to best utilize them. They had all learned quickly how to best use their God given abilities to their greatest advantages. Many learned how to bounce off another's powers to accomplish a greater goal.

Marnor sat at the top of an obliging fence and watched them as they practiced, amazed by the abilities of these people. His thoughts drifted back to the battle that had taken place just days ago where he saw each of them in action. Each peregrine, young and old, having a special gift to aid in their already skillful fighting abilities.

The way the Dragoman fought was unique unto themselves. Each one a skilled and masterful warrior. Simon could do things Marnor never would have believed just with a simple thought or action. He used his bare hands to shoot powerful beams of light, and the thin blade hidden in the staff he carried cut down any demon that got in his way. Malachai was capable of the same as well. Marnor wondered if it were also something he could learn. The women, Vashti, and Prisca, although they looked to be just average women, fought as fiercely as the others. The one called Safra, he understood to be an ordinary human like himself, but she fought as strongly and bravely as any of these chosen warriors with their special gifts. Perhaps Marnor could learn such skills? Should he ask to be trained? Or was it still too early for such a request? Perhaps, once he proved himself worthy, they would teach him.

Then there were the teenagers. Kids who could control any creature or beast to do their bidding. Although Bridget said it was more like asking than controlling. They showed the animals respect and asked them for their help instead of demanding it.

This new world Marnor had been fortunate to fall into was amazing, and not something he wished to give up. Perhaps his new-found faith in the God that they all spoke of would provide him a new life and a better future than the one he tried taking for himself. The pact with the demon allowing it to possess him was not something he would ever forget. He never wanted to experience such pain, hatred, and darkness ever again. He would do whatever it took to stay here on this remarkable island.

Simon watched Marnor every chance he got. He noticed the man seemed genuinely curious and watched everything that happened. He only hoped that it was for his own learning and not for some sort of treachery later. Safra had reported good things from watching him as well. She did say that he was bonding with Petra, but Simon wasn't certain that was such a grand idea either. Neither of them were solid believers. Simon wasn't even sure if either of them had accepted Christ. It was something he would have to discuss with both of them. Simon was shaken from his thoughts as Safra approached.

"Simon, I have something to discuss with you," she said as she stopped in front of him.

"Yes, what is it?"

"Well, I've noticed that all the Dragoman have been exceptionally busy lately and that the archives have been slightly neglected."

Simon sighed. "Yes, we haven't had much time to record anything. I hope we will remember the important details when we get around to writing things down."

"That's what I want to discuss. Why not let Petra and Marnor take over as scribes?"

Simon looked somewhat put-off by the idea.

"I'm not sure how that would work. Marnor is very new to this life, and Petra may not see things entirely correctly."

"You and the others could fact check their work after it's written. It would give them both something to do and would be a good way to begin letting Petra, and Marnor, prove themselves."

"Very true. Would you be willing to oversee them and make certain they didn't get into any trouble?"

"Yes. I have no other purpose here other than to fight when needed in battle. My healing abilities are rarely needed with Jason's gift of healing, and my tinctures and herbal remedies only take care of internal illness, which doesn't happen very often here."

"Well, than I see no problem with this. Thank you, Safra. I have been fretting a little lately over the archives. This, I believe, is an answer to prayer. You and I will go and speak with the other Dragoman, and if they concur, then we'll discuss this with Marnor and Petra at lunch today."

"Great. I'll gather the current archives and writing aids and place them on the center library table. We can show them how things are done after lunch, *if* they agree to do what is asked of them."

"Wonderful. Now let's go find the others."

Simon and Safra walked off to search for the other Dragoman, passing by Odessa as they did so, with her stopping them.

"Simon, I've had another vision."

"Yes. What is it?"

"It's about the Shields of Faith. I think I've been given the place, or places, where to find them."

"Go on," he prodded.

"Well, it's strange really. As I told you before, I was unsure as to the exact location, geographic wise. Now, I think the shields are in several different places. Maybe up to five. The scenery changes around each area, like it did when I was given the vision of the keys for the ancient archive books."

"But, unlike the keys, you all must be in attendance to locate the armor. You can't split up like you did to search for the keys."

"Are you certain about that?" Safra interjected. "They would all still be looking for the armor. They may not be in the same places, but they would still be searching for the same thing."

"Perhaps. But just in case, they all need to be together. I believe that is the best way to handle the search," Simon replied. "Odessa, meet with us about 1:00 p.m. and Safra can draw your visions."

"All right, Simon. See you both later."

Odessa left, and Simon and Safra continued on their mission to find the other Dragoman. They entered the main floor library finding Malachai, Vashti, and Dekker, still helping Heba and Renquin with the deciphering of the *Book of the Keepers*. Simon approached the table while Safra went in search of the items she would need to show Marnor and Petra after lunch, should the Dragoman agree to her idea.

Simon noticed Renquin seemed rather tired and off balance. As he reached the table, the man nearly fell over sideways.

"Renquin, are you all right?" Simon asked, forgetting the man couldn't speak English.

Heba quickly questioned her grandfather in their native tongue, turning to look at Simon with his reply. Dekker translated.

"She says he is becoming increasingly dizzy and light-headed."

"Hmmm. Let's lay him down over on one of the couches."

They each got on either side of him as Vashti fluffed pillows to lay him back, and Malachai lifted his feet onto the sofa.

Malachai looked at Simon and said, "I wonder what could be wrong with him? Perhaps we are over working him?"

"Possibly," Simon answered, "let's get Safra's opinion on the matter."

As Safra entered the library and placed the items on the center table, she noticed the commotion over by the couch.

"What's happening, Simon?" she asked.

"Renquin became dizzy and nearly fainted," he replied.

Safra knelt beside him, feeling his head and cheeks, looking into his eyes, and checking his pulse.

"I don't see anything unusual, but his breathing is a bit labored and his complexion is slightly pale." She looked up at Heba who seemed to be fine.

"Dekker, ask Heba if she is having any of the same symptoms as her grandfather?"

Dekker questioned Heba and gave her reply. "She said the first day she arrived she was a bit dizzy and lightheaded, but it quickly passed. She assumed it was from all the excitement."

Safra sat and thought for a minute. "Perhaps, but more likely he is suffering from the change in environment."

"How so?" Prisca asked.

"Well, they have lived their entire lives on the ocean floor buried beneath a mountain with no sunlight, fresh air, and a poor quality of oxygen. The difference between the two places is likely what's affecting him."

"I never thought of that," Simon stated. "We'll have to keep a close eye on him. Let him rest here for a while. Perhaps Heba can continue with the translations."

They all went back to work with Safra agreeing to tend to the elderly man. She sent one of the housekeepers up to her room to grab her medical bag, certain she had something in her tinctures that would help with his symptoms.

A few hours went by and the others began filtering into the house for lunch. Simon and Safra quickly related her idea to the other Dragoman who agreed to the plan, then they all entered the kitchen for lunch

Clancy and Shannon had already brought Petra down for lunch and had her seated at the table. Simon and the others sat down beside her as Safra found Marnor and pulled him over to join the conversation.

Marnor was nervous, thinking this was the end to his stay here on the island.

Simon began. "Marnor, Petra, we have an idea we wish to run by the two of you. Safra has recommended the two of you as scribes. If you agree, you will both take over the recording of information in the Dragoman archives. With everything happening lately, and our attentions pulled in many different directions, we are in need of someone to keep track of events and people. Would the two of you be willing to do this?"

Petra quickly answered. "Yes! Thank you! I'm going crazy in my room with nothing to do."

"This does not mean you have free reign just yet," Simon warned her.

"Fine. I understand. I'm just glad to have something to do."

They all turned to Marnor, who had yet to answer. He was nervous. He didn't read well and his spelling was even worse. But he wasn't about to let on to any of them lest they see him as completely useless and make him leave the island. "Sure, I can do that. As long as someone shows me what to do. And if Petra can help me learn?" he asked as she nodded her acceptance of his request.

"Safra will be aiding in the task as well. We'll explain how, what, and where the information is to be written this afternoon. We will check each entry for accuracy after you record it, and Safra will be in charge of the both of you. You've seen her fight, so I suggest you both be on your best behavior," Simon warned them. "We'll meet with you around four p.m. in the library."

They both shook their heads in agreement, Petra smiling at Marnor who returned a nervous half-grin. He hoped he hadn't agreed to something he couldn't do. He would have to spend more of his free time learning to read and write at an accelerated pace. He was catching on quickly with Bridget's teachings, but he had only had one lesson so far. He would confide in Bridget and pray she could help him somehow. Pray. That was a new word for him, and a completely new concept. Well, it couldn't hurt to start praying to this God. He supposed this was as good a reason as any to start.

Lunch went by quickly and the Dragoman instructed the Keepers to pack lightly for an undetermined amount of time in Zanchier. While the rest of the Dragoman packed for their trip, Simon, Safra, and Odessa sat in the archival library as Odessa described her visions while Safra sketched them.

Odessa related that one place the shields were located was known as the Cliff Palace in Mesa Verde National Park, in Colorado, in the USA. An ancient tribe had built a castle dwelling in the underside of the highest cliffs, carved out of the mountain itself in many places.

The next location was Cappadocia, Turkey, where an underground city was carved inside the mountainside, but this one ran beneath the earth's surface with many caverns, pathways, stairways, and rooms. The underground city of Derinkuyu was thought to date back as far as the eighth and seventh centuries BC.

The third location was in the abandoned city of Craco, Italy. A completely intact city high up on the cliff, left by its residence long ago for unknown reasons.

The fourth location was an old church known as St. Dunstan's in the East, in London, England. The church dated back as far as the twelfth century.

And the fifth and final location was the Al Khazneh in Petra, Jordan. A city of immense size and architectural detail lying inside the mountains of Petra, carved within the rock.

Simon decided it would be easier to inform the others of Odessa's vision at dinner, and had Clancy and Henry set up the large patio table. This made it easier to have everyone in one location, and to call an impromptu meeting.

They all had come to learn that when the large table was prepared, that something was going to happen.

It was nearing four o'clock and Simon, Safra, and the other Dragoman met with Marnor and Petra to explain the task that they had been given. After, dinner was close at hand and Simon disappeared to his room for a brief respite, to think about all the information they had discovered lately, all the tasks ahead of them, and where everyone was to be. It was hard being the only person truly in charge. Nuncio had carried much of that burden, and now that he was gone it seemed to fall to Simon, and it was exhausting him. He knelt and prayed that God would give him strength of heart, mind, and spirit to handle all that was required of him. He also prayed for the others and all they were soon to face. After which, he laid down for a brief nap for the next hour hoping for renewed strength upon waking. He needed his wits about him for tonight's meeting and tomorrow's journey to Zanchier.

Downstairs the activity level was normal with people moving and working in every direction. The kitchen staff prepared dinner while some of the Peregrines sparred in the fields. Some of the others helped the now limited groundskeepers and housekeepers with duties. Others worked with the Keepers in the stables with the horses and the building of the new forge.

The Dragoman, Heba, and Renquin worked at deciphering the last few chapters of the *Book of the Keepers*. Renquin's health seemed to be a bit better after a long nap so he rejoined the task. They all hoped to have it finished within the next two days.

Malachai, Vashti, and Prisca made notes on anything they deemed important about the Keepers, and the descriptions of the beasts that The Twelve were to face in the final battle.

Malachai noted some very peculiar details about the beasts that he was certain Simon would find interesting.

The dinner bell was rung, and people began filing outside to gather around the large, prepared table. Simon was nearly the last person to sit down, grateful the nap had done him some good.

They ate their meal amongst jovial chatter, and upon finishing, all visited in their seats as Simon stood to quiet them with a raise of his hands. The group quickly quieted down, and they all looked to the man they had all come to rely heavily upon for direction and guidance.

Simon began. "As you all know, we are about to begin the search for the final piece of armor, the Shields of Faith. Odessa has informed us that they have been separated into five different locations according to her most recent vision." Simon nodded to two of the housekeepers who began passing out folders to everyone. "Within these folders is information concerning the places, time periods, and other important information you all may need for locating the shields."

Zaccai asked, "Simon, can we all split into groups to search for them? Like we did for the keys to the books?"

"I'm uncertain about that, Zaccai. It was made clear that you all had to be together to find the pieces of armor."

"Yes, but when we were in Timna, and several went after the Belts of Truth, the rest remained in camp."

"True, but you were all in the same location."

"It would make the searching go much faster if we could split up."

Zeke chimed in. "Perhaps we could give it a try? We would all still be on the same mission, searching for the shields, just in different locations."

Simon sighed. "I suppose you could give it a try. But it may be a waste of time."

Jason spoke up next. "I say we at least try it. We can communicate with each other by way of the Portgens, and time travel is very easy now with them as well. If it doesn't work out, we can all meet up and continue on together."

"As you wish," Simon answered. "We Dragoman and the Keepers will be traveling to Zanchier to obtain the Rhenium and

Ruthenium for the coating and strengthening of the armor. The rest of the Peregrines retired or not, and any other members, will remain here. Safra will be in charge in my absence so if anyone needs anything you can go to her. Petra and Marnor are our new scribes and will record important information into the archives.

Bridget and Marnor exchanged a knowing glance at Simon's announcement. Bridget was a little worried about her brother's lack of reading ability. Writing would be a whole other challenge.

"Petra," Simon addressed the woman, "you will no longer be confined to your room. We have decided to trust you with your freedom. Do not make us regret our decision in giving you a second chance."

"I won't, Simon, I promise. I've learned my lesson. You can count on me," she assured him.

Simon looked at her with raised eyebrows and nodded, unsure whether she was telling the truth, but had little choice in the matter. They would find out soon enough if she would be true to her words.

He turned to address the rest of the group.

"You all need to prepare to leave in the morning. With the accuracy of the Portgens, and the places you will be traveling, you can decide for yourselves whether you wish to take the horses. You will also need to decide amongst yourselves who will go in each group and to which location. Seeing as how you have decided to split up, it may be in your best interest for some of the other non-twelve to travel with you. Strength in numbers you know. As long as Safra can handle things here on the island that is?" He looked at Safra questioningly.

"We will be fine here. Besides, you all will likely only be gone for a few days. I believe a few of us can handle things here if the others are needed elsewhere," she replied.

"All right then. Those of you who wish to travel with The Twelve, get with the others after this to plan who goes with whom. Jason, you, and the other leaders can figure that out. Now, does anyone else have any questions?"

Wade asked, "Are all of us Keepers going with you Dragoman tomorrow?"

"Yes. We may need you all due to the nature and size of the creatures on Zanchier. Some are still familiar with us, but I'm not leaving possible recognition as our only option for protection."

"Any other questions?" No one replied, so Simon closed the meeting.

"All right everyone, finish up your details and turn in early tonight. I believe we all have a few, long, days ahead of us."

Everyone who wanted to tag along on the next peregrination gathered around the leader's end of the table, while the others went on their way to prepare for their own journey or island chores for the next several days.

The leaders split nineteen people into five groups. Each group would search their given location for the Shields of Faith. They prayed that splitting up like this would work. If it didn't, then the searching would take them much longer.

They called the meeting done and everyone disappeared to pack and prepare for their next adventure to come in the morning.

Memnah would travel with Jason, Seth, and Caroline, and packed excitedly.

"Jason, I can't wait to go on the peregrination with you. For so long I've wondered what your travels were like. Where you went? What you saw?"

He walked over to her, grabbing her hand, and turning her to him pulling her into his arms. He smiled at his new wife. "It's not all exciting you know. We have frequent run-ins with demons. And fights happen no matter where we are."

"Well, since that is something I've already experienced, I figure there won't be many surprises there." She smiled at him and wrapped her arms around his neck. "I'm just so happy to be here with you and to be able to share your life."

"So am I, love."

They shared one long passionate kiss before Memnah broke away in protest.

"Jason, we need to finish packing," she said with a slight giggle.

"We're nearly finished. It can wait a little longer." He smiled at her, producing a smile from her as well.

Seth and Caroline were packing when she took a sudden dizzy spell, swooning and landing on the bed, shaking her head to clear it. Seth noticed his wife's sudden distress and went over to her.

"Caroline are you all right?" he asked, placing his hand on her forehead to check for fever.

"I think so," she breathed. "I just suddenly got a bit dizzy."

"You don't seem to be hot," he replied, checking the back of her neck as well.

Caroline suddenly grabbed her stomach. "I think I'm going to be sick." She stood and bolted out of the bedroom and across the hall to a bathroom.

Seth followed her, standing outside the bathroom door.

"Sweetheart, are you all right?"

"I'm fine, Seth!" came her muffled answer from behind the door.

"Can I get you anything?" Worry creased his brow. The door slowly opened.

"A cold glass of water would be nice." She walked across the hall to the bedroom, her hand on her stomach.

"Be right back." Seth took off toward the kitchen stairwell at the opposite end of the hallway, concern for Caroline niggling at his mind. He had never seen her sick before.

With Seth headed to the kitchen, Caroline sat on the edge of the bed, curious as to what could have made her sick and wondering if any of the others were feeling the same way. She took a few deep breaths, and realized she felt better. Just as she was about to get up and continue packing, Seth appeared in the doorway with a glass of ice water and some crackers. He handed her the water and placed the crackers beside the bed.

"I thought maybe the crackers would help settle your stomach. Gram always gave them to me when I was a boy with tummy trouble." He grinned lopsidedly at her, stroking her long silky hair, concern evident in his eyes.

Caroline took some long drinks and looked at him. "Thank you, Seth, but I'm fine now. Perhaps something I ate didn't agree with me. I have been feeling a bit tired lately. You know, I used to lead the quiet life of a librarian before this." She smiled at him. "Perhaps my body is just tired from such a drastic change of pace."

"Maybe," Seth agreed, still feeling concerned for her even though her color had returned. Perhaps it was something simple and he didn't need to make a mountain out of a molehill. "Let's try and get some rest. Hopefully you'll be right as rain in the morning."

"We need to finish packing first, Seth," she said standing.

"That can wait till morning," he admonished, standing, and taking her hands in his and looking down into her soft eyes.

"It will only take another ten minutes or so. Besides, you know I don't like waiting till the last minute. Things always end up being forgotten that way." She cocked her head and smirked at him.

"Fine. Let's make it quick then. I want you well rested and feeling one-hundred-percent better by morning." He leaned over and planted a kiss on the tip of her nose. They grinned at one another, finished packing, and crawled into bed with Seth wrapping his arms protectively around Caroline who curled into his side. Seth said a silent prayer for his wife, concern for her still niggling at the recesses of his mind.

Don't let anyone look down on you because you are young,
but set an example for the believers in speech, in conduct,
in love, in faith and in purity.

1 Timothy 4:12

Chapter 10

Morning broke clear and bright as the island breeze softly blew across the landscape, and the hustle and bustle of activities for the journeys soon to start filled the air.

The Dragoman and Keepers would venture on foot. The horses being an extra liability should the native creatures of Zanchier grow hungry for an abundant and easy target.

Jason, Memnah, Seth, and Caroline took horses as they were to travel to the ancient city of Al Khazneh in Petra, Jordan. From the modern-day pictures available on the web, they could see that the city was massive, and the rooms and hidden buildings went on for miles. Seeing that it was a major tourist attraction, they would have to try and pick a time-period where there were less, or preferably no people around.

Zaccai, Zeke, Sofia, and Rourke would also take horses as they traveled to the Cliff Palace in Colorado. They also would pick an earlier time period in hopes of avoiding tourists, yet late enough to quite possibly avoid the tribe that built the castle.

Alec, Odessa, and Oz were taking Craco, Italy. Historical records were unclear as to exactly when the city was deserted, but the latest materials said either 1963 or 1991. They would do their best to find a time period that was adequate, knowing it might take a few tries, but with the Portgen, that wouldn't be too bad.

Gabriele, Timothy, and one of the groundskeepers and housekeepers went to the underground city of Derinkuyu, in

Cappadocia, Turkey. The city was easily accessed by foot and the discovery was marked in historical records as 1963. Picking a date to return might not prove too difficult for them.

Sean, Kristin, Nick, and Nadia would take St. Dunstan's in the East, in London, England. Choosing a period in time when the church was lower in activity may prove to be problematic, seeing as how the church had always been a place of refuge for sailors, and an important support for the surrounding community since its erection in the 1100s.

Seth looked around at all the peregrination groups ready to take on the next task. He also watched Caroline closely this morning, still concerned about her health. She was a tad pale this morning and seemed sluggish to him, but at least she wasn't complaining of being ill.

Caroline took her pack and tied it to her horse's saddle bags. Her stomach felt as though it were going to roil again. She tried to play it down as much as possible. She knew Seth worried about her and didn't want him to know she still felt ill. After securing her bags she slowly walked back into the house until she was out of Seth's gaze. Then, she took off as fast as possible for one of the bathrooms located in the far rear of the large mansion, passing Safra on the way.

Safra watched as Caroline flew by her, holding her stomach. She decided to follow after the woman to see if she needed anything.

When Safra reached the bathroom door, she could hear Caroline inside retching.

Safra tapped lightly on the door. "Caroline, are you all right?"

It was a few seconds before she finished and answered.

"I believe so," came her winded, muffled, reply.

"May I come in?"

"Are you sure you want to?"

"Things like this don't bother me," Safra replied, entering the bathroom. " Is there anything I can do to help?"

"Unless you can stop me from throwing-up, I doubt it."

"Are you in any pain?"

"No. I just started feeling very sick yesterday evening."

"May I give you a quick check up?" Safra walked closer to Caroline.

"Please do. I have a mission to go on, and this will make it very difficult."

Safra stepped forward and quickly checked Caroline over, taking her pulse, checking her pupils and glands in the neck.

"Caroline, when was the last time you had a cycle?"

Caroline froze at Safra's question. Her eyes grew wide with understanding.

"No way!" Caroline threw her hands over her mouth in surprise and fell back against the sink. "This month's cycle is late but only by a few days. I never even really paid attention to it."

"I would say congratulations, but with the battle that you are soon to face, I'm not so certain it is such good news."

Caroline looked at Safra as the Final Battle came into her mind. "Safra, what am I going to do? If the Final Battle is still a while off, how am I supposed to fight with a pregnancy belly?"

"Well, I have some herbs that I can give you to help with the nausea. The rest is in the Lord's hands."

Caroline looked at her. "Please, don't tell anyone, not even Seth. I don't want him fretting over me the entire time. Especially since I am one of The Twelve."

Safra shook her head in agreement. "I'll be right back with the herbs. I'll meet you in the kitchen." Safra left Caroline alone in the bathroom.

Caroline stood still, shocked at what she just learned. She looked to the ceiling and silently prayed. *Lord, I'm not sure what you have in mind here, but, as happy as I am to be with child, I am also very frightened for our baby's life. Could this not have waited just a little while longer? Until after the battles I am to fight have ended? Please, Lord, Protect me and my child from harm.*

"Caroline!"

Seth's worried voice boomed through the house. Caroline gathered her composure and went to find him. He was starting up the massive staircase to the second story. When he saw her, he stopped and turned back down the steps.

"Are you sick again?" he asked her, taking her hands in his and looking into her eyes.

"Only a little. Safra has some herbs to help me get over the nausea. She asked me to meet her in the kitchen."

"All right, let's go."

"There's no need for you to go too, Seth. I'm a big girl, I can take care of the directions for use by myself." Caroline said with a slight, stiff smirk.

"Did she say what was causing the nausea?"

"I'm certain she has no idea," Caroline lied. She hated doing so but telling him the truth right now would drive them both mad.

"Then how does she know what to give you?"

Leave it to Seth to be so diligent for answers, she thought. "She said it was just for general causes of nausea. Please, go finish getting ready. I'll be back out in just a minute ready to go on our quest."

"All right. If you're certain. I'll see you outside." Seth leaned over, kissed her cheek, and left the house.

Caroline could tell he was on edge about all of this. If he knew why she was sick it would make him ill with worry and could quite possibly get him injured or killed if they faced demons again. He needed to concentrate on the task at hand and not be worried about her and their baby.

Caroline thought about that as she walked into the kitchen to meet Safra. She was pregnant with her and Seth's child. She so wanted to be over the moon happy about the pregnancy, but fear for the life growing inside her had wrapped around her heart, squeezing tightly. She only hoped that if they did see another fight, that she could fight as fiercely as before and not let worry cloud her judgment.

Safra was standing at the counter separating a powdery substance into small bags. She looked up at Caroline as she entered the room and stopped in front of her.

"Take one of these each morning upon waking, and each night before bed. It will quell the nausea. It might take a couple of doses before it starts to help, but it will work."

"Do I just pour it into my mouth?"

"You can, or you can add it to water. It has a slightly bitter taste at first but gets better quickly. If you can manage it under the tongue for a few seconds before swallowing, it will work faster."

"What does it taste like, just so I'm not surprised?"

"Like peppermint and ginger root."

Caroline did as Safra instructed, noting the taste wasn't too bad. She then downed the glass of water that Safra had placed on the counter. Pocketing the rest of the small packages, she said, "Thank you Safra. I don't know how I would get through this without you."

"Well, when you get back, come see me and perhaps we can come up with some other ideas to help you out during this time."

Caroline smiled at the woman, took her hands in hers giving them a squeeze and nodded. She left the kitchen and headed back outside. Her group was waiting on her just off the edge of the patio area. Jason and Memnah were already in the saddle, while Seth stood on the ground holding his and her horse's reins in his hands.

Seth looked at her with a questioning brow as he handed over her reins. She smiled at him, reassuring him she was fine. The relieved smile on his face melted her heart. It was going to be very hard keeping this from him.

Next to their group some of the others were ready to head out as well. Several of the groups had already taken off earlier on foot. Ready to go quicker from not having to prepare horses. The few remaining groups waved their goodbyes, voicing well wishes, and each disappeared through the Portgen toward their respective searches.

Simon watched the last of the Peregrines ride through their Portals, then turned to his group of travelers which consisted of the other three Dragoman and the four Keepers. He looked down at the youngest, Annabelle, wondering again how one so young could come to live such a life. But, regardless, she had been called by God and it wasn't Simon's job to question it. She had already had to experience so much pain and fear, and had to exude so much bravery, he couldn't fathom her mindset. But she appeared to be handling it all quite well since her first demon battle five days past where she experienced some shock and then broke into tears after returning to the island. But most of them had been in tears as well after all the loss of lives.

"Everyone ready to go?" he asked the group standing around him. Everyone chimed a yes or nodded, and Simon opened his Portgen to the time of year in which the instructions stated that one could pass safely both ways through Zanchier. The odd coordinates in which they found hidden in Hiram Burkes archive books were strange indeed, and Simon hoped they worked and that it wasn't some sort of trickery. Before the instructions were found, they had to get trapped within the portal of an intense storm to get to Zanchier. This would be their first journey through other means. Simon took a deep breath, shot up a prayer of protection and pushed the numbers and odd sequencing into the Portgen.

The device whirred and an intense light opened with some actual electrical pulses shooting through the center. Simon's eyebrows raised in question as he peered at the now brightly glowing hole in front of him. Unlike most Portgen travels, once the brightness passed, one could see what lay on the other side. This experience was unlike the others. He could see nothing past the occasional brighter blip of light that circled the edges within.

Simon squared his shoulders, closed his eyes in another quick prayer, opened them and stepped through, his feet fortunately landing on solid ground. He looked around at the strangely quiet and softly falling blue snow. *Was this Zanchier?* he wondered.

As the others filed through after him, Bridget took up the lead, obviously knowing where she was going. She waved them all quickly and quietly to the edge of the open valley they just exited into from the Portgen. They quickly obeyed her command and trotted to the line of trees.

Once hidden beneath the thick foliage, Bridget smiled and giggled softly.

"I've never seen it snow here before," she said, taking a handful of the blue, cold flakes and blowing at them. "It was summer when we were here last. I suppose you chose this time for a reason, Simon?"

"Yes, Bridget. I did. Your father's book stated that this was the only season when one could pass through the portal in the valley both ways. Perhaps the quieter season and weather allows for less rainstorms."

"Perhaps. It wasn't something I or Caroline ever discussed with Oz. I'm sure he didn't know about it or he would have left years before."

"Yes. Poor Oz and Sofia. Your father likely returned to Zanchier after their confinement here."

"I don't think so. He never really went anywhere once we moved to Dover. There were only a few times where he left me alone overnight. Just for one night of course, and I was older when he did so."

Simon watched as Bridget scanned the sky above, looking and listening for something. It wasn't long before a rustling came from the trees somewhere around them. As the Dragoman grew nervous, the Keepers watched closely, a wide smile soon breaking out on their faces.

Several of the large cat-like creatures appeared, their bodies so large that only their heads were visible through the tree branches. Simon knew them to be the Pagorinxes that aided in the war, but he had little chance to actually get a good look at them. Just then the sky above them darkened a little, and a shadow descended over them and landed just to the right of the trees. Bridget ran through the branches with the others close behind her. She emerged to find Cho landing in a small clearing.

Simon cleared his throat to capture Bridget's attention. "Now what, Bridget?"

"Simon, you and another can ride on Cho with me. The Pagorinxes will take everyone else."

Annabelle stepped up excitedly. "Bridget, may I ride with you and Simon? I haven't flown on Cho before."

"Of course, Annabelle." Bridget smiled.

"You're much braver than I am, my dear," Simon whispered to a giggling Annabelle. "I must say, I'm a tad timid about climbing on the back of this creature." Simon stared up at the sheer size of Cho, being so close to her now.

Simon stepped up to the massive bird-like animal. He remembered her from the battle. The very battle where she lost her mate, Han. Cho knelt low on the ground as they climbed upon her back. Annabelle sat between Bridget and Simon as they waited for the others to climb aback the Pagorinxes. They soon were off, headed for Oz's famed treehouse.

As they took flight, Simon's stomach turned, feeling as though hundreds of butterflies fluttered within him. They soon leveled out and his stomach quieted as he gazed out at the colors that streaked the sky which gave way to the blue snow-covered magnificence of the Xantifal Mountains. The hues of purples and golds the sun bounced off of were breathtaking, and the thrill of flying on the powerful creature was exhilarating now that his fears had quieted.

About half an hour later, they landed on the lowest platform of Oz's treehouse, arriving just ahead of the Pagorinxes. Everyone was chilled to the bone, the breezy run and flight through the snow-covered area taking its toll. Bridget quickly jumped down, bid Cho goodbye, and ran inside the tree. It was only a matter of a few minutes before they could smell the scent of smoke in the air. As they all followed Dominic inside the tree, he gave them directions where to step so no one tripped down the root-made staircase. They soon entered the large opening in the tree's center where a roaring fire was now beginning to heat and warm the room. Bridget had located several blankets for them to wrap around themselves, and she had already started a pot of water boiling over the fire.

They all spent the next half-hour warming themselves and taking in the strange treehouse where Oz had spent ten years of his life. Bridget had brought some tea from the island and made them all wonderful cups of steaming hot tea to warm their insides.

Simon sipped the last of his tea from his cup feeling quite pleasant now. He set the cup on the small table in the room's center.

"Now, Bridget, do you know where we can purchase the Ruthenium and Rhenium?"

"Well, I would assume from the Rhe Mines. We never discussed such things with Oz."

"Where exactly are these mines located?"

"I believe them to be about an hour-and-a-half to two-hours flight across the mountains toward Carpasmere."

"I'm sure we can find out from one of the villages I saw at the base of the mountain when flying over."

"Perhaps, but you must be careful here, Simon. The Scaithers have surely found themselves a new leader, and they are a cruel bunch."

"Yes, well, everyone stay together while here. Plus, we will have the protection of the animals."

"True. I suppose there's no use in hiding our abilities anymore. Most of the villagers saw us riding the animals across the open planes when we came to get them for the battle."

"We won't be staying long ourselves. Only to get enough minerals to coat the armor pieces and rebuild the swords."

"Oz did say once that there was a gypsy type fellow who he traded with when he needed supplies. Oz kept some of the minerals in his possession to barter with."

"Do you remember the man's name?"

"No, I'm afraid not."

"We should have thought of all of these questions earlier before we all parted ways."

"Perhaps the Portgen's communications option will work, and we can ask Oz about him?"

"Good thinking, Bridget. I have yet to use that particular feature."

Simon took his Portgen from its holder and pushed the appropriate buttons to locate Oz's Portgen, then pushed the call button. It beeped a few times and then Oz answered at the other end.

"This is Oz."

"Oz? Simon here. Do you have any advice or a name we can contact here about the purchases we need to make?"

"Well, the only place ta get the Rhenium and Ruthenium is the Rhe mines. I know a fella' that used ta' work the packin' a' the trucks. Name's Farnsmuth. Jilbin Farnsmuth. He an' I made a few side deals. Ya' know, the stuff that fell off the trucks. Tell 'im I sent ya' an' ta' keep it on the down low."

"What's the best way to contact him, and get to the mines?"

"He's a little fella'. Older too. Looks like a hairy bag a' bones walkin' 'round. The mines 're a northeast 'cross the moun'ains to'ard Carpasmere. Simon, you all be careful. Them people at the mines catch ya' and it'll be hard to get you all outta' there. The miners ain't like the Scaithers, but they don't care where they get their slave labor either."

"We will, Oz. Thanks for the information. No worries about any of that. We have things under control here." Simon was grateful that the Portgen's communications worked this time. He wasn't certain as to why, except for perhaps the ease of travel due to the seasonal change.

Simon disconnected the call and they sat for the next thirty minutes formulating a plan to locate Jilbin Farsnmuth, make the necessary purchases, and get out of Zanchier without getting caught by anyone.

They all put on more appropriate clothing for the cold winter weather, and Bridget called the creatures back to the treehouse. By the time they made the trip across the mountains to the Rhe mines it would be nearing the noon hour.

Malachai spoke up as they headed to the platform to mount the animals. "You know, Simon, we could just snatch whatever amounts of the mineral that we need. I don't think many people would chance going up against these creatures." He gestured to the three massive beasts.

"True, but I would rather pay for what we need. These people have a hard life here."

"I understand that. But if push comes to shove, then I say we snatch what we need, throw the money whichever direction it lands, and be off."

"Yes, you have a point. We certainly can't risk getting caught. Let's all keep our Portgens on the communications setting so that we can talk without having to call one another. We don't want to alert anyone to our whereabouts during any of this. If these people here get a hold of our technology, it could mean serious trouble."

"What do we use for currency here?" Prisca asked.

Simon turned to look at her. "I am unsure. Perhaps Bridget knows," he asked looking to her.

"No again, sorry. We hunted for what we needed, and Oz was pretty well stocked on everything else. We were only here for a month or so."

Vashti asked, "Did Sofia ever mention what the monetary system was here?"

Prisca said, "I remember her saying they bartered for a lot of things."

"Surely there is some sort of economy here," Simon stated. "Perhaps we should visit one of the valley villages before heading off to the mines. We can see what transpires, what they use for money, and maybe even find out a bit more about the mines and Mr. Jilbin Farnsmuth."

Malachai answered, "Sounds like a plan to me. Bridget, which village do you think would be safest?"

"Well," she said thinking as she sat on Cho's back, "there is a fishing village on the edge of Everly Lake. Perhaps that would be the safest place. Oz told us that a lot of different people come and go there from all over Zanchier. We would draw less attention to ourselves there."

Simon climbed up behind Bridget and Annabelle. "All right, then, Everly Lake it is."

Malachai and Vashti rode with Dominic on Paxton, who now was larger than Mother. Wade and Prisca mounted Mother, and the band of travelers were off once again. Searching for the best way to acquire the large amounts of minerals they would need.

The trip to the small village at the edge of Everly Lake took them just over an hour. They decided to leave the animals at the forest's edge and walk the remainder of the way into the village. For their safety, as well as the villagers. They didn't want to draw any attention to themselves until necessary. This was to be a quiet, watch and learn expedition.

They walked the lake village for the next hour, listening, watching, and interacting as little as possible. They noticed the currency to be some sort of coin. One man in particular carried bills and seemed to be further up on the social scale than most everyone else here. He also had a few servants that followed and watched over his purchases. His purchases were loaded into a cart pulled by a massive beast that resembled a horse. Unlike the horse however, this creature was much taller and broader. It had strange, straight, braided looking strands that fell from its neck like a mane and the same for its tail. It also had three split-toed hooves to support its massive frame. It wasn't as large as the Pagorinx, but it was much larger than a Clydesdale.

Dominic asked Bridget, "Do you know what that thing is called?"

"No. This is the first time I've been to a local village or even seen one for that matter."

Bridget concentrated just a bit and the creature began to prance nervously, turning to look at her. It's handlers grabbed at the reins trying to quiet the beast.

"Settle down, you daft beast!" one of the men yelled.

Bridget grinned to herself. "It's called a Yarequu."

Simon and the others looked at her in surprise. He asked, "How do you know that?"

"I just asked him what he was." She smiled at Simon.

Simon shook his head. "Your gifts amaze me, and I have seen a lot in my years. But to speak with animals… I just can't fathom it."

"I must say, I *truly* enjoy my gift."

Dominic, Wade, and Annabelle all shook their heads in agreement. Bridget smiled broadly at Simon and the other Dragoman, garnering a like response.

Prisca replied, "And we are grateful for your abilities. They have saved us much trouble many times now."

Malachai stated softly, "To God be the glory!" Making everyone smile once again.

After a few more minutes of watching, Simon said, "All right. I think we've seen enough."

"But how do we figure out where and how to get some of the local currency," Malachai asked.

"I have a plan." Dominic smiled.

Everyone looked at him with curiosity.

"I'm sort of a good pick pocket. Something my brothers taught me growing up. Just as a game. I never used it illegally, although a few of my brothers tried to get me to."

"Yet now you would do so?" Simon admonished.

"The way that man is throwing money around, and lording his power over the vendors, he won't miss it. Besides, he is cheating people. I've been watching him."

"Two wrongs do not make a right," Vashti added.

"No. But I won't feel guilty about taking from him like I would someone else. Besides, does anyone else have a better idea?"

Simon sighed. "No. I suppose this is the only way." He looked at Dominic seriously. "Don't get caught."

Dominic smiled assuredly. "I won't." With that, he walked off, blending into the crowd as he made his way toward the wealthy man and his servants.

Dominic grabbed what he assumed to be an apple off the end of one of the market stands. As he approached the Yarequu, he connected to the animal telepathically. The Yarequu turned its large head in his direction, snorting a reply. Dominic grinned mischievously as he got close to the beast, then stuck his hand out flat for the creature to take the offered fruit. The Yarequu took the offering and danced around a bit, backing up the cart making his handlers take notice of him and distracting his owner. As the hefty man yelled his discontent at his servants and the creature, Dominic took his chance. He passed by the man without being noticed, reached into his large, over-sized pocket, and plucked out his money pouch without a hitch. He quickly threw it into his own side pouch and slowly made his way back to his friends.

"I never would have believed it was so easy if I hadn't seen it with my own eyes," Wade exclaimed as his friend sat back down.

Dominic shrugged his shoulders and grinned.

Simon looked at Dominic over his spectacles and said with amusement. "Yes. Very sneaky indeed. However, it isn't a talent I want you using often."

"No Sir. I would never." Dominic feigned injury, holding his chest.

Simon raised his eyebrows in warning, unsure as to the real meaning of Dominic's playful reply. Dominic grinned broadly at him.

"All right. We've got what we came here for. Now let's get back to the forest and the creatures, figure out how much this is worth, and see about contacting this Jilbin fellow." Simon stood and the rest followed him out of the village and into the surrounding trees. As they walked, they could hear the exclamations of the angry man whose pouch of money had suddenly disappeared.

For I command you today to love the Lord your God, to walk in obedience to him, and to keep his commands, decrees, and laws; then you will live and increase, and the Lord your God will bless you in the land you are entering to possess.

Deuteronomy 30:16

Chapter 11

Craco, Italy, 1964

Alec, Odessa, and Oz walked the empty, overgrown, cobblestone streets of the once vibrant city of Craco. The city was forcibly abandoned just the year before due to natural disasters that had plagued the city for hundreds of years. The most recent being a series of landslides, causing the government to force relocation of the thousand or so remaining residents.

Alec turned to Odessa to ask, "Dee, where are we supposed to find the Shields? Did your vision give you any details as to how to find them?"

"Unfortunately, no. I think we just have to figure that part out." She turned at the sound of Oz's Portgen receiving a call and they all stopped walking for a brief moment while he conversed with Simon.

Alec jabbered frustratedly in French, then said in English, "This is a very large place to search." He threw his hands up to the heavens and stated, "Lord, we trust you. But is it too much to ask for a *little* more to go on here?"

Odessa smiled to herself. She did love her crazy Frenchman. Attitude and all. Their temperaments complimented each other well. She was glad she finally had the good sense to realize how important he truly was to her.

"Well?"

"Well what?"

"Did He answer?"

"Ha...ha...ha," he replied with a scrunched-up face as he approached her. Stopping nose to nose with her. "You Madam are a vicious tease."

"Yes. And you love me for it." It took all she could muster not to giggle at him.

"All right you two," they heard Oz bellow. "None a' that now. We're on a mission 'ere." He grinned as they turned to look at him.

"Spoil sport," Alec tossed at him.

"That's right, an' don' you ferget it," Oz tossed back.

The three of them ventured the streets once again, discussing possible places in which to find hidden religious relics.

ST. Dunstan's in the East, London, England, Present Day

Kristen, Sean, Nick, and Nadia marveled at the beautiful architecture of the once magnificent building. They wandered silently for a few moments just taking in their beautiful surround-dings.

The London Blitz of the early 1940's nearly destroyed the entire city and many other areas throughout London. The historic and centuries old St. Dunstan's Church was nothing more than a shell after the bombing by the Germans. The building was left derelict and unused for many years until the city turned the remaining shell into a beautiful city garden for all to enjoy.

Trees were planted throughout the courtyard which now laid within the unroofed walls of the old church. Vines and flowers crawled their way along the semi-cracked walls and beautifully arched windows, and benches and fountains dotted the open area.

Kristen loved all things nature related and historical. But this building held a special place in her heart.

"I remember seeing this church once in all its glory."

Sean asked surprised, "When was that?"

"When my medical troop was transported through the area on our way to the Western European Front during World War One. The US then declared war on Germany over the supposed Zimmerman Telegram in 1917. Our military was small back then and many people who weren't drafted volunteered to serve." For Kristen, that was just about two years ago. But where she stood today, that event took place more than one-hundred years before. *How strange it is sometimes to live this way of life,* she thought. The church of course looked vastly different now, but still strangely mesmerizing and beautiful in its brokenness.

Sean knew the memories this place must recreate for her. He knew that she still had nightmares sometimes from serving in that war.

"You know, as nice as this is, I'm pretty certain that we'll have to venture further back in time to actually be able to search the church. I doubt the shields would be hidden in anything that was left after the 1940's bombings."

"Yes. I agree. We'll likely need to go back before that," Kristen said.

Nick put in, "I'd say *way* before. As far as history is concerned, the earlier the better. Less people to interfere with our search."

Nadia looked at him. "True, but not too early. We have no idea when in history the Armor of God was separated."

Sean replied, "Yeah, but the armor was separated way before this church came into existence. How some of it ended up here is beyond me? This church had to have been established long after the Knights Templar existed in all their hay-day."

"Who knows," Kristen put in, looking up at the clear blue sky through what was once the roof. "Things get thrown out, misplaced, forgotten about over time. Only God knows how they came to be here. And what time period in which we can find them."

"We had best get started then," Nick stated.

They all agreed, picking an earlier period in time when perhaps the shields could be found. One where the church was still intact.

Cappadocia, Turkey, Underground City of Derinkuyu, 1925

Gabriele, Timothy, Alicia, and Trenton walked the long distance across the sands of Cappodocia.

"We should have brought horses," Timothy groaned.

"It isn't so bad." Gabby looked at him disbelieving. "A little walking never hurt anyone."

"Maybe, but it's really hot too," Timothy groaned again.

Trenton teased, "Too bad your armored skin doesn't cover temperatures as well."

Timothy shot a snide look at the older man.

Alicia and Trenton exchanged amused glances.

"It isn't much further." Gabby smirked at him.

"Are all these pointed, elongated tubes part of the city?"

"No. Derinkuyu is completely underground. The entrance is literally a hole in the ground with steps leading into it. There are several of those apparently. The underground caves are supposed to run for miles in every direction, connecting other cities together. But I suppose that depends on what time in history you visit the city."

Trenton supplied the answer to his question. "These tubes are made of the same material as the city below. Most of these tubes did supply homes or business for people though. They may have lived above ground until trouble arose, then disappeared below for protection."

"We're here," Gabriele announced as the group came to an abrupt halt.

"How do we know that no one is still living down there?" Alicia asked.

"Well, we can't be certain that no one is. But according to the information given to us by the Dragoman, the last inhabitants were in 1923. All we can do is hope."

With that, Gabby began the descent into the underground city, pulling her flashlight from her pack before walking below the earth's surface, the others doing the same.

Mesa Verde, Cliff Palace, Colorado, USA , 1888

Zaccai looked up at the cliffs above them, scanning the area for the famed Cliff Palace.

"Zeke, it's sort of hot. Can you give us a little cloud cover? It would make it easier to scan the cliff tops as well."

"Sure, give me a few seconds," came his reply.

Sofia said, "I guess Fall in the desert is about the same as Summer." She fanned her perspiring skin as she shrugged out of her lightweight jacket.

Rourke looked at her and grinned lopsidedly.

"This kind of weather doesn't really bother me. Being a cowboy from way back, this feels like home to me."

"Well Yippee-Ki-Yay for you," she responded sarcastically.

Rourke laughed. "My, my, my, aren't we a bit testy."

"Sorry. I get like this when I am exceptionally hot and uncomfortable."

Just then, a large mass of clouds rolled in, covering the entire area in a blanket of shade.

Sofia sighed. "Ahh…bless you, Zeke."

"Yes. Thank you, Zeke. I was beginning to fear for my life with Sofia's present mood." Rourke teased.

Zeke smiled. "Happy to oblige. Don't want anyone dying over some excessive heat."

Zaccai smiled broadly at the banter of her companions.

Suddenly Zeke's horse stopped moving as he whistled lowly. "Would you look at that!"

All eyes turned to where he was looking. High up the cliffside they could make out the top part of the Cliff Palace. They all sat stunned for a brief moment. The information and photos they received about the place didn't quite do it justice. The sheer scope and size of the palace, and the fact that it was built on the underside edge of a cliff was truly something to witness in person.

"Now *that* is impressive," Rourke stated.

"No joke," Zaccai said. "I can't wait to scale that cliff and get a closer look."

They spurred their horses forward, wondering what would be the best angle from which to approach the palace.

"Should we drop down from the top or climb up from the bottom," Sofia asked.

Zaccai replied, "Let's take a look around and see what we think would be best. There's got to be a way up. Someone built the place, so it has to be accessible."

They found a place to tie off the horses and began the climb up the side of the cliff, able to use the growing vegetation to help pull themselves along.

Zeke glanced upward. "I think this might take us a few hours to scale."

"Well then," Zaccai replied, "I suggest everyone dig in, pull up your big boy pants, and start climbing."

"Can't you manipulate the plants to help us somehow?" Zeke asked.

"I can make them grow, but I don't see how that would help us," Zaccai replied.

"Maybe you could make a bridge or something all the way up?" Sofia said.

"Hmm…that might be an idea." Zaccai stopped her climb, looked at the best possible access and began weaving the local limbs, vines and plants to form a path to easily pull themselves up the cliffside toward the palace. A few minutes later they had what looked like a rope bridge all the way up.

"That was a good idea you guys," she said, admiring her handiwork. "I forget that my powers can be used for things other than fighting demons.

"Impressive work," Rourke stated.

Zaccai turned to him and grinned. "Thanks."

The four of them once again began the climb up the cliff. Hoping that instead of two hours, the rope bridge would cut it down to one.

Al Khazneh, Petra, Jordan, 1800

The horses meandered through the desert sands between the large rock cliffs as the group rode through the Siq; the entryway into the city of Petra. The rocking and bouncing motion thankfully having no effect on Caroline. Either the powder was working, or the nausea was just nonexistent at the moment. She hoped it was something that would pass quickly and not hang around for weeks or months. She was grateful for the powder Safra gave her, and that it wouldn't harm the baby in any way.

"Would you *look at that!*"

Jason's exclamation of surprise shook Caroline from her thoughts, as she gazed at the enormous size and beauty of the carved building in the city. It had six huge columns, carved decorative windows, and stone etchings and figurines that went from the ground up the side of the mountain, hundreds of feet straight up. The sands below dotted with few other nomads there, trading and wandering through the city.

Memnah grinned at his response. "I have seen this place many times in my day."

"Really?" Seth asked.

"Yes. My people traded with other tribes along this route. Many different people would frequent here, as well as the nomads who would come and go. Petra is but a day's walk to

Timna, or half a day by horse or camel. My people know these desert lands well."

"In that case," Jason stated, "anything you can tell us that might help us locate what we came for?"

"Perhaps? I have been inside Petra a few times. Not all of the ancient city was accessible due to cave-ins or certain tunnels being sealed off. I do remember overhearing stories when I would come with my father. I was just a small child then, but the whispers of buried treasure deep within the mountain city captured my attention, as well as several other children. We would make up stories and games about looking for the buried treasures of Petra." Memnah finished her story, her wistful expression and emotion in her voice relaying the joy of the memory she had shared.

They stopped the horses, dismounted, and tied the reins around an obliging carved surface of the rock. They all walked beneath the massive opening of Al Khazneh -which translated to the Treasury- into the massive room. The room was a square block carved into the mountain. Jason noticed Memnah's pause at the door.

"Memnah, are you coming?"

She breathed in deeply and exhaled slowly. "It was always forbidden for the children to enter here. Only my father ever came inside."

"Things are different now. Remember, we are on God's mission. What He deems good, is good."

She smiled at her husband's wisdom. She looked around the room once more, still hesitant to move forward.

"Sorry, years of behavior being ingrained into me makes it hard to take these leaps of faith as you do."

"I understand," Jason said, extending his hand to her. She reached out and took it, allowing herself to be pulled into the room. Jason asked as they walked, "Do you maybe know what we might be looking for? A particular place or room? This place is pretty empty except for these large pottery pieces and urns."

The main room of the treasury was very large in size and rectangular in shape. There were three other doors off of each of the other walls.

"I doubt you'll find much more in any of the other rooms. This city has been looted for thousands of years."

Memnah and Jason walked into one of the other rooms, while Seth and Caroline searched the other two. They searched anything that looked as though it would hold a large item like a shield. They found nothing, meeting back in the main hall.

Seth stood with his hands on his hips. "Well, looks like we need to try another building."

Jason answered, "Yeah. Let's go explore some more of the city."

The four of them left Al Khazneh, mounted their horses, and rode through the narrow gorge toward the open area of the city.

Reader's Island, Present Day

Safra was in the archival library that morning when Heba appeared looking upset.

"Heba, is something the matter?"

Heba babbled frantically in her native tongue as Safra tried to understand what she said as she pointed to the back of the house.

Just then, Dekker appeared, quickly walking over to calm his friend. He asked her what was wrong and when she had answered, he turned to Safra.

"Renquin is sick again this morning. And she says he is much worse than yesterday."

"Let's go see." Safra motioned for Heba to lead, and they followed her to the servant's quarters in the cottages at the back of the house.

They walked in to find Renquin lying in his bed. Safra bent over him, his forehead feeling cold and clammy to the touch.

"I believe we must return him to Akrotiri. His body can't take the change in climate."

Dekker related the message to Heba who replied, and he translated.

"Why is Heba not sick as well?"

"Perhaps it has to do with her age. She is much younger than he is."

"How are we going to return him to Akrotiri without Gabriele being here. I thought we needed her gift?"

Safra stopped and thought a minute. "When we were there, my Portgen got opened up by some local children. If that was possible then, perhaps we can find coordinates for that position in my Portgen. I'll be right back. I need to go see Ryan."

Safra left the cottage and went to the computer room where Ryan mostly stayed.

"Ryan, I need you to see if you can find some coordinates on my Portgen." She explained to him what had happened while in Akrotiri, and what they needed to do now with Renquin.

Ryan took the device from her. "I can try, Safra. It sh…should have them saved so…somewhere in the m…memory."

"Thanks Ryan. Work quickly though. We need to get him home as soon as possible."

Ryan pushed some buttons, turned a few knobs, then plugged the device into his mainframe computer. In a matter of minutes, Ryan had exactly what they needed.

Safra returned to the cottage with the information.

Dekker looked at her worriedly. "What if the Portgen won't work that way?'

"We won't know until we try," Safra stated.

"Isn't it dangerous?"

"Again, we won't know until we try. It's either that, or we leave him here to die."

"All right," Dekker sighed. "I suppose we need to get him up."

Heba and Dekker each grabbed Renquin under an arm, as Safra punched in the coordinates that Ryan had given her. A portal opened in front of them, but they were unable to see through to the other side.

"Let's go," Safra said, stepping through. The others directly behind her.

Craco, Italy

"Hey fellas, come look in here," Odessa stated, entering the doors to what appeared to be a sort of church. The room was relatively small in size. Barely large enough for twenty people standing shoulder to shoulder.

Alec and Oz peered inside behind Odessa.

"Looks like a good place ta hide somethin' religious ta me," Oz said.

"Yes. What better place than a church." Alec stepped inside, perusing the outer edges of the room along the walls, gazing at some artwork hanging there.

Odessa walked to the stone altar in the center of the room near the back. It stood near chest height, about five feet, was about three feet wide and four feet long. She felt the edges of the top which protruded out over the base of the altar. She then bent down and peered up at the top from underneath. She called Oz who stood nearby.

"Oz, come take a look at this."

Oz walked over, bent down to take a look at what was so interesting. It appeared that there were small pieces broken around the top of the base, and that the solid top flat piece was actually some sort of lid.

Odessa looked at Oz. "Do you think it's this simple?"

Oz answered with, "Not *ever'thin'* has to be difficult does it?"

"I hope not." She smiled.

"You two find something interesting over there?" Alec asked as he approached them.

"Alec, grab th' other end there, will ya'?"

Alec stood on one side of the stone top of the altar, with Oz on the other.

"Lift on three," Oz said.

The two men hefted the heavy stone slab up and over to one side, grunting and groaning as they did.

Odessa quickly peered down in the base of the altar, reaching down to clear away hundreds of years of cobwebs. She smiled broadly as she hefted out two shields from the altars hidden open base, leaning them against the outside of it.

"I think we found them," she nearly sang in excitement, brushing at the grime and webs to reveal the embossed symbol on the front of one of them. One symbol was for the tribe of Reuben; a bunch of flowers raised from the center. The other shield was for the tribe of Asher; a goblet sat in the shield's center. The shape of the shields were in a teardrop design that was wide at the top and narrowed to a flat bottom, half the width of the top, just at knee height. They were pretty large in size, although amazingly light in weight.

"Alec, help me put the top back on." Oz stated. When they had finished, Oz grabbed one of the shields while Alec grabbed the other.

Alec smiled triumphantly. "Great! Now we can return to the island. This is the fastest mission I think we have ever had."

"All right, boys, let's head home." Odessa smiled.

The three of them left the church building, pulling the doors closed behind them, each feeling joyful over the ease of the mission. Just as Odessa was about to open the Portgen for home, ten demons appeared, walking out of the barrier, all around them.

"You have *got to* be kidding me," Alec said, securing the shield with a rope and throwing it around his back.

"So much fer easy," Oz stated, doing the same.

The demons charged and a battle ensued. Odessa, Alec, and Oz all split up, running through the streets of the city of Craco, demons hot on their trails. Three following each Alec and Odessa, and four taking out after Oz. They needed to somehow level the playing field. They were all gifted warriors, but to fight with more than one at a time with no back up was tough.

Alec yelled to no one in particular as he looked back at the demons running after him. "We should have stayed together!"

He searched frantically for an advantage point from which he could fight better. Noticing a spot just a tad higher above the street, he teleported himself there, leaving the demons behind in a stupor as they stopped and searched for him everywhere. Alec crouched behind an obliging, low, stone wall and thought for a moment about his plan of attack.

He peeked over the low wall, spied one of the demons, who unfortunately saw him at the same time, took aim with his pistol and fired. He struck the demon between the eyes but alerted the other two to his location. He took aim again, standing and firing at them, one after the other, killing them both.

The next street over, Odessa's premonitions gave her a few seconds advantage over her attackers. She could see what was coming up. She ducked into a building to hide as the demons ran past her, stopping when they realized she had disappeared. Just as they turned to look for her she stepped out.

"Looking for me," she asked as she laid one to the ground with a swing of her katana as the other two attacked her from each side. She swung and leaped into action, running quickly and jumping up on the wall and pushing off, flying through the air, spinning, and slicing at another demon who had changed to its true, hideous, form and flew at her. Each flap of its wings blowing the awful stench of death all around her. It too soon fell to the earth, dead.

As she fell to the ground landing on her feet, but having to regain her stance, the third demon lunged at her. Its thin blade at the top of its weapon catching her on the bicep and cutting the flesh. She twirled, whipping her katana around her body like the samurai warrior she had been trained to be, slicing at the beast, killing it.

As she stood there catching her breath, the demon remains dissipated and floated up into the sky and were whisked away by the breeze. She resheathed her weapon, took a quick look at her arm, and ran off in search of the others.

Oz, who decided to stand his ground and stop running, took out one demon with his sword, another with his power to liquefy them from the inside out, and fought with the other two, a sword in each hand. While he was fighting one demon, the other grabbed the shield at his back and yanked, cutting it free from the rope which secured it. Oz was surprised by this but had to do battle with the beast in front of him as the other ran off.

Oz sliced at the creature killing it, then took off after the other demon which had suddenly disappeared somewhere in the city. As he ran around searching, he heard the squeal of the beast and ran in the direction of the noise. Rounding the corner, he saw Odessa picking up the shield which the creature had stolen from him.

"Lose something." She smiled at him, holding the shield up and throwing it over her shoulder, across her back.

"Glad ta see ya there, Lass. I sure didn' want ta 'ave to run after that thing. Not as young as I used ta be ya know." Oz smiled at her, leaning over, breathing hard.

Alec suddenly appeared from around the corner, taking instant notice of Odessa's arm.

"You're hurt," he said, coming to look at the wound.

"It's fine. Nothing that can't be patched up," she replied.

"Then let's return to Reader's Island and do just that," Alec replied.

Odessa removed her Portgen and the three of them returned to the island. As they walked through to the other side, they were quickly met by Ryan who told them of Renquin's illness, and

Safra, Dekker, and Heba's mission to return him to Akrotiri early this morning. He explained the details of his discussion with Safra.

Oz looked at Odessa and Alec. "I hope they actually made it. I fig'red the only way down there was by the barrier."

Odessa looked worried, "Let's hope that whatever coordinates that Ryan found on Safra's Portgen worked."

Alec asked, "It is nearly noon, why do you think they have not yet returned?"

Odessa sighed heavily. "I have no idea. And Simon isn't here to ask what we should do."

Oz answered, "We'll give 'em a bit more time. Then, we'll get those co'rdinates from Ryan, and go lookin' fer 'em ourselves."

And without faith it is impossible to please God, because anyone who comes to Him must believe that He exists and that He rewards those who earnestly seek Him.

Hebrews 11:6

Chapter 12

St. Dunstan's in the East, London, England, 1200 AD

St. Dunstan's church was all of one-hundred-years old and the building looked vastly different than it had only moments earlier. The church itself would undergo several makeovers throughout the years to come, due to fires, invasions, and natural disasters. But it was the oldest church in London in present day, surviving more than nine-hundred years.

Sean had chosen this particular era because of the Knights Templar. They lived and thrived in this era, and since they had also possessed the Breastplates of Righteousness then perhaps they had also had a hand in hiding the Shields of Faith. And what better place to do so then in a church?

They opened the doors to the main building, calling out to anyone who might answer. No one replied. They hoped that meant that whoever stayed and ran the church might be away at the moment.

"Well, what now?" Sean asked, glancing at the wooden beams of the ceiling and the tall, graceful windows.

Nick said, "I guess we split up and see if anything calls to you."

"Right," Sean stated flatly.

They all went in opposite directions in the church, looking closely at anything that looked large enough to hold a shield or two. They opened doors, lifted lids, peered under pews, tapped the floors wooden surface for any hollow sounds, moved tapestries to the side for any hidden safes. Unfortunately, they came up with nothing. Just as they gathered in the center of the large room, the main doors opened and in walked two men in robes.

The men stopped suddenly, looking them over, amazed by their strange clothing and the weapons they carried.

"Can we help you?" one of the monks asked cautiously.

Nick answered, "Yes, father. We are weary travelers who have come to see St. Dunstan's Church which caters to travelers such as us."

"Well, we'll do our best to assist you in your needs," he answered.

Just as Nick was about to speak again, a hoard of demons burst through the door of the church, many in their true forms. The monks were taken by surprise and shock. They ran for cover and began praying heavily and loudly as a battle broke out between the travelers and the demons. They took shelter behind whatever safety was available as they peered out at the scene before them. The travelers were surely gifted by God to fight such evil.

Nick whispered to his friends, "keep your gifts hidden. These men will claim us to be witches."

Everyone nodded their head in agreement as the demons came at them quickly. There were about twelve in all, leaving them all to fend off about three each. Not being able to use their powers was something they weren't used to, and they had to concentrate to keep from doing so. Sean hadn't really been able to use his much anyway since most of their recent battles had been in the desert.

The battle went on for about fifteen minutes, while the monks shook in fear, but were unable to look away. When it was finally over and the remains of the demons began to dissipate and float out the door on an underlying current, the monks stood and just looked at the four people before them, unable to speak for a bit.

Nick and the others put away their weapons and nervously began to walk toward the monks. The two monks quickly and nervously approached them, shaking their hands briskly and gratefully.

"I don't know who you people are, but you are obviously sent of God. I would have never believed it if I hadn't have seen it for myself."

"Nor I," the other man said. "How can we be of service to you?"

Nick began to explain to them what they were really doing there, leaving out the time-travel part.

"We are warriors for God, traveling across the earth to battle the very evil you just witnessed."

"Yes, this I truly believe! How can we be of help in your mission?" the first monk all but stuttered.

"We've been sent here to retrieve something. A very important piece of armor to aid us in our battles."

The two monks exchanged looks and then turned to Nick once again.

"I believe we may have what you seek."

Nick looked at the others who grinned ever so slightly.

"Where?"

"Follow us," the monks stated, leaving the main sanctuary through a side door that opened into a narrow hallway leading toward the back of the building. "We were given explicit instructions by our predecessors to keep the shields safe until a time when The Chosen would appear to claim them. We truly believe you all to be those people, but we must ask you to reveal your marks. It is written as such."

The monks walked through another door into a small room, summoning them all to follow.

"Before we go any further, we need to see your marks."

They each showed their marks to the men, who seemed satisfied. They looked at Nadia who did not have one to show.

"What about you?" they asked her.

"I am one of the chosen, but not like them," she said, nodding toward Kristen, Sean, and Nick. "I have not been marked by God for this particular need."

"We thought there would be more of you. Twelve to be exact."

Nick cleared his throat. "There are twelve. But the others are on missions such as this to find the shields that are located in other parts of the world. They also travel with those like Nadia who have been chosen to fight the good fight."

"We understand. Besides, we only have three of the shields here. We have no idea what became of the others."

They pushed a bookshelf to the side, revealing nothing more than a stone wall. One of the monks then proceeded to push on one of the stones until a pressurized sound released and a click was heard. Part of the stone wall popped open enough to place a hand behind and swing the rest of the heavy stone door open.

Nick turned once again to look at his friends, excited to find the shields so quickly.

The monks reached into the dark hole and pulled out three parcels wrapped in burlap and linen cloth.

They took the packages and laid them on a nearby table and began to unwrap them.

"We have wanted to gaze upon these for decades, but never had the courage to do so. We were given explicit orders to never open the wall unless for the Chosen."

They laid open the last pieces of material to reveal highly polished and well cared for shields. The symbols embossed in the center of the shields were for the tribes of Simeon — a gate upon a sword, Joseph — shafts of wheat, and Gad — a tent camp.

They all gathered around the table to gaze at the beauty and craftsmanship of the shields. They had obviously been taken well care of over the years. All three polished to a high shine. Each shield had a few dents and dings from the many battles in which they had obviously been used.

Nadia reached out to touch one of the shields. "You've taken great care with these." She looked up at the two monks.

"All we did was hide them. Whoever first put them inside the wall was the one to take such care of them. I must say, for weapons of war, they are beautifully made."

The other monk spoke. "Yes, very. We'll be sad to see them leave. Like part of our mission is over."

Sean said, "That may be true. But you can rest assured that your diligence has paid off, and that these shields will be used to save mankind."

"We are only humble servants of our Lord and Savior. Peace be with you all, although I dare say, peace isn't what you'll get."

Nick smiled at the man's jest.

"You are very right. But once this battle is over, then the world should be at peace, for a time anyway. We also are only humble servants as well."

As Sean, Kristen, and Nick each picked up a shield, they all walked out of the room, back through the sanctuary, and out the front doors. The monks followed closely behind them bidding them farewell.

"Go with God my friends," one yelled as they disappeared around the corner and into the woods.

Once they were out of sight, Nick opened a portal to return to the island.

Cappadocia, Turkey, Underground City of Derinkuyu, 1925

Gabriele shined the flashlight all around, watching where the twisting, volcanic-ash carved staircase went as she descended the steps down into Derinkuyu. Timothy followed, with Trenton and Alicia close behind.

Once below in the first level of the city, it opened up into many rooms, each leading off in every direction through carved doorways. They chose one and walked through, turning around to look at the room. Leaning against the wall by the door opening was a huge, round, boulder which was obviously used to seal off the entrance in times of invasion or possibly adverse weather conditions. It had to take several large, strong, men to move it.

"Which way do we go from here?" Gabriele asked the group.

"How are we supposed to know?" Timothy questioned.

"Maybe we should take a look at the map we were given. From what I understand this place is pretty large."

Trenton chimed in. "Yeah. Large enough to house twenty-thousand people."

Gabriele handed the map to Alicia who unfolded it and held it open for all to see. They scanned the map for possible locations and information that might help lead them to where the shields might be hidden.

"What about this area here?" Tim asked, pointing to a place below on the second level on the map. "The legend says that this was a religious area used for ceremonies and a school."

Gabriele nodded. "Seems like a good place to start."

They refolded the map and placed it inside Gabriele's pack. As they walked, everyone pulled out their own flashlights to guide their way. There were occasional spurts of light here and there, apparently from vents in the city's ceilings that ran all along each level. They also occasionally felt puffs of air as they walked along, passing by the ventilation tubes that ran through the city's walls.

They reached the room in question, noting the size and the vaulted ceilings with smaller rooms located off the larger center area. They all chose rooms and began searching through them for anywhere to hide something as large as shields.

Thirty minutes later they were no closer to finding them and returned to the map once again.

They all scanned the map carefully when Gabriele said, "What about here," she pointed. "Three levels down from here is another church."

Trenton asked, "Why are we only searching religious areas? The shields could be hidden anywhere. Like a stronghold?"

"True, but this place is really huge. They could literally be anywhere. I'm just trying to rule out the most likely places first."

"Exactly. Wouldn't thieves also search those places as well?"

"Yes, if they were looking only for the shields. But if they were looking for valuables, most commoners wouldn't know the value of the Shields of Faith. And most religious leaders, I believe, would want to keep a religious relic safe within the walls of a religious house."

"That's true, possibly thinking that God would protect whatever they sanctified, like the Armor of God." Trenton added. Everyone shook their heads in agreement.

"We can search as we go down, but, like I said, it's a big place," Gabriele offered.

Timothy put in, "We can split up and take separate floors."

"I suppose that would make it go faster," Gabriele stated. "All right, Trenton, you and Alicia can stay here and search this level while Timothy and I search the lowest. We'll work our way up as you two go down. Perhaps when we meet up somewhere in the middle, someone will have some good news. If we miss each other, we'll meet topside of the city in two hours. That should give us quite a bit of time to look."

Trenton agreed. "Sounds like a plan." He and Alicia took off to search more of the second level, while Gabriele and Timothy took a vertical staircase that led to the cruciform church below.

"We'll search the church first, and if we come up empty handed, then we'll go through the rest of the level."

"Lead the way," Timothy said, following her further into the underground city. The staircase twisted and turned a few times as they passed the other levels and continued on lower.

When they reached the level in question, and found the church as shown on the map, they split up.

Gabriele instructed, "Look for anything unusual. There might be a hidden wall or area. Pull and push on anything that might look like it could open a secret passage or wall."

"Got it." Tim walked slowly to take in every little nook and cranny.

"The city, believe it or not, was only abandoned two years ago," Gabriele stated.

"That must be why there is still so much pottery and other items down here."

"Can you imagine having to hide down here to avoid religious persecution?"

"No. We have it pretty good I suppose."

"Yes, we do. We can go anywhere we want in the blink of an eye almost."

"True, but our lives aren't our own. And we battle demons at the risk of death most days."

"Yes, I suppose. But these people had no special gifts or abilities. They lived out their faith without seeing the power of God as we do. Yet they still chose their faith over a normal life."

Timothy thought about what she said. "That's not likely something I would have ever done before peregrination. I was one selfish and self-centered person." Timothy looked at Gabriele who was just across from him, turning her attention to him at his declaration. "That has only recently changed I'm ashamed to say."

"But *it did* change. That's a step in the right direction. Our faith and belief isn't an instant personality change. We still fail, even as Christians. But we have the Holy Spirit to guide us and help us to grow to become more like Christ. We are not perfect, just forgiven."

Timothy looked at the young woman whom he had come to respect greatly. The more he knew about her, the more he liked her.

"How did you get to be so wise for someone so young?"

She shrugged and animatedly said, "Just another gift I guess." She smiled at him.

They exchanged amused looks, both chuckling a little at her exaggerated words. They turned away from one another and went back to the task at hand. Thirty minutes later, after the entire area had been searched with no luck, Gabriele turned to Timothy, a little exasperated.

"Well, where shall we go next?" she asked, pulling the map from her pack once more.

"Let's take a look at this and see," Tim answered, going over to stand beside her. They both decided to sit on an obliging rock. When they did, the rock moved slightly, and they heard rock scraping rock as something opened somewhere within the room.

They quickly shined their flashlights all around them trying to find where the sound was coming from.

Gabriele noticed the movement just behind a solid, tall, stone table in the rooms center. "Tim, look." She pointed to where her light was shining. The center of the stone table had slid open to the left, revealing an opening large enough to squat into. They both stood to walk over to the opening, and it began to close.

"Wait," Gabriele halted. "One of us needs to stay here and provide pressure to the lock mechanism."

"All right, you stay, and I'll go check it out under there."

"I don't think you'll fit Tim. It's a pretty small area. Why don't *you* stay here, and *I'll* go check out the opening?"

"All right. Just be careful. We don't know what's down there. It could be a trap."

"Then you'll figure out a way to rescue me," she said bravely.

Tim could only smile at her gumption as she walked over and peered down into the hole. There was another small staircase that led down into the underside of the table, off to the right. She stepped inside, being able to stand up fully after taking a few steps down. There was a small room located beneath the table about ten feet square. In the corner sat a few items wrapped in dingy, dusty, old cloth. She walked over to see what it was and partially unwrapped one. She smiled, knowing what she saw to be the shields. She hefted the two items, throwing the sacks over her shoulder and carried them up the staircase. She pushed them through the stone passage and climbed out herself.

"Is that what I think it is?" Tim asked grinning.

"It sure is." Gabriele smiled.

"Let's have a look then." Tim stood and walked toward her. The stone door slowly resealed itself with the release of Tim's weight on the rock.

They fully unwrapped the shields, shining their flashlights to take in the details.

Gabriele looked at the raised emblem in the centers. "This one must be for Naphtali. See the stag. The other is for Issachar."

"Is that a pack donkey?" Tim asked bewildered.

"Yes." She smiled at his amused disbelief. "One translation for the name Issachar is 'for hire'."

"How do you know all of this stuff?"

"My parents were big into religion. Father was a sailor and a scholar. I learned a lot from both of them. Plus, I do take it upon myself to study. The things of God interest me greatly."

"Now I feel bad again." He stated flatly. "I guess I need to do better in a lot of areas."

"It certainly wouldn't do you any harm," she said pointedly, standing up and picking up one of the shields.

Timothy followed her example, and the two of them left the room headed back up to try and locate Trenton and Alicia. Their mission was now over, and they could head back to Reader's Island.

Mesa Verde, Cliff Palace, 1888

Zaccai led the expedition up the mountain, reaching the top in record time. The four explorers breathed heavily over the exertion of the climb. The vine bridge made the climb easier, but they still had to pull themselves almost straight up the cliffside.

"Whew," Zeke breathed, "that was some climb. I say we take a little break and grab some water before we go exploring."

"Good idea," Zaccai stated. Sofia and Rourke not protesting.

They sat quietly for a few minutes, drinking from their canteens, and slowing their breathing and heart rates.

Zaccai looked around the ancient dwelling. She broke the silence.

"Anyone have any idea where to start?"

"Not a clue," Zeke replied.

"I'd say, wherever looks safest," Sofia said.

Rourke put in, "I'm not sure *safe* is an option. There's a lot of loose rubble lying around those ancient structures."

"Let's keep that in mind shall we?" Zaccai said, standing. "We certainly don't want to get caught in an avalanche of rock and stone."

"Agreed," Zeke stood to follow her, Sofia, and Rourke directly behind him.

They walked the cliff trying to stay on the backside of the loose rocks lying about, the large rock overhang above their heads providing shelter from the scorching sun.

Sofia noticed a tug at her laces. She looked down realizing her shoe was untied and she had stepped on it with her other foot.

"That could add to the already serious trip hazards out here," she said, stooping to tie her boot.

At that moment, an arrow whizzed above her head. She looked up and yelled at the others. "I think we have demons on our tails!" She hurriedly secured the loose lace.

Everyone took off running for the safety of one of the interiors, making it inside as arrows flew by, bouncing off the stone walls.

"Everyone all right?" Zaccai asked.

"Yeah," they all replied.

"What is with everyone's demonic perception lately? We used to be able to sense these things coming?" Zeke replied.

"We used to be more alert on missions too. Before our powers, we relied heavily on our skills. Perhaps we need to start paying more attention," Zaccai stated.

"We can't hide in here all day," Rourke said. "Aren't they usually more up front with their attacks."

Sofia said, "Maybe it's not demons. It could just be a local tribe protecting their home."

The others looked at her.

"Could be," Zaccai replied. "Maybe that's why we didn't sense demons?"

They changed positions, going to another window linked with the same dwelling. Zaccai scanned the adjacent clifftop, while the others looked to the tree and bush covered landscape.

"There," Zaccai motioned with her head. "Just on the lower part of the ridge. I saw movement. Who or whatever it is, is slowly making its way toward us."

"I see movement on the other side too," Rourke put in.

"Then let's get ready to do some battle." Zeke took up his sword.

"We don't want to kill the locals," Zaccai admonished.

"No, but I don't wish to be killed either. It's them, or us," Zeke answered matter-of-fact.

"Give me a minute to determine what we're dealing with here," she replied.

Zaccai raised her hand toward a small bush growing near where the approaching person slunk through the shrubbery. The bush's began to grow, reaching out toward the man and entangling him in its branches. He struggled for a brief few seconds before his form changed to a winged beast that tore through the vines with its claws and the force of its powerful wings.

"Demons!" Zaccai stood up from her crouched position, pulling her bow and an arrow from her back. She ran through the doorway, her loaded bow in hand. Everyone else followed her, doing battle against the demon hoard that suddenly fell upon them.

Zeke sliced at a beast, the rocks slipping below his feet, but aiding in saving his life from the demon's blade. He swung at its legs, severing one as the beast fell over and he pierced it's chest.

Rourke was running along the top walls of the Palace, a gun in one hand and a whip in the other, while Sofia ran below, each in a battle of their own. Rourke leaped, flipped, and rolled in battle against the winged creature. Finally winning the fight as his whip wrapped around the beasts neck holding it in place long enough for Rourke to shoot it between the eyes. As it fell toward the ground dead, Rourke's whip wouldn't release it's hold, pulling him down with it. By the time he let go of it, he was dangling from the top of the wall with one hand, trying to best gauge where and how to fall without breaking his neck. All of a sudden his body was being lifted off the wall by a large vine which sat him down on the ground. He looked around to see Zaccai, fighting a demon and saving his life at the same time. He smiled at her, tipped his hat, grabbed his whip from the now disappearing demon and took off after another beast.

The fight lasted another five minutes, with Sofia slaying the last demon. They all looked at one another, tired and a little worse for wear, each of them baring new wounds.

"Let's find these shields and get out of here. I'm ready to fight the Final Battle and get on with my life," Zaccai stated wearily.

"These demon wars seem to be almost every few days now. Anytime we step off the island they attack," Zeke said.

"Let's get on with it then. I say we all split up. We can search faster that way."

"Groups of two," Zaccai said. "This place could come crashing down around us if we make the wrong move."

They agreed. Sofia and Rourke went one way, while Zaccai and Zeke went the other.

Akrotiri, Present Day

Safra, Heba, Dekker, and Renquin walked through the portal into the city of Akrotiri, grateful that the coordinates that were locked into her Portgen were viable. She had hoped that it wouldn't send her into whatever world the young Akrotiri boy had entered into.

The good thing was they were in Akrotiri, the bad thing was that they were a two hour walk across the city and outlands to Renquin's village and home, and there was no way the man could make that in his weakened state.

"Dekker, do you have your Portgen on you?" she asked him.

"Yes. Why do you ask?"

"I'm going to run to Renquin's village, load my coordinates and you can pass easily through."

Dekker translated for Heba.

Heba began speaking in Akrotirian.

Dekker addressed Safra, "Heba says to take him to her home. She will care for him there. It is much closer."

"How much closer?"

"Less than an hour."

"Do you think he can make it that far?"

"I'm not sure." Dekker looked at the pale man.

"Well, then, I'll run to Heba's instead. Once inside, I'll open the Portgen to these coordinates here, and you can all walk through. Give me about fifteen minutes."

"Can you run it that quickly?" Dekker asked surprised.

"We're about to find out."

"Safra, do you remember where she lives?"

"I think so. I'm not one-hundred-percent positive, but God will guide me."

Safra took off running as fast as her feet would let her in the mostly unfamiliar terrain. She prayed as she went that God would quicken her pace, guide her in the correct direction, and allow them to save Renquin's life.

But how is it to your credit if your receive a beating
for doing wrong and endure it? But if you suffer for doing
good and you endure it, this is commendable before God.

1 Peter 2:20

Chapter 13

Petra Jordan, 1800

Caroline looked around at the carved façades of the ancient stone city of Petra. A look of peaceful joy on her face.

"Seth, isn't this place amazing? I can *just imagine* the hundreds of generations that have lived here."

"Yes, it certainly is ancient."

"Ancient is right. The name itself means stone in the Greek language. I've read articles in the library that said Petra is believed to be one of the cities the Israelite people passed through when they wandered the desert. Perhaps they passed through the Siq."

"Your knowledge never ceases to amaze me." Seth smiled.

"Isn't it interesting to think that we are traveling the same path that they did thousands of years ago."

"Yes, I guess it is," he answered appreciatively. "Not to change the subject, but I'm glad to see you're feeling better. Your nausea seems to have left. The medicine Safra gave you must be working, or your over whatever it is that was making you ill."

Caroline swallowed hard, pasting on a quick smile. "Yes. I'm feeling quite well now."

"Good. You had me worried there for a bit."

"I'm fine Seth. Really. You have no need to worry about me."

He smirked. "Unfortunately, worrying about you is not something that ever fully goes away. Especially with the sort of life we lead."

She smiled at him. "I know what you mean."

They rode a little further until they came to more places with tombs carved into the sides of the mountain. Stopping to look at the information given to them, they dismounted to discuss their next step.

"So, what are all of these holes all over the place?" Seth asked.

Memnah answered him. "Most are tombs. Especially the ones that are higher up."

"I doubt the shields are hidden in a grave," Caroline said.

Jason asked, "Well, according to the information given to us about the area, what would likely be the best location for them to have been hidden?"

"What about here," Seth said pointing. "There is a Monastery located right here." He lifted his head to compare where they were on the map to the location of the building.

"It looks to be a good way up those steep rock steps," Caroline said.

"Yes, Al Dier. That is the Monastery up there," Memnah stated. "I know just where it is located. But the climb is not an easy one. It will likely take us a few hours."

"Do you think we should check out everything down here first?" Caroline asked. "Just so we don't have to walk back down again if we find nothing up there."

"That's a good idea, and we can't use the Portgens. Someone here would likely see us," Seth offered, watching the strained look on Caroline's face.

Jason said, "Well, we are here to search for the shields, and the most likely place to hide a religious item would be a religious center, building, or temple."

"The Great Temple is just a bit further down the street. It is the religious center for Selah," Memnah stated. They all looked at her questioningly. She smiled at her mistake.

"Sorry. Selah means rock in Hebrew. As a child we knew this place as Selah. The Gentiles call it Petra."

Everyone shook their heads in understanding.

Jason asked, "Where exactly is this Great Temple?"

Seth looked over the map. "It looks to be up that way just a bit."

"I can show you where everything is here." Memnah smiled.

"Great." Jason smiled. "Lead on, wife!" he teased, making her smile even bigger.

Caroline was feeling a bit more tired than usual, attributing it to being a result of the pregnancy. She was grateful not to have to walk the eight-hundred and fifty steps up to the Monastery. If she were already starting to be affected by this pregnancy, how in the world was she supposed to fight a dragon in the coming weeks or months? *Lord, I need your strength and guidance,* she silently prayed.

Everyone rode along, quietly enjoying the beauty and majesty of the desert city. Caroline was feeling like the horse rode her instead, but she was trying to look normal or Seth would start questioning her again.

Jason asked Memnah, "Did your father bring you to the Great Temple when trading in Petra?"

"A time or two, yes. But it was mostly the religious leaders who met there. Each tribe present would meet and discuss business. We children mostly played on the steps up to the Monastery, or in the city center until our fathers returned. Sometimes, on rare occasions, mothers would come along to reign us all in while the men tended to business."

Memnah smiled at the memory.

Jason enjoyed listening to her memories, noting the difference in what she described and what transpired around them now. "It seems so empty. Even though it is a mere forty years earlier. Why do you think there are so few people here?"

"It is between seasons. The summer trading has ended, and the fall harvests are now being gathered. We have actually come at an opportune time. In a few weeks there will be many people here trading. It would have made our quest very difficult. Many prying eyes and questions from the religious leaders."

They rode through the large stone gate and began their ride down the colonnaded street. Broken columns lined the sides of the half sand, half stone road. The remains of what was once buildings, some now only crumbling heaps of stone, dotted each side along the road as well.

They road along the street eventually coming upon a very large structure. The Great Temple, even though worn as well from the elements and the years of raids and takeovers, was still in decent shape.

"Let's leave the horses here," Memnah stated, dismounting.

They all did as she suggested, following her lead around the side building into an arched stone passageway that slanted upward, implementing some steps along the way.

"This leads to the Propylaeum, the Cryptoporticus and the Lower Temenos."

Caroline smiled at the questioning looks from the men's faces, so she explained. "The entrance to the temple, a covered passageway, and the open sacred area surrounded by a low wall."

Her explanation lent understanding to them and they shook their heads.

Jason asked Memnah, "Sweetheart, could you speak in layman's terms please. Then Seth and I wouldn't feel so mentally outranked by you two."

"Sorry," Memnah stated sheepishly. "I've just heard these terms my whole life. That is what I know them by."

They passed through the Cryptoporticus and out onto the Lower Temenos, which was a large open courtyard area. The area was flat and empty with stone steps leading to the Upper Temenos, theater, and residential living quarters. They walked the stone steps to the upper level, taking in the scenery. Each searching a different area for anything that looked like it could hide a few armored shields. Once on top they all separated and went in different directions to search deeper into the area. Thirty minutes later, they all met back at the top of the stairs, empty handed.

"Now what?" Caroline asked, getting hot and agitated by the glaring noon-day sun.

Seth noticed her mood. "Why don't we find some shade and have some lunch."

Jason answered. "Sounds like a good idea. We can go back down to the covered passageway and eat. It's close to the horses, and we need to give them a drink as well."

"Yes, we can pull them into the shade of the entryway with us." Memnah led the way back down and they sat for the next hour, eating lunch ,and resting beneath the coolness of the stone archway overhead.

"Where do you all think the shields could be?" Seth questioned.

"I'm not sure," Jason replied.

"How about the tomb of Aaron?" Memnah questioned.

"Such as, *'the Aaron'*, brother of Moses?'" Caroline asked surprised.

"Yes. The very one," Memnah stated.

Jason sat up. "Is his tomb one of these here in the valley?"

"Well, not exactly in the valley here, but on top of the mountain."

"Great! Lead the way." Jason stood up, picking up his pack and placing it back in his saddle bags. Everyone else did the same. Caroline moved with disdain at having to travel so far up the mountain in the heat. She wasn't usually so agitated about such things. Her hormones must be raging for her to feel so discontented at the moment.

Seth noticed that Caroline was not herself this afternoon, and his concern for her began to grow as he watched her agitated body language.

"Memnah, it's a pretty long ride up the mountainside, right?"

"Probably a few hours at least."

"Isn't this the hottest time of day here?"

"Yes. It would be cooler to make the trip later this afternoon. For the horses as well."

Jason said, "Yeah, but the sooner we find the shields the sooner we can leave."

Seth looked at Jason with a slight nod no. Jason looked slightly confused but decided to ask him about it later.

"But I suppose we can wait until it cools off. Let's find a place to rest in one of these big buildings in the façade of the mountain."

"There is a place we can rest near the staircase to the ridge," Memnah said.

"Lead on," Jason stated, looking back at Seth. The look on Seth's face was one of concern as he closely watched his wife.

Seth watched Caroline fanning her face. He knew it was hot, but she was always one to be cold natured. The heat didn't seem to be affecting anyone else like it was her. He'd have to talk to her about letting Safra look her over when they returned to the island.

They all mounted their horses once more and followed Memnah as she led them across the colonnaded street and through the street of façades to where they would rest for the next few hours until traveling would be easier on Caroline.

He didn't know what was going on with her, but when this mission was over, he hoped they could find out.

Derinkuyu

Gabriele and Timothy, each with a shield strapped to their backs, climbed the narrow, vertical, staircase looking for Trenton and Alicia.

"Trenton…Alicia!" Gabriele yelled, her voice bouncing and echoing through some of the rooms on the fourth level.

They listened for a few seconds. After which Tim called for them once more, getting no reply.

"They probably didn't make it down this far yet. We'll likely meet up with them on the third level."

"Maybe," Gabby replied. "I wonder if our Portgens will work down here? I have yet to use the communications feature."

She pulled out her Portgen, turned it on and pushed the call button. A blip suddenly appeared on the screen and was moving rather quickly.

"Tim, does this look like they could be running to you?"

Tim leaned over, looking at the small screen.

"Maybe. The location pins are so small it's hard to tell. But, since they are so small, the fact that there is movement at all might suggest that *they are* running."

"That's what I thought," Gabby said frantically.

"You think they are in trouble?"

"Most likely."

The two of them climbed the staircase as quickly as they could with Gabriele watching her screen, trying to locate which direction the ping was coming from. When they reached the third level, the blip moved to the west on her screen.

"This way," Gabby said, running toward the blip. "I think we are getting close." She pulled out her weapon, as did Timothy.

Just at that moment, Trenton and Alicia appeared nearly directly in front of them.

"Run!" Trenton yelled at them.

They all took off toward the east, trying to find a place to hide quickly, and having a very hard time seeing where they were going.

"What are we running from?" Timothy yelled over his shoulder to Trenton.

"Demons!"

They came into a medium-sized room with crates stacked against the walls and rotting hay lying about.

Gabriele stopped and turned to fight.

"We can't keep running. Let's just get it over with."

They were soon overtaken by the handful of demons which entered the room.

Gabriele threw up her shield, covering herself, Trenton, and Alicia, whom she noticed was limping. Gabriele battled a beast with her free hand.

Timothy jumped out in front, no fear of the demons blades even scratching his armor-like flesh. They fought hard and long in the small room, Trenton, and Alicia each being pushed off into another separate room or area to fight a beast alone.

Timothy had slain one while another turned its attention to him. Gabriele was fighting off two, deciding to let her shield go and use both hands.

They heard a scream from the other room, catching their attention. Gabriele quickly killed one demon while Timothy, finished slaying his own, turning to kill the other one she battled.

They both ran in the direction that the scream had come from, finding Alicia lying on the floor. They both yelled for Trenton, waiting to hear him yell back.

"Over here!"

Gabby and Tim took off again, finding him with his back to the wall, and three demons wailing against him.

"Hey fella's what say we even up the odds," Timothy said, running over and knocking one to the ground, stabbing it through the heart. Gabriele took out another one as Trenton finished killing the last demon.

They stood there for a brief second, before Gabriele turned and ran back to where Alicia lay, quickly followed by Tim, and Trenton.

Gabriele bent over trying to see if there was any sign of a pulse, but there was none. Another friend and ally claimed by the demon hoard.

They all stood there in silence for a few seconds, not knowing what to say to one another.

"We need to take her back to the island for a proper burial," Gabriele said.

"I'll carry her," Trenton said, his voice thick with emotion.

"I'll help," Tim stated.

The two men exchanged looks and Trenton nodded his thanks.

They picked up Alicia's limp body while Gabriele tried the Portgen.

"It won't open down here. You'll have to carry her topside." She looked apologetically at the two men.

The three of them hefted Alicia's body out of the underground city. Once outside, Gabriele immediately opened the Portgen and they were home on the island. Unfortunately, they had one more loss to this terrible ongoing battle with the dark forces that were trying to destroy the world and everything in it.

Reader's Island

Oz, Alec, and Odessa were still discussing the possibility of having to fetch Safra and Dekker from Akrotiri, when Gabriele, Tim and Trenton appeared from a portal, carrying Alicia.

"Not another one?" Oz said, running out to meet them, followed closely by Odessa and Alec.

"Le' me guess?" Oz questioned. "Demons?"

"Yes. Unfortunately, we didn't all make it back alive." Sadness and frustration masked Gabriele's emotions.

"Let's take 'er up ta the house," Oz said. "Put 'er in the libr'ry on the table. I'll talk ta Shannon and Clancy 'bout what ta do." Oz walked away toward the kitchen to find Clancy.

Some of the housekeepers and groundskeepers suddenly appeared, mourning the loss of their friend. Gabby and Tim decided to give them some peace. They discarded the shields on the table next to Alicia's body, and then went up to their rooms to leave their packs.

Gabriele sighed heavily, frustration lacing her words. "I'm so tired of losing people to this war!"

"Yeah, I know what you mean. I'm not particularly close to anyone here, but watching everyone die, and the sadness it leaves behind…well, I've had enough myself."

"Maybe the Final Battle is close at hand and we can finally end all of this." Gabriele stopped in front of her room; her arms crossed over her chest.

Tim reached out and pulled her face up to look at him. "I hope so Gabby. I just worry about you, and the others of course, having to fight four dragons." He slid his hands down her arms and pulled her in toward him to give her a hug.

They stood there for a minute, just leaning on each other. Gabriele finally pulled back and looked at him.

"I think I need some time alone. I'll see you downstairs later." She stepped out of his embrace and disappeared into her room.

Tim did the same, taking a few minutes to lie back on his bed and spend some time in prayer. It was something he was growing accustomed to doing, and he could feel the comfort of God's presence more and more each time.

Akrotiri

Safra ran as fast as her feet would carry her, jumping and leaping off any surface that got in her way. She was close to reaching Heba's home, remembering now where it was. She had been running for nearly sixteen minutes now and had to be very close. She rounded a corner and nearly passed it up. She turned quickly, kicking the door in, and running inside. She opened her Portgen to where she had left Dekker, Heba, and Renquin. Thankfully, a portal opened and they quickly hefted the ailing man through the portal and deposited him on Heba's bed.

Safra took her medicine bag from Dekker and began administering to the needs of Renquin.

Dekker and Heba stood discussing what they could possibly do to aid his failing health.

Heba was so distraught she began crying. Dekker tried to comfort his friend.

"Dekker," Safra said, "let her know that I believe he will be all right after a good night's sleep. He is resting and seems to be breathing a bit easier now. Perhaps being back in his native environment was all he needed."

"Perhaps," Dekker replied. "His old body may have not been able to handle the oxygen rich air."

"Most likely. It could also have been overexposure to the sun. He isn't used to that kind of heat. He likely is experiencing some dehydration as well. Ask Heba to get me some water. Let's see if we can get him to drink."

Dekker translated and Heba grabbed a pitcher and ran outside. She soon returned with a full pitcher, grabbing a glass from the counter, and pouring some water into it.

Dekker and Heba helped Renquin sit up, while Safra guided the glass to his lips to drink. He took a few sips of the cool liquid before they laid him back down.

Safra watched Heba. The woman's facial expression conveyed her worry, but she seemed to be handling it better now. Safra considered their situation. She and Dekker would have to stay longer than predicted. Perhaps she could take the Portgen and return to the island just to let them know what was happening. If she knew Simon, he would likely send out a search party for them if they didn't return soon.

"Dekker, you stay here with Heba and Renquin. I'm going to return to the island to let them know we are staying until he gets well. I'll return shortly. Anything you need me to grab for you?"

"That's fine, and no. I have all I need here. If we have to stay longer than a night, we can go tomorrow and grab some clothing and bath essentials."

Safra agreed. She tried to open her Portgen right there in Heba's home, but unlike last time, it wouldn't work. She would have to walk back through Akrotiri to the same spot they had entered through.

"I'll see you all later." She left the house, and an hour later she walked through the portal, and back into the library where they had peregrinated from. She looked around at the commotion in the room, noticing people gathered around someone lying on the large table at the center of the library. She walked over, noticing that one of the housekeepers named Alicia was now dead.

"What happened to her?" Safra asked stunned.

"Demon raid," someone bounswered.

She turned sharply. "Not here on the island?"

"No. She was with the Derinkuyu party looking for the shields," someone behind her answered.

Safra sighed deeply. "Will this ever end?" she asked no one particular. "I'm assuming some of the other parties have also returned?"

"Yes, Oz, Gabriele, and Nick's groups are all back already," answered the one called Katerina, who stood sniffling over her friend's untimely death.

Safra left the library headed toward the kitchen, first checking the rooms she knew people would likely be located. As she entered the kitchen, she saw Clancy and Henry preparing the dinner meal.

"Clancy," she called, "Dekker and I will be staying over in Akrotiri until we are certain how Renquin is doing. Would you please let the others know of this decision? I don't want anyone worrying about us."

Clancy grinned stiffly in her direction. "Sure thing, Safra. I'll announce it around dinner."

"Thank you. I'm going to grab some more of my medicines and other supplies then leave again."

"No problem."

"I saw what happened to Alicia. I'm sorry for your loss, Clancy, Henry." She looked at the men. "I know she's been working here on the island for a long time."

"Yes," Clancy said, heavy hearted. "But so did so many of the others."

She excused herself and went out to the staff quarters where she had been staying, lost in thought as she went.

Safra understood his mood but couldn't truly mourn the loss much. Her older-self surely could have, but at her current age, she had spent little time in the presence of many of those who had perished. She had known a few from several occasions here and there, but Simon was the only one she truly knew well. And strangely enough, Seth, from when she was but sixteen and he, a boy of nineteen; cocky and headstrong. Enough so as to be talked into a large tattoo. She smiled at the memory, finding a small piece of joy in one of the few memories she had of these people.

Speaking of Seth, she wondered how Caroline was faring with the morning sickness. She would check back as early as she could tomorrow. Perhaps Caroline's group would be back by then, and she could see if she needed anything else, or if the nausea powder had worked.

Safra gathered her things and opened a portal back to Akrotiri, praying the old gentlemen would recover from his recent exploits.

Do not conform to the pattern of this world, but be
transformed by the renewing of your mind. Then you
will be able to test and approve what God's will is.
His good, pleasing, and perfect will.

Romans 12:2

Chapter 14

Zanchier

Simon was growing accustomed to riding on the back of the
Kabihanxu. The colorful plumage lending explanation to its
common name, the firebird, used by the people of Zanchier. It
was amazing to think that such a massive creature could be
gentled by the Keepers. Some mere children, young men and
women called by God. They were all very brave in Simon's book.
Never before in the history of the Dragoman archives had he ever
found where people so young were used before now. Perhaps
children were more drawn to animals and less likely to fear them
as adults do. Perhaps that was why they were all called to serve
so young.

Bridget telepathically instructed Cho where to go, leading
the group toward the Carpasian Mountains and the Rhe mines.
Only this time, instead of flying overhead they would have to be
more evasive. They would land in the wooded area south of the
mine's entrance and loading area and walk the remainder of the
way so as not to frighten everyone into hiding for fear of the
Firebird. They needed to locate Jilbin Farsmuth as quickly as
possible.

Cho slowly descended into the massive tree canopy below,
hopping down through the branches to light upon the forest

floor. The Pagorinxes met up with them on the ground only seconds later.

Bridget turned to speak to the animals.

"All right you three, stay here in the woods until we return. No eating anyone, understand?" she gently admonished them.

Cho and Paxton nuzzled her and the other three Keepers with their heads, signaling their understanding. All three animals curled up on the forest floor, tucking their heads into their bodies to rest and wait on their return.

Simon waited for the keepers to join their traveling party before addressing the group.

"We all stay together if possible. I don't think demons are an issue here in Zanchier, but we certainly don't want to run into any Scaithers either. When we get to the forest's edge, we stay hidden until we locate Mr. Farnsmuth. We'll formulate the rest of the plan as we go."

They walked as quietly as possible through the forest, being only a few hundred feet from the edge line. The loading area lay just south of the mine's main entrance. The road in and out of the mines was between the loading area and the woods. The group squatted in the brush, peering out at the activity in the loading area where a six wheeled wagon pulled by four Yarequu was being loaded. It took only a few minutes to locate the man Oz instructed them to find. Jilbin Farnsmuth was just as Oz had described him. Older, slightly hunched over, thin, wiry, and dusty looking. His beard was nearly as long as his entire body, thick and scraggly, almost touching the ground. The hair on his slightly balding head stuck out in all directions. The color of it was hard to distinguish, but it appeared to be light in color, probably light gray beneath the mining soot and road dust.

Simon took his glasses and pointed them at the sun, letting the glare reflect off the glass, creating a glint of light at the forest's edge. He aimed the light at Jilbin Farnsmuth, hoping to catch the man's attention. And it appeared that he had. The man looked in their direction, shook his head and kept walking, turning a corner around a wagon currently being loaded and disappearing out of sight.

Simon sighed heavily. They sat still, waiting for Jilbin to reappear. Just a minute later he came back around the large wagon and Simon tried his glasses once more. Jilbin Farnsmuth noticed the glint again. The man looked around, back over his shoulder and made his way cautiously across the road.

Simon and the others looked at each other with small grins of hopeful triumph on their faces.

As Jilbin got closer, he stopped fifteen feet before the edge of the forest.

"Who's that there?" he questioned cautiously.

"Oz sent us," Simon said, standing so the man could see him.

Jilbin's bushy eyebrows shot up. "I ain't spoke to Oz in a bit. Why didn't he come hisself?" Jilbin questioned curiously.

"He isn't in Zanchier anymore. We are very old friends of his from somewhere else. We are in need of a great deal of Rhenium and Ruthenium. He said you could help us."

"He did, did he?" Jilbin scratched his thick dirty beard. "Well, how much we talkin' about here?"

"I'm not sure. How much pure minerals remains after refining?" Simon questioned. "We need enough to coat twelve suits of armor, plus weapons."

"Hmm." Jilbin thought for a minute then looked around to make sure no one was approaching . "That'll take quite a bit. How you gonna' carry that much out a' here?"

"Don't worry about that. We have transporting the minerals covered."

"That kind of supply will cost ya' a lot a Rhedons."

"Is this enough?" Simon asked, tossing the satchel of money at the man.

Jilbin caught the satchel, opened it, and peered inside. His eyes lit up and he smiled, revealing a near toothless mouth.

"You can buy *me* fer *this* much Rhedons." Jilbin laughed in a high-pitched cackle.

"We only need what I requested. You can keep the rest as a bonus."

"I'll have to see how to smuggle out that much product. I'm sure I can figure it out though. I'll leave yer purchases here tonight. Right behind the bushes yer hidin' in."

"Thank you. We'll be back then," Simon stated.

Just then, a large, leather-clad man appeared at the wagon, and Simon quickly disappeared behind the bush.

"Jilbin!" he yelled. "What are you up to, old man?"

"Just takin' a leak! Can't a man go to the bathroom in peace anymore?" Jilbin said; doing exactly that.

The women behind the bushes quickly turned away, trying to cover their astonishment by throwing their hands over their mouths and eyes. Wade and Dominic did all they could not to burst out laughing. Simon and Malachai tried shushing them so as not to blow their cover. They too also trying to keep their amusement intact.

"All right, you old coot!" the man yelled. "Hurry it up and get back to work."

Jilbin waved the man away, finished his business, and whispered, "See ya' after sundown." He then turned and walked back to the mines.

They walked back into the forest toward the animals.

"So, what do we do for the next four hours?" Malachai asked.

"Good question," Simon replied.

Prisca answered with, "I think we should just curl up here with the animals and all take a little nap until tonight." She sat upon the forest floor, leaning up against Mother who purred at Prisca's touch.

Bridget looked up at Cho who began nervously dancing around and looking to the sky hidden above the trees.

"Cho seems to be getting anxious for something. I think she needs to return to her nest. I'll go with her and return before the night gets here."

"Can I come with you, Bridget?" Dominic asked.

"I suppose so."

"Bridget and Dominic climbed onto Cho's back, and the firebird climbed the upper branches of the trees until she reached the top and was clear to fly.

They soared through the sky for hours, coming to a high and secluded cliff area where the Northern Xantifal and Southern Bakrashan Mountains collided. Bridget had only been here once before, but late at night. Cho circled the clifftop, coming to land on a niche tucked neatly under a high cliff. Bridget and Dominic slid from Cho's back as she went over to a large nest and turned over the three, large, yellow eggs, covered in colorful orange, red, and purple spots.

"Cho, your eggs are so beautiful. Will they hatch soon?" Bridget walked over to lean on the edge of the nest and peer inside. Cho bent down to nuzzle Bridget and lowly squawked.

"Now that Han is gone, you have to take care and raise them all on your own." Bridget sadly touched the smooth surface of one of the eggs, her eyes filling with tears threatening to spill over. She sniffed as her nose began to run. Cho leaned into her once again to comfort her.

Dominic sat and watched the exchange. Realizing just how close Bridget had become to the animals here in Zanchier. She had a very special bond with all of them.

Cho sat upon the eggs for the next half-hour, warming them, as Bridget and Dominic sat on the edge of the nest chatting and looking out at the striking countryside below. They had to be in the highest point in the whole of Zanchier and could see almost all of it from this angle. Bridget had thought the treehouse was the highest point, but the firebird's nest was higher still. After Cho had finished her motherly task, she covered the eggs with the loose materials lying about her nest. Then the two of them climbed onto her back, and they flew out across the Bakrashan Mountains and lower territories toward the Northern Carpasian Mountains and the Rhe mines.

When they reached the area in the woods where they had left Simon and the others nearly six hours earlier, they found them all sitting around and chatting while Mother and Paxton drank from an obliging stream just a little way off. Cho deposited her riders on the ground and went to the stream to do the same.

"Where have you two been?" Wade asked.

Dominic answered. "Cho took us to her nest. Her eggs needed tending too."

"I should have gone with you two. I would have liked to have seen them again."

"As would I," Annabelle said excitedly.

"They are very pretty." Bridget told everyone all about their experience. They sat and talked for the next few minutes until Simon stood up and announced that it was time to go.

"We'll have to take the animals with us this time to carry the minerals. If what Jilbin said is true, we'll have quite a haul."

"At least the sun will have gone down by then and no one will see them," Malachai stated.

"We hope anyway. Of course, if any light shines our way, they might likely see eye-shine from the Pagorinxes," Simon replied.

"Do you suppose Jilbin will have left by then?"

"Let's hope so. I have a feeling he won't react well with us having the animals."

They walked through the forest as quietly as possible. The Pagorinxes were stealthy as usual, but Cho, not being used to walking anywhere for very long, had a harder time being quiet. Her large body had to squeeze through some rather tight areas, and she was becoming agitated by it. The four Keepers tried to calm her and help as much as possible.

Simon turned to Bridget.

"Bridget, keep Cho here until we return. We'll take the Pagorinxes with us. Surely the two of them can pick up the rock."

Bridget nodded her agreement.

"Dominic and Wade, you two come to control them. Annabelle, you stay here with Bridget."

They left and walked the remaining one-hundred or so feet to the edge where the minerals were waiting, stacked in eight, large, crates with woven rope tied around each one.

"Good grief," Simon exclaimed. "How are we to carry all of this back. I'm not sure the animals can handle the weight, plus us."

Malachai said, "Well, all we can do is try it."

Wade said, "Paxton should be able to carry two and Mother two. If we can get the other four to Cho, she surely can handle the rest with her four claws."

"Let's take the four to her first and then we can come back to get the rest," Dominic suggested.

"How do we get them onto the animals?" Vashti exclaimed.

Dominic took one of the loose pieces of rope and tied it around Mother's neck, making sure it wouldn't slip and choke the animal. Then he tied one of the crates to the other end of the rope. Wade had Paxton lie down beside the crates, and Dominic led Mother, having her heft the crate until it laid over Paxton's back. They continued until they had four crates tied across Paxton's back. They walked back into the forest, dropped those to Cho, and went back to continue in this manner until all crates were loaded. Cho picked up the four crates. Two with her beak and two with one front leg and one with a back leg so she could climb the trees and take to the sky.

They walked back into the woods, climbed onto the animal's backs, and an hour later were headed back to the Bakrashan Mountains and Storm Valley. They would head directly home, not wanting to unload and reload the crates again. The traveling would take them longer, as they didn't wish to tire or injure the animals. What normally took two hours, taking them three.

They returned to the island by seven that night and unloaded the crates near the barn and the forge with the help of the others there on the island. Then the Keepers returned the animals to their homeland of Zanchier, bidding them farewell once more.

Mesa Verde, Cliff Palace

Zaccai searched through the lower places of the interior buildings on the right side of the city, while Sofia searched the left. The men took the high places of the city, splitting it into two sides as well. Zaccai walked out of one of the lower rooms surfacing on the ground floor level. She and Zeke appeared in the same room.

"Any luck?" she questioned.

"Nope. You?"

"Nothing that even resembled a hiding place. Maybe Rourke or Sofia found something."

"Let's hope so."

They walked around the medium-sized room, finding nothing, and exited out onto the open courtyard. Rourke was coming down one of the lower broken walls where they converged.

"Any sign of Sofia?" Zaccai asked him.

Rourke answered, "Last time I saw her was about fifteen minutes ago when she disappeared underground near the end over there." He pointed to a walled recession in the ground.

"Maybe we should go check on her?" Zaccai stated, walking in the direction he had pointed.

They reached the recessed area, noticing an opening leading into the rock below. Zaccai stepped down and climbed into the hole.

"Sofia!"

"Right here," came a voice behind her, startling her.

"Warn a woman, will you?" Zaccai stated, breathing hard.

She looked down at Sofia's hands. "You found them!"

"Yes. They were in an underground tomb belonging to what I believe must have been a religious leader amongst some of the people who once lived here."

"Awesome. Now let's get out of here. It's nearly evening and I'm ready for a nice hot shower and my comfy bed back on the island."

"I hear you sister."

They climbed out of the hole, passing the shields off to the men to admire. They had found two shields representing the tribes of Benjamin—a wolf, and Manasseh—a horned anvil.

"Time to head home," Zaccai stated.

The men held onto the shields as the four of them climbed down the braided vine bridge. Once at the bottom, Zaccai commanded the vines to return to their original state of being before they mounted their horses and rode through the portal and onto Reader's Island.

Petra Jordan

Caroline slept soundly in the cool darkness of the cavern while Seth, Jason, and Memnah sat up watching her.

Jason asked quietly, "So what's happening with her Seth?"

"I have no idea."

"Maybe she's just worn out?"

"Maybe. But why? No one else seems to be affected this way."

"We don't know that?" Jason stated. "We haven't really been around anyone else much lately."

Memnah sat and listened, throwing in what she believed might be the answer. "Could she be pregnant?"

Both men turned to look at her, then quickly turned to look at Caroline's sleeping form. Seth abruptly turned back to look at Memnah.

"She was nauseous early this morning, and last night."

Memnah shrugged her shoulders. "It could be pregnancy. But I'm sure if that were the case, she would have told you."

"Maybe she doesn't know it yet?" Jason stated, as the three of them looked back and forth between themselves and Caroline.

Seth stammered, "Surely it's not that. Maybe it's just a little virus, or she's just really tired."

Memnah smiled at his failing abilities to explain away the mysterious illness with which Caroline was dealing.

Seth nervously looked at his wife again, then turned to them and asked, "Do you really think she could be pregnant?"

Memnah smiled broadly. "Anything's possible, Seth. I mean, you two have been married for six months now."

"Yeah but, we were separated for four of those."

"And reunited for two." She smiled and chuckled at his dumbstruck face.

"Why now?" he asked confused.

Jason asked, "What do you mean?"

"She's one of The Twelve, Jason. She has to fight in a battle against dragons. Dragons that may be *so fierce* that if we fail, we apparently lose the fight to save mankind. Don't you think God *could* have waited for *just* a little longer?"

"Look, Seth, that might not even be what's wrong with her. It could just be that the heat today got to her on top of some… temporary illness."

"Let's hope so."

Seth was stunned that pregnancy could even be on the table *at all* at this point in their lives.

They sat and talked about other things for the next four hours while they waited for the hottest part of the desert day to pass. Caroline's current possible state of being never leaving Seth's mind as she slept nearly the entire time. When she finally woke, her color and attitude seemed to be better.

Seth wanted to ask her if she could be pregnant but decided to wait until after this mission was complete, and they could get back to the island.

"Feeling better?" he questioned.

She stretched her long frame while walking over to stand where they sat.

"Yes. I feel much better." She grabbed her canteen and took a long cool drink.

Jason spoke up and said, "It seems to be cooling off some outside now that the sun is beginning to go down. Let's get to Aaron's tomb and pray the shields are there. I'm ready to get home."

"Me too," Seth replied.

"Me three," Caroline stated.

Memnah simply smiled. She was used to this way of life. This area technically was her home up until just a few days ago.

They all stood, grabbed their packs and horses, mounted up and rode up to the top of Mount Hor.

Aaron's tomb was marked with a white mosque and made of stone bricks. They tied the horses to a small tree that stood about thirty feet from the tomb and walked up the small staircase onto the platform that sat at all four sides of the sand-worn, half-white painted building. They walked around to the door and entered the tomb. Once inside, they marveled at how large it actually was. The rounded, concaved ceiling of the domed roof led to slightly pointed archways supported by large columns at either arch. The floor was faded with decorative tiles in one area, and rectangular, smooth, stone pavers in others. There were a few small stone decorations. One looked like a chest carved from one solid stone piece. It was about three feet high, four feet long, and two feet wide. It had small, arched, false windows carved in the sides and square columns on each corner with domes on the top. A crack started at the floor and ran up the middle of the center window, ending where the curved roof met with the sides. A center steeple rested on one end of the box above an arched stone impression of a door that looked as though it opened but was sealed tightly and smoothed over with concrete.

"Do you think the shields could be in there?" Caroline asked.

"Maybe, but let's have a look around first before we have to break into something like that," Jason answered.

They walked the room, descending down a set of stairs that led to a lower level of the tomb, searching anything that looked to be of interest.

"I believe you're right, Caroline," Jason stated after a few minutes. "That chest on the other level must be where the shields would be hidden. It was certainly large enough to hold something of importance."

Seth said, "Well, let's go see if we can get it open."

They walked the steps back into the room, stopping at the stone chest.

"Now what?" Caroline asked.

"I can easily break it open," Seth stated.

Memnah protested. "You cannot! It is sacred to the tomb!"

Jason said, "Well how else are we supposed to get into the thing?"

Caroline had bent down to examine the sealed front of the chest.

"It appears there is a cutaway around the door here. We'll just have to chip away at it until we can open it. See here, near the bottom on each side. The seal doesn't go all the way to the bottom of the chest."

Everyone bent down to look at what she described.

"We will need a hammer and chisel for this," Seth observed.

"How about a small knife? I think I have just the thing." Jason smiled and pulled out the jewel-handled knife that Memnah had given him when they had first fallen in love and had to say goodbye. "A gift from someone very special a few months back."

He and Memnah exchanged smiles as Jason began digging at the mortar that plastered the edges of the door. The task took them half an hour with Seth and Jason taking turns picking and prying at the mortar little by little until the door was free.

Seth picked up the stone slab door like it weighed nothing and set it aside, leaning it against a parallel wall.

Jason took his flashlight and shined it inside the interior of the box, pulling out three wrapped parcels, all the size of the very shields for which they searched.

"I think we're in luck." He handed them off to the others as he pulled them from their resting place.

"I wonder how long they have been in there?" Memnah said in awe.

"There is truly no way of knowing," Caroline stated.

Seth, Caroline, and Memnah all began unwinding the rope from around the cloth covered items. They held three shields, each one representing one of the twelve tribes of Israel. Caroline held the shield of Levi; the Ephod embossed on its center. Memnah held the shield of Zebulun. A large, detailed etching of a ship graced the front. The very shield that Caroline would carry. Caroline smiled when she saw it, exchanging shields with Memnah. Memnah handed hers to Jason. Seth unwrapped the last piece of linen cloth to reveal the shield of Judah. A mighty lion roared on the embossed surface of the shield. He gazed at the image, running his hand over the smooth, cool, metal surface.

"Whew!" Jason whistled lowly. "These are something."

"They are absolutely beautiful!" Memnah exclaimed.

"Great. We've got what we came for, now let's head home," Jason stated, standing.

Memnah objected. "We must first replace the door back in the chest."

"We have no way of resealing it," Jason stated.

"We do not have to. Just put the door back into place." She insisted.

"Fine. Seth, would you do the honors," Jason asked.

"Sure, hold this." He handed Memnah his shield and set the heavy stone door back into place in the stone chest.

They grabbed their packs, walked out of the tomb into the edge of darkness and mounted their horses. Caroline was last to get on and pulled up the rear of the group.

Just as she had gotten situated in her saddle, she was lifted off her horse and into the night air.

"Seth!" she screamed.

Seth and the others turned around to see Caroline being lifted into the air by a winged demon. She struggled to reach her knife in the top of her boot.

Memnah pulled back with her bow and arrow and released a shot at the beast, making it turn toward them. Several more demons appeared out of nowhere and a battle ensued.

Seth tried to keep his eyes on Caroline as he fought. He turned just in time to see her flung into Memnah, both the woman tumbling to the ground. Memnah from her horse from the force of Caroline being thrown into her. Seth slayed the two beasts he fought against and ran to Caroline's aid. The thought of her possible condition caused fear in his heart.

She and Memnah stood, each engrossed in battle with demons themselves. Seth quickly killed their tormentors, rushing to Caroline's side.

"Are you all right?" he asked her, grabbing her upper arms.

"Yes, Seth, I'm fine," she stated.

"Are you sure? Nothing's wrong. Nothing hurts anywhere?"

"Yes, Seth. What's wrong with you? Why are you acting so crazy?"

Their conversation was interrupted by more fighting until the last beast was done in.

"Seth? Are you going to answer my question?" she pried.

"I'm just concerned. That's all."

"I can see that. What I don't know is why."

"Can we discuss this when we get back to the island?"

"Why can't we discuss it now?"

"Fine. I was worried about, you know…," he motioned to her stomach.

"No, I don't know." She crossed her arms over her chest and waited for his explanation.

"We just thought that maybe, since you've been so sick, you might be pregnant?"

Caroline's posture changed, and she dropped her arms to her side. Seth could see the truth of it written on her face.

"You are pregnant!" he stated loudly. "And you know you are? Why didn't you tell me already? Something really bad could have happened Caroline!"

Caroline sighed heavily. "Because, Seth, I didn't want you freaking out and treating me like an invalid. Or worrying constantly about me while we fight demons, or dragons for that matter. You know, like you are now!"

"That isn't exactly something I can control. Excuse me for caring about my wife's life and that of our unborn child!"

"Neither of us can control what is going to happen, Seth! I *still* have to fight as one of The Twelve. Pregnant or not!" She picked up the shield which was slung off her back when she had been thrown to the ground. She walked over to her horse, jumped back into the saddle, and opened a portal for Reader's Island. Seth, Jason, and Memnah followed quietly as Jason slapped Seth on the shoulder for comfort.

But store up for yourselves treasures in heaven,
where moths and vermin do not destroy, and
where thieves do not break in and steal.

Matthew 6:20

Chapter 15

Reader's Island, Present Day, Nighttime, Late Evening

Caroline rode toward the stables, noticing eight huge crates stacked near the forge end of the barn. She dismounted from her horse, leading it inside and began removing the saddle and tack to brush the animal down. She was throwing the saddle over the stall wall when Marnor walked in. She sighed heavily, in no mood to deal with anyone else tonight.

Marnor noticed her agitation but spoke anyway.

"I'll do that for you."

"I can manage…thanks."

"You've had a long day. Besides, it gives me something to do. A way to contribute."

Caroline looked at him for a few seconds, finally conceding.

"Fine. It's all yours." She handed over the reins, grabbed her pack and the shield, and briskly walked toward the house.

Seth watched the interaction intently, hearing their conversation. He still didn't like the man, but at least he was trying to do something to help out. He noticed Marnor did whatever needed doing. No questions asked.

Seth watched Caroline stalk away in agitation. He had put his foot in it again. But, he had a right to be angry as well. She had known she was pregnant. *How long had she known?* he wondered. He never thought Caroline would keep such a secret from him.

Marnor looked at Seth and held out his hand.

"I'll take care of all the horses." He then turned to Jason and Memnah so they would understand that he meant theirs as well.

Seth handed over the reins, nodded his thanks, grabbed his pack and shield, and headed off after Caroline trying desperately to catch up to her before she could lock him out of their room again. They needed to hash this out tonight. He was not about to let this one go. He was not in the wrong this time.

The two of them quickly strode past the others gathered around the library and headed straight for their room. Caroline gathered clean night clothes, ignoring Seth as she passed by him. He too grabbed some clean clothes and they both headed for the showers.

Jason and Memnah thanked Marnor and left the stables. They slowly walked toward the house far behind Seth and Caroline.

Jason spoke. "Trouble in paradise again."

Memnah smiled. "We've already had our fair share of those problems and we've been together far shorter a time than they have."

Jason laughed. "Isn't that the truth. But I'd rather fight with you any day than to ever live without you."

Memnah smiled brightly. "I feel the same way, my love."

As the two of them passed by the library they noticed the activity within. They soon found out they had lost another warrior to demon wars. They decided to just skip dinner and turn in for the night, both taking quick, hot, showers to wash the desert sand away. They passed a freshly showered Caroline and Seth, in the hallway, both still sulking from their earlier fight. They watched as they both stormed into their room and shut the door.

Caroline went to sit on the edge of the bed to towel dry her long, strawberry-blond, hair.

Seth watched her for just a moment before speaking. He walked over to her side of the bed and sat down beside her.

"Caroline?" he softly spoke her name. She didn't answer. It was unlike her to ignore him. He reached out to stop her increasingly rapid movements before her hair became a tangled mess. At his touch, she stopped moving all together.

"Sweetheart, we need to discuss this. Tonight. We aren't sleeping on this one."

Caroline sighed deeply and turned to look at him.

"Why didn't you tell me you were pregnant?"

"We already went over this, Seth."

"Yeah, we did. But your answer wasn't a good one."

She stood up and started pacing the floor. "I thought it was a great one. Seth, you could get hurt in battle if you constantly worry about me and the baby. You don't need the distraction and I don't need the added problems of worrying about you worrying about me."

"I can't help worrying about you Caroline. I always worry. Even before this." He motioned to her stomach again.

He reached out to stop her pacing, taking her wrists gently in his hands. "It wasn't fair for you to keep this from me. How long have you known you were pregnant?"

"Just since this morning. It never even occurred to me that was what was wrong until Safra said so."

"From now on, you have to tell me things, Caroline. You can't keep stuff like this from me. I have a right to know. It's your body, but this," he placed a hand on her stomach, "this is half mine in here."

Caroline softened at his touch and the emotion in his voice when talking about their child.

"I know that Seth. But regardless of my being pregnant, you have to focus on what you need to do, and please, don't worry. I'm doing enough of that for both of us. All day long I've second guessed every move I make. It's hard enough for me to deal with this without you constantly jumping down my throat or freaking out in a battle."

"I'm sorry. I promise to try harder if you promise to not leave me out of important things like this in the future."

Caroline grinned slightly, leaning toward him. "I'm sorry too, Seth. But *you* have to promise to not make this any harder on me than it already is."

"I'll try." He pulled her into his arms, wrapping them around her waist and planting a kiss on her stomach.

"I don't want anyone else knowing just yet. I don't need more mother hens all clucking around me every waking moment."

"All right. I'll tell Jason and Memnah first thing in the morning."

"Let's hope we can catch them first," Caroline said.

"I'm pretty sure that after the fight we had tonight, they won't be saying anything until they clear it with us."

Caroline giggled lightly. "You're probably right about that."

"You know, I wish I could be more excited about this new development in our lives."

"I know what you mean, Seth. I do too."

They slid into bed, curling up with one another. Intertwining their hands on-top of Caroline's stomach. They both fell asleep silently praying that God would protect them all, especially the new, little, life that grew within Caroline.

The next morning, Seth woke early; dreams of a little girl and boy invading his sleep. He slipped out of bed and went downstairs to the kitchen to make a pot of coffee. After he started the pot to brew, he walked into the grand dining room to gaze out at the moonlit front yard of the estate. The breeze blew gently through the tops of the palm trees, stirring the plants all around the yard. A few leaves from the different types of trees drifted across the patio and pergola, carried away on an ocean breeze. Fall had already started, and the cooler breezes off the ocean could now be felt during the nights.

Seth figured the coffee was done by now and returned to the kitchen for a large cup. When he entered, he was surprised to see Marnor sitting at the counter with an opened Bible and a cup of coffee.

Marnor looked up to see Seth come into the kitchen. He lifted his cup. "I hope you don't mind me helping myself."

"Not at all. I made a large pot knowing everyone else would be up soon." Seth moved to the pot pouring himself a large cup. He then went to sit across from Marnor at the counter.

The two of them sat quietly for a while. Seth noticing Marnor quietly struggling with the words he read. Confusion and frustration were written all over his face.

"Need some help?" Seth asked as nonchalantly as he could. He didn't want Marnor to think that he was judging him on his inability to read.

Marnor looked a little nervous at the realization that Seth had figured out his secret.

"I'm not good at reading. It wasn't something that was taken seriously for my status of people where I'm from. I'm trying to teach myself, with Bridget and Petra's help."

"Well, I'm no bookworm myself, but I can read. If you need help, I might be available sometimes."

"Thanks." Marnor looked confusingly at the huge man across from him.

They sat quietly, drinking their coffee while Marnor sifted through recognizable words in the book. The sun began its morning climb as more people began wandering into the kitchen, claiming the scent of the coffee wafting through the house called to them.

Seth left the kitchen to go upstairs to wake Caroline and see how she was feeling. He passed Jason and Memnah on the stairwell.

"Hey," he said, stopping to chat.

"Morning," they both sang.

Jason asked, "So, how are things with Caroline?"

"Fine. But she doesn't want anyone else to know, so if you two would keep it quiet for now."

"Sure," they both agreed.

"Seth," Memnah said, placing a hand on his, "if she needs anything, just tell her I'm here for her. Whatever it is. We are sisters after all."

"Thanks, Memnah," Seth grinned. He went back upstairs while they continued their descent toward the kitchen.

Simon made his way downstairs, thinking about the day. The first item on today's agenda was the funeral service for Alicia. Then, they would have a meeting to discuss the finding of the shields, the purchasing of the minerals to plate the armor pieces, Safra and Dekker still being in Akrotiri, the continuance of the forge's enhancements, and the making of the swords based on the descriptions of them in the *Book of Armor* and the now translated *Book of the Keepers*.

Simon walked into the already noisy kitchen as half of the house's inhabitants were up.

"Good!" he shouted. "Most of you are present. Don't anyone leave just yet. We'll wait a little longer on everyone else to make an appearance before we discuss today's happenings."

The mumbled agreements flew around the table as Simon grabbed some coffee and a plate of food, and sat down at the counter across from Clancy, Shannon, and Henry.

"Good morning, all," Simon said.

"Good morning, Simon," Clancy said, followed by the others.

"I hate to start the morning off with such conversation, but has Alicia's body been prepared for the funeral service?"

"Yes," Shannon answered. "I and some of the others took care of that last night. Alicia was a sweet woman. She'll be missed."

Simon shook his head in agreement.

"We'll hold the service early this morning and then get on with our day. I assume everyone had time to mourn yesterday?"

Clancy answered, "I believe so. The peregrination group she was in got back relatively early yesterday."

"Yes. I'm sorry I wasn't here to help with that," Simon sighed.

"Simon, you can't be here for everything. There are plenty of people here to see to things. You just need to delegate a bit more."

Simon smiled. "You always could read me like a book, Clancy. You're right of course. I could put others in charge of things. Especially the other three remaining Dragoman. Safra already has her hands full."

"Hmm, yes. I certainly hope Renquin gets better now that he has returned home." Clancy took a bite of eggs.

"I'm sure if there is any way to help him, Safra can do so. However, I do hope she and Dekker can return today. We need to finish up the forge's improvements so that we can get on with making the swords."

"Oz is here. I'm sure he could start the process."

"Perhaps. But Dekker was sent here for a reason. I'll not overlook his purpose here. No, we'll wait on our master black-smith to return. I don't wish to overstep what God has put into place."

"Good point." Clancy smiled before noticing the new group of people entering the kitchen. "Well, guess I'm back at the stove." He glanced at what was left on the counter and table. "Yep, most of its gone already. Talk to you later, Simon." Clancy, Shannon, and Henry got back to feeding the newcomers while Simon sat and watched everyone pile in wherever they could.

He watched as Seth and Caroline had a seat at the counter next to him. He noticed that they seemed at odds last night when they arrived back from their peregrination. He smiled. They seemed fine this morning, although Caroline didn't look like breakfast was too appealing to her.

"Caroline, are you all right? You look a bit…pale."

Caroline tried to brush off his concern, but this morning's bout of nausea was exceptionally strong, and she had left the draught that Safra had made her upstairs.

She smiled at him and said, "I'm fine, Simon, thank you." But no sooner had she gotten the words out of her mouth, than she had to hit the floor running for the nearest bathroom. Which fortunately the small bathroom near the kitchen at the back of the house was close by.

Unfortunately, her hasty retreat grabbed the attention of everyone in the room. They all looked at Seth.

Seth's eyes grew wide as he searched for a quick explanation. "She's just a bit under the weather."

Most everyone accepted his reply and went back to their breakfast. Not everyone was so easily fielded though.

Simon cleared his throat, making Seth turn to look at him. Simon's questioning gaze, raised eyebrows, and concerned expression, told Seth that he was not to be fooled. Alec and Odessa, who approached the counter as well, were not persuaded either. They looked questioningly at Seth, small grins gracing their lips.

"What?" Seth asked, playing it down.

Odessa smiled brightly. She leaned forward to whisper, "Is Caroline pregnant?"

Seth didn't know how to answer the question. He didn't want to lie, but he couldn't betray Caroline's request either. Caroline entered the room again during the inquisition.

"What makes you think that?"

"All the nausea she's having lately. Plus, she's looking a bit tired as well."

Caroline approached the table and sat down. Seth looked to her for help.

"What are you all discussing?" she asked.

"You," Alec stated. "Dee thinks that you are with child."

Caroline sighed and went somewhat limp. Her elbows supporting her head in her hands.

"You are!" Dee squealed, trying to contain her excitement.

"So much for keeping it quiet," Caroline groaned.

Seth defended himself. "I promise, I didn't say a thing."

She looked up at his worried face and smiled to reassure him.

"I know, Seth. I don't blame you. I blame this nausea that I can't seem to get rid of."

Dee was almost bouncing up and down with excitement. Caroline couldn't help but smile at the woman who had become a close friend.

"Why are you trying to keep this a secret?" she excitedly whispered.

"Well, this isn't exactly the most opportune time for a Peregrine to get pregnant. Especially not one of The Twelve."

"No, you're right. But if you let everyone know, then we can at least try and help you," Odessa said in a low voice.

"I'm afraid of being smothered by everyone's help," Caroline replied honestly.

"Just tell us to back off when it gets to be too much." Odessa shrugged like that was all it would take.

Caroline doubted that things would work out that way, but with the way her pregnancy was going, she apparently wasn't doing a good job of keeping it hushed, and it had only been twenty-four hours since she herself had found out.

Caroline rolled her eyes. "Fine. I guess I should let everyone know." She turned to Seth. "You've got my back? You aren't going to let anyone be overbearing or overprotective, right? Including yourself?"

"I can't promise, Beautiful, but I'll do my best."

Caroline shook her head in understanding, then stood up on her knees on the high stool and cleared her throat.

"Everyone," she shouted, "can I have your attention for a minute. Seth and I have an announcement to make. BUT, before we do, I just have to ask that everyone not be too over-protective, please." She looked at Seth and nodded to him to say it.

Seth stood, wiped his sweating palms on his jeans and nervously announced, "We're having a baby."

The entire room was shocked for a second, all except for Odessa who was jumping up and down before Seth even finished speaking. Jason and Memnah, who knew what was coming, sat smiling broadly at the announcement. Soon the entire room was in an uproar of excitement. Most running over to congratulate them and chattering about what it was going to be like having a baby on the island. The first one ever to be born here, or more importantly, the first to ever be born to active Peregrines.

Simon grinned at their news, but he was also very concerned for Caroline and the baby's health. She was, after-all, one of The Twelve, and the upcoming battle against a dragon would be even harder for her in her condition. Simon glanced at the ceiling and asked in a low voice, "Lord, what are you doing here?"

After ten minutes of congratulations and exclamations of joy and excitement, Simon stood up and began to calm everyone down for the impromptu meeting.

Seth signaled he would be right back, running upstairs to get the nausea medicine for Caroline so she could eat something. When he returned, Simon began the meeting now that all were present and accounted for.

"First, let me start by saying that we will all be praying for Caroline and Seth. But mostly Caroline while she carries her pregnancy in these difficult times."

Everyone chimed in, agreeing to pray as well, suddenly understanding just how inopportune her pregnancy was.

"Next, Alicia's service will be at 9:00 this morning near the prayer gardens. Then, we need to count the shields. I haven't gotten to speak with everyone yet, but since you're all back, I assume they were all found."

Alec said, "We found two."

Nick put in, "We have three."

Gabriele raised her hand. "Two here."

Zaccai said, "We have two more."

Jason finished the rounds. "That puts us with the last three shields."

"Wonderful. Where are they?" Simon looked about the room.

Seth said, "Two are in our room. We were a little distracted last night when we got back." Laughter flit across the room.

Jason said, "The one I had is also in our room. I didn't know where I should put it."

Everyone else said the same thing. Each Peregrine had just taken the shield to their personal quarters. Except for Gabriele, Timothy, and Trenton. Their shields were still in the library where they had laid them when bringing in Alicia's body.

"All right then, when the meeting is over you can all collect them and place them in the archival library so we can have a look at them later. Now, I'm sure you all noticed the rather large crates by the stables. They are full of the minerals we need for the coating of the armor. We need to unload the crates and begin the refining process. I have the Goddelikheid Crucible which we will use in the refining of the minerals for the pureness of the metals. It's a bit small, so it may take a little time to refine such a large amount."

Ryan spoke up. "Simon, I might be able to al...alter the crucible to m...make the rrr...efining go fff...aster.

"That would be most appreciated, Ryan. Thank you. I'll bring it to the computer room after this meeting."

Ryan nodded his acceptance.

"Now, with Safra and Dekker still in Akrotiri for an undeterminable time, we will need to finish the adjustments and upgrades to the forge. Oz, you are familiar with the setup. Could you please oversee this?"

"Sure thing, Simon."

"We won't make any of the swords or mess with the armor until our God appointed blacksmith returns. However, we *can* have everything ready for him to begin."

Everyone agreed once again.

"Malachai, and Vashti, would you two please look up the descriptions for the swords in the *Book of Armor* and the jewel mounting in the *Book of the Keepers*. That message that came with the jewels said they went in the hilt of the swords, but we need to know exactly where."

"We can do that, Simon," Malachai replied. "I will even sketch what I think the description states and we can analyze it together before we start on them."

"Great. Now, Vashti, Safra has taken on quite a bit of responsibility for many things here. Can you tend to some of those until she returns? I would also like you to oversee the making of the capes when Heba returns. *If* she returns that is. If we need to take them to Akrotiri for her to finish them, we know that we can do that easier now."

"Certainly, Simon. Whatever you need," Prisca nodded.

"Thank you everyone for your attention, and I will likely see all of you in the library to look over the shields after the funeral."

Some left the kitchen while some finished eating.

Caroline was finally able to eat something and keep it down. Bridget stayed close to her friend during breakfast, both excited and nervous for Caroline.

"Caroline, have you picked out any names yet?"

Caroline chuckled. "Bridget, I just found out yesterday that I was pregnant."

"Oh yes, sorry. I just can't wait to meet him, or her."

"Well, it is going to be a while still."

"Oh, I know that. But it's so exciting. A baby. My very first little niece or nephew. I am going to be auntie Bridget aren't I?"

"Bridget, the baby can call you anything you wish." Caroline smiled at her young friend, giving her a hug. "I'm sure this baby will have so many aunts and uncles that it will be completely confused."

The two of them laughed and joked about the whole situation until it was time to leave for the funeral.

Alicia's casket was decorated with flowers from all over the island. It was a quick ceremony, with people saying a few words over her about her life. The groundskeepers laid her to rest in the ground beside the others they had lost. Dinah had been the first to be buried on the island, but she certainly had not been the last.

Everyone made their way to the library to look over the shields. They all marveled over the design and beauty of the embossed centers and the inlaid jewels, colors, and other ornately designed artwork.

After that, they all returned to the stables to begin the unloading of the boxes and the rebuilding of the forge and the molds for the pieces of armor.

The rest of the day was long, hard, hot work, but they were on the island, safe from demon attacks and the risk of anyone else dying for a time. They could at least rest peacefully; for now.

But now you are laden with the judgment due the
wicked; judgment and justice have taken hold of
you. Be careful that no one entices you by riches;
do not let a large bribe turn you aside.

Job 36:17-18

Chapter 16

Everyone was so busy working that the kitchen staff had brought lunch to the stables. They ate picnic style then got right back to work. The forge was coming along nicely with the newly added quench tanks to cool the large pieces of armor after being dipped in the refined Rhenium and Ruthenium.

Seth, of course, unloaded the heavy rocks from the crates. The other men, trying to help, grabbed the smaller, less heavier ones. Some pairing up to carry them inside. Seth smiled at them, tossing the large rocks around like they were light as a feather.

Now the afternoon was growing late, and the sun was beginning to go down on the island.

Gabriele stopped working and began looking around the island.

Simon noticed her curious behavior.

"Gabriele, is everything all right?"

"I'm not sure Simon. Anytime I'm near anyone else's Portgen, and they open it, I can somehow sense it."

"Hmm…when did that start?

"After the first time I connected with them; during the Timna demon battle."

"Interesting. I can't imagine who would be going anywhere? Perhaps Safra and Dekker have returned?"

"Maybe," she said turning and getting back to work.

"I'm sure they'll appear quick enough when they know where we all are."

They continued on with their work until Simon called for a break for the night. It was nearing dinner time and he didn't expect the meal to be brought to them again.

"All right everyone, let's knock off for the night. See you all in thirty or so for dinner."

Everyone, tired and dirty from the day's work, walked toward the house ready for nice hot showers.

Bridget, Wade, and Annabelle sat outside on the patio waiting for their turn in the bathrooms. Marnor sat next to Bridget also, chatting with her about some words he didn't understand from his readings. Bridget had stood up and walked over to the table to get a cold glass of ice water when she heard her name whispered from somewhere in the bushes.

She stood there, looking at where she thought the sound had come from, but shrugged it off thinking she was just hearing things. Then, she heard it again. She walked over to the bushes to listen more carefully.

"Who's there? Dominic...are you playing with me?" she giggled as she ran toward the shrubbery. When she walked around the end of the tree cluster she stopped abruptly, completely in shock.

"Father?"

Standing before Bridget was none other than Hiram Burke, just as she last remembered him.

"Hello Bridget."

"But...how?" she asked shocked.

"Uriah came to get me before my life was taken. Can't your father get a hug?" he said, holding his arms open.

Bridget ran into her father's arms, sobbing.

"I'm so happy to see you, Father."

"And I you. But I need you to come with me now."

Bridget stepped back, unsure what he was asking.

"Father, we need to go to Simon and the others. Let them know you're here. You can make amends for those things you did. We can be together and work like we were supposed to."

Hiram stepped back a bit, grabbing her by her biceps and holding her in front of him.

"No Bridget, I can't do that."

"Why not, Father? They'll understand. You just have to mean it when you apologize."

"I don't plan on apologizing to anyone, Bridget. I plan on starting a new life, and I want you to come with me."

Bridget pulled out of her father's arms. "What do you mean when you say, 'starting a new life?'"

"You don't have to worry about that. Let me do the worrying. Just come with me."

"I can't do that. I have important work to do here."

"You can still do that, with me."

"How? Is what you're doing part of God's plan?"

"Would you stop questioning me, Bridget and just do as I say? I am your father after all!"

"I know that. But if you're up to the same things that you pulled in the past, then I can't go with you."

"Doesn't your precious Bible tell you to 'obey your parents for it is right'?"

"It also says to put no other gods before Him. If I follow you, Father, knowing you are doing wrong, then you become my god over the one true God. I'll not leave my calling like you did. God is my first priority, and I don't think you follow Him at all."

"Now you listen here young lady…"

"No! You listen Father. All my life you hid this from me. You stole my life away and refused to let me live my destiny. Now you try to *command* me to go with you when you are up to something bad. I love you, Father, but I can't do that. And I won't let you do it either. I won't let you hurt my friends and family."

"No one here besides *me* is your family," Hiram stated angrily.

"You're wrong Father. Marnor is here."

Hiram's face went white with shock. "How…?"

"The same way you came. The Portgens. Not just Marnor, Father. These people have become my family. You left me all alone, living your secret life, which you wouldn't tell me anything about."

"I will be murdered by these same people you call family. I kept this life from you for your own good, Bridget!" Hiram said, trying to keep his voice down. "You're too young to be making a decision like this. I demand that you listen and come with me. I'm still your Father!"

Suddenly, Marnor appeared around the corner.

"Bridget, are you o…?" Marnor's words trailed off when he saw Hiram standing before them.

Bridget, unflinching, continued her questioning.

"Who is to murder you?" she asked shocked.

"It doesn't matter now. Just come with me!"

Marnor grabbed Bridget by the arm. "No, don't do it, Bridget."

Hiram seethed, shooting Marnor a deadly look. "Stay out of this, Marnor! It has nothing to do with you."

"No, it never did. Not even when you took Mother and left me all alone at fourteen."

Bridget looked at Marnor, realizing the truth of what he said.

Hiram ignored Marnor's words. "Bridget, I don't want you to get hurt. If you don't come with me now, I can't promise that I can protect you."

"What do you mean, Father? Protect me from what?"

Just as she asked the question, a sudden outburst of yells and screams came from somewhere on the island.

Bridget and Marnor ran back toward the house, seeing Annabelle and Wade under attack from strangers. She didn't understand how these people got here or who they were, but the island was full of invaders.

She and Marnor ran to assist Annabelle and Wade who were being attacked by two men. Marnor ran between the men and the kids. Wade stepping up beside him.

A fight broke out between them. Marnor and Wade overtook the two men, knocking them out.

"Bridget, Annabelle," Marnor instructed, "bind their hands and feet behind them. Then get inside and out of danger." The girls found some rope lying over a fence post and did as told, while Marnor and Wade ran off in the direction of the approaching invaders.

Bridget quickly ran into the house with Annabelle, taking her into the large living room and hiding her behind a couch.

"Stay here, Annabelle. Understand?" Bridget warned.

Annabelle shook her head yes and watched Bridget grab someone's bow and arrows leaning on the wall in the corner of the room and run back outside.

Annabelle slunk over to one of the large windows and watched the fighting outside from her safe place.

Wade looked about at the chaos. People were coming from every direction, wielding swords, and guns. He ducked when someone pointed a gun at him, the bullet just missing him as it whizzed past his head. Just then he saw Simon appear on the front lawn just outside the door. He had his staff in hand. Simon used the staff and pushed away from him, the force taking a handful of offenders and throwing their bodies into nearby trees and bushes.

Some of the other Peregrines and Dragoman were already outside on the lawn, engaged in a fierce battle. Others were running from inside the house, their weapons in hand.

Were these invaders to the island demons? Wade wondered. He was quickly approached by a woman carrying a sword. He leaned back, dodged her blade, then grabbed the woman by the shirt, headbutting her in the forehead and knocking her out cold. He ran off to fight another.

Simon looked about, wondering where the one person who could be responsible for such an attack was? Just across the lawn standing by the open portal of the Portgen, while invaders continued to run through, was Uriah Mose. Simon began his quick approach toward Uriah. Uriah saw Simon's intended approach as the last invader passed through the portal.

Uriah harnessed his Portgen and raised his hands. Bolts of electricity shot out toward Simon. He blocked the electrical charge with his powers but was then attacked from behind by non-other than Hiram Burke.

Simon was shocked by the revelation that Hiram was alive. Simon did all he could to fend off both attackers but was beginning to fail. Just as he thought that this onslaught would be the end of him, Timothy appeared and stood between Uriah's constant onslaught of lightning. Sean appeared behind Uriah and rained a wave of ocean water down upon him, picking him up in a whirlpool and slamming him into the ground. Uriah shook it off and fought back, throwing a bolt of lightning at Sean who used his sword to deflect it, but it knocked him backward to the ground. When he got back up, Uriah was nowhere to be seen.

Timothy was picked up by Hiram's powers and thrown away from Simon. Hiram continued his barrage on the man, the two men now locked in a mortal battle against one another as the remainder of the island continued their fight against the invasion.

The Peregrines soon realized that these people they fought were just that. Ordinary people who were most likely paid mercenaries for Hiram and Uriah. The retired people of the island and some of the Peregrines who were around over fourteen years ago, did recognize some of the invaders as past Peregrines. Those who helped Hiram Burke in the betrayal all those years ago.

Bridget couldn't help but watch between fighting as her father fought against Simon, determined to kill the man. Why was her father so angry? She just couldn't understand how *so much* hatred had overtaken him.

Uriah managed to sneak into the back of the house and up the steps to the second floor. He snuck over to Petra's bedroom door, finding it unlocked, and her nowhere to be found. He went down the steps of the main staircase, ready to use his power to throw aside anyone who dared get in his way. He walked through the house and across the hallway toward the main entrance. He was suddenly surprised to find Petra coming from the direction of the kitchen. She stopped suddenly in fear when she saw him.

Ryan hid just in the shadow of the staircase, listening and watching Uriah and Petra. His trusty baseball bat held firmly with both hands.

"Uriah?" she breathed.

Uriah smiled nastily. "Petra. There you are. I've been looking for you."

"For what," she asked shakily.

"I wanted to say how sorry I was. We need you on our side. I need you." He coaxed as he walked slowly toward her.

"That isn't what you said when you left me behind. As a matter of fact, I remember a very different conversation," Petra bravely said. She stood still, watching him slowly approach her, standing her ground.

Uriah was glad to see that she wasn't backing down to his approach, even if she was fearful. He still held her in his power, even after the way he treated her when he left. He grinned nastily, now standing in front of her. He grabbed her by the shoulders, sliding his hands down her arms, smiling cockily at her.

"I knew you couldn't resist me. All those years we had together are hard to forget. Surprisingly enough, I missed you. I never thought I would, but I did." He slid his hands around her waist.

She slowly raised her arms, lifting them to where he couldn't see her hands. She smiled seductively at him.

"Well, that's so sad because, I didn't miss you," she spat, plunging the knife she had hidden behind her into his back between his shoulder blades.

Uriah screamed in pain and stumbled away, reaching toward his back to try and pull the knife free. The look of shock on his face was also one of emotional hurt and surprise as he fell to the floor, throwing one last bolt of electricity which struck Petra.

Ryan blanched at the action, not sure what to do. He stepped over Uriah's twitching body toward the door headed outside. He heard someone running just outside and suddenly became frightened and quickly backed up beside the opened door, his bat ready to swing.

Marnor had watched the whole scene play out through the opened double doors. He raced to Petra's aid as she fell to the floor in a fit of convulsions.

Ryan began to swing the bat as Marnor flew through the door.

"Hey, hey, Ryan, wait!" Marnor yelled as he ducked to miss the bat.

"Oh, s…sorry, Marnor," Ryan said and ran outside to help fight. Ryan hid behind one of the tall porch columns. Anytime an invader ran by, he stepped out and swung, knocking them out.

Marnor knelt beside Petra, picked her up, and carried her out the door, frantically looking for Jason. He spotted him not to far away.

"Jason!" he yelled.

Jason looked around for whoever had called him. He spotted Marnor waving to him and kneeling on the patio, holding someone in his arms. Jason ran over and realized it was Petra, looking a little singed.

"I don't know that I can heal this Marnor."

"Please, just try."

"What happened to her?"

"Some guy. I think it must have been that Uriah fella' she told me about. He hit her with lightning, from his hands," Marnor said surprised. He had seen these people and their powers, but it still took him by surprise when he witnessed new things.

"Where is Uriah?" Jason asked frantically.

"Last I saw, I think he was dead, or close to it. Petra plunged a knife into his back right before he did this to her."

Jason did what he could to heal her, then helped Marnor take her inside and lay her on one of the couches.

Jason then went to see about Uriah Mose. The man lay dead upon the floor near the base of the main staircase, a knife sticking out of his back. Jason reached down, pulled Uriah's Portgen from its pouch at his side, then went back to the fight outside.

Simon and Hiram still went at one another. Each one using their powers as Magi, locked in a battle to the death as war waged all around them.

With one swing of his powerful fist, Seth literally broke the necks of any who dared run at him.

Timothy's armored skin repelled bullets, dropping them at his feet. His adversaries, after emptying their clips, fled in fear at this revelation and were quickly overtaken by another of the chosen.

Although there were many invaders, they stood little chance against the Chosen. Their skills and gifts far above that of these mere men and women. Although using their gifts in any fashion other than to fend off attacks was strictly prohibited against any of these people, except for the Fallen, those who had turned their backs on God's plan to follow and do evil. And even still, some of the more deadly gifts would not work against them.

Jason spent most of his time healing the serious wounds that had been inflicted on the islanders, like gunshots, piercings, or large cuts. He tried to keep an eye on Simon when he could, but his attention was often taken somewhere else.

On another part of the lawn, Nick searched frantically for Annabelle after his fighting was done, worried something had happened to her. As he yelled her name, she heard him from inside the house. She ran outside and into his opened arms.

"Thank God you're all right," Nick said, holding the young girl tightly.

She smiled at him. "Bridget hid me in the living room and told me to stay put."

"Bridget is a very smart young woman. And so are you for listening." Nick smiled and kissed her on the forehead.

Those who had finished fighting watched the epic battle between the two Master Magi, unable to look away from the fight. All of them praying that Simon would come out the victor. Simon threw one last ball of energy at Hiram knocking him backwards. Hiram stumbled and turned to catch himself and landed onto a spear sticking up in the air from one of the very mercenaries he had hired to overtake the island. Hiram looked stunned as the blade pierced him through his chest. He stood, pulled the spear from his body, and stumbled toward the barrier, passing through it to Dover England in 1578.

Bridget ran after her father, passing through the barrier behind him before anyone could stop her.

Dominic watched her go. "Bridget!" he yelled and was about to run after her when someone placed a hand on his arm to stop him.

"This is something she has to do alone," Zaccai stated.

When every invader had been killed or captured and the battle was finally done, they made the prisoners do the majority of the work and set about cleaning up the bodies. Unlike demons, this required physical work. These people however would not be buried on the island, but their bodies wrapped and tossed into the sea on the opposite side of the barrier. Then they took the prisoners through the barrier to whatever world they had come from, warning them to never return.

Dover, England, 1578

Bridget ran after her father, as fast as her feet could take her. She was crying so hard that she could barely speak, the calls to her father breaking on her lips before she could get them out. She finally screamed his name, making him turn to her only for a second. He then limped into the house they had shared for her entire childhood. She slowly walked to the small house and peered into the open window from the darkness of night. Realization suddenly dawned on her as she watched the scene unfold before her.

Her father lay on the floor of the small house, blood oozing from the holes in his chest as a younger, more frightened version of herself knelt over her father, crying.

She remembered that night all too well. That was the night she had lost her father. She had always thought he had been murdered by the strange people who would sometimes visit, whom she now knew to be Uriah Mose. Or by the demons she overheard them speak about when she would eavesdrop on their conversations.

But none of that was true. Her father had been murdered by his own greed and hatred for the very people who once were his friends and loved ones. Bridget sniffed, feeling sorry for the torment her younger self would go through for years, until one fateful morning when God would deliver her by dropping Caroline Jager in a ditch by her house. She slowly backed away from the window, pulled the Portgen from her holder, pushed the button for Reader's Island, and walked back into her future with a greater understanding of her past.

Reader's Island, Present Day, The Next Morning.

The entire group slept well into the late-morning hours, having just gotten into bed well after midnight when most of the clean-up had been finished, and their prisoners sent home. It was closer to noon before people began trickling downstairs into the kitchen for much needed coffee and food.

Clancy, Shannon, and Henry spent the first hour throwing out and cleaning up the dinner meal that no one got to eat the night before. Clancy and Henry then began cooking breakfast for the hungry hoard of people who would soon fill the room.

Marnor had sat up with Petra most of the night until he was certain his friend would be all right, causing him to sleep especially late.

Simon sat at the counter sipping a large mug of coffee when Bridget entered the kitchen. He had wanted to speak to her ever since his battle with Hiram yesterday. He called her to come over so they could talk. He was relieved when she didn't seem to hesitate.

"Bridget how are you feeling this morning?" he asked as she sat down on a stool next to him.

"Well," she sighed wearily, "other than reliving my father's death all over again, I suppose I'm fine."

"About that. I'm sorry Bridget, for being the cause of Hiram's death."

"Oh, no Simon!" she turned to lay a hand on his arm, "I don't blame you at all. My father chose a life separate and indifferent to God all together when God chose differently for him. My father's death was his own doing."

"That is a very grown-up way to see things, Bridget. I'm very proud and impressed with how much you've grown lately."

"I've had a lot of things to make me do so since leaving Dover." She weakly grinned. "You know Simon, when I followed my father last night, I had no idea where he was going. But when I found him, he had returned to Dover, our home. It was the exact same scene that I lived two-and-a-half years ago when I found my father murdered at fourteen. I watched the whole thing through a window. It was so strange, standing out there looking in at the worst day of my life."

"Just the same, I wish I could have spared you that."

"Thank you, Simon. You know, after experiencing the love and kindness of everyone here, I've come to realize that my father, although he took care of me and was never cruel or anything, never truly showed me any honest love. It's strange to think back to my childhood and see things so differently now than I did before."

"I'm sorry for that as well. No child should feel unloved by a parent."

"I don't exactly feel like he didn't love me. He just had no idea what real love was. His was a selfish love. Not like the love of God."

Simon smiled at her answer. Again, a very grown-up answer. How could a man with so much hatred raise a young woman with so much understanding, faith, and love?

Bridget and Simon grinned painfully at one another.

"I still love my father, Simon. I just understand so many things so much better."

Simon just sat and listened to her talk as they chatted over breakfast and several wonderfully-hot cups of coffee. The kitchen began to fill as more and more people began to enter the room.

They all stayed in the kitchen to eat. No one wanting to have breakfast on the blood covered lawn.

The groundskeepers and some of the others decided they would spend the afternoon trying to wash down and clean what they could. They needed their peaceful island and safe haven back.

Jason entered the kitchen and walked over to Simon.

"Simon," he said, with a nod, "I took this off of Uriah last night. I didn't want it getting into the hands of any of those hired thugs. I'm sure they all saw him use it, and I'm pretty sure I saw a few checking out some of ours as we sent them packing."

"Thank you, Jason. I'm glad you had the forethought to take care of that. I'm shocked that we had to fight a battle right here on our island. It feels different now. No longer our safe harbor."

"Well, I doubt we'll have any more visitors now that they don't have a Portgen. And since all the fallen Peregrines and Dragoman died yesterday in battle, we won't likely be troubled by them any longer either, especially since the two leaders of the NKRO are dead as well," Jason said, looking at Bridget and feeling a bit of regret at his words. "Sorry Bridget. I mean no disrespect."

"Oh, I know Jason. I understand. It's fine." Bridget got up and walked away to let the men talk as she went to sit beside Caroline and Seth.

"How's she doing?" Jason asked Simon.

"Remarkably well considering. That is one very impressive young woman."

They watched as Bridget sat and jovially interacted with the others; a hint of sadness evident in her mannerisms. Simon decided then to say a special prayer every night for the healing of Bridget's heart.

Chapter 17

Ryan brought the newly altered Goddelikheid Crucible down to the stables to show Simon the finished product. He had fashioned several overflow bowls made from the same materials that would attach to the outside of the crucible and each other, catching any pure metals that ran over. This would allow them to place as much rock into the bowls as they could. They could place all the crucibles on the fire at the same time to allow for faster smelting and refining.

Seth, Jason, Nick, Zeke, Rourke, Wade, Sean, and Timothy began using sledgehammers and wedges to bust up the massive pile of rock to make pieces small enough to fit in the crucibles. They had been slaving over the rock pile for an hour when Kristen walked by, looking frail in comparison to the group of large men. Noticing what they were doing, she stopped. She motioned toward the rocks with her hands and concentrated using her earth powers. The entire pile of rock began to shake and break apart, until it all crumbled into much smaller pieces. The hot sweaty men all turned and looked at her.

Nick asked, "Where were you earlier?"

Kristin drawled in a thick southern, lady-like manner. "Well, all you had to do was ask. I would have been happy to help."

The men watched their banter with amusement.

"If I had thought you would have been capable of tackling this, I would have," Nick breathed heavily.

She sighed dramatically as she began walking away, tossing her hair over her shoulder and saying, "Glad a little ole gal like me could be of assistance."

They all began laughing, some seriously and some sarcastically, throwing the hammers to the ground. Needing water badly, they went in search of some.

"Well, at least we got that done," Nick said, clearing his throat. Making the men laugh even harder.

"Yeah, only because *little ole Kristen* walked by. We'd have been there for days," Jason replied, smiling.

Nick blanched. "Don't let her hear you say that. She already has a big enough head." They all laughed at his joke as they went off to find the next place they might be needed.

Sean watched Kristin walk away. She turned to look at him and blew him a kiss, making him smile from ear to ear.

Timothy caught the exchange and slapped Sean on the shoulder, grinning and pulling him along.

Inside the stable, Simon barked instructions. "Oz, fire up the forge and have the quench tanks filled. We can soon begin the melting process for the rocks and the refining of the metals. We can quench the refined metals and store them until they can be used."

"Sure thing, Simon," Oz bellowed. "All right, boys, and gals!" Oz winked at Bridget and Annabelle. " Ya' heard th' man. Get them tanks filled."

Several of the younger people set out with multiple gallon jugs of oil that were sitting at the opposite end of the stables.

Sean was walking by and watched with interest as they began carrying them across the stables. He smiled broadly. He walked over and opened the jugs. Realizing oil was like water, he then tried to instruct it to flow into the quench tanks directly from the jugs, walking inside to monitor when they were full. Everyone smiled, dropping the now empty jugs on the ground as they watched the flow of oil seemingly float on air and fall to its destination. Sean soon had the tanks full.

Oz smiled at him. "Now that's usin' yer head instead a' yer back."

Sean beamed, cockily. "Yeah, well, intelligence *is* one of my better virtues." Sean smiled. Nick laughed in the background somewhere.

Oz leaned over the front of the forge, loading wood and coal into it to light. "Now where did I put them matches?" he said, patting down his pockets.

"How's this for using your head?" Nick asked, walking by, and shooting fire from his hand into the forge to light it. "And… it didn't require any intelligence." Nick looked at Sean and laughed while Sean made at face at him.

Oz shrugged and said, "That'll work too, thanks." He ignored the playful jabs between the two long-time friends.

"Yep." Nick replied with a nod of his head as he went about collecting the busted rock from the piles outside the stables to begin adding to the crucibles. They shoveled the now small, loose, pieces; thanks to Kristen; into the wheelbarrows and wheeled them inside, leaving them beside the crucibles.

Sean's wounded pride made him stand there and sulk. Kristin happened to walk by at that time. "Well *I* think you're a genius." She planted a kiss on his cheek then walked away.

That bolstered his spirits some, making him stand up a little taller.

Gabriele and Timothy exchanged grins over the antics playing out around them. Shaking their heads at all the lovey-dovey exchanges between Sean and Kristen today.

The atmosphere in the stables continued in the same manner throughout the rest of the day. The rocks were being melted down and the minerals refined, quenched, and stored in sealed containers for later use.

Simon was beginning to worry that something was wrong with Safra and Dekker. They had been gone for nearly two days now.

"Ryan my boy," Simon announced, entering the computer room. "I need the coordinates for Safra's location. I plan on making a trip to check on them."

"Okay, Simon." Ryan clicked his computer keyboard a few times, wrote the coordinates on a piece of paper, and handed it to Simon.

"Thank you." Simon looked at Ryan over his glasses. "Ryan, you stay cooped up in this room too much. What say you join me on the trip to Akrotiri? There's so much of the world out there to see. And you see very little of it."

"I, I, don't know, Simon." Ryan began stuttering. "I l…like my computer room."

"Yes. And it's a very nice room. But you need some air, my boy, and a change of scenery. It won't take long. Maybe a few hours or so. Come have a small adventure with me." Simon smiled.

"You can just call her on the Portgen," Ryan supplied.

"True, but I think I'd rather go see how Renquin is doing for myself. Besides, you could do with a break."

Ryan shuffled his feet, thinking about Simon's request. "I guess I, I can go for a lll…ittle while, *w…with you*, Simon."

"Great." Simon grinned. "I'll just get my Portgen and meet you back here in a few minutes."

"O…oookay," Ryan stammered, a bit nervous about this adventure.

Simon left the computer room, notified Malachai and Vashti in the archive library of his plans, grabbed his Portgen, and went to get Ryan, hoping he hadn't changed his mind.

"All right, my boy, let's go." Simon opened the Portgen and walked through. Ryan stood nervously watching, unsure he still wanted to go. "Come along, Ryan. It will be fine. Trust me."

"O…okay." Ryan stepped through to the other side with Simon. He was instantly drawn to look around at the ancient city from their crumbling boundary position. He could see the tall, columned buildings and the King's Palace over top of all the smaller dwellings and businesses.

"This way, Ryan," he heard Simon call.

Ryan followed closely to Simon, making sure to keep up. He didn't want to get lost in the strange city so far from home, even though his trusty Portgen with the *home* button hung at his side.

"Do you k,know where to gg…o here, Simon?"

"I believe so, Ryan. The closest place to where we came through the portal would be Heba's. We'll check there first before going all the way to Renquin's village."

After thirty minutes of walking, Ryan questioned Simon again. "A…are you s…sure you know wh…where you're g…gooing, Simon?"

Simon smiled at the young man's forthright question.

"Yes. It's just a bit of a walk to get there. Just enjoy looking around at the scenery. It shouldn't be but another thirty minutes or so."

"Okay." Ryan sighed. He didn't take much pleasure in things like traveling. Especially since the strangely dressed people they passed by stared and whispered about them. They looked nice enough, but Ryan didn't like people staring and pointing at him. So, he looked up instead and noticed the absence of blue sky and clouds. It was curious how there didn't appear to be sunlight down here, but some strange sort of light glowed mysteriously above them, giving a sort of daylight experience. Ryan was very curious as to what that could be. His mind was a whirl of thoughts and ideas as they walked, curious as to what could be causing the glow. The city around him faded as he concentrated on the light above.

Thirty minutes later they arrived at Heba's. Simon knocked on the door.

Heba opened the door with a surprised smile on her face. She stepped back to allow them inside.

Dekker announced, "Hello Simon, Ryan. What are you two doing here?"

Simon smiled back. "Just coming to check on everyone. We haven't heard from you today and wanted to make certain that everyone was doing well." He finished the sentence while looking at Renquin.

The older man was resting in bed, but his color looked much better and he seemed to be more alert.

Dekker translated for Renquin and Heba. Renquin replied that he was feeling much better. He enjoyed his adventure and the island, but knew his place was here in Akrotiri. He did voice the wish that Heba not be stuck below the earth's surface as he had his whole life. He wished for her to return to the island if she so wanted.

Simon glanced at Heba who nodded yes, then turned back to Renquin. "I have no problem with that, as long as that is what she wants. And, with us being able to return here more easily now that we've found an accessible portal on the outskirts, she can come back to visit often."

Safra looked at Heba. "I think we can leave now. Your grandfather should be back to normal in a few days."

Dekker, of course, translated for her as they prepared to go back to the island with Simon and Ryan.

Heba thanked them in Akrotirian and asked Dekker to check on her in a few days. Dekker relayed that message to Simon.

"Yes, that will do. We still need the capes finished after-all."

Dekker again translated, and she replied that they could bring them to Akrotiri where she could work on them.

Simon said, "Perhaps. We will likely send them back later today or tomorrow."

Heba smiled and shook her head yes, as Dekker relayed the message.

The party of four said their goodbyes and left Heba's for the outskirts of the city, and the accessible portal to the island. As they walked Simon noticed how quiet Ryan had become. He looked back at the young man who still seemed very interested in the strange light source this far below the mountain. He didn't disturb him, only watched him. Simon could see the wheels of Ryan's mind turning, trying to figure it out. If anyone could, it would be Ryan. They finally reached their destination and returned to Reader's Island.

Simon and Ryan had only been gone for about three hours. When they returned, Oz and the others had gotten quite a bit of the rock melted down and a good stock of pure minerals separated and stored.

Dekker was thoroughly impressed.

"Well, it looks as if you've all been very busy."

Simon smiled. "Yes. We have a good bit with which you can begin working. We even looked through the ancient books for descriptions of the swords. Malachai was fortunate enough to come upon a description just this afternoon, of which, our young artist Dominic did an extraordinary rendition. I'll retrieve that picture for you in a bit. We've already cast the forms for pouring. You should be all set to go."

"Great. I'll get started right away then." Dekker headed in the direction of the stables.

Dekker began remelting the already pure minerals in the dipping vat to begin coating the armor pieces.

Oz and some of the others were instructed to disassemble the leather straps from the shields while he took measurements from the women to refashion their suit of armor to fit them. As Dekker looked over the armor pieces for each person, he realized that some of the men's needed a refashion as well. Very few of them actually fit into the armor pieces in their current state. Seth and Oz would need a substantial amount of metal added to theirs to cover and protect them properly.

While Dekker did this, he instructed the others to build a drying rack for the armor pieces after they had been dipped in the heat resistant metals and quenched.

Dekker took one of the suits of armor that belonged to the women, heated it, and began hammering and refashioning it to the women's smaller frames. Nearly everyone on the island that walked by gave him special instructions to make sure that Caroline's was especially sturdy around her torso, Odessa finally explaining why.

Simon and Safra stood outside the stables watching the activity inside as they discussed recent events.

"Safra, you missed quite a bit of happenings while you and Dekker were away."

"Really? Other than Alicia's death?"

Simon sighed. "Yes, unfortunately. First, we found out about Caroline's pregnancy."

"Already?"

"You knew?"

"She had never even considered pregnancy until I pointed it out to her. I also gave her a nausea tincture to help with her symptoms before they left on peregrination."

"Ah. Well, after that, we had an all-out battle with Uriah Mose and Hiram Burke here on the island. They led a large group of mercenaries through a portal using Uriah's Portgen."

"Really!"

"Yes. It was a nasty fight that lasted about twenty minutes. The both of them are now dead of course, but it was an awful night. Especially since we had an immense amount of clean up to deal with afterward."

"A girl leaves for a few days and *everything* falls apart."

"Literally." Simon smiled.

"Well, what would you have me do?" she asked. "It looks like things are humming along nicely. Everyone seems busy at something."

"Yes, things are happening quickly. I would ask you to just continue with Marnor and Petra and the archive entries. Petra, by the way, is a little worse for wear after an encounter with Uriah. She did him in but got hit with his powers in the process. She's fine I think. However, a bit singed around the edges and moving a little slower today. "

"All right. I'll go check on her. See you later." Safra walked off into the house while Simon continued to the stables to check the progress.

The forge fires would burn long and hot for days on end, trying to get each of the metal pieces annealed, making them workable for refashioning. Then Dekker would harden the pieces, and then temper them making them strong. After that task was finished, he would spend time making the swords.

There wasn't a huge amount of room in the forge area of the stables, so everyone took turns helping Dekker with whatever was needed over the course of the following week. Some went off to take care of other chores on the island, while others spent time wearing whatever armor pieces were finished so they could get used to fighting in them.

Simon and some others took a trip back in time to gather some much-needed chain mail to wear under the armor in the more vulnerable areas where the pieces met but did not cover completely. He also had to take the capes to Heba for finishing.

More than a week had passed on the island with all the armor having been finished, and the sword for each of The Twelve remade and polished to a high shine. The jewels which were inset in the end of each hilt glinted in the sunlight.

Simon looked at the twelve Peregrines who wore the armored suits in full. The only thing left to add were the capes, and he and Dekker would go back to Akrotiri today and hopefully bring them back. He was overtaken by the powerful picture they made and what they represented.

The Twelve were ready for battle against the great evil that plagued the earth. He prayed they would all survive the fight. He only wished he could be there to help them somehow. He knew he couldn't go with them. His was a different kind of fight. He knew what was expected of him and when.

Safra interrupted his thoughts.

"Simon, I feel we should have a ceremony anointing The Twelve before they leave for battle. My spirit is saying this strongly."

The two of them began walking up toward the house.

"Yes, well, it never hurts to anoint God's people. Especially if He's telling us to do it." Simon smiled. " Of course, we don't know yet when they are to leave or where they must go. The location for the four dragons hasn't yet been revealed."

"Do you think they will have to battle all four at once?" Safra asked concerned.

"I certainly hope not. I can't see that working out well for our warriors at all."

"No, neither can I. Well, I can start planning the ceremony to anoint each one of them. Where would you like to have it?"

"I believe the prayer gardens and temple would be the ideal place. When do you think that you can have this ceremony ready?"

"How about tomorrow night? That will give me the better part of today and tomorrow to acquire everything we need, and make sure all the plans are ready."

"That sounds like a very good idea. Thank you, Safra. I'll have Clancy prepare a special feast for the occasion. We'll have the ceremony first then finish off with dinner."

"All right. I'll see you later. I need to get started." Safra left him at the patio and disappeared into the house. Simon headed straight for the kitchen where he found Clancy preparing the day's lunch meal.

He filled Clancy in on tomorrow night's plans. Then went in search of Dekker to plan a trip back to Akrotiri to retrieve the capes. He hoped they would be finished in time for the dress ceremony.

He found Dekker cleaning up in the stables where the forge was located.

"Dekker, would you mind taking a trip to Akrotiri with me?"

"Not at all, Simon. Are you hoping the capes are finished?"

"Yes. I figure since you finished refashioning and dipping twelve suits of armor and made twelve swords in a week and a half, then surely Heba has the twelve capes finished."

"Yes, but I had a load of help with all of that. Heba only has herself."

"You have a very good point there." Simon was deep in thought.

"Are we in need of them soon?" Dekker asked.

"Yes, actually, we are. Safra has suggested we have an anointing ceremony for The Twelve tomorrow night. I had hoped they would be in full dress for that."

"Well, let's hope she is finished then. If not, then perhaps we can pitch in and help her. We have a day and a half to finish them."

"Yes. You're right."

"You probably need to be here to plan the ceremony though," Dekker said thoughtfully.

"Not really. Safra is taking care of that. But I do need to have some private time with the Lord over what I should say at the ceremony. Figure out what sort of ritual needs to take place."

"Let's get to Akrotiri then and get you back." Dekker smiled.

"We'll have a good lunch first. All this activity lately has me starving." Simon grinned. The two men set out for the kitchen, had a quick lunch, then left for Akrotiri.

By the time Simon and Dekker reached Heba's, she was finishing up the last of the capes. They only had to wait an hour before she was done and had them packaged and ready to go.

Simon invited Heba back to the island to witness the ceremony now that her grandfather had gone back to his home and village.

The three of them left Heba's home, each carrying four packages in carrying bags Heba had sewn for them to throw across their bodies, carrying them on their backs. They returned to the island by mid-afternoon, giving Simon plenty of time to prepare for tomorrow evening.

He sent word to The Twelve, by way of whoever passed by, to meet with him in the archive library. He wanted to hand out their capes to them.

They unwrapped the packages and laid the beautiful, silken, hand-sewn capes spread out on the long table. Each cape was a masterpiece of work. Heba had made them fit for kings and queens. Which they would all be one day when this was all over.

Each cape was fitted to the size of each Peregrine. Seth's and Oz's looked very large in comparison to the women's. Each Cape was the color, or colors, that represented each tribe as outlined in their research. The material they had gotten from King Solomon's temple back in Timna Valley, flanking the back wall in the king's throne room, had been the exact match for each tribe.

The Chosen Twelve began trickling into the library, oohing and aahing over the beautiful capes. Heba beamed with pride as they all thanked her for her work.

"How do we know which belongs to who?" Caroline asked.

Simon answered, "Each tribe had a color that they were represented by in their tribal flag. I'll list them for you. Reuben is silver, Simeon-gold, Levi-purple, Judah-brown, Issachar is the blue-violet, Zebulon-pink, Manasseh-yellow, Gad-red, Asher is gray, Naphtali-green, Joseph is white, and Benjamin is Black.

The capes were thick and well made, yet surprisingly light in weight, which would help to ease the burden some from the weight of the armor. Each cape had a thin, smooth, braided tie at the neck in the same deeper color as the cape itself. The length of each falling at the middle of the calf.

The rest of the afternoon was spent polishing all the armor to a high shine and finding tight fitting clothing that each Peregrine would wear beneath the armor. They would carry their armor with them on the mission until it was time to do battle against the prophesied dragons. They prayed they would have time in between finding the beasts and having to fight the beasts.

The next morning, Clancy, Safra, and Simon sat in the kitchen before everyone else awoke discussing the plans for the ceremony that night.

"I have my old bagpipes in our house. I can play something on the pipes to commemorate the evening as The Twelve walk up to be anointed. A processional walk, so to speak."

"That would be a grand idea, Clancy," Simon replied.

Safra agreed. "Yes. This should include fanfare. These people are sacrificing their lives for mankind. The kings of the Bible always prepared and met with God before going into battle. Many fasting and praying."

Simon shook his head. "Yes. After the ceremony, we will give them all time alone with God. They can enter one of the prayer temple's rooms for as long as they feel it necessary. That prayer time will end the evening when the last of the twelve emerges from the rooms. Then we will come back here to feast."

A thought suddenly struck Simon. "You know, I never really thought about the significance of the twelve separate rooms at the temple until now."

Safra adjusted in her seat. "Yes. I see your point. It is humbling to see how God works everything out far in advance for His plans."

Clancy put in, "But what about the Keepers? Aren't they also important in this battle?"

"Yes, they are. I'll instruct Bridget and the others to dress up tonight. They too should be anointed. Thank you for that reminder, Clancy."

They sat drinking coffee for a while longer before the room slowly filled with jovial banter. Dominic entered the room first and Simon called him over to instruct him in what needed doing tonight. He told him to pass the word to the other three Keepers.

Prayer Gardens and Temple

The evening hour for the ceremony was at hand. The preparations were complete, and everything was in place. The prayer gardens were decorated with hanging lights in the trees, and torches lined the path The Twelve would walk.

Simon and Safra stood at the center of the prayer temple dressed for their part in the ceremony. Her special brand of incense filled the air with fragrance.

The Twelve entered the prayer gardens in a processional line as the sound of the bagpipes filled the air with their minor song. The Twelve were lined up according to their position on the Ephod. Alec was first in line followed by Odessa, Gabriele, Seth, Wendel, Caroline, Sean, Nicholas, Jason, Zaccai, Kristen, and lastly, Ezekiel. The four Keepers were in line behind them.

Each carried their shield in front of them in one hand and their sword behind that. They did not wear their helmets, but instead carried them underneath one arm, tucked neatly inside their elbow. As Alec approached, Safra handed Simon a bottle of oil. Alec knelt down as Simon anointed his head with oil and Safra prayed over him. He then entered the first prayer room starting on the building's left. They continued in this fashion until everyone had been anointed and the last person entered the prayer rooms. Then, Simon had the four Keepers kneel on the ground upon the four large pillows placed there for them several feet apart. He and Safra anointed them with oil and prayed over them as they stayed in that position and prayed.

The sound of the bagpipes stopped and there was serene quiet on the island as those outside the temple prayed and beseeched the Lord for the safety and success of those who would battle against the four beasts.

When Alec exited the temple, he knelt on one knee outside his door until all of his fellow warriors exited their prayer rooms. Each one taking a knee as Alec had. When the last exited, they all stood. Simon spoke.

"Each of you must remember that you are chosen and anointed by God. What you are about to face, no man has had to do so before. Trust in His care, His grace, and His guidance. May the Lord be with you all."

Everyone split apart as they all walked back to the house in high spirits, charged by the evening's events. The night was one of laughter and joy as each of The Twelve, and the four Keepers, had changed into something lighter for a relaxing evening. They all exited the house onto the patio, equally decorated, to enjoy a feast fit for kings. Now, they only had to wait to be given further instructions on finding the dragons, and the fight that was soon to come.

And the Lord said to Gideon, "The people who are with you are too many for Me to give the Midianites into their hands, lest Israel claim glory for itself against Me, saying, 'My own hand has saved me.'

Judges 7:2

Chapter 18

Odessa awoke in a fit of sweat and anxiety, the nightmare feeling so real. She sat up in bed to clear her thoughts. Had it been a dream or a premonition? She wasn't sure. She looked at the clock beside the bed which read 3:00 a.m. She laid back against her pillow breathing heavily, trying to calm her jittering nerves.

She decided to get up and go for a glass of cold water. She slung her robe across her shoulders and padded barefoot downstairs down the back staircase into the kitchen. She entered, grabbed a glass and some ice, and filled the glass from the sink. She quickly drank the glass and filled it up once again, turning to sit at the counter. It wasn't long before she was joined by Safra.

That was not a good sign. More than likely, Safra had had the same vision, or one like it. Safra looked at her, grabbed a glass of ice as well, filled it and joined her at the counter.

The two of them just looked at each other over the rim of their glasses as they took long drinks from them.

Safra broke the dreaded silence. "You too?" she asked. Knowing Odessa had the same type of dream.

"Yep. What was yours?" Odessa asked.

"It was scary. A very large, very angry, fire-breathing beast, whose tail spikes were nearly bigger than our warriors."

Odessa exhaled heavily, throwing her head back over her chair and staring at the ceiling for a few seconds before looking back at Safra to speak.

"Sounds like it wasn't just a nightmare after-all."

"Oh, it was a nightmare all-right. I just fear they will soon come true. Did you have any locations revealed to you?"

"I'm not sure I can recall. The size of the beasts in the dreams and the struggles of those that fought kind of scared the life out of me. If He did reveal locations, I think I forgot them."

"I remember one. Perhaps tonight will reveal more. Or we can try hypnosis?" Safra offered.

"You do hypnosis?" Odessa asked.

"Yes, but I can't do it on myself."

"Who would perform it on you then?"

Safra took a long drink. "Simon. He is gifted in many ways."

"That I do know." Odessa smiled. "But I've never seen him use hypnosis before. I've seen him wipe away someone's memories to save our lives."

"That isn't something he does often," Safra stated. "So, are you up to it?"

"Hypnosis?" Odessa asked, as Safra shook her head yes. "Sure, I'm game. As long as you don't make me cluck like a chicken."

The two women chuckled at Odessa's response and the visions it conjured. They finished their water and returned to their rooms to try and get a bit more sleep; neither one quite capable of managing it.

Safra soon found Odessa again outside under the pergola watching the sun come up, coffee cup in hand. They sat quietly, enjoying the serenity that came with the early morning songbirds and the rising sun in all its splendor and colors. An hour later, when others began appearing outdoors, Safra spotted Simon.

"Well, looks like I'll go have a chat with Simon. I'll see you in a bit." Safra stood and walked away.

She returned just a few minutes later.

"Simon has agreed to hypnotize us both right after breakfast. He said that he would have Dominic record and draw whatever we say. You know, since I usually do that for you," Safra stated.

"All right. Let's go grab some breakfast then and get this show on the road."

The two women went inside, grabbed some food, and sat down at the kitchen table along with a few others. When they had finished eating, they went outside to locate Simon once more, finding him in the same spot as earlier. They sat down at the table next to him and waited for him to finish his breakfast, and a conversation he was having with Dekker.

He turned to them. "All right, you two. Are you ready for this?"

"As ready as ever," Odessa stated a tad nervously.

"Let's go inside to the archival library where we won't have as many disruptions. I'll grab young Dominic on the way."

Dekker asked, "Mind if I tag along?"

"Not at all," Simon answered, "you just need to keep quiet."

Simon stood up, followed by Safra, Odessa, and Dekker.

Alec watched the group with interest. Especially since Simon grabbed Dominic and it involved Odessa. He pushed his near empty plate away, took one last drink and followed them inside, catching up to them.

"Dee," he called to her, "what's going on?"

She turned to him and nervously said, "Hypnosis."

"Really?" Alec asked excitedly. "You think Simon will let me watch?"

"Probably. As long as you're quiet."

"Great. Now, who's being hypnotized, and why?"

Odessa explained to him about her and Safra's nightmares and that neither can remember too many details.

They entered the library, pulling out two chairs for the women to sit in. Simon faced them away from the door to limit the amount of distractions.

Dominic ran upstairs to his room to grab his pencils and sketch pads and a notebook to write in, returning quickly.

"Dekker, close the two large library doors would you?"

"Certainly, Simon."

Dekker and Alec each took a side and slid the large, heavy, sliding doors into place. Then they each went to sit on the opposite side of the table to watch the women.

Dominic handed Dekker the notebook telling him to write down any details they gave while he sketched their visions. Dekker agreed with the shake of his head.

Simon began the session, having both women sit quietly, close their eyes, and breathe deeply a few times to clear any tension from their bodies. He then instructed them to keep their eyes closed and listen to the sound of his voice, going through a series of commands for a few minutes. Then he began.

"Clear your minds and concentrate only on the sound of my voice. Listen only to me. Concentrate on what I am saying. Now, Odessa, tell me about your dream last night."

Odessa, in a trance-like state, calmly began describing her dream.

"We found the dragons."

"Who is we?"

"Zeke, Caroline, Bridget, and Me."

"Where are the other Chosen among the Twelve?"

"Fighting the other dragons."

Simon looked at the others in the room. Not liking what he was hearing.

"So, The Twelve must split up?"

"Yes."

"Where was the dragon, Odessa?"

"In the clouds."

"What do you mean by 'in the clouds'?"

"High up the floating mountains. Where the lightning comes from. "

Simon couldn't understand what she meant by that. He had never discovered any such place in all his years of peregrinating.

"Do you know where the others are?"

"They fight the Behemoth, on the land."

"Who fights the Behemoth?"

"Seth, Jason, Kristen, and Wade."

"What land? Where is the land they fight on?"

"Tanmoyaro Draconamai."

"Odessa, repeat that name."

"Tanmoyaro Draconomai."

"Where is this place, Odessa?"

"The fifth dimension, in the Ring of Fire."

Simon had never heard of such a place before.

"And the other two groups?"

"I don't know where they are."

"All right, Odessa, rest for a bit. Clear your mind and rest."

Simon turned to Safra.

"Safra, what was your vision last night?"

Safra spoke slowly.

"The dragon of the sea, the Leviathan."

"What about the Leviathan?"

"The Chosen were in a great battle with the sea dragon."

"Can you tell me where they fight this dragon?"

"The Ring of Fire."

Simon was still unsure what they meant, but at least she and Odessa's answers lined up here.

"Can you tell me who the Chosen are that battle the sea dragon?"

"Yes. Zaccai, Wendel, Alec, and the Keeper,"

"Which Keeper, Safra?"

"Dominic."

"What of the other Chosen? Where are they?"

"They fight below the surface. In the belly of the mountain."

"Which mountain?"

"Tanmoyaro Draconomai."

"Who fights in the belly of the mountain?"

"Nicholas, Sean, Gabriele, and Annabelle."

"Where is this mountain, Safra?"

"The fifth dimension, in the center of the Ring of Fire."

Simon shook his head.

"All right. Odessa, Safra, I want you to clear your minds. Concentrate only on my voice. Focus on what I tell you. I will count backwards from three to one. You will wake on one. Three… two… one."

Odessa and Safra both suddenly woke and looked around.

"Well?" Odessa asked Simon.

"We got a good bit of information. Although I must say, some of it is a bit confusing."

"Like?"

"Well, you both mentioned a place I have never heard of in a dimension we only speculated about. We think that Zanchier may exist on the same plane as this other place."

"Well, what's the name?" Odessa asked frustrated.

"Let me see if I get this right. Tanmoyaro Draconomai."

"That actually came out of my mouth?" Odessa asked unbelieving.

"I'm afraid so."

Safra sat thinking for a minute. "Simon, I think I've heard of that place before."

"How could you have possibly heard of that place?" he asked shocked.

"It was an old legend my father used to tell me for a bedtime story when I was little."

"Can you remember the story?"

"Maybe. Let me think a minute."

Safra closed her eyes and drifted back to when she was very young. "My father used to say there was a place where the dragons of old lived called the Mountain of the Dragons. He also once called it Tanmoyaro Draconomai. He said the ancients told of a mountain that stretched to the clouds, and also touched the earth's core. The island was home to four dragons, and each one controlled the seasons, and the weather. The Wind Dragon lived in the floating mountains of the region. The Water Dragon swam the island's borders. The Land Dragon wandered to and fro, from one end of the island to the other. The Fire Dragon lived deep within the earth's core, in the farthest recesses of the island. All four dragons are in the same place, sort of. The legend stated that the four dragons were once peacekeepers of the earth and were gentle with the people. Then man destroyed their peace, and they rage against him now and forever, until those who will rise come and give them back their peace."

"And you're *just now* telling me this legend? You never saw the similarities between what we do and the story?"

"Sorry. I just now *remembered* that legend because of Tanmoyaro Draconomai. He only told it to me a few times before mother made him promise not to mention it again. I had a very vivid imagination as a young child. I gave myself horrid nightmares for months."

"Well, it seems your father Sage was a very wise man. I don't know how he knew of the Mountain of the Dragons, but he heard it from somewhere. Which means, we need to find a way to locate this mountain. Would your father maybe have any information about this in any of his books? He had to hear of or be told about the legend somewhere."

"It's a possibility. Father had so many ancient texts. Most of which are related to herbal remedies. And most of which I never searched through because he taught me himself. We didn't need a lot of them."

"If we don't find anything in any of the ancient archive books then we may need to go back before he died and see if he can tell us himself about it. That may be the easiest way to approach this."

Safra shook her head in agreement.

"Well," Alec put in, "God has led us this far. I am certain He will give us that information as well. No?"

They all smiled at the annoyingly positive Frenchman. One of the newest Christians on the island, yet wise in his faith and trust.

"Well, Dominic, we didn't give you much to go by, but were you able to give us an idea of what we are looking for?"

"I think so, Simon. Just give me a few more minutes. I really only had enough information to render a drawing when Safra started talking about her dad."

Dominic sat sketching frantically for the next several minutes, trying to finish the drawing. He finally stopped, sat back, looked at the paper, and then stood up.

"Here." He handed it to Simon. "This is the best I could do."

Simon held a rough sketch of an island. The center had a tall, volcanic, mountain stretching to the heavens. Clouds, smoke, and lightning encircled it, and pieces of land floated around the highest peak. Lower down, the mountain continued beneath the water, all the way to the ocean floor and beyond. At sea level, the land spread out widely on either side of the mountain, stretching out almost equally on either side. At the top of the mountain, a dragon sat upon one of the floating pieces, peering down at the ground. In the center, below the ocean floor in a cavern, sat another dragon. Another creature, the leviathan, swam around the island, while on another side, a large dragon stood on the land. Above the photo read the words, Tanmoyaro Draconomai, Mountain of the Dragons, Ring of Fire.

Simon was thoroughly impressed at Dominic's speed and skill to draw something so quickly yet so thoroughly.

Simon handed Dominic's drawing to the women to look over. "Was it something like this?" he asked them.

Odessa and Safra both looked at the rendering.

"From what I could see in my vision, it could be. This is really very good Dominic," Odessa said.

Safra shook her head as well. "Yes, very nice. Only, I didn't see this much of it. Only the caverns going into the earth. I could see a red glow, feel some of the heat from it, and hear the piercing roar of the dragon. When I rounded the corner, I saw a massively large, very ugly, very spikey-looking dragon. If what I saw is what we are up against, God is the only way we are going to win these fights. Especially since there are four of these beasts."

Odessa said, "My main concern is for the Keepers. The twelve of us have armor to protect us. The Keepers have none of that. What is their purpose in all of this, and how are they supposed to help us fight what Safra just described without any kind of protection for themselves?"

Simon shook his head. "You raise a very good point there. One to which I have no answer. We may need to make the Keepers some sort of shield at least. I only hope we aren't missing something. Perhaps we should look through the *Book of the Keepers* translation more closely. We honestly haven't done a thorough inspection of the ancient books yet. We've been so consumed by other things. Perhaps it's time we Dragoman take whatever time we have, and thoroughly check the information in the books before we send you all out to fight these dragons."

Everyone left the library, except for Simon and Dekker, Simon asking them to send the other Dragoman to the library, along with Heba, to help with more of the translations. After spending so much time with her grandfather, Renquin, deciphering the ancient language, she had learned a lot and could now figure it out without his aid.

They would spend every waking moment with the books until the time for the Final Battle was at hand. He knew what his role, and that of the other Dragoman, would be during those battles. The Scroll of Rubric was instructions for the Dragoman, and Simon had been preparing for it ever since Alec and Odessa had found the scroll seven months ago.

Malachai, Vashti, Prisca, and Heba entered the library. Simon explained to them the plan, showing them Dominic's sketch, and explaining Safra and Odessa's dreams. The six of them got busy, each one taking one of the ancient archive books and carefully going over any areas they had just skimmed through or skipped all together. Heba and Dekker got busy with the newly translated *Book of the Keepers*, carefully looking at the use of words in the translation and their ancient meanings.

Simon used the intercom system to call the kitchen and had a large pot of hot coffee and some cakes brought to the library. They were going to be there for a while.

Shannon brought the requested items into the library fifteen minutes later. As she left, she slid the large doors closed so there wouldn't be any distractions for them.

While the Dragoman worked inside the house, the Peregrines and Keepers worked outside. They dressed in full armor as they sparred with one another, getting used to the feel of it. The kitchen staff delivered a cool picnic lunch of cold sandwiches, cucumber salad, and grapes instead of a hot meal.

Simon had instructed them not to wear their capes when they went up against the dragons. The capes were for ceremonial wear only, never for combat as they could cause some hazardous situations.

Caroline spent time trying to get her defensive movements down to protect her torso even more than before. The armor was cumbersome. Especially since they had trained to fight using nothing but the bare necessities. Now she was having to learn to fight wearing an entire suit of armor, and they had to face massive dragons that surely had some sort of power and abilities. She normally wouldn't put so much thought into it, but now she had another life to consider. Since Dekker had fixed the armor to fit each of them properly, she worked tirelessly whenever possible to get used to it. Working tirelessly was also a lot easier to do before the pregnancy. Now, most mornings she awoke tired. After a long day of sparring in full armor she usually crashed right after dinner. A few nights last week she had even passed out before dinner. Seth just let her sleep on those nights but had made certain there was something she could eat sitting beside the bed if she happened to wake in the early morning hours. He was so supportive of her and her needs at this time. The whole island had been. Everyone made sure she had everything she needed at all times. Whoever happened to be walking by brought her extra water and snacks three or four times a day in between meals. That's probably why she had passed out before dinner a few times. She wasn't lacking for food at all, and so likely was much more tired than hungry. Simon had even gone into a current time-period to find her the latest and best in prenatal vitamins and care to make sure her body didn't wane in health and nutrition. The kitchen staff would ask her every morning if she had any cravings and would gladly, and with excited smiles, fix her whatever she wanted at each meal. She was certainly taken care of and very blessed with so many people willing to see to her and the baby's health. So far no one had gotten pushy, but she wasn't even close to showing yet.

Seth watched his wife practicing. She had spent the last week trying out her armor as the pieces were finished. He noticed she had also started learning new defensive moves. She was still fierce in battle, but she worried about the baby. He knew and understood that. Heck, *he* worried about the baby. When it came time to fight the dragons, Seth would make certain to protect Caroline as much as he could. She and the baby were his top priority. He at least had some control there.

It was nearing dinner time and Jason and Seth decided to call the training done for the day. Seth went to walk home with

Caroline, carrying most of her armor for her. She seemed out of breath and looked worn thin.

"I can throw this armor down and carry you?" Seth asked teasingly, but very serious about the offer.

Caroline grinned weakly. "Thank you, Seth. But surely I can make it to the house on my own. I'm hoping this is just an adjustment period and my body will react better soon."

"Maybe the vitamins just need a little bit of time to get into your system."

"Probably." She smiled, linking her arm with his. "I think I'm going to just grab something simple, take it upstairs, shower, and crawl into bed."

"Just don't forget to eat. That isn't good for either of you. And it's definitely not good for your energy level."

"I know. I promise to eat my supper like a good girl."

Seth bent down to plant a quick kiss on her lips. They walked into the house and into the kitchen where Caroline made her requests known. Shannon was happy to oblige.

"You go on up to shower dear and I'll have your meal on a tray by the bed waiting for you."

"Thank you, Shannon. That's very kind and much appreciated." Caroline and Seth went upstairs to clean up. Caroline retired to their room, and after making sure she was settled in and didn't need anything else Seth went back to the kitchen for dinner.

Simon and the other Dragoman had finally made an appearance after being locked in the archival library all day studying. Seth could tell they had something to tell everyone, so he grabbed a plate and sat down at the large table beside Jason and Memnah.

Simon looked around the room, making sure everyone was accounted for before he began.

"Everyone stay here after your meal. We have some news to share about what we found in the books."

Everyone chimed in or nodded and went back to eating. Twenty minutes later, everyone had finished dinner and sat around with coffee and cake, waiting on the Dragoman to fill them in on what they knew.

Simon addressed the group.

"As you all know, we've spent nearly the entire day going through the books with a fine-tooth comb. And, we still have a lot to search through. This morning, I hypnotized Odessa and Safra because of a dream they both had last night. We've discovered where the dragons are, how many there are, and who is to fight which."

Zeke raised his hand. "You mean we have to split up?"

"Yes. I'm afraid that is exactly what I mean."

"Why? Wouldn't it be better if we all worked together?" Kristen asked.

"I thought so, but apparently that isn't the way it works."

Jason asked, "So we're splitting into four groups?"

"Yes, exactly. Three Peregrines and one Keeper for each."

"Do we just choose the groups?" Zaccai asked.

"I'm afraid not. Odessa and Safra's visions were very clear on the groups and which dragon they were to fight." Simon cleared his throat, watching Seth with caution. He knew Seth wasn't going to like what he was about to hear, especially now. He decided to save that announcement for last.

"First, let me start by saying that you will all basically be fighting in and around the same place. There is an island in the center of the Pacific Ocean called Tanmoyaro Draconomai. Translated, it means Mountain of the Dragons. It sits in the Ring of Fire —which describes a highly volcanic area of the Pacific Ocean. The island apparently got its name from each section of the island being home to one dragon. In the highest part lives the wind dragon, which probably controls the rains and winds. On the land at ocean level lives another, the behemoth, the earth dragon —controlling earthquakes, landslides, and storms of that nature. The ocean around the land is home to the leviathan — the water dragon — likely controlling typhoons, hurricanes, and such. And lastly, the fire dragon, which lives in or near the earth's core in the deepest part of the mountain. Surely it is responsible for volcanic eruptions."

Sean asked, "So what you're saying is, these dragons control the weather and storms that affect the world?"

"If Sage Driscoll's bedtime story for Safra when she was little is correct, then yes. After extensive study of the *Book of the Keepers,* we've found that the Keepers job was to take care of the nature dragons. I first believed that our four Keepers were the first ever to exist. I now find that to be incorrect. There were four others before, long ago. We don't know what happened to them or the extent of the Keeper's job."

Seth asked, "So how do we find this island?"

"Well, it appears that the island may exist in a different dimension. Much like that of Zanchier."

"We can get to Zanchier pretty easily now. Surely this place won't be that difficult."

"That is true, Seth. But, we have to find where it is in the fifth dimension. We still have some more of the books to look through, and we will spend most of the night doing just that."

"What about the groups, Simon?" Nicholas asked.

This was the part that Simon dreaded.

"In both visions, this is the way you were all divided. Nicholas, Sean, Gabriele, and Annabelle will fight the fire dragon at the core of the mountain. Zaccai, Wendel, Alec, and Dominic are to battle the leviathan, the sea dragon. I don't think you will have to be in the water for this. I can't see God giving you armor to wear beneath the water. Seth, Jason, Kristin, and Wade will fight behemoth, the land dragon, and Zeke, Caroline, Odessa, and Bridget the wind dragon."

Seth stood up immediately. "Now wait just a minute Simon. Are you telling me that I won't be with Caroline?" he asked, his voice tinged with disbelief.

"I'm afraid not, Seth."

"Well that just won't do. My wife is pregnant, Simon."

"I know that Seth…"

"Then switch someone around."

"I can't do that, Seth," Simon said, almost pleading.

"Why not?" Seth's voice was becoming more and more agitated.

"I didn't make the order, Seth. God gave the women these visions."

"I don't see what difference it makes! If all groups have three Peregrines, than surely we can just switch someone with her. I'll not leave my pregnant wife alone while she fights a dragon!"

Ezekiel got a little testy at that. "Thanks a lot man. What exactly am I? or Odessa and Bridget for that matter?"

"I didn't mean that in an ugly way, Zeke. But she's my wife."

"And we will take care of her. Not to mention, she is fighting for God. He put her there for a reason, man!"

"Yes! I know all that. But I need to be where she is!"

"That's enough a that!" Oz boomed, standing up and facing Seth. "We all know how ya' feel Seth. Ya' think we ain't thought 'bout all this too? I love that gal like she's my own daugh'er. Yer gonna' drive yerself crazy if ya don't trust God ta take care of 'er."

"Right. I've seen the Chosen die, Oz. I'm not willing to lose her. *I* intend on taking care of her. Where she goes, I go."

"Ya' ain't got a choice, boy. She's one a' the Chosen. God'll send 'er, and you, wherever He chooses."

"We'll see about that," Seth said, storming out of the room. He ran upstairs, taking them two at a time, calming down enough before quietly opening the door to their bedroom. The lights were out, and Caroline was sound asleep on the bed. Seth crept over to the bed lying down beside his wife. He stared at her sleeping form for a long while, worry driving him mad. He finally gave in and began to pray.

"God, why? Why the baby now? Why can't I be allowed to protect her?" Seth fell asleep praying and beseeching God to change His mind and allow Seth and Caroline to fight side by side. For God to allow him to protect his little family.

Finally, be strong in the Lord and in his mighty power.
Put on the full armor of God, so that you can take your
stand against the devil's schemes. For our struggle is
not against flesh and blood, but against rulers, against
the authorities, against the powers of this dark world and
against the spiritual forces of evil in the heavenly realms.

Ephesians 6:10-12

Chapter 19

Jason decided to have a talk with his brother before everyone gathered for breakfast that morning. He walked down the hall to Seth's room and knocked on the door.

Seth opened the door, looking a little aggravated to see Jason standing there.

"We need to talk," Jason stated.

"Fine," Seth answered nonchalantly.

Seth said, "Caroline, I'll see you at breakfast. I need to speak with Jason for a minute."

"All right," came her reply from behind the dressing screen.

The two men walked down the hallway to the second-floor library and sitting room. Jason closed the large doors behind them. Neither men bothered to sit down.

"Seth, I've got to ask what last night was all about?"

Seth turned to look at Jason. "It's about exactly what I said it was. I don't see what the harm is in putting me and Caroline together."

"Well, for one, it isn't anyone here's decision to keep you apart.."

"Okay then. Just switch out someone in the group with Caroline."

Jason thought for a minute. "Okay, say we do that Seth. Everyone disobeys God for *your* comfort. What if the entire mission goes wrong because of that one decision? What if switching people around is the very thing that causes us to lose?"

Seth breathed in slowly and exhaled hard. "Look Jason, I understand what you're saying. I just want to be with her. To protect her, that's all."

"Protecting her isn't your job, Seth. That right belongs to the Lord. That may be the very reason He separated the two of you."

"Yeah? Well it isn't like I'm going to be able to concentrate any better not knowing what is happening to her."

"But at least your focus will be on the task at hand and not watching every move Caroline makes. It's likely for the good of both of you that you *aren't* together."

Seth slid his hands over his face in frustration, trying to wipe away the odious feeling he had. His hands fell to his side, and he slumped onto the couch, resting his elbows on his knees.

"I know what you're saying is true, Jason. It's just that, I've watched her over the past week. How tired she gets, and how worried she is over the baby. I just want to ease her burdens some and be there for her. I'm afraid this fight will be too much for her."

Jason walked over and put his hand on Seth's shoulder. "I understand how you feel, brother. But God has a plan, what that is, we don't know. We just have to do as we are asked. Trust Him, Seth. If you're going to trust Him, you have to trust Him with everything. Even Caroline and the baby."

Seth sat pondering for a second before standing. "I know you're right. But I can't say it's going to be easy."

"The Bible guarantees that our walks with God won't be easy. It's our faith in Jesus that sees us through the tough times."

"Thanks, Jason. Now, I have some apologizing to do."

The two men left the library and walked into the kitchen. Most everyone was there already so Seth apologized to the whole room, stopping to speak to Simon and Zeke personally.

Seth noticed that Caroline watched him with a look of curiosity after his public announcement. She was obviously wondering what she had missed last night. Seth grabbed a plate of food and went to sit with her, explaining himself and the events of the night before.

"Oh Seth. I know you're worried. I am too, but we have to trust that God knows best. I'll be fine. It's not like I'm going in alone."

"I know that Caroline. I just wanted to be able to help and protect you."

"So, trust that God will protect me, and my mission partners will help me."

He slightly grinned at her gumption and faith. She had lived her whole life with faith. This trust thing was new to Seth. He wasn't used to giving up handling a situation to anyone. Let alone an invisible God. He knew God was real, and He had already given Seth several miracles since becoming a Peregrine. And likely many more in his past life. But letting go, knowing what could happen was a whole new kind of faith for him.

They ate breakfast in peace amongst the chatter in the room. Seth knew he had no choice, but his mood hadn't yet improved, and likely wouldn't until this fight was over and Caroline was safely back home with him.

Simon stood and announced a meeting that afternoon.

"We'll meet at the patio table for lunch. We have some new information concerning the Final Battle. We would tell you now, but we want to check some details first. We were up half the night figuring things out. You all have this morning to prepare yourselves. This afternoon, the hunt for the dragons and Tanmoyaro Draconomai begins. Prepare your armor, your weapons, your spirits, and your resolve. See you all in a few hours."

Simon left the kitchen and went about preparing himself for the role he would play in all of this. He caught the attention of the groundskeepers and Dekker, wanting to talk to them about building a metal bowl in the center of the prayer gardens to hold fire to light the prayer gardens for reading. They would also need four pedestals, each having a slightly, slanted platform at the top in which to lay a book. These pedestals would ring the metal fire bowl he asked them to build. It all needed to be finished and set up by late-afternoon. He also asked that Dekker and a few of the other men search through the wardrobe room for suitable shields to give to the Keepers. They didn't have time to fashion any, but Dekker would have time to coat some from the wardrobe room with the heat resistant minerals to give them some sort of protection. Simon wasn't sure they would need such a thing, but he and everyone else would feel better if they had something.

The job for himself and the other three Dragoman during the Final Battle would be to pray and read the names of the saints. Those Peregrines and Dragoman who had come and gone, giving their lives for the cause. What this signified, he wasn't certain. He just knew that the names, and the meanings of the names of each person had something to do with the Final Battle. They would start reading when the Spirit revealed it to them, and they would read until the Spirit told them otherwise. Each would read from their own archive books first, and then, if led to continue, they would begin reading from the books in the island's archival library.

The Scroll of Rubric was an instruction manual for the Dragoman during the Final Battle. Some of what it said had confused Simon when he first read the scroll. But now, with the recent findings and details, it made much more sense.

After speaking to Dekker and the others, he went to the wardrobe room to find proper attire for the other three Dragoman. Ceremonial robes would be perfect attire for such a thing. Much like the one he wore for the anointing ceremony last night. He located what he needed, grabbed the Scroll of Rubric from his room where he had been looking over it early this morning, and went down to the archival library to speak to the other Dragoman. He found them all sitting at the table looking over the books again.

Simon laid the robes and scroll on the table.

"I've found each of you ceremonial prayer robes to be worn tonight during the ceremony."

Malachai replied, "Thank you, Simon. I suppose we should see if they fit." He picked them up, looking for the larger of the three. He slipped it on while Vashti and Prisca did the same with the other two robes.

Prisca stated, "I suppose we should prepare ourselves as well. We need to gather all of our personal books, correct?"

"Yes, starting with the most recent one and working backwards."

Vashti asked, "Why do you think that is? What is the significance of reading the newest entries first?"

Simon shook his head. "I'm not sure. I just know that is what the Scroll of Rubric states. Perhaps it has to do with The Twelve being the ones to actually fight the beasts. Maybe their names, or meanings of their names, hold some power over the creatures. More so than those who have come before them."

Malachai agreed. "That sounds like as good an answer as any."

They prepared for the noontime meeting just four hours away, and all that they would discuss.

Seth and Caroline sat in their room, spending as much quiet time together as they could. Both were uncertain as to what the future held for them, but they knew they would have to trust God to take care of each of them and the baby.

They made sure that all their armor was intact, all the weapons were ready, and that they spent time in prayer. They both knelt beside the bed and prayed together that God would grant them favor.

Down the long, second-story hallway the same sort of preparations were happening in every room.

Jason and Memnah talked while each of them polished a piece of armor. Also ending their time before lunch in prayer.

Alec made his way to Odessa's room after preparing his own armor. They too prayed and talked, both worried for the other.

Sean and Kristen finished their armor and prayers, then decided to go walk the beach and spend some alone time together.

Timothy visited with Gabriele, helping her take care of the things she needed. They weren't a couple, but Timothy hoped that in the future they might become one. For now, he would help and pray for his friend.

The Keepers all huddled together on the patio furniture outside, holding hands and praying. Each comforting the other, and all trying to help calm the very nervous and youngest member of their group, Annabelle.

Nadia knocked on Nick's door, hoping to spend some time with the man she had come to respect greatly. After he had finished with his armor, the two of them went in search of Annabelle to pray for her and encourage her in her up-and-coming role. They found all the keepers outside near the firepit, sitting on the couches and wondering what their roles in all this would be. Nick and Nadia asked to join hands with them to pray. Each of them standing on either side of Annabelle.

Zaccai and Zeke sat outside on the covered patio of the front porch, talking, and praying with one another. Their burgeoning relationship still in its infancy.

Oz finished polishing up his armor and went in search of Prisca, finding her in the library with the other Dragoman. They too took a long walk, taking the time just to be with each other.

The rest of the island prepared for the evening, the long night ahead and the next morning. Each person tossed up their own prayers for safety and guidance for all those facing the beasts only hours away. Marnor, Petra, Safra, Sofia, Rourke, the kitchen staff, and housekeepers all helped Dekker and the groundskeepers to prepare for the battle at hand. Some carried books out of the library to the prayer temple to prepare for the Dragoman to read from them. Others helped to build the pedestals and fire bowl, while others helped to prepare food and water to send with each Peregrine, paying special attention to Caroline's needs. No one was sure how long this battle would take, or how long the Peregrines would be gone.

Lunch time came as everyone began gathering on the patio beneath the fragrant veranda. The islands beauty and aroma tended to make one forget about the troubles of the world. That is, until they have a meeting like the one they were about to have.

Simon breathed deeply after filling his belly with the delicious lunch Clancy and Henry had prepared for them. He looked around the table. Everyone's spirits weren't quite as jovial as usual. No doubt every one of them were thinking about the Final Battle and being separated from their loved ones for an undisclosed amount of time. He knew it was time to get started with the meeting, and so stood as he usually does to get the attention of everyone there. Normally he would have to speak to get their attention, but today they were all on high alert, waiting to hear when it would all start.

Simon cleared his throat and began. "We have deciphered how to get to Tanmoyaro Draconomai. First, you must all travel to Zanchier, entering Storm Valley. There you will all pick up Zanchier creatures which will aid you in battle against these four dragons. Your Keepers know best and will decide which creatures are best for each group. This must be done quickly because the portal to leave Zanchier and enter another fifth-dimension plane will occur in Storm Valley just at sunrise tomorrow, when the light flashes over the mountains. It will be marked by a distinctive light. The books do not give any further information on that. Only, that it will remain open for only thirty seconds, so you must all ride through the portal quickly."

Jason asked, "Simon, will this portal take us to Dragon Mountain, or do we have to find another way there?"

"Of that, I am uncertain," Simon stated. "I assume you would exit the other end of the portal onto the island."

"Well, how do we know if we've found the correct island?" Sean asked.

"Another good question, to which I have no answer. I assume you will find the beasts quickly. You may very well be in a battle at the point of entry. The dragons may sense your arrival, so be prepared to fight when you ride through; just in case."

Kristin asked, "Well what about the animals? How can they survive the attacks by these dragons? If the dragons breathe fire, then won't the animals be killed or harmed?"

Simon turned to Bridget. "Bridget, would you like to answer this question? You know more about the Zanchier creatures than most anyone else here."

"Certainly, Simon," she answered, turning to look at Kristin. "Most of the creatures of Zanchier have a certain amount of fire retardation to their pelts and skin. This will protect them more so than the protection we ourselves will have."

Zeke said, "A lot of us here have never been to Zanchier. What should we expect? Those cat-like things and four-legged bird-type animals are pretty large. How can we be certain they will take direction from us? You know, during the battle. I don't want to be fighting with whatever I'm riding when I need to be fighting the dragon."

"They'll listen to you. Besides, each group will have a Keeper with them should any problems arise."

Oz interrupted, "I don' think you'll 'ave ta worry 'bout that. After the girls left Zanchier, me an' Sofie still used th' animals when we needed 'em. A' course, we're both telepathic, but we can't talk with 'em like Bridget does."

Caroline stated, "Yes, that's true. I spoke to them as well, without a reply or an understanding. All I can tell you is when I gave a command, whether telepathically or verbally, they did as I asked. Not saying some of the younger ones like Paxton didn't wander off at times chasing something interesting, but I doubt we'll be using any juveniles for this trip."

"True," Bridget reiterated. "We will not use juveniles for this trip. Although, Paxton is no longer a juvenile, so we will use him."

Zeke was a tad nervous. "So, we have to ride these things?"

Simon replied, "Technically no, you don't have to ride them. But it will benefit you greatly. Especially your group Zeke, as you will have to scale the mountain all the way up to where the clouds form and the atmosphere grows colder. Not to mention the floating pieces of mountain up that high may make it very hard to navigate around while fighting a flying dragon."

"Okay, okay, I get it. Ride the birds."

Simon smiled as Bridget corrected him. "They're called Kabihanxu or firebirds."

"Got it," Zeke stated uncomfortably.

Bridget grinned at his obvious qualm. "Don't worry Zeke. It's very easy to ride them. They're such large animals, falling off is an improbability."

Her statement made his eyes widen at the thought of falling. He cleared his throat. "I'm just not crazy about heights."

"Then God must be stretching your faith." Bridget smiled.

Caroline put in, "Zeke, if I can do this, so can you."

Zeke grinned at Caroline, shaking his head in agreement. He knew her situation was far more complicated than his.

Seth watched Zeke, the man's fears making him nervous again. He needed someone in control by Caroline's side. Not a man who feared flying. It was all Seth could do to hold his tongue.

Simon looked about the table. "Anymore questions?"

No one replied.

"Now, when you reach Tanmoyaro Draconomai, if the dragons don't come looking for you, you'll have to search them out. We know that the entrance to the cave to the core is located on the center mountain. There may be more than one mountain on the island, so search for the one that reaches the heavens. It should also take you to the earth's core."

Gabriele asked, "Do we know how far it is in either direction? How far up and how far down?"

"I'm afraid not. I'm sure you'll find out the closer you get to each dragon's lair. But you'll all be riding creatures that can travel much quicker than you can yourselves."

"I'm going to say that the land group and the water group will most likely begin their battles much sooner than the other two. Assuming the journey up, and down through the mountain will take you all longer to make."

Odessa asked, "When do we leave?"

Simon looked at her. "As soon as our meeting is finished."

Everyone looked around the table. Seth held Caroline's hand in his. He looked at their locked fingers, bringing her hand up to his mouth and planting a kiss on the back of her hand. They looked at one another, knowing they would soon part ways.

Simon watched the couples around the table. This was why he never got involved with anyone while living this way. It did make for a lonely life at times, but it was best that way.

"Now, if there are no more questions, then everyone can go get ready to leave. I'll meet you all back here on the front lawn. Just know, that I and the others who stay behind will be praying for success for each and every one of you."

They adjourned the meeting, and everyone disappeared inside to get ready to leave. They packed their armor and strapped on their weapons and packs.

The Dragoman also prepared to head to the prayer gardens to await their own tasks. They would need to be ready and in place when the Final Battle began.

Everyone met on the lawn as Simon instructed. The Twelve and the four Keepers, stood together as Simon opened the portal with the coordinates to Storm Valley in Zanchier. Everyone waved one last goodbye, with well-wishes for luck and safety, as they all walked through the portal and disappeared.

Simon so wished he could have gone with them. But he knew his place and it was at the gardens.

"All right everyone, let's get some rest and be about our business. It could be a very long, early morning task. You all know what to do."

The kitchen staff was prepared with food and drink to keep everyone awake and alert. The other Peregrines would stand by the Dragoman as they read and hand off books as needed. The groundskeepers and housekeepers would transport any other needed items from the house. If the Dragoman read through the first archives, then they would transport more to the garden.

Zanchier, Fifth Dimension Plane

The Keepers were the first to step through the portal and into the valley. Bridget instantly, telepathically called to Cho, some of the other firebirds, and Mother and Paxton, and several other

Pagorinxes. They had a large group of people, most of which needed to learn to ride the animals.

Bridget would need to choose which mature creatures to use in this battle. She didn't want any of them to suffer death as Han had. She would also have to find some other beasts that would serve their cause. She chose Pagorinxes, which would be good for the caves because of their ability to see in the dark. The Kabihanxus would do well for the floating mountains. *What other creatures could be of use,* she wondered.

Cho, Paxton, Mother, and several other creatures like them appeared in Storm Valley, taking some of the Peregrines by surprise. They all came to a stop just in front of the group, several coming forward to nuzzle the people they knew and had missed. Bridget, Dominic, Wade, Annabelle, Caroline, Oz, and Seth all patted the beasts, talking to and scratching their ears and necks.

Oz said, "All right, enough a' that now." He smiled as Paxton nudged his back. "Let's get out a' this valley an' up ta the tree house. There still be Scaithers 'bout down here."

They all mounted the animals, the newer creatures following the leads which were Cho, Mother, and Paxton. There were six Kabihanxus, in which the Keepers doubled up to ride. Four Peregrines flew on the others. Seth had flown before and convinced Jason to join him. Bridget suggested that Zeke and Odessa ride the other two to get used to flying. Oz and Caroline road mother and Paxton, while the others cautiously climbed onto the backs of the Pagorinxes.

When they landed on the treehouse platforms, or dismounted at the ground level where the Pagorinxes stopped, they all marveled at the size of the tree in which Oz had lived for so long. Oz showed them the way inside beneath the massive root system of the tree, entering the large wooden and iron door that Oz had made long ago to keep unwanted creatures out. They all walked up to the platform of the treehouse where the firebirds had landed to drop their passengers.

Alec looked at Bridget and said, "I see why you like this world. It is a beautiful and magical place."

Bridget smiled. "Yes, I hope to live here one day. This place holds a very special place in my heart."

"Perhaps when the barrier fades between worlds as the prophecy states, God will grant your wish."

They smiled at one another and everyone gathered around awaiting their next orders.

Jason looked at Bridget. "So are we to use only the firebirds and Pagorinxes in the battle?"

"No. I don't believe so. I know of one other creature, the Yarequu, which would also benefit us. I think they will do nicely for battling the land dragon. Now, just to find another creature that can handle both the water and the land for fighting the sea dragon. Dominic could you call to the Yarequu? You've actually had an experience with one."

"Sure Bridget."

Dominic called to the Yarequu he had met at Everly Lake market just a week or so earlier, connecting with the creature telepathically. Dominic called to it, sensing others near to where it was stalled. He called to three more of them as well, asking them to come to Storm Valley.

Bridget looked at Oz.

"Oz, you've lived here longer than any of us. Do you know of a creature that lives in water and on land? Large enough to ride into a battle?"

Oz stood scratching his beard for a few seconds. "Well, I did see somethin' mighty strange once when I was out at market over by Everly Lake. I went ta' buy some seafood, when I looked 'cross the lake an' saw what looked like rocks at first, then they moved. They stood up, shook inta a hairy ball a fur, an' then walked inta the water. I ask'd a fella at the market what they were, and he said they were called the Monshokto."

"Monshokto? How strange," Bridget stated. "I'll take Cho and check it out."

"That's a good ride over ta Everly Lake an' back. I don' think we have the time fer that," Oz stated.

"True. I'll try calling them telepathically. Perhaps they will come because I am a Keeper. We should meet them halfway at least. Get them used to us." Bridget looked to the other Keepers. They all shook their heads in agreement.

"Let's hope so," Oz answered. "I su'pose you four should git then."

The four Keepers hopped on the backs of two firebirds and were off in the direction of Everly Lake and a spot to meet up with the creatures known as the Monshokto.

The rest of the group waited on them, enjoying a tour of the treehouse and the Xantifal Mountain ridge. Oz explained the strange rumbling sounds heard every once in a while, letting them know the Shifts didn't reach that far up the mountain.

Forty-five minutes away, Bridget, Dominic, Wade, and Annabelle flew over the land on the firebirds. They could see four large hairy beasts, sandy gray in color, walking two legged through the tall grasses headed in the direction of the treehouse.

'That must be the Monshokto. Cho, land please.' Bridget telepathically instructed the massive bird.

As they began to land, the Monshokto looked up to the sky, and began running on all four legs in fear.

"What are they doing?" Dominic yelled to Bridget.

"I'm not sure. Perhaps they're frightened by the Kabihanxu?"

"Who isn't," Dominic replied in understanding.

Bridget and Dominic called telepathically to the Monshokto to calm their spirits and let them know that they were in no danger from the Kabihanxu.

'Wade, ride your firebird to the other side of the clearing to turn the Monshokto around and back toward us,' Bridget telepathically instructed him.

Wade did as he was asked, he and Annabelle landing the large bird on the edge of the valley between the Monshokto and the forest behind them. The large creatures turned in fear, back toward Bridget and Dominic. When they saw the other firebird land in the valley, the Monshokto stopped, unsure where to go from there. Some turned to face Wade and Annabelle behind them. All four began bellowing lowly, the reverberating sound echoing across the valley, causing the Firebirds to flap and squawk in agitation while Bridget, Dominic, Wade, and Annabelle covered their ears and fell to the ground.

Bridget and Dominic both again called telepathically to the creatures to stop. To let them know they were in no danger.

Bridget stood against the onslaught of vibrating, ear-piercing, sound waves. She pushed toward the Monshokto, speaking to them telepathically, urging them to stop.

When Bridget reached them, just a few feet away from the hulking, hairy animals, she stopped and fell to the ground again. She pulled one hand away from her ears and held it out in front of her, palm facing up. The largest of the beasts stopped bellowing and snorted, panting deeply. She sat there, her hand raised, finally opening her eyes to look at the beast in front of her. All the Monshokto were now quiet, following their pod leader's example. Bridget dropped her other hand to her side as she and the Monshokto just looked at one another. Cho squawked loudly, making the beasts skittish, stomping the ground in protest.

"Shh…it's all right," Bridget said as she stood. "Cho or the others won't harm you. I called you. We need your help. The world is in danger, and we need your help to save us all. Including your kind."

The Monshokto's large dark eyes fluttered, and its breathing began to regulate.

"You're not a predatory animal are you? You're a vegetarian. You eat plants and fish?"

The Monshokto bobbed its head up and down in reply.

Bridget smiled. "You have a wonderful defense mechanism. You'll need it to go up against the water dragon. Can you help us fight against the evil?" She slowly walked the distance between her and the animal.

The Monshokto made a small bellowing noise in reply. Bridget stopped just a few feet before she reached the beast. The Monshokto stood on its two rear legs and walked to her, making up the rest of the distance between them. The large creature bent down and allowed her outstretched hand to touch his head just under a single horn that was mostly hidden by the massive amount of hair the animal had.

"Thank you for your trust and help. It will be dreadfully scary I'm afraid. But I think you and your, Pod? Is that what you called them? Will all do wonderfully. Will you allow me and Annabelle to ride upon your backs? You see, I must take the four of you to Storm Valley, where we have to take a time portal to an island where we must fight the dragons I spoke to you about."

The Monshokto nodded its head. The other three Monshokto watching the leader of the pod. Bridget motioned to the others to come forth. They walked slowly so as not to frighten the creatures.

They all spoke to the beasts as they inched forward, following Bridget's example as they did, and holding one hand out in front of them. They introduced themselves to the beasts as they carefully approached, making friends with the creatures, and garnering their trust.

"We must get going. May I and Annabelle now climb upon your backs?" Bridget asked.

The Monshokto in front of each girl, laid down on the ground allowing the two of them to climb up. The Monshokto then stood up on two legs, as the girls held tightly to the fur about its neck, their legs dangling over the creatures massive shoulders.

Wade and Dominic turned and went back to the firebirds and mounted them.

As the large beasts ambled along the valley, Bridget was growing impatient.

"I'm sorry, but we have to hurry. Can we go faster?"

The largest, which she rode upon, leaned forward, landing on all four feet. The others did the same. They were soon off at a steady run, traveling at round fifty miles an hour, the long legs of the Monshokto taking large strides. Wade and Dominic flew high above them on the backs of the Kabihanxus. Bridget figured they should make it back to the tree house within the hour.

It said to the sixth angel who had the trumpet,
"Release the four angels who are bound at the
great river Euphrates."

Revelation 9:14

Chapter 20

Zanchier, Treehouse

Caroline peered out over the valley below the treehouse platform.

"I think I see them coming, and there is something else approaching from around the same area, just ahead of them."

Oz came to look. "I wonder what that could be?"

"More animals hopefully," Caroline stated. "Didn't Dominic call to some creature called the Yarequu?"

"Yep. Could very well be jus' that. Ya' ever seen one a' them Yarequu?"

"Can't say that I ever got the chance," Caroline answered.

"They're strange lookin' beasts. A' course, not much stranger 'an anythin' else 'round these parts." Oz smiled at her. "They resemble a horse. Except they're a might bigger. I saw one once while travelin' that was twen'y-five hands high, an' eight hands wide 'cross the chest. Their colors vary a bit, but they're mostly light charcoal er black. Most a' the ones I saw had streaks a' white an' teal 'round their eyes, ears, an' mouth, an' a few other places on the body."

The movement through the brush and up the mountain side drew everyone's attention. They all began gathering on the platform, looking out over Storm Valley below. It wasn't long before the Yarequu burst forth out of the forest that encompassed the valley, coming to a halt in the open field. The Yarequu pranced around, tossing their heads, and waiting on whoever it was that had called to them.

They all stood around watching the animals, fascinated by their appearance. Just seconds later, Dominic and Cho landed in the valley. They could all see him interacting with the Yarequu, trying to calm them from the sheer fright of a firebird landing near them. It didn't take Dominic long to calm them before Wade and the other firebird landed as well. He jumped down to help Dominic stay the Yarequu once again.

Zeke said, "I sure hope these kids can get all these animals to work together. Those horse looking things look mighty scared of the Kabi…thingys."

Zaccai smiled at his failure to learn the animals names. "Kabihanxus," she corrected. "Just call them firebirds if you can't remember."

"Not sure I can remember that either." He grinned.

"Wasn't it fun riding one?"

"I wouldn't exactly say fun."

"Well, you best get the hang of it. Because now that the Keepers are back, we have to get this show on the road." Zaccai's eyebrows rose at how uncomfortable he looked with the idea of flying on the Kabihanxu again. She walked away with Zeke following behind. He exhaled loudly and shook off the feelings of anxiety that wanted to take him over.

By the time everyone made their way to where the animals had gathered, mounted them, and made it to Storm Valley, Bridget and Annabelle were riding in on the Monshokto.

Seth's eyes grew wide. "What in the world is that?"

"Well, I assume it's the Monshokto," Jason replied.

"How do you remember the odd names of all these creatures?"

Jason smiled at Seth, raising his hand as he spoke. "Veterinarian, remember?"

"Still, it's impressive."

Bridget and Annabelle rode to a stop, with each group of animals staying within their own packs.

Bridget and the other Keepers all chatted with the animals, warning the predators not to try and eat the non-predators.

Bridget spoke to the group. "All right everyone. Let's get each of you familiar with your creature. I wish to try something. A sort of experiment between rider and beast. I'll come around later and show you what I mean. The sky, or wind group gets the Kabihanxus of course. The land or earth group will be riding the Yarequu. Wade, take the others over and introduce them."

"You all heard the lady, this way." Wade waved them over toward him.

"Now, the Pagorinxes will go underground with the fire group. They can travel quickly in darkness with their eyeshine. Annabelle, I believe you are that group's Keeper. Take them and introduce them."

Annabelle smiled to actually be in charge of showing the adults what to do.

Bridget looked up at the docile beast beside her. "The last group, the water warriors, will get to ride these sweet creatures."

Alec stepped up to them with a questioning look on his face. "Bridget, are you certain that these big, hairy, things can actually be beneficial while battling a dragon?"

"I've already seen a little of what they can do. Plus, they like the water."

"So do turtles, but I doubt they would be much help."

Bridget smiled at Alec in a reprimanding way.

"I'm positive that you will be pleasantly surprised."

"I sure hope you're right. I can see a dragon setting these things on fire and these furry things running for the hills." Alec squinted as he looked them over.

"I doubt a water dragon breathes fire." Bridget giggled.

"That makes sense. I hear dragon and I assume fire-breather."

"Dominic will help you all get familiar with them. I need to go see about my own group."

Bridget left them and walked over to Zeke, who didn't look too sure about what to do with the Kabihanxus.

"Zeke, I'll let you ride Cho. She's very familiar with people riding her, and she won't give you any trouble at all."

"All right. If you say so." Zeke said following Bridget over to the large animal.

As Zeke stepped up to Cho, she turned her large head to look at him. Zeke stopped in his tracks and looked her in the one large eye that was peering at him. Just one of her eyes was as large as his hand. Cho must have sensed his reservations about her. She moved her large beak down toward the ground and used her head to rub up against Zeke.

Zeke stiffened at first, tightly closing his eyes, unsure what to do.

Bridget smiled at his discomfort. "Zeke, she's trying to make friends with you."

He opened one eye and looked at the bird still peering at him. He lifted one hand up and slowly began petting her. She cooed and moved a tad against his hand, reassuring him that it was okay.

Zeke relaxed a bit, realizing that the massive beast was gentle and understood his discomfort.

"Uh…okay. This isn't so bad." Zeke relaxed some more.

"I said earlier that I wanted to try something. Are you game?"

"I suppose so," Zeke answered a bit hesitantly.

"Trust me, if this works, it will benefit you greatly." Bridget placed two fingers to her temple, and using her other hand placed two on Zeke's temple. "All right Zeke, I want you to place your hand on Cho's head, right between her eyes."

Zeke did as she asked.

"Good, now close your eyes and concentrate on Cho."

Zeke did what she said.

Bridget began instructing him again. "Now give Cho a command but do it with your mind, not your voice."

Zeke told Cho to lay down and she obeyed. Zeke was astounded that it worked. Bridget smiled brightly, taking her hands away. "Now, give her another command either verbally or telepathically."

Zeke told her to stand and she obeyed.

"Yes! It worked! You are now connected with your animal."

"This is really cool," Zeke said excitedly.

"Good," Bridget stated. "Now, climb on her back."

Zeke looked at Bridget, not too sure he was ready to fly off on Cho and fight a dragon. Yes, he had flown on one of these to the tree house and then back to Storm Valley, clinging onto the things neck for dear life. He was not yet a confident rider. But he had best learn to be, and quickly.

"Okay, I can do this," Zeke said, trying to bolster his confidence.

Oz called out across the valley. "Zeke, these things used ta try an' eat me fer breakfast! If I could get used ta ridin' 'em , you surely can!"

"Eat you!" Zeke said, now unsure again.

"Zeke…" Bridget admonished him by only using his name.

"I'm going, I'm going." Zeke squared his shoulders, took a deep breath, and climbed onto Cho's back. She stood up instantly, with Zeke bouncing around just a bit.

"Whoa, big girl!" he nervously called.

Bridget looked up at him in all seriousness. "Zeke, you have to trust Cho. Move with her, lean the direction she leans. Feel the rhythm of her breathing. She can sense your feelings. The more you relax, the better the two of you will work together."

"Yes Yoda!" Zeke saluted.

"What's a Yoda?" Bridget asked confused.

"Never mind, I'll tell you later." Zeke forgot that Bridget was from the year 1580 and wouldn't understand the reference.

Bridget went around the valley doing the same connectivity trick that she did with Zeke. Now everyone could communicate with their animals. She stood back and yelled as loudly as possible. "All right everyone, you have a few hours to bond and get used to your animals before sunset. Use the time wisely."

Zaccai asked, "Bridget, do we know anything about the Monshokto that will help us?"

"The only thing I have discovered, is when they feel threatened, they make a low vibrating sound that can bring you to your knees. The waves reverberate off the body of their attacker and repel it."

Zaccai shook her head in appreciation. "Good to know."

Seth asked, "What about the Yarequu?"

"I have no clue. Perhaps they move really fast?" Bridget shrugged.

"That's it? That's all you got?" Seth asked shocked.

"Sorry. I'm sure there are things you'll discover about each while in battle, so don't be too surprised should something unusual happen."

"Sure. They get fire-breathing birds, sound repelling hairy things, and sabertoothed cats. We get, what? Basically just a glorified horse," Seth said sarcastically.

His Yarequu threw its head around, whinnied, and danced about in agitation.

"Sorry!" Seth said to the beast. "I'm just saying. If you got it, show me something."

The beast snorted indignantly at his demand.

The next several hours was spent as Bridget suggested. Everyone bonded and got to know their creatures.

They decided to take a little break before the sun went down and grab a bite to eat. Everyone making sure that Caroline ate and was feeling well.

Sean used his water gift to bring some fresh water to the animals from a nearby spring, allowing them to drink the water right out of the air. The Monshokto, after drinking, ran through it, splashing and wetting their coats. There wasn't a huge amount for them to play in, but they tried none the less. Making Bridget and their riders realize that they not only liked water, but they probably needed it as well.

Bridget looked at Zaccai. "We may have found something else they have. Oz did say he watched them swimming in Everly Lake. Since you're fighting a water dragon, that is obviously important."

"Well, being able to ride them in water will hopefully be beneficial. Not sure how this armor is supposed to help with that though."

"Is the armor very heavy?" Bridget asked.

"Surprisingly, no. It's a bit stiff, but I'm getting accustomed to it now. Do you think the difference between salt water and fresh water will harm the Monshokto?"

"What do you mean?"

"I'm assuming that Everly Lake is a fresh water source, unlike the Pacific Ocean."

"I'm not sure. But I do know that these creatures are the ones that God brought me to. So, He must know something we don't."

"Let's hope so." Zaccai grinned.

Dominic watched the group of people sitting upon the creatures backs and had a thought.

"I think we need to make some sort of harness or saddles. It might be hard to stay on the animals in a fight."

Oz looked at him. "Ya' got a point there, Dom'nic. I got some leather an' rope up at the treehouse. We can use that t'night ta make what we need."

Caroline chimed in. "I suggest we get started. We have to leave at first-light." They all spent the better part of the next four hours doing just that.

The large group rode up to the treehouse, gathered the materials they needed to make the necessary accessories for their creatures, and got to work. They measured and fit their harnesses to their creatures making certain everything was right before falling into their bedrolls on any available treehouse surface.

The next morning, after a long night of working leather and rope, and getting about five hours of sleep, the Peregrines and their creatures appeared back at Storm Valley just before sunrise.

Jason watched the sky with interest. "All right everybody. Pay attention, it's almost time to leave."

Everyone watched the sun and the valley for signs of a portal. Several watched the horizon, while everyone else picked a different direction of the valley to scan.

The sun glinted over the mountains, and near the center of Storm Valley a portal appeared, glowing brightly in glittering hues of gold, green, and blue.

"This way!" Kristin yelled.

Everyone turned to follow her, racing across Storm Valley and through the portal. When the last Peregrine and beast ran through the portal, it stayed open only a few more seconds before closing.

Tanmoyaro Draconomai

The group of travelers exited the portal onto an island, lush and green, resembling a tropical jungle. A large mountain loomed far above with large waterfalls cascading down the steep sides and splashing into large pools of water surrounding the base of the mountain where they stood.

Nicholas looked around. 'Well, you all think we're on the right island?"

Caroline answered, "If that mountain is any indication, I'd say we are in the right place."

They all looked up at the tall, looming, mountain that appeared to have no end.

Odessa's premonition gift gave her a vision.

"We're in the right place," she said nervously. "Everyone get ready. I think we're about to have a visitor."

Jason replied, "Which means the rest of us need to get going and find our own dragons."

Seth quickly turned to Caroline. "You be careful Beautiful. Take care of you and baby J."

Caroline smiled crookedly at his reference. "I will. You be careful too, Seth."

Everyone looked to their significant other, giving a knowing look, or an expression of love mixed with caution to each other. Then, each group rode off in different directions. The sound of a far away, deep, roar penetrating the air.

The wind dragon group on the backs of the Kabihanxus climbed high and fast up through the sky, staying close to the mountain.

The group on the Pagorinxes rode around the circumference of the mountain at breakneck speed on the agile, and quickly moving animals, searching for the entrance to the cave that would take them to the earth's core. They needed to find it quickly before the land dragon appeared. They didn't want to fight a battle that was not theirs to fight. As they rounded another section of mountain, another roar rang out over the air just when they found a massive opening in the rock. They entered the dark cave, with only the Pagorinxes to rely on to find their way.

As the daylight waned, Nick yelled out "I wish I could see something!"

"Me too!" Sean answered.

Gabriele thought a minute about their request. She used her shielding ability to create a barrier in front of all of them as they moved. The shield in front of them acted like a curved, two-way mirror.

"Nick, use your fire ability to merge with my shield power!" she yelled.

"What?" He yelled back, confused.

"Shoot your fire at my shield! I want to try something!"

"All right," Nick answered, unsure about what she expected to happen.

When he did as she asked, the fireball from his hands hit and spread out over the shield, illuminating it all around out in front of them. Their two combined powers worked like a giant, red-orange flashlight beam. Allowing them to see what was in front of them. They were amazed at how agile the Pagorinxes were in the quickly changing interior of the cave. Although, the size of it shook them to their very core, knowing the size of the beast that must come and go through these passageways.

The Surface

On the surface, the two groups on land searched for their adversaries as well. The land group held their position, knowing that Odessa's vision meant that the dragons likely knew they were there and were waiting and searching for them as well.

Jason told the group. "Let's push back into the trees to give us some cover until this thing gets here." As they did, they realized that the Yarequu's flesh began to change and take on the colors of the jungle, giving it camouflage abilities. What's more, its riders were also given the same camouflage by way of proxy. Anything that touched it's flesh in this state received the same.

Seth smiled, patting the large beast on the neck. "Now that's what I'm talking about."

His Yarequu huffed and lowly whinnied in response to the appreciation for one of its defense mechanisms. The group of riders all searched for one another, smiling at the discovery. Each able to make out only slight impressions of the others outlines.

In another area of the island, the water group rode across the land as fast as the Monshokto could run, headed for the coast and the open sea. They assumed the water dragon would be in the ocean waters that surrounded the island. They were still unsure how they were to fight something like that in the water; all of them hoping the fight would take place from the shoreline.

The Sky

Back at the mountain, the Kabihanxus rose higher and higher. Their massive wings pushed them and their riders through the sky. Their riders held onto the quickly-fashioned harnesses, locking their legs on the underside of their wings. They were going at such an angle that the Peregrines were nearly standing up straight.

The air around them began to grow colder and colder the higher they flew. Each one now realizing the necessity for the thermal undergarments that Simon insisted they all four wear beneath their clothing and armor .

Caroline was curious as to the strength of her armor against the bone chilling cold and ice, compared to the heat treatment with which it had been forged. She looked over at Bridget through the opening of the helmet. She seemed to be handling the cold just fine. However, they weren't quite to the top where the air would grow colder still. Caroline was thankful for the face protection of the helmet, yet worried about her young friend being so exposed to the extreme and sudden change in temperature.

Bridget shivered slightly at the force of cold air that rushed against her body. She pulled up at the scarf she wore about her neck, pulling it up over her cheeks and nose and around her ears. It wasn't an easy task to do with one hand while traveling at the speed and angle they were.

As they climbed higher, they began to see clouds forming above them. Or was it smoke of some sort? They heard a loud screech penetrate the air, clouds rolled out from the mountains center, and lightning flashed inside the darkening mass.

As they flew into the clouds, Cho, the lead firebird let out a squawk and suddenly spun, cutting to the far left. The other firebirds followed her lead.

Caroline and the other riders realized that she had sensed the floating mountains of the peak and had cut left to avoid flying into the underside of one of them. They too had sensed or seen with an internal eye what their firebirds were seeing and sensing. The gift Bridget was able to bestow on them back in Zanchier becoming more and more evident as to its uses and benefits.

The Kabihanxus leveled off, stationary amongst the clouds that were so thick they couldn't see each other, let alone a predator that could be coming at them from any direction. They all pulled their weapons and clung onto the birds with the free hand that was laced through the leather straps of the shields which now sat snuggly on their forearms.

The firebirds were slightly winded due to the flight straight up the mountain, so each one located the edge of one of the many floating landscapes and lighted to rest while they could.

Zeke watched the horizon with a trained eye. Any movement he saw he would alert the others. But how? *'How am I supposed to communicate with the other flyers?'* he wondered, not daring to make noise.

'I can sense you Zeke.' Caroline remembered when she first learned she was telepathic and had a hard time concealing her thoughts from others.

'Caroline?' Zeke questioned.

'Yes,' she replied.

'How is this possible?'

'It must be Bridget's gift.'

As they spoke telepathically, all the other riders entered in the conversation with them. Odessa was already telepathic as was Bridget. Zeke was the only one who hadn't had the gift before now.

Zeke smiled. *'Well, this is certainly fortuitous. Do any of you see anything through this heavy coverage?'*

Everyone answered no. Just at that moment, Zeke noticed a stirring and what he thought might have been the back of a dragon, flying around the edge of the floating land.

'I think I have a visual. Hold steady Cho.' He commanded the now nervously prancing firebird.

Suddenly, a massive dragon flew upwards out of the clouds about fifty feet away from where Zeke and Cho sat. It was ice blue in color at the thinnest parts and melded to a frosty white that covered its entire body. It had four long legs and two very large front wings which extended out quite far. At the top of the wing joint on both sides, three fingerlike claws protruded from the top. It's tale was long, with icy barbs protruding upward in three directions. It stopped just above the clouds and looked at them. It suddenly opened its mouth revealing sharp teeth that looked like black, curved, icicles. It drew in a deep breath making a hissing noise and then blew out, sending ice spikes flying from its mouth straight at them.

"Fly Cho!" Zeke screamed.

Before he could get the words out of his mouth Cho had already moved. Flying upward away from the spikes and toward the dragon, blowing fire from her mouth. The dragon flew back, screeching in fear, sending streaks of lightning out from its body in every direction. Cho absorbed some of the lightning, protecting Zeke from being struck.

Zeke was shocked that Cho was capable of that. He could feel the electricity flowing through her veins, the charge giving her strength, and him as well.

The other riders appeared by his side.

"That way!" Zeke pointed in the direction that the dragon had flown.

All four of them flew downward into the cold, misty, clouds, cautiously searching for the beast.

'We can't see in this stuff,' Odessa stated telepathically.

Zeke thought for a second. Weather was his gift. He laid his sword across his lap, lifted his hand, and concentrated on the mist that surrounded them, making a pushing motion with his hand. The air around them began to swirl and the clouds began to clear away as the dim brightness of the setting sun began filling the space where the clouds once were, filtering in between the now bare spots. Within seconds the cold mist was nearly completely dissolved away, and the floating mountains were revealed in their entirety. The wind dragon sat upon one of the largest peaks, smoke billowing from its nostrils. It peered at them, angry that its cover had somehow been removed. It let loose a loud, angry, roar that vibrated the snow-capped mountains, making some of the snow slide down the sides and fall toward the earth far below.

Zeke grabbed his sword. "All right ladies, here we go."

They all flew at once toward the dragon, it too leaping into the air, charging these invaders who dared to trespass upon its homeland.

Reader's Island

Simon stood in front of the pedestal. The fire in the metal bowl lit the area that would soon be completely dark within the hour. He felt the charge in the air, signaling that the hour for battle wasn't too far away.

"You all have the next six hours to rest before the battle begins. We don't know if the time between realms is different, so I want you all to be back here by four a.m. They all left, headed back to the mansion for a good night's rest before warfare would begin in the early morning hours.

Their sleep was fitful. No one was able to rest well knowing that they faced a spiritual and a physical battle just hours away. They all played an important part and therefore must all do their jobs well. Three a.m. rolled around, and everyone got up to prepare. They would need to be at the gardens by four, most of them making their way there earlier, just to be safe.

Simon was already there of course. He waited for Malachai, Vashti, and Prisca to stand before their pedestals.

"All right everyone, it's time to open the books. Be ready to read very soon. The Final Battle is about to begin."

The Dragoman readied themselves while the rest of the island began praying for the safety and success of their friends who battled the great evil that plagued the world.

They stood silently, waiting for the Spirit to lead. Suddenly, they all felt the Spirit tell them to begin reading the names of the saints who had come and gone while under their mentorship. Starting with the most recently deceased who had lost their lives for the cause over the last six months. The names of the fallen saints filled the air as each Dragoman read simultaneously from their books, calling out the full given name of each and every one.

In that day the Lord will punish with His sword
-His fierce, great, and powerful sword-
Leviathan the gliding serpent, leviathan the coiling
serpent. He will slay the monster of the sea.

Isaiah 27:1

Chapter 21

Tanmoyaro Draconomai, Present Day
Pacific Ocean, Fifth Dimension Plane,

The Land

Seth watched the trees around the clearing for signs of the dragon headed their way. It was a large area, and if they could lead the dragon into it, they would at least be able to see it fully. Seth looked around noticing a rather wide area like a dirt road that cut through the trees on either side of the large clearing. He wondered where it went, and who would live here amongst these dragons to even use such a thing. Then reality struck him.

"Jason, you remember when they said these things were large."

"Yeah," Jason answered, not taking his eyes from the horizon.

"You see that?" Seth pointed at the worn area that ran far along the mountain's base.

Jason looked at where Seth pointed. The worn path that this beast often roamed across was so wide that two eighteen wheelers could fit end to end across it.

"Lord help us," Jason said, so shocked by the width of it that his words weren't much more than a whisper.

The ground began to shake around them with each approaching step of the large animal. Both Jason and Seth counted between each small shake, trying to gauge how big this dragon truly was.

Seth's eyes grew large. "Five seconds, Jason, between each tremor."

"Either he's really slow, or truly gigantic," Jason replied.

"I vote for slow. Slow is good," Seth added.

"Me too, Brother. But I don't think that's the correct answer."

The beast roared again, this time sounding close. The earth shakes began to feel stronger as each large step the beast took grew closer. Then, they saw it.

The mud brown and mossy green colored behemoth lumbered toward them, its square shaped head and long neck far ahead of its massive, log-style torso. It bellowed again, its torso contracting in large heaves as it rang out across the island. It's large tree stump legs and massive tale swished back and forth, toppling trees like toothpicks. Its spiky toes clicked out in front of it. They all looked up, shocked by the size of the beast. Its square head had two eyes on either side, giving it a view of one-hundred-and-eighty degrees. Its powerful bone-crushing jowls held large, round, slightly sharp teeth, except for four. The two bottom canines were larger, razor sharp, and jutted out over the top lip, extending upward. Directly in front of those two were two more that extended downward over the bottom lip, a bit longer and just as sharp.

They all looked at one another in shock and disbelief.

"I'm afraid this is going to be a long morning," Kristen said lowly.

Seth said, "Wade, anytime you want to do your thing, have at it."

Wade replied, "If I only knew what that was, I'd be happy to oblige. Maybe."

The beast stopped moving and let out another massively loud roar that made them want to cover their ears.

They all inhaled and exhaled one last steadying breath.

"Time to go I think. Try not to die," Seth said to everyone, being the first to ride out of the safety of their camouflaged environment toward the beast whose attention he was about to capture.

The Shore

Zaccai, Wendel, Alec and Dominic sat at the shoreline looking out at the expanse of water before them. The Monshokto they sat upon started making gurgling noises and began fidgeting with excitement over the large amount of water. However, they appeared a bit frightened by some of the larger waves that broke against the shoreline.

"Steady boy," Zaccai patted the beasts neck. "This is no time for a leisurely swim. Just as she sat back again she and the others spotted a rather large looking mass of water being pushed in their direction.

"I think we got comp'ny comin'," Oz stated dryly.

They all watched anxiously as the wave of water got closer. The more the beast traveled forward, the shallower the water became and the more the beast was revealed. They could see two large split fins, deep blue in color that they assumed ran down its back. The Monshokto began to grow wary, feeling the anxiety of their riders, and sensing danger ahead.

"If that's company, then I say we go out for dinner and leave the company to itself," Alec joked. No one, not even himself, laughed.

"Too late fer that! 'Sides, we were the ones ta come callin'." Oz pulled his sword from its sheath and slapped his helmet down into place.

Everyone followed his example, except for poor Dominic who had little more than a shield and a sword. Neither of which was from the Armor of God. He had no idea what his role in all this was supposed to be, but he was feeling poorly equipped for whatever it was he was to do to help them fight the huge monster before him.

As the leviathan grew closer, it suddenly stopped in front of them. It slowly stood in the shallow water, rising high into the air, roaring in protest at being disturbed. It had six, long, crab-like legs which attached to its torso, and a thick exoskeleton that covered its chest and abdomen down to the tail. The long tail split into three sections near the end, with large round balls on the ends of each tail, all three covered in a thick exoskeleton. Its top half was like the flesh of a mammal over which the long fins on its back ran from the base of its skull to its haunches. It had long, tentacle like arms, the bottom of which were covered in suction cups like the tentacles of an octopus. It had little to no neck and its triangular shaped head stared down at them with large piercing black eyes. Barnacle encrusted spikes attached to the edges of its face and jowls stuck out like black and blue knives in every direction. It had two rows of sharp pointed teeth, a shade somewhere between the black and blue of its body; like shiny black pearls. Its body was so wide that it blotted out the rising sun which streaked the sky in every direction behind the creature's hulking form.

"What are we supposed to do against that?" Zaccai asked, stunned.

"Whatever we can," Oz stated, taking a ready stance to do battle as the beast roared and began moving forward.

The Cave

The Pagorinxes traveled quickly, deep into the long passage down into the earth. They reached a point where they started to slow down, nearly stopping altogether when approaching a series of massive caverns all linked together by a series of openings strewn about. The Pagorinxes growled lowly, sensing something foreboding. They stood their ground, all looking in one direction. Their riders all looked to one another, realizing they had likely arrived at their destination.

They listened intently, searching for any sound to come from one of the many caverns. They could hear a low rumble like a deep growl, but much larger than that of the Pagorinxes.

Nick telepathically told his Pagorinx, '*Slowly, boy. Move forward slowly.*'

His Pagorinx obeyed, followed by the rest of the pack. They entered one of the caves on the right and as quietly as possible slunk their way through the inky darkness.

Sean telepathically asked, '*How are we supposed to see down here to be able to fight this dragon?*'

Nick answered. '*I'm not sure. Look for some torches or something to light. Gabby is going to have to free her hand to fight. She can't hold the light-shield forever.*'

They all searched the walls of the cavern for anything that resembled a torch. They found nothing.

A deep, raspy, rumbling voice pierced the darkness. "I'll light your way for you. Just to make your deaths easier."

They all looked at each other in surprise.

"I can hear your thoughts, and I can sense your fears," the voice said again.

Annabelle asked, "Where are you?"

"Keep coming. You draw nearer."

"What are you?" she asked the voice again.

"You know me little one. Am I not who you came to destroy? We've been waiting for you. We sensed you when you entered the island."

"Who is we?" Nick asked, searching the caverns interior.

"My sisters and I," the voice droned out.

"There is more than you down here?"

"There is just me here. My sisters are above the ground. However, do not think that I need their help or fear you."

As they slowly walked through the massive cavern, the voice let out a roar and fire shot from its mouth, making them all jump. It lit a nearby stalagmite which protruded from the ground. It obviously emitted some sort of fuel source from somewhere in the mountain. The dragon did this several more times around the perimeter of the cave until the entire inside of the cavern was visible. The walls of the cave now sparkled in the firelight. Precious jewels that had been forged over the years from the dragon's fiery breath upon the caverns walls flickered like hundreds of tiny mirrors.

In one corner, in the furthest part of the cavern, they saw something that appeared to be rock move in the firelight. The creature twisted and turned until its entire form was unfurled.

The huge dragon before them breathed heavily in and out. Its massive chest and torso expanding and contracting, revealing a red-orange light which was visible between its large scales with each breath. The light faded into a yellowish color further from its chest. It stood high above them, peering down at them with large, red-veined yellow eyes.

"Are you impressed by me?" she vainly asked. "I am rather large, and quite intimidating I am sure." She strutted around in front of them, shaking her large head and unfurling her twisted and disfigured wings. She sensed what drew their attention. "Yes, my wings are not so impressive anymore. They have grown weak from lack of use. I've been stuck in this cave for nearly a hundred years. Unable to get to the surface."

"Why?" Annabelle asked innocently.

The dragon's head came down toward her, its pointed nose sharp with spikes jutting out along the sides. Its sharp teeth and rank breath now very close to the small girl and her Pagorinx.

"Because of your kind," it answered. "Now, I grow weary of this talking. And it's been years since I've had such a willing meal. I don't need my wings for the likes of you tiny creatures." The dragon straightened back up, took a deep breath, and belched out a great mass of fire toward the group.

The Sky

The dragon hissed and belched ice spikes at the riders. The Kabihanxus dodged the flying ice spears. Several let out screeches of fire, two riders and their firebirds each taking opposite sides of the dragon to attack as it flew between them.

Caroline and Zeke each reached out and struck the dragon. One on the wing tip and one on its leg. The dragon screeched in pain, as lightning flashed all around it.

Bridget noticed something where they had struck the dragon.

"Did you see that!" she yelled, as her firebird stopped and turned, hovering in the air.

Odessa flew up next to her. "See what?"

"Each time the dragon was struck, there was a flash of light."

"Well, keep an eye out. It could be important." Odessa flew off, ready for another attack by the dragon, which was turning widely in the air, circling back around toward them.

The dragon came back again, slinging its tail up over its head as sharp, cold, shards of ice flew at them again. She hissed again, also blowing icy spikes at them. They dodged the spikes as best they could, Odessa's Kabihanxu screeching in pain as one landed in the birds shoulder. Odessa reached down, trying to pull the icy spear from the firebird's shoulder as it clumsily flew down to one of the floating mountains. She dismounted, pulled the spike from the Kabihanxu's shoulder, and then remounted her.

The other three Kabihanxus flew at the Dragon, all three of them blowing fire at the beast as the dragon flew away circling the floating mountains, trying to find a temporary place of hiding. Suddenly the dragon disappeared somewhere amongst the floating mountains and the tip of the stationary mountain peak.

They all flew back to where Odessa had landed. Bridget leaned over her Kabihanxu's wing to inspect the wound of the injured bird.

"It doesn't look to bad," she stated. "Can you fly," she asked the firebird.

The creature threw its head up and down in the air, giving itself one good shake, making Odessa sway from side to side on its back.

"Good." Bridget looked at Odessa. "If not you can both fight from the mountain here. We'll do our best to keep the dragon in this area."

"Sounds like a plan," Odessa replied, stroking the feathers of the injured creature.

Zeke turned to them. "Anyone see where that thing went?"

Just as the words left his mouth, Cho turned at the sound of hissing, and shot another blast of fire from her mouth, melting the spikes before they could harm anyone.

The four of them were off again, chasing down the dragon. Odessa's bird flew a bit slower due to its injuries. The firebirds chased closely behind the dragon, spitting fire, and singeing her tail and wing tips. As the fire went out upon the dragon's skin, wispy smoke swirled up from the charred areas, followed by golden streaks of words shot across the dragon's body, inward toward her torso, making it shriek even more.

"Look, there!" Bridget yelled and pointed. "What is that?"

Caroline replied, "It appears to be words!"

"Words?" Odessa asked, confused.

"It seems that every time we strike her, the area where she gets hit streaks out in golden glowing writing of some sort!" Bridget confirmed.

Zeke yelled across to them. "Can anyone read what it says?"

"No!" they all yelled simultaneously, looking at him with disbelief.

Zeke shrugged off their reply. "Let's get busy then." He and his firebird flew forward chasing after the dragon, followed closely by the other three. The dragon swooped and turned between the floating mountains, hoping to shake its predators. It flew into a dark cave on the underside of one of the floating mountains. The darkness of the cave made it impossible to see where the dragon had gone.

The Land

Seth and his Yarequu, followed closely by the others, rode out toward the massive, treelike, creature. Seth realized that the Yarequu's defenses had kicked in again and they were now the color of the ground beneath them. He looked over at Jason who rode beside him, able to only make out his outline as they sped past the tree-line far off the clearing's edge.

Seth smiled, knowing no one could see his expression. And that meant that the behemoth before them couldn't locate them either, hopefully. The animal was so tall, they could ride underneath it and not touch the belly. Seth decided that was exactly what he'd do.

He lifted his sword and cut a line from one side of the beast's torso to the other, noticing a golden line of words appear as he did so. The behemoth bellowed in pain, thrashing its tail, and standing up on two hind legs, kicking it's front legs in pain. It landed with an earthshaking crash, as the water in the pools surrounding the mountain crashed and splashed against the rocks and over the edge onto the ground.

Jason and Kristin stabbed and sliced the beasts hind legs, making it roar out in pain once more. They too noticed words that appeared as glowing streaks up the beast legs.

Wade was surprised to hear speaking when the beast cried out the last time.

'Who dares challenge me? The behemoth formed by the Creator!'

Wade wasn't sure what to do. Should he answer the beast?

It spoke again. *'I sense you,'* she hissed. *'I smell your fear, your doubt. Why have you come here? Your kind is unwelcome.'*

Wade decided he should answer. Perhaps he could keep it busy while the others fought it.

"We were sent here by God! You are destroying the world!" he yelled, happy to still be concealed by camouflage.

'My kind is destroying the world? Nay, it is you and yours that are guilty of that sin. Man's sins have caused great convulsions in nature. We are nature. Man's sins have corrupted us. Made us like what you see. You turn us into evil with your sins yet wish to punish us for your own evil deeds!'

Jason, Seth, and Kristin realized that Wade was speaking to the behemoth. And apparently, it was speaking to Wade! They rode wide, circling the beast, trying to judge where to strike at it next.

"What do you mean man has corrupted you? Who is this 'us' that you speak of?" Wade yelled back.

'My sisters and I. The keepers of the seasons. We were once young, and beautiful. Until man's sins twisted our hearts and caused ugliness, pain, envy, deceit, greed, and many others to take hold within us. Our Keepers, like you, were supposed to care for us. Keep us away from the ugliness of the world. They too became corrupt. Feeding us lies, and hatred until they perished in their ugliness, leaving me and my sisters alone. We grow with the hatred and evil, and we lash out at that same hatred and evil that seeks to destroy us.'

"What is the evil? Perhaps I can help?"

The behemoth roared loudly, yet Wade heard it as laughter. *'You are that evil! Man is the evil that we must destroy. We send storms, rain, winds, earthquakes. Yet we have failed. Man still lives.'*

"God, the Creator doesn't wish for man's destruction."

'Hah! The Creator abandoned us long ago. We do not follow the creator. The evil one is our master now, and we seek to do his work!'

The behemoth lifted one massive leg and stomped the ground, making the earth shake and crack beneath her, large crevices in the land shooting out all around her.

Kristen noticed this, barely missing a split in the earth that nearly claimed her and her Yarequu, and the others as well.

Kristen called to the others telepathically. *'Move, quickly, back to the trees.'*

As the others rode back into the underbrush as she had told them to, she looked to the mountain beside her. She sheathed her weapon and used her free hand to summon the rock from high up on the mountain. A loud cracking noise was heard, as huge rocks gave way. A massive rockslide slid from above the behemoth and bounced its way down the slope, sliding and tumbling all around the behemoths left side. The large boulders slammed into the beast, sending her tumbling over onto her right side. She was down and covered in heavy rock.

The men took the opportunity to ride at the beast, striking at her again and again, golden words streaking across her flesh as she roared and thrashed in pain. They got in a dozen or so more strikes before the beast was able to right herself. Now limping as she lumbered about, searching for her attackers. About one-fourth of her flesh was now covered in glowing words.

Wade could somehow see the words with his mind. He was able to read them, yet he still didn't know what they meant.

The Shore

Oz, Zaccai, Alec, and Dominic quickly separated, some taking cover behind some large pieces of driftwood.

The leviathan slowly made its way onto the shore, yet never fully left the water. It reared its head and screeched a high-pitched, ear-piercing sound that shook the ground and fallen trees around them. The sound was multifaceted, like a sonar wave of sorts.

This gave Oz pause. He looked at Alec who was squatted beside him. "I sure hope that wasn' a call fer help?"

"Surely not. There cannot be two of these things!" Alec protested in disbelief.

"Let's hope not." Oz steeled himself, adjusted his armor a bit and said, "We might as well git goin'." He and his Monshokto rode out toward the leviathan, sword raised.

The leviathan watched his approach, throwing its head back and roaring as if to laugh. It turned toward Oz and began its approach.

Oz's Monshokto stopped, planted all four feet soundly in the sand and began to bellow deeply. A deep reverberating sound emanated from its throat, pulsing, and vibrating toward the leviathan.

Alec and the others had begun their approach, shocked by what they saw. The leviathans approach had been slowed by the sound waves holding it back. Their own Monshoktos joined with Oz's beast. The loud vibrations from all four beasts began to push the leviathan back into the water.

Oz telepathically said to everyone, *'This is all well an' good. But we gotta' fight this thing at some point. Ifn' we jus' push it back, we ain't doin' what we came here fer."*

Zaccai replied, *'True. What do you suggest?'*

'We go in after it!' Oz stated.

Dominic's eyes grew wide. *'Why don't we just back off and let it come on shore. In the water, I'm sure it would have a massive advantage.'*

Alec said, *'I agree with Dominic. Let's try that first!'*

The four of them pulled back on their Monshoktos, turning and heading inland toward the dense jungle just beyond the sand.

The leviathan screeched in agitation, beginning to climb out of the water once more, chasing after the small creatures who dared challenge it.

The four of them gathered in the jungle, trying to make a plan.

Dominic asked, "What do we do? How are we supposed to fight that thing?"

The leviathan began speaking, yet only Dominic heard its voice.

'Come out and fight! You cannot hide from me. I will crush you and your puny creatures.'

Everyone watched as Dominic's face was overcome with disbelief.

"What's wrong with ya' boy?"

Dominic looked at him in questioning shock. "Did you not just hear that thing challenge us and say it was going to crush us?"

"Nope, didn' hear a thing. Must be why yer here. Ta' communicate with the beast."

"What am I supposed to say to it?" Dominic squeaked in question.

"I don' know. Fig're out somethin'. Distract it so we can come up behind it."

Dominic sat there on his Monshokto, not sure what to do or say. The others rode off as quietly as possible to do as Oz suggested.

"Can I talk to you for a minute?" Dominic audibly pleaded with the beast so that the others could hear him.

'There is nothing to talk about. You have come to destroy us. We have expected you for many years. Now you are here. There is no need to talk. Only to fight. And for you to die.'

"Die!" Dominic yelled. "I don't wish to die. I don't wish to kill you. I just want to talk."

'Perhaps that is your cause, but those with you have other plans. My sisters and I all yearn for death, yet we fight to live. We cannot give up the hate within us. It is strong and wills us on. It keeps us going, feeding on man's sins.'

"We can give you peace. You can rest, giving over man's sins. We can take the pain and hatred away."

'I doubt that. Ugliness has been with us for far too long. It is who we have become. There is no turning back! We must die to be released! And though we wish for that release, we will not go quietly!'

The leviathan swung its long tentacled arms into the trees just above Dominic's head, sending palm trees, plants, and sand flying into the air. He and his Monshokto turned and ran, running underneath the leviathan's torso and belly to meet up with Oz, Zaccai, and Alec who came in swinging from the other end of the beach.

The leviathan screeched and turned to catch its prey. It reached out toward Dominic and the Monshokto with one long tentacle. Dominic looked back over his shoulder, yelling for the beast he rode to hurry. The Monshokto turned and faced the leviathan, its one horn in the center of its head creating an electrical barrier around itself and Dominic. The leviathan's tentacle pad reached out to grab them, screeching, and pulling away in pain as it's pad sizzled at contact with the shield. Oz, Zaccai, and Alec each swung at its crab like legs, severing the smallest part at the base, making the animal fall slightly onto the sand. Glittering gold words flashed against the severed leg and curled upward and around the beast's exoskeleton toward its abdomen.

The all looked puzzled by this but didn't have time to think much on it. They all continued to swing at the creature from beneath it. Fighting with everything they had in them. Alec momentarily left the back of his Monshokto as one long tentacle flew around at them. He teleported himself up onto the leviathan's back, striking downward into the flesh of the creature. Again, the golden glittering words appeared, webbing out along the creatures back in every direction.

The leviathan screeched piercingly at the contact that Alec had made with the Sword of the Spirit. It reared up, but not before Alec stabbed again and again, piercing it deeply. Alec began slipping from the leviathan's back as it stood up on its hind legs, trying to shake Alec from its back. Alec dangled over the sand below, his sword still stuck in the creatures body. Alec pulled the sword free, and as he fell, he teleported back to his Monshokto and the two of them took off, slashing at the beast's tail from beneath its haunches.

The leviathan raised the three forked tail high in the air, bringing the large round exoskeleton-covered balls hard against the ground. The earth shook beneath them as a wave of water pushed back into the sea then rose up from the water and rushed forth at them.

The four warriors were washed further inland. Then, the force of the water pulled them and their Monshokto, back out into the ocean. The leviathan turned and dove into the ocean waters, searching for its enemies. Now having a definite advantage over those who sought to destroy it, even in its weakened and battered state.

Those who oppose the Lord will be broken. The Most High
will thunder from heaven; the Lord will judge the ends
of the earth. "He will give strength to his king and
exalt the horn of his anointed."

1 Samuel 2:10

Chapter 22

Reader's Island, Prayer Gardens

Simon and the other Dragoman read the names from the books
as quickly as they could, knowing that the meaning of the names
of the saints is what held the power.

Long ago, Dragoman from hundreds of years before had
discovered the power of a name. The Bible often spoke of how
important a name was. Most names given to people in the Bible
were related to their character or a physical trait. The Dragoman
and Peregrines were no different. The names they read had
meanings. They were the given birth names of each of the chosen.
These men and women, who over the years, through time and
space, had been chosen for a higher calling. They all had fought
in one way or another for the Lord, many losing their lives in the
process. Those saints were being avenged today by the Lord their
God. While The Twelve laid metal to beast, the saints were
avenged and the beasts were weakened, being defeated by their
very Creator. With each swing of the blade or strike upon the
dragons, the meanings of their names were imprinted into the
flesh of the beasts. Once that flesh was covered over by the
meaning of the names, the beasts would be no more and The
Twelve would win the fight.

Simon and the others had no idea how long the Final Battle
would take. They had already been reading for nearly an hour.
Meaning, The Twelve had been fighting for that long, or near to
it.

Clancy, Shannon, and Henry made sure the Dragoman had water to quench their parched throats from all the reading. As things continued on Reader's Island, they also continued on Tanmoyaro Draconomai.

Tanmoyaro Draconomai,
The Cave

The dragon belched fire, spewing its hot breath back and forth inside the large cave. The riders and their Pagorinxes scrambled to take cover behind an obliging boulder or stalagmite. The Peregrines had their shields and armor, as did Annabelle, but they weren't certain how the Pagorinxes would fare against heat that intense.

As the dragon continued to blow fire, Nick and his Pagorinx took an opportunity to sneak around behind her as she concentrated her attention toward the others. His Pagorinx leaped upward, bounding off the rocks in the cave and landing on the dragon's back between her wings. Nick struck downward into her back, and the Pagorinx bit at her wing, shaking its head violently.

The dragon roared loudly in pain as the walls of the cave shook, small bits of rock crumbled from somewhere up high. Nick and his Pagorinx quickly leapt away to the safety of the ground and an obliging boulder in which to hide, but not before he had caught a glimpse of something strange. Golden words flew out from the wounds that he and his Pagorinx had inflicted. There was no blood, only a spider web effect where his sword entered the dragon's flesh, and where the Pagorinx bit the wing. He looked at the dragon over the top of the rock, trying to look and see if what he had seen was real. Sure enough, across the dragon's back in swirling golden letters were words trailing in all directions, across and over her hide, and traveling toward her under belly.

"Huh, that's interesting," Nick said to himself.

"What's interesting?" Sean asked, riding over to where Nick hid, making Nick jump.

Nick fussed in a hushed voice, "Warn a man will ya'!"

Sean smiled. "Sorry, but hey nice moves. And, what's interesting?"

"Look at the dragon's back. See where I stabbed it?"

"Yeah, its like some kind of light coming from under the skin. Weird."

They peeked over the top of the rock to gauge their next attack and saw Gabriele and her Pagorinx out of hiding and facing the dragon. Gabby's shield was up as they ran at the beast. The dragon roared, blowing fire at her. Her shield blocked the fire that licked at it, wrapping all around her and her Pagorinx. They rode beneath the dragon, slashing at her underbelly with her blade, but not making a scratch. The dragon's hide and scales were too thick and tough for such a move. As they came to a stop on the other side, Gabby pushed her sword into the dragons flesh on its rear right leg. Another golden spider web of words flew across the dragons body in all directions. The dragon belched fire and roared once again in pain, kicking out at its offender. Gabby and her Pagorinx flew across the cave and into a wall.

Nick and Sean watched the dragon turn toward Gabby. They both leapt from their hiding places and each took a side to attack, both piercing the creatures flesh again.

The dragon swung her mighty tail, roaring in pain and anger. Her attention now diverted to her two attackers. Her thick tail knocked Sean and his Pagorinx away and across the floor. They quickly righted themselves and attacked once again.

Gabby and her Pagorinx gathered their wits and took out after the dragon. The beast didn't know where to look. It was being attacked on three sides.

Annabelle hid and watched the warriors fight the massive dragon. She was frightened and had no idea what she was supposed to do. Her shield was nearly as large as she was, and the sword she carried was heavy and hard to wield, much less fight with. So she hid, hoping God would tell her when to move and what to do.

The Sky

The riders and Kabihanxus slowly and quietly glided through the floating mountain cavern. Small specks of light from holes around the narrow passage filtered through, giving little light with which to see. The Kabihanxus were able to see where to fly with their night vision, but the Peregrines and Keeper had no such abilities. They could only trust their creatures to know where they were going. They soon came to the other end and the outside of the mountain. As Zeke and Cho flew out of the cave, there was a hissing noise and icy spikes flew at them taking them by surprise. Zeke searched for where the dragon was hiding, not paying attention to Cho who turned quickly. She leaned left, while he leaned right, losing his grip on the harness. He slipped from her back and began spiraling through the air, downward toward the quickly approaching mountain peak below. Suddenly something grabbed him. He looked up to see the underside of one of the Kabihanxu which had snatched him up in one of its large front claws.

Zeke went limp with relief as the firebird lighted on a nearby mountain, setting him upright. He looked up to see Bridget looking down at him.

"Didn't I tell you to move with your bird?" she admonished him as Cho landed next to them to retrieve her rider.

"Yes Yoda, it won't happen again. I promise. And thanks for saving my life."

"You're welcome. And why do you keep calling me Yoda?"

Zeke smiled. "If we survive this, you and I are going to have a movie marathon."

Bridget, still not understanding his meaning, shrugged her shoulders and they took off again hunting for the dragon. They rounded a floating mountain to see Caroline and Odessa engaged in a battle with the beast in the air. Caroline struck one side, while Odessa the other. They soared close to it as it tried to outrun them. It twisted and turned in the air, lashing at them with its massive, sharp, tail, and screeching loudly as lightning streaks flew at them. Zeke and Bridget joined the fight, Zeke attacking from below and Bridget from above.

The dragon screeched in pain with each strike of the swords, its body becoming more and more covered by the glowing words.

As Bridget and her Kabihanxu flew over top of the dragon, it blew out a blast of fire upon the dragon, laying the last of the golden words across its flesh. There wasn't a spot anywhere upon it that wasn't cracked and glowing.

The dragon twisted and turned, clumsily flying down toward the peak of the Mountain of the Dragons. They followed it downward, knowing it to be injured beyond fighting. It landed in a high area near where its nest lay, collapsing upon the snow-covered ground, breathing hard and slow.

The riders and their firebirds landed, cautiously watching the dragon. Bridget jumped down from her firebird and slowly approached the dying beast.

Zeke and the others yelled at her, asking what she thought she was doing. Bridget ignored their calls and followed the calling of the Spirit. She somehow knew what she was supposed to do now. She walked up to the dragon's head, kneeling in front of her and looked into her eyes.

The dragon lay there, taking long, deep, labored, breaths. It opened its eyes as it sensed Bridget's presence.

The compassion on Bridget's face and the tears that streaked her cheeks surprised and softened the dragon's heart as Bridget spoke to her.

"I'm sorry you are in such pain. I can feel your agony."

The dragon let out one labored breath. *'I know you feel it. I feel yours as well. The pain of hurt and betrayal from those you loved. We too felt such loss long ago when your kind once cared for us and then abandoned us for their lustful ways and greed. The Creator sent you to release us, I sense this now. I was growing so very tired. The sins of man has burdened our souls greatly, turning us from kindness to hatred. Hatred is such a heavy burden to carry.'*

"I know. I'm so sorry that man has done this to you. I know what I am to do now. I promise that I will take great care of your successor."

'See that you do. Only one season dragon can live at a time. So as I die, my egg shall hatch and live. It will now rule the sky, controlling the winds, and rains. See that you take greater care with its heart than your predecessor did with mine.'

"I promise I shall," Bridget said, reaching out and touching the dragon's nose just below her eyes.

The dragon took one last labored breath and passed into death as the glowing words on its flesh glowed even brighter, until in a flash of light the dragon was changed. She had been returned to her former self, beautiful to behold even in death.

The others stood there, shocked at what they had seen, hearing the words that Bridget spoke to the dying dragon as it drew its last few breaths knowing that Bridget must have been speaking to her.

Bridget stood and approached the nest which lay tucked on the side of the mountain. The large white and lavender egg wiggled with life. She knelt down beside it as the others approached behind her, curious about the creature that would emerge from the large, wiggling, rough surfaced egg.

They all watched in wonder as the sunlight illuminated the egg from behind as it suddenly split apart. A small, lightly-colored, lavender, and white baby dragon shook loose its wings as it unfurled from its long sleep inside the egg. It stood and looked about at those that were watching it. It sneezed, and a small puff of billowy white cloud floated up from its nostrils and mouth. It stood about two feet tall, about three feet long, and had small wings, which it couldn't use just yet.

Bridget reached out to it. "Come little one. I am your Keeper, and I shall take care of you."

The small dragon walked toward her and nuzzled her hand. Everyone knelt down beside Bridget to pet the beautiful little creature.

Bridget gathered the wind dragon in her arms and the warriors climbed on the backs of their Kabihanxus for the long flight back down the mountain.

The Land

The behemoth thrashed wildly, its log like tail whipping about, wiping out half the trees and jungle in the area as it did. Its long tail struck Jason and his Yarequu, knocking them apart and disengaging the Yarequu's defenses. Jason and the Yarequu were now both visible to the behemoth, its large piercing eyes on the right side of its massive head each focusing on the both of them. It slung its head around to try to snatch the Yarequu up off the ground before the creature could stand up again. Jason took the opportunity to lunge at the beast, his blade piercing the tip of its nose. Golden words flew upward, and across its face. One strand running across the eyes of the behemoth blinding the beast on the right side. It roared and lifted its head in pain, taking Jason into the air with the motion. It flung its head back and forth, sending Jason flying through the air. Fortunately for him, he landed in the freshwater pool beside the mountain. Unfortunately, his sword was slung out of his hands in the process, landing in the water in another area. He swam over to where he thought it had landed and quickly searched for the sword beneath the surface of the water.

While Jason was busy with the front of the behemoth, Seth and his Yarequu rode up the tail and back of the beast, their camouflage no longer working since they rode along its tail and back. While the behemoth thrashed its head to shake Jason, Seth rode high, up toward its shoulders. He jumped from his Yarequu and thrust his sword into the beast's back. The behemoth reared up in pain, landing hard upon the earth once more. It threw its head around toward its back, coming from the left side now that its right eyes were blinded. It opened its large mouth to grab Seth.

He swung his fist into the jaw of the beast, knocking its massive head out and away from him and his Yarequu, dislodging one of its massive lower teeth. Golden words again flashed across the flesh at the contact, the long spiky tooth flying through the air.

Wade yelled out in fear as the sharp canine landed beside him, pointed side down into the ground, sticking firmly. The thick part of the broken tooth protruding up from the ground. He shook his head in disbelief as he watched Seth on the behemoth's back, stabbing and pounding its flesh with his sword and fists.

Seth mounted his Yarequu once more and the two of them rode as quickly as possible down off the behemoth's back. It began lifting its tail into the air to prevent Seth from getting away. The behemoth's long, thick, tail lifted higher into the air as Seth and his Yarequu rode along the twisting flesh trying to stay upright. As they reached the end, the Yarequu leaped into the air, and a set of fan shaped wings appeared out of the spikes around all four legs at the knee joints. The four, small, wings were hard like iron and worked more like gliders, the wings allowing them to soar toward the ground, disappearing the moment the Yarequu's hooves made contact with the earth.

Seth let out a loud whoop, appreciative of the Yarequu's abilities!

"Sorry I gave you such a hard time before, you are full of surprises." Seth appreciatively patted the Yarequu's neck.

Kristin lashed at the large legs on the right side of the behemoth, laying more injuries to the beast. The behemoth lifted its large leg and stomped at the ground, just missing Kristin, as its long tail came around and struck her and her Yarequu. They flew apart, flying underneath the torso of the beast. It began stomping, trying to squash her and the Yarequu. Seth rode up to it and punched the behemoth in the side, making her stagger to her left. As she did, she slipped on the pile of rock that Kristin had thrown at her before, tumbling over onto her left side, her massive frame sliding down the rocks, almost sliding over Kristin. She whistled for her Yarequu which ran up to her and she leaped onto the creatures back. They rode away from the behemoth, turning to gauge where to strike next.

Jason had climbed out of the water after finding his sword and ran toward the back of the beast which lay over on the rocks. He stabbed at the creature's neck, sending golden words in every direction. He pulled his sword out and struck again as Seth and Kristin stabbed at the beast in any area where the golden words did not cover. They didn't understand the significance of them, but they knew they somehow weakened the beast. The behemoth thrashed about, trying to stand but was unable.

Wade suddenly had the urge to be brave. He rode up to the behemoth, staring into the eyes on its left side as its head lay on the ground, the last of the golden words covered its body. The behemoth breathed hard, both of its eyes watching Wade. The Peregrines had stopped their onslaught of the beast, now standing still; tired and breathing just as hard as the behemoth did, which was trying to catch its last few remaining breaths of life.

Seth, Jason, and Kristin had all approached to stand near where Wade now stood. All surprised to know he was communicating with it once more.

Wade reached out, laying a hand upon the beast's head just in front of her eyes. They stayed that way for just a minute as Wade spoke to her as if answering her.

"I will," Wade said. He turned to the others. "We need to ride back toward the edge of the mountain, down that trail. We need to go quickly." He turned, taking the trail, and riding hard, but the others watched for a moment longer as the behemoth's flesh exploded in beams of light which sparked and trailed upward upon the wind. What lay before them now was a smaller, beautiful, creature, the horrid behemoth now gone. They all turned and rode fast to try and catch up with Wade.

The Shore

The water swirled around them, tossing the Peregrines, the Keeper, and their beasts out into the ocean. Fortunately, the waves had not been so large that they pulled them too far into the sea.

Zaccai swam to catch up to her Monshokto, the creature seeking her out and swimming underneath her. Once she was seated on its back, it took off in the water, moving faster and more agilely than it did on land.

Oz swam upward toward the surface of the water, his Monshokto just above him. He noticed the webbing underneath attached to its torso and extending to each massive leg all the way to their feet, normally covered by the massive amount of hair on the animal's legs. The Monshokto looked like a giant flying squirrel from his vantage point. He surfaced, gulping air, and climbed onto the Monshokto's back. The creature took off toward the other three riders, now reunited with their own creatures.

As they began to converge in the water, the leviathan broke through the surface between all four of them, reaching upwards into the sky as water splashed down around them, pushing them outward and away in all four directions. The leviathan screeched in its piercingly high voice.

The Monshokto pod all faced the beast, bellowing their song beneath the water from separate directions. The leviathan screeched more in pain yet was unable to move. It tried to push against the deep reverberating sounds of the four Monshokto, with little effort. Each Monshokto swam slowly forward toward the leviathan. The closer they got, the less the leviathan could move. It managed to throw out one long tentacled arm which Oz managed to slice at and sever from its body, the golden words encircling what was left of the tentacle. The Monshokto all had to take a deep breath before continuing their onslaught, allowing the leviathan a split second to get free. It thrashed out in all directions, but the Monshokto engaged their horns and protective electrical shields. As the leviathan reached out to grab the four creatures and their riders, its tentacles connected with the electrical shields, electrifying the water around it, electrocuting the large beast. As sparks flew in and around the leviathan, golden words flew across its flesh and exoskeleton. The leviathan screeched and shook with pain as it thrashed out of the ocean toward the beach, followed closely by the Monshokto and their astonished riders.

The leviathan lay in the shallow part of the water, its barnacle encrusted face lying upon the sand. Dominic could feel the creature pulling him closer.

'Come forward,' it called to Dominic.

As Dominic began approaching the leviathan, the others called out to him.

"Dom'nic! What 're ya' doin'?" Oz asked in caution.

"What I'm supposed to do," Dominic answered, not slowing his forward motion.

"It might jus' wanna' eat ya' ya' know?" Oz warned.

"No. It's dying. It needs me." Dominic didn't take his eyes off the massive creature as he and his Monshokto slowly approached its head.

Alec, Zaccai, and Oz all approached behind him. Each getting into a position to attack the creature once again if needed.

Dominic's Monshokto stood up on its hind legs, reaching far up the side of the leviathan's head. Dominic reached out and placed his hand on the beast, and it began to speak to him.

'I will show you where to find the egg. You must go quickly if you wish to bond. You must take care of the waterbeast, the ruler of the sea. Do not abandon her as the last Keeper did to me.'

"I promise."

Suddenly in his mind, the location of the leviathan's egg and her successor was revealed to him and his Monshokto, as they were telepathically connected.

"We have to hurry!" Dominic yelled to the others. His Monshokto threw up a protective barrier around Dominic and dove under the surface of the water. The other Monshokto following the pod leader, doing the same for their riders. The Monshokto knew their riders couldn't breathe underwater and were able to provide a bubble of air this way. They could also feed that bubble with their own oxygen if the need arose while underwater.

The Cave

The dragon let out an earthshaking roar, mingled with pain and anger at losing the battle. It could feel itself growing weaker with each strike of its enemy's blade.

'*Help me Keeper. It is your job to protect us. You gave your promise to us long ago, yet you stand by and watch them destroy me.*' The dragon called to Annabelle, playing on her sympathies.

Annabelle stood there, shocked at what the dragon said to her.

"I can't. I have to do what God commands."

Nick was fighting close by and could hear her speaking to the dragon but could not hear what the dragon was saying.

'*Did not the Creator make you to care for me? Is that not His commands for you?*'

"Yes, but He sent me with the others to destroy the evil that plagues the earth."

'*I am not that evil. These men and women you fight with are the evil. Will you not help me, child? If I perish, who will control the seasons? What beast will care for the earth and control its lashings and groanings?*'

"I...I don't know. I'm confused," Annabelle stammered, still unsure as to her purpose here.

'*Come out of your hiding. I will not harm you. You are my new Keeper. You shall restore me.*'

Annabelle slowly stepped out from behind the rock and into the open before the dragon. The creature twisted and thrashed in pain as her attackers continued their onslaught.

The dragon saw the young girl before her. Now was her chance to kill the Keeper. They looked into each other's eyes, Bridget seeing the truth that the dragon was hiding from her. The dragon let loose a fiery breath at Bridget, but not before Nick could run up beside her, placing his and her shield out in front of both of them, kneeling to the ground. The dragons fiery breath flew all around them, bouncing off the shields, heating the air around them to a stifling hot temperature making it hard to breathe.

Sean and Gabriele both screamed in protest, as they leapt onto the dragons back and stabbed at the beast until her hot breath escaped no more and she crumbled to the ground, beaten, and battered.

The dragon drew one last breath before she exploded into millions of sparkling pieces which floated up and disappeared against the ceiling of the cavern. What was left of her was beautiful, her flesh now unmarred by the hideous sins of man.

Annabelle stood and threw her arms around Nick's neck while he scooped her up into his arms, hugging her tightly.

They looked at one another before he set her on the ground.

"Over there." Annabelle pointed.

"What's over there?"

"It's the new earth dragon. She didn't want me to know. She tried to save herself instead."

Annabelle walked over to another cave that glimmered inside with colorful gems scattered throughout the walls, light shimmering from the gas fires of the larger adjoining cavern. In a nest in the center of the room lay one egg. It was large and swirled with colors of red, yellow, and white.

As she approached the egg, it wiggled and cracked. When she reached out to touch it, the egg broke apart revealing a beautiful little dragon. It huffed out a puff of smoke as it peered at her. It crawled toward her and into her arms, curling up against her chest, purring and tucking its head into its body.

The others watched incredulously at the scene before them.

"I think I have what I was sent here after." Annabelle smiled, cuddling the small creature in her arms.

They all mounted the Pagorinxes and began the climb out of the center of the earth, the long journey ahead now taken in casual strides. Their fight was finally over and the peaceful journey home their only destination.

The Land

Wade rode at breakneck speed, trying to reach the nest before the egg hatched. He couldn't miss his chance to bond with the new beast. He could sense where it was he had to go, and knew he was close now.

As his Yarequu approached, Wade told it to slow and stop. He jumped down from its back and walked over to the large nest in the jungle's center. He knew the massive nest held only one egg. He ran up and climbed over the edge, peering down into it. The egg had already hatched, and the small dragon bellowed in protest, searching frantically for its mother.

Wade climbed over the edge and slid down into the nest, startling the little dragon. It turned and screeched in fear at Wade. Wade slowly approached the little beast, cooing to it and holding his hand out in front of him. The little dragon danced around and backed away, trying to decide where to run.

Wade stopped moving and sat down in the nest. He called to the little creature, trying to reassure it.

"I won't hurt you, little one. I am your friend. I'm your new Keeper. Come on, come here."

The little dragon stopped moving and sniffed the air in Wades' direction. It bellowed a little and cocked its head, still unsure about the man that sat before it.

"God sent me to you. I'm supposed to take care of you. I'm sorry I was late getting here." Wade spoke to it as he inched forward. "You see, I was trying to get to you. I was just further away than I thought I was."

Wade stopped moving, now only inches away from the thick little creature that peered up at him. It sniffed the air and Wade's hand and bellowed happily, jumping into Wades' arms, and licking him all over his face.

The other three Peregrines stood and watched the scene before them from the top edge of the nest. Jason remained standing while Seth kneeled down, and Kristin took a seat, her legs dangling below her. They all three looked at one another and smiled, as they watched the gentle giant of a young man bond with his baby dragon.

The Sea

Dominic and his Monshokto raced to the bottom of the sea. He was taken by surprise at how fast the Monshokto could travel underwater. The Monshokto raced around the mountain, sliding into a cave that ran along the ocean floor. It turned upward into the mountain and the two of them surfaced in a small underwater cavern that held fresh air. The cavern glowed brightly with bioluminescent light which sparkled from the rock walls and glistened in the materials that made up the nest. The cavern was basically only large enough for the leviathan to have entered long before it grew as large and disfigured as it was.

Dominic and his Monshokto swam up to the edge of the nest. They both climbed out and shook the water from their bodies. As Dominic stood gazing upon the now hatching egg, the others and their beasts entered the cave and began to climb out of the water, curious as to what Dominic was looking at.

Dominic knelt beside the egg just as it split open. The smallish creature inside pushed at the shell, breaking free from its hold. The strange looking little sea dragon looked little like the leviathan which had laid the egg. The little dragon had four flippers, two small, undeveloped fins on its back, and no exoskeleton or tentacled arms. It was a soft black and teal blue in color, fading into white along the barely noticeable fins on its back. It blinked at Dominic who smiled at the beast. It barked at him in reply, hopping up and down with joy. Dominic gathered the creature in his arms, and the party of nine now ventured back to the surface of the island to find their friends, and hopefully make their way home.

Reader's Island

Simon and the other Dragoman fell onto the benches that graced the prayer gardens, sensing the battles were over. They were mentally and physically exhausted. They had read through nearly three Dragoman archives each that morning, the battle taking nearly four hours. If they were exhausted he couldn't imagine how much more each of the Peregrines and Keepers were. He only prayed that each of them would return to the island. He didn't know if he could handle any more losses to the cause.

Once they had rested a bit and had some nourishment, they all stood and made their way back to the main house. They would wait outside on the patio for the return of The Twelve.

It was near the noon hour, when a portal opened on the lawn of the island and all twelve of the chosen, all four Keepers, and four little beasts stepped forth.

The island erupted in cheers as everyone welcomed the warriors home.

Memnah happily cried that Jason was safe, Prisca exhibiting the same emotions for Oz as all the others smiled and hugged one another, joy at the success of the Final Battle finally being over. No one else had lost their lives for the cause, and the world was now saved from destruction.

As they all stood there rejoicing, sighs of relief escaping their lips, the barrier around the island began to dissipate and fade away, and all realms and worlds began to appear, no longer separated by the barrier. They would all now live in harmony, side by side.

The ceremony to appoint the kings and queens of new earth would take place that very evening. Each Peregrine and Dragoman taking their rightful place upon the thrones.

The bridges between worlds would now be easily passable by each ruler with a simple thought or word as to where they wanted to go. The Portgens had served their purpose, along with the gifts of the chosen. They would rule as ordinary men and woman, yet still stronger and wiser than any others upon the lands

Chapter 23

The New Kingdoms of Earth
One Year Later

The air was ripe with excitement as each nation, kingdom, and realm prepared for the festivities. The Unity Festival, the first annual celebration of the uniting of all the realms and planes was about to commence. All the kings and queens were coming together in the high Kingdom of Judah to mark the celebration. People from every plane and nation traveled to see the heroes and heroines that had saved the world, all wanting to pay homage and catch a glimpse of each one. The main festival would begin in the kingdom of Judah, and on the second day, would take place at one of the other high kingdoms, allowing all to celebrate. This would continue until each kingdom had been visited by all the rulers.

The kingdoms of the earth and all the realms and planes, although now connected, were each ruled by one of the chosen, or divided up by couples who ruled together.

The Twelve were given the highest seats in the kingdoms, supremely ruling over all the lands. The other chosen Peregrines, and all the retired Peregrines who once fought and still served were given the lower kingdoms to rule over, seeking the council of the upper kingdoms. The Dragoman sat in high council positions as advisers to the kings and queens of all the realms.

The Keepers lived in a large castle on Tanmoyaro Dracono-mai and ruled over the island and all the creatures. Bridget ruled the animals of the sky, Dominic ruled the animals of the sea, and Wade and Annabelle ruled the animals of the land.

Their main job was to care for and train the Season Dragons to love and live in peace and harmony. The Keepers spent time with the dragons daily, helping them grow in nurturing love.

The veil between worlds had been removed and all the worlds now could see the power of God. The scribes and story-tellers went throughout the lands, telling the stories of the great kings and queens who had saved them all from destruction, telling the fantastic stories of the great battles they had fought and the beasts they had slain.

Marnor and Petra sat in charge of these people, traveling along with many servants and assistants to each land, heralding the tales and reading the stories from the archive books. Children and adults alike lined up waiting to hear the tales of the rulers.

Seth and Caroline, rulers of the Kingdom of Judah, had welcomed the newest members of their little family, Prince Matthew, and Princess Esther. The twins were a few months old now and very healthy. They were adored by their many aunts and uncles throughout the lands.

Jason and Memnah were also expecting a little prince or princess of their very own in the Kingdom of Asher.

Alec and Odessa had gotten married, along with Sean and Kristen. Each couple ruling over one of the high kingdoms together, the Kingdom of Reuben and the Kingdom of Naphtali.

Zaccai and Zeke also ruled in adjoining kingdoms, and shortly after being appointed to their thrones also married, combining the two Kingdoms of Manasseh and Benjamin.

Nick and Nadia had married as well, and the two of them along with Annabelle made a nice little family in the Kingdom of Gad. Annabelle worked on Tanmoyaro Draconomai, but until she was older, would live with Nick and Nadia.

Gabriele ruled the Kingdom of Levi as supreme ruler and Timothy sat just below her as ruler of the lower kingdoms, both taking their friendship and budding relationship slowly.

Simon had finally given into the feelings that he and Safra had shared for so long. No longer having to choose between being a Dragoman or having a relationship.

Simon was also able to retrieve all his artifacts from his safehouse at Barrier's Edge, but of course, the barrier was no longer there. He turned his safehouse into a museum, displaying all the artifacts that all the Dragoman for all time had collected over the years.

Oz and Prisca ruled together in the Kingdom of Issachar, along with her council position as a Dragoman. They were vastly happy together, finally being able to actually live together after ten years of secretly being married and thirteen years of being separated. They had missed out on so much in life, but it was a sacrifice they had both willingly made to serve the Lord. Because of this, God saw fit to give them children in their older ages, however not in the traditional sense. While out in their kingdom one day, they came across a little family of three orphaned children, one boy of twelve and two girls, one eight and one five. Their hearts were so stirred with love for the children that they adopted them.

Malachai and Vashti also were expecting a baby. A much-awaited event. Vashti had worried she might be too old now to bare children, but Malachai reminded her that with God all things were possible.

Rourke and Sofia ruled side by side; their kingdoms bordering one another. Rourke making certain that was how it worked out. He was wearing her down and hoped one day soon he would convince her to trust him enough to marry him, making their two kingdoms into one.

Clancy and Shannon, Henry, and all the other retired Peregrines and Dragoman each were given one of the lower kingdoms to rule over, but Henry decided to stay with Clancy and Shannon instead and be high advisor to the king and queen.

Ryan was given his own special laboratory to invent and construct new technology for all the kingdoms. He had many who worked beneath him, Simon, Safra, and Dekker often visiting and stepping in to help the young man with governing his responsibilities.

In the Palace of Judah, in the private sector reserved for the royal family, the events of the morning were playing out.

"Seth, could you take her for just a moment?" Caroline called to her husband.

"I have my hands full with this one," Seth answered. He sat on the living room couch, looking down at the sleeping little boy in his arms, waiting for his wife to finish dressing. Joy in his heart for his two children.

"I'll take her, Caroline." Bridget entered the room, smiling brightly. "Come see Auntie Bridget my sweet, little, Esther."

"Bridget! I'm so happy to see you!" Caroline leaned over to hug her young friend after passing her the baby. "Thank you. I need more than two arms to tend to both of them." Bridget went to sit beside Seth so she could look at baby Matthew as well.

Memnah walked in smiling, overhearing Caroline's words. "You have plenty of arms. I offer mine anytime." She bent over Seth and Bridget's shoulders to peer down at the babies.

Caroline laughed. "Yeah, right, yours will be full soon enough."

Memnah looked down at her large belly, lovingly smoothing the silken material over her swollen abdomen.

"Too true," she said smiling brightly, Jason entering the room not too far behind her.

"What about us?" Alec announced entering the room. "I want to hold my beautiful little niece or nephew!" He walked over to Seth and took Matthew in his arms. He and Odessa sat down and smiled over the sleeping little boy who began to stretch and yawn.

"My turn, Bridget," Kristen announced upon entering the room.

"But I just got her!" Bridget protested.

"Fine, five more minutes and then I want to hold Esther."

They agreed and sat smiling over the baby. Sean followed Kristen and stood behind her, looking down at the two little sleeping infants; their naps being disrupted by all the fawning people entering the room.

"Where's my gran'babes!" Oz boomed as he and Prisca entered the room. They walked over to gather around the quickly filling couch to peer down at the twins.

The infants never flinched, as they were used to Oz's booming voice.

"And my Godchildren." Simon and Safra entered the room, searching through the growing mass of people hovering around the babies.

Zaccai and Zeke entered directly behind Simon and Safra. Zaccai walked over to Alec. "Alright, my turn with the little prince." Alec smiled and gave him over to Zaccai's arms as both he and Zeke played with the now awake baby, cooing, and making baby noises.

"You're all going to spoil them rotten," Seth said nervously.

"That's what uncles and aunties and grandparents are for," Jason put in.

"Just remember you said that when it's your turn," Seth said with a wicked smile, nodding toward Memnah's belly.

The two men smiled at one another.

Gabriele and Timothy showed up coming into the room in grand fashion.

"Caroline!" Gabriele called.

"Over here!" Caroline answered from her vanity table as she tried to finish getting ready.

"I have a gift for the babies. It's an album of lullabies that I wrote for them. I put them on a jump drive so you can play them from nearly anything."

"Thank you, Gabby. What a lovely gift. And they get to hear their Aunt Gabby sing to them every night."

"That's the idea. I have to get in early with them if I am going to get the chance to be their favorite aunt." She winked and smiled playfully at Caroline.

Caroline laughed out loud at her statement.

"You have a lot of competition for that prized role I'm afraid."

His arms now free, and being completely ignored, Seth walked over to help Caroline with her necklace. He and Caroline looked back at the scene in the living room as Gabby and Tim went to get their turn with the babies. They smiled, grateful for the people in the next room; their rather large, rather loud, family. And they wouldn't trade a single one of them. Even quiet Uncle Ryan, who had somehow shyly snuck into the room, walking over to peer at the little babies, unsure what to do with them.

The private living room of the king and queen filled up quickly with even more of their family of friends; each coming in to see the babies and have some long overdue conversations with one another. The parade would soon start, and they would all become busy with the festivities for the rest of the day and well into the night. Then tomorrow, it would all start over again, and each consecutive day thereafter until all the kingdoms had been visited to celebrate The Unity Festival.

That morning, the parade of Kings and Queens was soon to start. Each would pass by the large hoard of people gathered to participate in the festivities. First the parade with much fanfare, music and dancing would pass through the streets that ran to the palace. At the palace, the Dragoman would first recognize the Father in heaven for his wisdom and grace, and for loving the world so much that he put forth all things in motion to save them all, giving them the chance to accept his son Jesus before death. They would then recognize each King and Queen who ruled on high, then those who ruled the lower kingdoms. After that, the Storytellers would tell the tale of the final battle that united the worlds. The Season Dragons and their Keepers would make a grand appearance, telling of how man's sin had nearly destroyed the earth and the beasts that ruled the seasons. There would be games and fun for the rest of the day, followed by a large feast for the entire kingdom to end the night.

Seth and Caroline sat in the back of the first carriage to pass, which was pulled by Seth's Yarequu. Their seats sat higher above the driver so that the people could see the King and Queen and the new little prince and princess. They waved to the people as they passed, tickertape, confetti, and flowers flew about the air as happy people paid tribute to their wise and just rulers.

Each carriage passed in the same manner, pulled by the very beasts that also played a part in saving the world. Trumpeters blasted joyfully, and the drums thundered loudly, providing the beat to which the marchers and banner carriers marched. The Flag of each Kingdom flew above the flag bearers, two for each carriage. But the flag that flew the highest and which was given the most reverence of all, was the flag of the trinity; the flag of the Father, and the Son, and the Holy Spirit.

The kingdoms would be ruled for hundreds of years by the wise and just rulers of the new earth, and their successors. And the world would live in peace, for a very long time to come.

Your gates will always stand open, they
will never be shut, day or night, so that people
may bring you the wealth of the nations
-their kings led in triumphal procession.
Isaiah 60:11

About the Author

S.G. Boudreaux is a stay-at-home mom, who has homeschooled her three children for the last twenty years. Her oldest two have graduated. She has been married to her husband for twenty-five years. They live in the country in Southwest Louisiana, where they have pets and a quiet, yet sometimes busy life. She and her husband are both active in their local church where they have attended for twenty-three years. The ideas for the Peregrination Series came about in the summer of 2017. She began writing that fall and published the first in the series with a vanity publisher in early 2018, having it released in December 2018. She has since republished book 1: Earth in early 2020 as a second edition, self-publishing the last four books herself, writing and releasing two books in 2019, and the final two in 2020, this being her last. Look for her new series to come in 2021 known as Zanchier. To find out more about her and her books, go to:

www.sgboudreaux.com

SG Boudreaux

Other Book in the Series

Book 1: Earth

Book 2: Wind

Book 3: Fire

Book 4: Water

Other books by author

Zanchier Series of Books

Subjugation Book 1

Uprising Book 2

Anarchy Book 3

Search other Nonfiction books by
Shawna Boudreaux